THE STONE HOUSE DIARIES

by

ROBERT C. MOORE, JR.

The Niagara River Above the Falls.

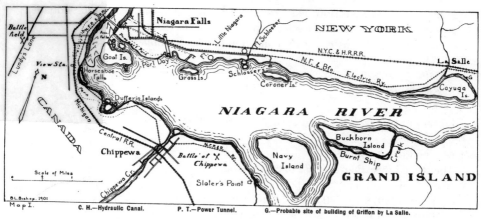

Map I. C. H.—Hydraulic Canal.   P. T.—Power Tunnel.   G.—Probable site of building of Griffon by La Salle.

D1089615

The Local History Company
publishers of history and heritage

Pittsburgh, Pennsylvania, USA

The Stone House Diaries
Copyright © 2006 by Robert C. Moore, Jr.

Published by
The Local History Company
112 North Woodland Road
Pittsburgh, PA 15232
www.TheLocalHistoryCompany.com
info@TheLocalHistoryCompany.com

The name "The Local History Company", "Publishers of History and Heritage", and its logo are trademarks of The Local History Company.

Maps on title page and page 1 are from *The RedBook of Niagara, A Comprehensive Guide to the Scientific, Historical and Scenic Aspects of Niagara* by Irving P. Bishop (Charles A. Wenborne publisher, 1907).

Map on pages 2-3 is from *The New Guide and Key to Niagara Falls,* John Edbauer, editor and publisher, 1921. Courtesy of Niagara Falls Power Company.

Map on page 4 courtesy of the collection of *Charles Rand Penney.*

ISBN-13: 978-0-9770429-3-7
ISBN-10: 0-9770429-3-6

Library of Congress Cataloging-in-Publication Data

Moore, Robert C., 1956-
The stone house diaries / by Robert C. Moore, Jr.
     p.   cm.
  ISBN-13: 978-0-9770429-3-7 (pbk. : alk. paper)
  ISBN-10: 0-9770429-3-6 (pbk. : alk. paper)
  1. Niagara Falls (N.Y.)—Fiction. 2. American loyalists—Fiction.
  3. Stone houses—Fiction. 4. Dwellings—Fiction. I. Title.

PS3613.O5667S76 2006
813'.6—dc22
               2005025873

Printed in USA

d e d i c a t i o n

To Steph, for patience—it's been a while but it's finally done.

To Dad, for teaching me to love my hometown.

To Mom, for helping me to see it from a distance.

And TB2G for the perseverance to finish it.

And to Niagara Falls, New York, and its history, which has been so fascinating to me.

a c k n o w l e d g m e n t s

To read Niagara Falls' history, one can find parts of it on the web and in books in libraries around the country, but if you want to dig deep there's ultimately one best source for it: the local history department at the Niagara Falls Public Library. Don Loker and Daniel Dumych assisted me during their respective tenures as local historians. Dan's scholarly work in books and his Website were valuable sources. And Maureen Fennie, the current local historian, not only helped with research questions, including some last minute fact-checking via email, but read Power City (after I begged her) and offered very valuable technical and editorial suggestions, improving it greatly. Thanks very much, Maureen.

Don Glynn of the *Niagara Gazette*, and John Hanchette, (formerly of the *Gazette*) now a professor of journalism at St. Bonaventure and contributor to the *Niagara Falls Reporter*, provided very helpful answers to my questions about urban renewal and Mayor Lackey.

I also made use of materials from two Canadian institutions, the Welland Public Library and the Pelham Historical Society. My thanks to these fine institutions.

As a librarian myself, I thank librarians in many places who helped me. We're the best!

Robert Moore

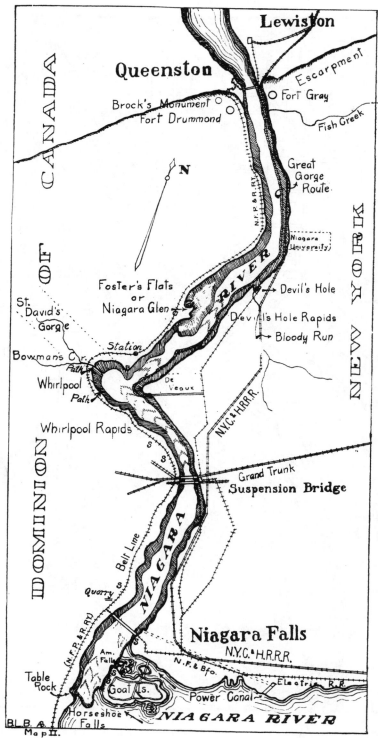

Niagara Gorge from the Falls to Navigable Water.

Circa 1920.

1

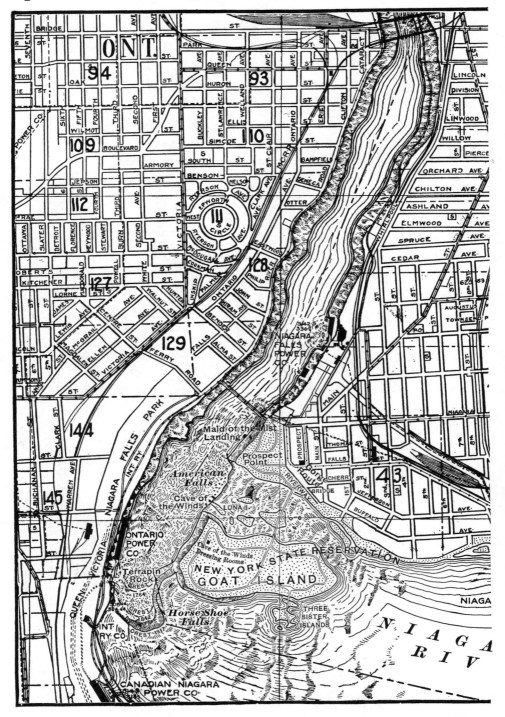

This page and next: Niagara Falls, showing the South End, circa 1920.

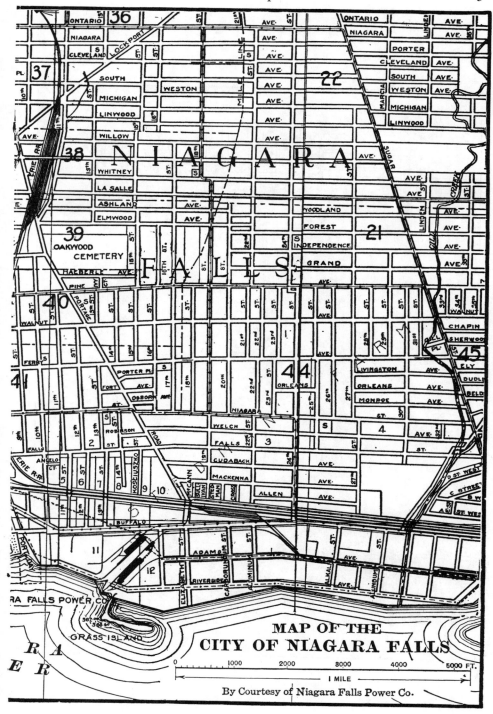

MAP OF THE
CITY OF NIAGARA FALLS

By Courtesy of Niagara Falls Power Co.

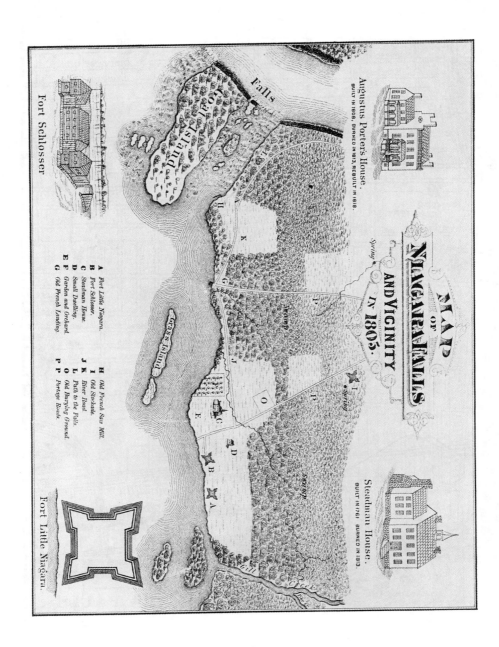

Fort Schlosser

Augustus Porters House.
BUILT IN 1806, BURNED IN 1813, REBUILT IN 1818.

MAP
OF
NIAGARA FALLS
AND VICINITY
IN 1805.

Spring

Steadman House.
BUILT IN 1761 BURNED IN 1813.

A   Fort Little Niagara.
B   Fort Schlosser.
C   Steadman House.
D   Small Dwelling.
E F Garden and Orchard.
G   Old French Landing.

H   Old French Saw Mill.
I   Old Stockade.
J K River Road.
L   Path to the Falls.
O   Old Burying Ground.
P P Portage Roads.

Falls

Goat Island

Grass Island

Fort Little Niagara.

The War with the States I

My life was not simple. I have my regrets, but in the end I can think of nothing I would change.

In the summer of 1812 I was twenty years old. I stood just under six feet tall, with my late father's dark brown hair and brown eyes and my mother's high cheekbones. From eight years of working as a clerk on the Portage Road around the Niagara Falls, helping load and unload wagons and keeping count of the freight, I was strong and brown from the sun. Schooled until I was twelve, I was literate.

I learned in June of the war when a wagon driver on the Portage tossed me an old newspaper.

The heat of the sun at ten that morning was making me sweat from every exertion. Humid, positively steaming, the air was like a wool blanket. A light breeze was blowing the refreshing mist from the falls west to the British side of the river that morning, giving me no relief, and there was no rest. Every hour or so a wagon rolled out of the woods, into the clearing, the end of the Portage Road, and I had to help load the freight into a boat.

Augustus Porter, or Judge Porter as he came to be known, part owner of the Portage, charged me with keeping accurate counts of the goods that traveled the road. At one time everything that went into and out from the wilderness traveled down that road. Now it was barrels of salt mostly, for the Salt Exchange in Black Rock, but I also saw barrels of pork and bread, and rum, whiskey and ale, to provision the forts in the Northwest Territory, and almost every fur traded by Indians or trappers in the Northwest Territories came back that way, headed for John Jacob Astor's Manhattan business. Casks of gunpowder; nails, hammers, hatchets, axes, tools of all types, anything made of metal, some of it from small foundries in New England but most still from England. Cloth in bolts, coffee and tea. But mostly salt. And I had to keep track of it.

The road was busier before the Revolution, so I was told. When all of North America was British, one road to bypass the falls was adequate. With the river now the border, another portage followed the other bank of the river, and though the traffic seemed endless to me, the Judge was brusque when I reported my counts every evening, surly that traffic was down.

It was common knowledge that the Judge was set on building an empire here. The company he helped found built and owned most of the ships on the lake. Porter himself had built a rope works, a carding machine, a gristmill, a tannery, and he ran the post office. He built a barn for the oxen that pulled the wagons and a few cabins for wagoners and the boatmen who had families. One of the few businesses in the village he didn't own was the inn my father built.

Manchester was a small settlement. Our neighbors included John Sims, who piloted a pole boat ferrying goods from the portage, the Pruitts, who did some farming and John Pruitt ran the gristmill, and the Isaac Bartlett family. They left during the war, and only Sims ever returned. My first blush of love was for Heather Pruitt. She was a nice girl, red hair and a wide, smiling mouth, and at the age of eleven she was my first kiss, but she was wooed more successfully by a soldier at the fort and left with him during the war.

I'd been schooled until twelve, when a wildcat killed my father. It had been attacking the few farms in the area, killing sheep and goats, then a calf. As part of a hunting party, my father surprised the cat feasting on a dead sheep. My father was dead by the time they brought him back to our home, lying in the bed of a wagon.

As I remember, Father was a quiet man, spare in his opinions and his praise, but he taught me to shoot and to find myself in the woods. He knew a few words of Seneca, for the periodic visitors from the tribe, mostly greetings and compliments. The day after the wildcat slashed his neck open, the day after we buried him, Judge Porter called me to the Portage Landing. "Your father paid to have you schooled," he said, "did it stick?"

"I think so," I got out. The Judge was physically a big man, and I knew he was important, and I was afraid of him.

Though he periodically visited our inn, as a child I had never spoken directly with him. Children being entities to be seen and not heard, I caught his eye on occasion, and he left me with the impression of a busy man who ordered people about. He was a latecomer to the falls in 1806, my family having been here three years before I was born. Just as he took over the Portage, so did he take the old Stedman house, empty since John Stedman, master of the portage, crossed to British Canada after the border was settled. Porter started as a surveyor who, once he saw the falls, set out to buy as much of it and the surrounding land as he could. His wealth and power impressed Mother, and his wife, Lavinia, was my mother's friend.

That day he handed me a chunk of chalk and a slate. "Write your name." I did so, writing the formal version I'd labored to perfect. 'Nehemiah Cleary.' He nodded, then asked, "to provision three hundred men at Fort Schlosser, allowed fourteen cents a day, how much will you spend in a week?"

"I count it as two hundred and ninety-four dollars." I did the sum in my head; I was good with figures.

He smiled. "Very good. Your father was a good man, Nehemiah. And you appear to have learned something in school. So I'll give you a leg up. You've seen the wagons from Lewiston coming down the road."

"Yes sir," I said. The wagon drivers, when they reached the river at sunset, often stayed in the stone house my father built, with extra rooms to be an inn, and I had seen all manner of traders pass through.

"It's important to keep good accounts in business," the Judge tutored me that day, standing right where I was standing now, waiting for another wagon. "Every bale and barrel must be counted and their contents noted. Business is what will build this country. And business will make our village prosper. And if you prove yourself reliable and accurate, you will never want for employment while I'm alive."

Mother was so grateful. I was happy enough to get out of school, at twelve.

Eight years later it had become a tedious, onerous routine. I helped empty the wagons, drawn by oxen, helped load the freight into the pole boats that carried them east, and helped unload the boats and load the wagons for freight heading into the wilderness. By 1812 I was praying for a way out of Manchester.

Perhaps it was seeing the goods? Nails are just nails, but the merchant's name from Connecticut, the bills of lading from New York; these were daily reminders of the world. Once in a while a book or newspaper came my way, and I could read news from New York, or from Boston. A year ago a trader gave me an English paper, already four months old, which carried stories from Europe, from places of which I'd only read. I kept that paper by my bed at home, to pick up and read when I felt the need to escape. I memorized it. There was an ad for a suit by a London tailor, an imitation uniform, with brass buttons and gold trim. I would look so smart in that suit. It cost thirty dollars, which was impossible to save. But it gave me something to dream about.

Old Shultz, one of the wagoners, brought his third load of the day down the road near sunset the last Friday in June, 1812. The wheels squeaked, and I could see that Schultz, paid by what he hauled, had loaded his wagon until his springs were flat. "Couldn't squeeze anymore in?" I asked, irritated.

He looked to the west and the setting sun. "Your day won't be much longer," he said. Old Schultz was rheumatic and slow as molasses.

Even resting a bit between loads I carried four times what he did. "If you can't carry your freight you're too old to work this road," I said unkindly. He said nothing, just hefted a barrel with a grunt and rolled it down the bank. "If that barrel bursts, it's your account, not mine," I warned him.

When we were done he reached under his seat. "Sorry I made you work so hard, young Master Cleary. But I got a treat for you. The fellow what gave this to me said it had news. Important news. But the bastard knows I can't read and he just laughed when I asked him to read it. What's it say?"

Embarrassed at the gift after how I'd spoken to him, I picked up the paper, unfolded it and scanned down until I saw the headlines. "It says we're at war," I read, surprised. "With Great Britain."

Schultz scowled. "I ain't surprised. From what I hear, the American government and the King have been spoiling for a fight like two angry boys." He and I looked across the river. "Wonder how bad it'll be?"

A thrill was pouring through me like water through a burst dam. I handed up the paper.

"You keep it," Schultz said, "at least you can read it."

So I read it. Instead of the swim I had promised myself to wash off the sweat from unloading that wagon, I sat and read in the waning sunlight. The paper was filled with column after column of calls to arms. Stories told of young men volunteering in Baltimore, in New York, and in Washington. Young ladies lined the city streets as newly formed brigades marched along, offering their handkerchiefs as mementoes for the young men. Scented handkerchiefs.

I'd never smelled a scented handkerchief but I bet they smelled wonderful. Made, probably, of silk, a fabric I'd felt once when it came through as freight. And scented with perfume, carrying the warmth and cologne of a beautiful girl's body with it. With so few available young women in Manchester, well, I'd not yet lost my virginity.

Scented handkerchiefs. Uniforms. Baltimore, Washington. The thrill cascaded through me again, telling me that I'd found my way out.

And then I heard the grunt of another wagon creaking towards me down the road, casting long shadows in the setting sun. It was Mad Bear, one of the few Indians hired as a driver, and his wagon was also loaded high. *This has to be the last one,* I promised myself. I got a drink of water and began planning how best to explain to my Mother my plan to enlist.

Mad Bear was too late for the pole boats, but he preferred to sleep by his wagon, so that night it was just us. Mother and Electa and I ate chicken stew around the kitchen table. "Pour your sister some milk," Mother asked, dipping into the iron pot to ladle stew into our bowls.

We had a milk cow and I'd milked her before leaving for work. I'd put the milk into a clay jug, lowered it into our well to keep it cold, then drew it up for dinner. "Mother," I began after my first bowl was empty, "I saw a newspaper today, Old Shultz brought it by on his last trip."

Mother looked up from her food. She was just forty, but careworn as a widow raising a family and running an inn. "What did it say? Anything interesting?"

"It said we're at war. With the British."

Her eyebrows arched, then knit in worry, then furrowed in irritation. "War with the British? Are you sure? Do you still have the paper?"

I'd taken it to my room, but I got it and gave it to her to read. She read slowly, struggling with the text while I finished my second bowl. Electa wanted more so I dipped more stew for her. Mother turned a page and read more. She was shaking her head in exasperation. "I don't understand these people. I just don't understand what they want."

"The British?" I guessed.

She looked up at me, with a look I'd never seen on her face, a touch of guilt, perhaps of embarrassment. "It's time I told you about how your father and I came here." I sat and listened carefully; Mother found talking about father to be painful. She had been a girl of sixteen, he a man of forty-six, when they were wed. "As I think you know, your father's family and mine come from Western Massachusetts. He inherited a hundred acres of good land from his father, when he passed away in 1773." I nodded. "Your father was barely sixteen, but a smart lad. Then the Rebels started the war with our sovereign."

I'd never heard Mother speak of politics. I'd never heard her use the phrase 'our sovereign'. "The rebellion started without promise, and every prosperous man in the state, including your father, was pressed to support them. The rebels wanted cattle and money."

Mary Cleary's green eyes focused on the fire in her hearth as her memories were allowed a rare breath of air. "Your father refused." She allowed herself a proud smile. "Several of the families near us refused. The saying was common among those loyal, 'better one tyrant a thousand miles away than a thousand tyrants a mile away.' We had our disagreements with England, to be sure. Your father believed an American parliament, loyal to the King, would solve this country's problems." She smiled again, a tribute to his memory and good sense, then frowned. "The patriots were a mob. They drank in public, they burned stuffed effigies, carried on like the lowest kind of people. Not the sort you would want to gamble your future on." She pursed her lips. "A bunch of lawless smugglers. They wanted an end to order, an end to law, they preached all sorts of anarchy. Usually most of the Patriots," she treated the word as a profanity, "were men of no property, no learning, men who had little to lose. And you know, even so, your father defended them to me."

"It'll be all right if they let us live in peace, that was what he said. Your father was not blindly in love with our sovereign, but he preferred an ordered, lawful society to their alternative. 'Just let us live in peace,' he asked of them when they came to our house that autumn. But they wouldn't." She hissed with old anger. "Then the war began, and the committees declared themselves the law, and we watched civilization retreat from disorder. The Patriots passed ordinances making it illegal for those loyal to engage in trade. Illegal to buy or sell cattle, illegal to lend or borrow money. Illegal to sell our own land." She shook her head in anger at the memory. "Our second year married, your father heard from friends that such restrictions were about to be enacted in our town. He sold the farm to a neighbor, Giles Hanson, a good man, a mild patriot, not one for the streets but he had given money and supplies. He gave us half what the farm was worth, but your father was happy to get it. And then we got in the wagon and rode west."

"So Father supported the King," I said.

"He was loyal," Mother clarified. "He admired one or two of the patriots, men of learning who wrote about the rights of men, which he did believe in. But when he had to choose, he was loyal."

It filled in a blank space. I had never heard my father speak a word about politics. About fixing things broken, about land, about farming, about money, about his God, about his love for us he'd spoken, but hardly a word about politics. 'That's Judge Porter's business,' he used to say, as though it were a nasty chore of which Porter was relieving him. Then again, I was just twelve when he died, a little young for trading political opinions.

Mother continued. "We came as far as Canandaigua, and I wanted to stay there, where there was a town, but Father felt it wasn't safe, we were still among Patriots. Fort Niagara was a British fortress, and Butler's Rangers were stationed here. So we kept going until we reached the Niagara, to be under the protection of the fort." Mary took a drink of water, her mouth dry from remembering. "We were both in awe of the falls. And it was quiet, no mobs. Other than the soldiers and the wagoners and the traders, there were hardly any people at all. But the Portage was running and your father saw the chance to start the inn. So we built our house here."

"But we're Americans now."

She nodded ruefully. "We never believed the rebels would actually win, but when they did, we felt wise to have moved this far west. When the treaty was signed, when we learned in '96 that the river was the border and we were on the American side, oh!" She shook her head at the memory. "Your father and I argued whether to cross the river, and start over again a second time. Captain Stedman left and advised us to leave. But Father, he wanted to stay. I," she looked at her wedding ring. "I was his wife. We'd just finished building this house, which took more than a year. The land was cleared. We knew that with peace there would be more business for the inn. And this was just starting to be a village. We were just God-fearing people making our homes and raising our families." She shook her head in dismay at old regrets newly recalled. "Yes, we became Americans, but it didn't seem to matter. The people we see from across the river, they're British and we're American but it doesn't matter. And that's how it's been." She lifted the first page of the newspaper. "Until today."

We said nothing of importance the rest of the evening and I went to bed. I didn't sleep much that night. I'd learned as much about my father that evening as I'd known all my life. That I was the son of a Loyalist made my ambitions to join the New York militia feel queer, to say the least. But when I fell asleep I dreamt of the uniform I'd be wearing, and my fantasies of young women were wild and untouched by politics, and when I woke the next morning I was determined to quit the Portage, determined to join the militia.

I left home on July 11th to enlist at Fort Niagara.

Mother sent me off with a winter coat that was much too heavy for that day. "The war can't last beyond December," I said. "Our enlistments are just for six months."

"You'll have need of it," she said, pressing it into my hands. She also gave me a packet of biscuits and some dried venison and some cornmeal, all tied up in a bundle and I tied it all up in the coat, which made a bulky sack to hold on a hot day. "Son," she said, standing at the doorway, "I know you're chafing to see something of the world and I'm not stopping you. If you've inherited your father's good sense, you'll come through this, and maybe then this little village will be enough for you." She looked in the direction of Lewiston. "Over in six months, eh? If you're still at war when the river freezes, you'll know that you can't always believe what you read, or what you hear." She sounded resigned, and blinked away tears. "And whatever happens, whatever you must do, come home as soon as you can."

I remember a long line on a hot day. Too excited at leaving home that morning, I'd skipped breakfast and ran the first mile through the woods. Finally, winded and hungry, I reached the Fort late in the morning, starving, and ended up gnawing on the venison and biscuit, trading another biscuit for a cup of cider and thinking of the breakfasts I wouldn't be eating for a while.

We waited, a crowd that grew all morning, sitting and talking and smoking and playing cards on the bare ground outside the main gate, waiting for the recruiter to come out. "About time," rippled through the crowd when, the sun at noon, a drummer boy preceded the recruiter and a surgeon out the gate. They set up shop, the recruiter borrowing a peddler's wagon and the surgeon installing himself in a tent. The recruiter was a sharp looking sergeant in a royal blue jacket and cap, black boots shined to reflect the sun, and the drummer boy pounded out a march. "Good morning," he called out, "I am here to sign up free men for the New York militia. We are at war with our old nemesis, England, and it's going to end the same way it ended last time!" He smiled broadly. "The English navy seems to believe they are entitled to replace their deserters by taking sailors from any other ship that crosses its path. They seem to especially like American sailors. They can't stand the smell of freedom and victory. We cannot tolerate their abuse." He paused, expecting perhaps for us to cry out in outrage. There had been no such outrages on the inland sea; there was no outcry. He went on. "The fighting will take place across the river, and that's where we'll all end up at the end of the war. With British land!"

There was still land available in this country. Across the river was the same dirt as here and there were more British than us. But knowing that, I still stood there and smiled and waited to enlist. Such is youth. I saw puzzlement and frowns in the crowd around me, and heard others mumble about land and British. Still, no one left.

He pressed on. "Your term of service will be for six months. Can't take longer than that to beat 'em. There's nothing over there but some starved Americans married to British, and the ones that don't join us as soon as we arrive, they'll run away for the second time when they see our flag."

I was beginning to feel my intelligence insulted. We'd had a few British through, and they were polite and paid their bills and smelled better than the traders. The only pretty girl I'd seen in the past few months was the young wife of an Englishman. I divorced her each night in my mind. "Just shut up and sign us up," I said, mostly to myself.

An older man, just behind me, chuckled and patted my shoulder. "Tell him, lad," he said, smiling.

"Line up by the tent," the recruiter called out, red-faced by now from ale and sunshine, "get the good doctor's approval." Inside the tent, the surgeon inspected us to be sure we were fit. As the day grew longer the surgeon got drunker and the inspections went faster, until it seemed one man pulled open the flap and stepped in, and the previous man stepped out the rear, and the time lapsed was no more than it took for the man to walk through the tent. On the other side of the tent the men sat in any shade they could find, waiting for the end of the day to write their names in the muster book.

"Are they looking for any ailments?" I asked the man behind me in line. "Does the surgeon reject many?"

He shaded his eyes, brown eyes set deep, and looked ahead at the line almost a hundred men ahead of us. After a minute he said, "nope, he hasn't rejected anyone yet." He had a beard speckled with gray. "The surgeon makes sure you got at least two teeth, one upper and one lower, to tear open cartridges. Then he thumps your lungs to hear if you've got consumption and looks at your legs and feet to be sure you can march a hundred miles a day, and you're fit," he joked.

"A hundred miles?" I didn't get the joke. "Will I pass?" I asked.

"You'll pass," he said, realizing then how naive I was, "you're healthy as a horse, from what I can see."

My trip through the surgeon's tent was so quick the surgeon couldn't have testified to much more than that I had two legs. At around three o'clock, when all the men were cleared, the sergeant got on a peddler's wagon again. "Raise your right hand and repeat the oath," he announced. We swore our oath to defend New York State for the duration of the War. Defend New York? When the recruiter was telling us we'd be in Canada soon?

Behind me in line was the same man I'd asked about the surgeon. He reminded me of my father.

"Howdy," I introduced myself; "I'm Nehemiah Cleary, from Manchester, near Fort Schlosser, just up the road."

"Lucas Ames," he responded, his face broad and wrinkled at the eyes and the corners of his mouth, and extended his hand. "From Cherry Valley."

"You've come a long way," I said. I wanted to ask why, but sensed he would tell me without being asked. While we stood in line for the sign-up bonus I asked, "do you really think we'll end up in Canada after the war?"

"Well, the oath we just swore was to defend New York," he said. "So if you go by that we won't be fighting the British unless they come here. But we'll see how it all comes to pass." Then he dug out a pipe and lit it, and I took that sign to be quiet.

Then we lined up to sign the muster book. We got twenty dollars for signing, easily the largest piece of money I had at that time earned, and the promise of a hundred and sixty acres of land upon victory, presumably British land. The signing went pretty quickly, the sergeant passing out money from a stack of coins, drinking more ale with his face now beet-red. Pointing to the line under the last signature, he inked a quill and held it. My hand shook a little. I was proud of my handwriting, and may have taken a little too much time. "All right, John Hancock. Next," he said, handing me my bonus.

I stepped back, and watched Lucas sign the book. I held the money tightly in my palm, the only part of the day that made sense, feeling the thickness, the coolness of the metal. And yet, it wasn't the money either.

I followed him to a shady spot and sat by him. "Well, we've done it now. Why'd you join?" I asked Lucas.

"For the twenty dollars," and, I came to learn later, because he had lost his parents and older sister years back to Butler's Rangers. "I apprenticed as a blacksmith but my master was an evil bastard. I decided soldiering was no worse than the life I was living." He lit his pipe again.

"For the money. And maybe for revenge." He didn't look angry, though. He didn't look twisted by hatred. He looked like my father.

We were marched, if two hundred untrained farmers walking at their own pace can be said to march, upriver to camp near the Lewiston commons. "Why not stay here, at the fort?" I asked Lucas.

"The regulars don't think much of us," Lucas observed. "So we're moving upriver a few miles."

I learned the routine fast, starting with Sergeant Pitt, who we met in Lewiston. Each morning we would be awakened by Sergeant Pitt's voice, or his boot or the riding crop he liked to use instead of a hand. We would assemble on the drilling field. We answered to a roll call. And once that was finished, the sun having risen enough to light up the field, Sergeant Pitt would give us the news of the day. Stepping up on a pine stump a couple feet tall, he would wait for complete silence. A newspaper might be poking from his coat pocket, but usually the news was just orders. "Dispatches," Pitt would growl, making each syllable known, dis-pat-chess. "Lights out means lights out. The Captain of the Watch observed candle or firelight showing from several tents last night. The next infraction will mean a loss of rations for a day and confiscation of candles." He would fold up that paper, shove it into a pocket, and look up to be sure he had his audience. "Washington has ordered that English vessels still in American ports are to be regarded as hostile and prizes of war." He smiled slightly, his jowls most of his face. "Not that we'll have much opportunity for that." He'd say a joke like that, but you didn't dare laugh. "So much for the news of the day."

The first week we had no cover and slept on the ground. It being July, the open air was preferable to being inside. One end of the camp was low land and the mosquitoes there bit something fierce, so we crowded together on the high end, though with little improvement. When it rained we tied pine boughs together as a lean-to. It was life in the open but it was no hardship, yet.

Pitt called me to his field table one morning. On his table was a new ledger. "Cleary, read this." He held up a label for soap.

"It says 'Pingrass Fine Soap, best lye soap for the money,'" I read.

"What's this column of numbers add up to?" he asked, and then I realized I was being tested. I did the sum in my head, though he offered a stub of pencil.

"Three hundred and seventeen, Sergeant."

Pitt's jowls moved as he smiled, ever so slightly. He was mostly bald under his broad hat, which almost never came off. "The company needs a clerk, and I think you're the man for the job. Anything to say?"

I had left home, signed myself into an army, and I was back counting supplies? "No, sir."

"Good. Use this ledger," he handed it to me. "When you hear that supplies have arrived you will make a count of them, and enter the number and type in this ledger. Then give the ledger to Captain Williams. Understand?"

"Yes, sir."

Since supplies arrived fitfully, days passing with no deliveries, I was also assigned as orderly to Captain Williams, a young man from Canandaigua, recently graduated from a school there. When not learning to march I killed flies and polished Captain Williams' pistol until it shone. I was also privy to officers' conversations.

Pitt smiled in a fatherly way the day he made me clerk. I guess he felt he was honoring me, and Pitt was a good sort, so I tried to smile and remembered to salute as I stepped away. Counting bales and barrels and boxes again. Damnation. And that very afternoon I was called from the drilling field to accept the first load.

As clerk of the Portage I often saw kegs of salt pork preserved in brine, emptied of the brine by lazy laborers who carried the half-as-heavy barrel to the other end of the road. Then they refilled the barrel with fresh water so it would weigh the same. The meat spoiled and would be riven with maggots by the time hungry men elsewhere opened the barrel.

"We've got a delivery," Pitt called to me that day, as I swept out Captain William's tent. And it rolled into camp, courtesy of Old Shultz the portage wagoner.

"I heard you done joined up," he said, looking at me like the dunce he always suspected I was. He had just unloaded the last barrel when I opened the first.

"Hold up," I said, prying up the barrel lid to show a cluster of maggots swimming in the watery ham. "This is spoiled."

Shultz got down with some trouble, his rheumatic joints causing him visible pain. He looked, sniffed, then spat. "Same as it usually is." He was a grizzled old fellow with three teeth, an Indian wife and a dozen kids. "I got trapped in a snowstorm last winter near Oneida Lake and I had to crack open a barrel to keep body and soul together. The bugs just wash right off." He wanted to be back up at the Portage by nightfall. "Just sign this receipt that you got the barrels," he said.

He was right; boiling made the pork clean, if tough, and baking killed bugs. But for years I'd shared crude jokes with Shultz and the other drivers at the sight of the hungry soldiers when they opened those barrels. I didn't relish the thought of my turn eating that meat. "Just wait here, I have to see my captain."

Captain Williams was, as usual, playing cards in his tent with two other officers and an enlisted man. I explained the problem.

"Just sign for it," Williams ordered, irritated at the interruption. "That's how it always is. You're the clerk." Williams and most of the officers ate their meals at the tavern in Lewiston.

Returning to Shultz with my signature on the invoice, I warned him, "Tell Judge Porter that I won't sign for any more shipments that come like this. Tell him," and I thought of my old boss, a large, powerful, and important man, but one who expected me to eat this offal. "Nehemiah Cleary said so."

He smirked at my attitude. "Oh, yes sir, Mister Nehemiah Cleary," and slapped the reins on the horse's back. "Be back in a few days with some more."

We spent an hour at drill practice each morning after breakfast. Drill, the skill of marching together, stepping in unison, turning in unison, and stopping in unison, as barked by Sergeant Pitt. The hardest part was marching shoulder to shoulder in a crowd and trusting everyone to turn at the same time. Hearing the order to turn right, I'd hesitate a moment. So did some of the others, but not everyone. We'd bump into each other, then those that had turned reversed their turn, and those that hadn't, turned, and we bounced off each other.

"Halt-ya-morons!" Starting over, trying the other direction, Pitt would yell, "Dress-left!" Same results. Our drill manual was a translation of a French drill manual that Napoleon had written, or at least used. Perhaps something was lost in translation. Whichever turn it was, we missed, and we'd hear Pitt yell, "halt!" Then he would pick out the ten or twelve of us who were the most confused, who kept turning left instead of right, and we would stand there as the others smirked.

"Do ya know yer left from yer right? This," the sergeant would kick the nearest right foot, "is yer right! What would that make this foot?" he kicked the other foot. "And when ya hear 'halt' you put yer damn feet together!" The older men tended to know the drills; they took a break, sat in the shade, and watched us bumping into each other, doubling up with laughter.

Our army grew. Based on the supplies I helped hand out, and the entries I made in the ledger, some numbers stick in my memory. By the end of the summer we numbered a thousand. By September the 22nd, when we were chafing at the bit to attack, we were two thousand.

With so many hungry men gathered in one place, the woods got hunted thin and the money we had, mostly our bonuses, was spent on whatever the farmers would part with. Each man got a ration of bread, corn meal, and salt pork, and we built fireplaces from stone and clay. The corn meal cooked up with fat made a morning cake, the bread was a utensil, and the meat we cooked with whatever kind of potatoes or turnips or other root we could find or, if pressed, buy. When we spent our bonuses, and were without pay, we foraged and the farmers harvested their crops and guarded them, without much luck.

A week after Old Schulz delivered the first load of supplies, Judge Porter delivered the next load. I saw him from a distance the day he drove in and my stomach grew butterflies. I wasn't just a clerk on the Portage, I was the company clerk, and if the supplies were shoddy I should refuse receipt. But after I'd shot off my mouth, the sight of him, the owner of everything in Manchester, cut me down to being a boy again.

"Is that you, Nehemiah?" he called out in a voice of false cheer, then climbed down, looking irritated. "Old Shultz told me you were unhappy with the last shipment of supplies. Said 'the youngster that used to work for me said the supplies were spoiled and he wouldn't accept any more'," Porter recited, angry.

"That's what I said," I said, realizing only for the second or third time in my life that right does not overcome might. "There were maggots in the pork. That's from replacing brine with—"

"I know how it happens," Porter said. "Point is, boiling cleans it up. The soldiers out west have been living off those supplies just fine. No one's died from the pork, so long as you boil it good. Sign this." He held out a bill in the same strong hand that had counted out my salary for years. The easy choice was to sign it.

I hesitated. Porter crossed his arms like a stern schoolmaster. He was a few inches taller than I, and broader. "Boy," and the term stung, for by now I felt I was certainly a man, "you may have worked for me for eight years but you didn't learn much about business. If I have to I'll go to your superior, or to my brother in Congress, if necessary, to get this signed. And if I have to do that it'll be the sorriest day of your life." He stepped closer to me and said, "Remember, I knew your father. He was a good man, but he was the King's man. How long you think you'll last in this camp when they find out your father was a Loyalist?"

In hindsight I see that his threat was threadbare. Most of the countryside shared my checkered upbringing. But I was young and naïve, and already scared of the Judge, and he knew it. Knowing he would likely prevail, burning with shame, I signed the bill. Porter tucked it into his coat, climbed into the wagon and kicked the barrels off. "That's more like it," he said. I pretended I was alone as he rode off.

We became soldiers.

"Dispatches," we heard Pitt call one steamy late July morning. "General Hull of the United States Army has invaded Canada at Sandwich, near Detroit. Three cheers for the United States!" We were a little ragged on the first cheer, and Pitt scowled at us. By the third he seemed satisfied. "And if we can master our left from our right, we can join our brothers in Canada without embarrassing ourselves."

After morning drill, we'd compose something like lunch, and then the squads would assemble and we'd drill together some more. The squads would form our platoon and we'd practice some more. Later in the afternoon the company would gather and try walking together some more. It took us weeks, took us the summer, actually, but we finally got to understand the orders, and to turn in unison. We started to feel more like soldiers. By September some coats arrived, not enough and odd sizes, so some of us looked the part—a benefit of being clerk was my mates got coats. "When do we get proper muskets?" I heard more and more.

We never got proper muskets.

While waiting for muskets, we were issued pikes. "This ain't going to buy me much time unless the British agree to fight with them too," said Stump McCartney when Sergeant Pitt gave us a demonstration. Stump was named stump because he looked like a. . . stump.

Pitt, having just beheaded a gourd on a pole, swiveled his pike and knocked Stumps' pike from his hand. It flopped end-over-end and, after

Stump stopped staring at his empty hands, he looked up to see the point of the Sergeant's pike a few inches from his throat. "Once that British soldier fires his musket, you've got twenty seconds to get to him with this. And it's a lot easier to work with than the bayonet on your musket," said Pitt. Looking at us, pleased that he'd earned respect for the pike, he said, "of course, Private McCartney has a point. If we're still holding pikes instead of muskets when the order to charge is given, I promise you all I'll take up the issue personally with our commanding officer."

"Dispatches," Pitt called out one August morning. "We are pleased and honored to welcome our commanding officer, General Stephen Van Rensselaer, recently commissioned by Governor Tompkins. Assisting the General will be his brother, Colonel Solomon Van Rensselaer. Three cheers for the General!" Out of respect for Pitt we cheered.

"Van Rensselaer?" I asked Lucas. "Who's he?"

"A politician," said Lucas, frowning. "Just a damn politician. His brother's got some training, that's the good news."

As we'd just been taught, we stood at attention.

I wish I could say he was an inspiring figure there, but he wasn't. Dressed in a uniform newly sewn by his Hudson Valley tailor, he wore a ridiculous hat with ostrich plumes. "Has anyone told him an ostrich took a shit on his hat?" asked Stump, and we choked back our chuckles.

"Good morning, men," the general said, in his educated, New York voice, "after reviewing our brother soldiers at Fort Niagara, and seeing your fine marching, I wish to inform you that I will be making my headquarters in the village of Lewiston."

I guess it was supposed to be a compliment. For reasons of his own, the General chose to camp with us volunteers at Lewiston, and so undermined his own appearance of authority. For the entire campaign, the militia would be treated as louts, as uncouth fools barely able to march, and far from an army, and Van Rensselaer as our incompetent leader. Not without reason.

"Our young country has suffered numerous humiliations at the hands of the British navy. They stop our ships when they've lost too many to desertion, and they kidnap our sailors. The honor of our flag, of our young nation, must be defended." He said some more things, about the militia and a promise that we'd be paid soon. He also promised the war would be over soon.

Two days later, Pitt ascended the stump. "Dispatches," he announced with less ring in his voice. "British General Brock has met General Hull in battle, near Detroit. There have been regrettable casualties. Several Indian tribes have allied themselves with the British, and their brutality in battle is legend, hence the American forces were driven back by sense of humanity."

We'd run. Our first engagement, with what I later heard was a smaller force, and we'd skedaddled.

A rumor ran through the camp the following week that Van Rensselaer got orders for a diversion to help Hull. But Van Rensselaer's response was a letter explaining that we were not ready to fight. 'Supplies are short, their quality is dismal and we are virtually untrained.' He promptly added two more hours of training to our day.

"I thought he liked our drilling?" complained Stump that evening as we ate around our campfire. Stump was the worst of us, but even he could dress-right. He'd also gotten handy with a pike.

Then, under white flags, British officers rode into camp. You could have knocked us over with a feather. There were more visits. We watched from the drill field in late August as our commander and his aides rode off to cross the river and meet with the British. On the 20th, Pitt stepped up on the stump. "Dispatches." He took a deep breath, looked up at us as if to gauge his safety should we not like the news, then, in precisely spoken words, said: "A state of ar-mis-tice has been declared between the United States and Britain."

"Armistice? What about our honor?" asked Stump, by then the most patriotic in our tent. "When do we get to defend our honor? When are we going to attack?" I saw most of the others agreeing with him, nodding their heads. Even I was vaguely angry. "Damn British think they own the world. This is the new world. They belong back in the old one." I might have enlisted out of boredom, but as we'd trained and drilled and become an army, we'd acquired a sense of purpose as well. We got through the drilling that day but the whole point of it seemed gone.

Perhaps we weren't much of an army. A week later we had our noses rubbed in it. American prisoners from Detroit, the wounded in open carts, were marched along the River Road in plain view of us. "If we cross, we can set our own troops free and we'll outnumber them," I heard another sergeant, a younger, more urgent fellow, say to Pitt. Even Lucas stood on the riverbank with most of the militia, yelling across the river. "Yellow bastards! Hiding behind your Indian slaves! Face us on the battlefield like soldiers!" That night around the campfires I heard men talking of attacking Canada, with or without our officers. "They're just a bunch of gentlemen cowards anyway," said Lucas. "Afraid to get blood on their uniforms." As I recall, he'd been drinking.

Neither our general nor his brother favored the war. The armistice was their attempt to stop it. But for one opposed to the war, Van Rensselaer took good advantage of the three weeks it lasted to ship in supplies and more troops. Six regiments of regulars joined our camp, and several heavy cannons were laboriously hauled up to the Lewiston heights to Fort Grey. I was grateful to be a company clerk that day; I decided it was a good day for checking inventory when they needed strong backs to haul those cannons up the hill.

When the armistice ended, we were a stronger force. And when General Brock learned of it, so I've read, he was beside himself with anger.

By this time the local gardens had given their last. With the harvest consumed we actually had to survive on the issued supplies. That was when sickness began tearing through us. The camp was wracked with diarrhea, the result of a miasma. Lucas nagged me to walk well into the woods to relieve myself. "Don't drink the water in the trough," he warned me one day soon after the first cholera appeared, "the water out on the drill field is drawn from the pump and it's too near our camp. It'll be tainted soon. We need to walk on down to the river and fill our bottles there."

The diarrhea caught up to us anyway. By the first frost I had to empty my bowels about three times a day. So did most, and it was harder and harder to find clean leaves. I thought of going home, just for a couple of days of good food, regaining my health and returning. But that would mean desertion. And that was punishable by death.

Drained from stomach spasms and the eruption in our bowels, we would drag ourselves to the drilling ground. Once there we lay down and made ourselves comfortable, waiting for perhaps an hour, while the officers finished their morning rituals, dawdling, in no hurry to begin drill instruction. Small wonder, feeling drained, that when an officer finally arrived, we would be resting, sitting in the shade, smoking and talking, playing cards or tossing dice. Then the officers would start bellowing at us, and we wouldn't feel much like getting up, and the tension would mount.

Probably the meanest was Lieutenant Dawes, from Yonkers, a protégé of Van Rensselaer's and anxious to look smart. The army was his means to advance himself. Early on he insisted on being the first on the field each day, at dawn, and would order the drummer boy to summon us.

In our tents we'd hear the drummer. "What's the matter with him?"

Someone would raise the tent flap and look outside. "Dawes is out there."

"Is Pitt there?" The Sergeant knew better than to show up at dawn. "Dawes can go to hell."

We'd finally show up and sit in the shade.

"Are you lazy bastards deaf as well as weak?" he would taunt us. "I will crack my sword over the backs of any man not on his feet by the count of ten." He would dismount, stand with his arms crossed, start the count and we would join in. "One!" we yelled out. "Two!" By "ten" we'd all sing it out, and by looks and signals be sure nobody was standing.

"I will have every one of you disobedient bastards court-martialed!" he would yell at all of us, and after a moment remount his horse and ride back to the camp. This happened several times, usually after dispatches telling us how badly the war in the west was going.

He would return in a half hour, after Sergeant Pitt came out and actually got us to stand. He would give the order, Pitt would repeat it, saving Dawes face as we followed orders. He did this every day for two weeks in August, until even he grew tired.

By September there was only one officer, Lieutenant Sims, who I'd known from the Portage, who was generally respected, and that because he sympathized with us and never ordered more than a slow march. "C'mon, lads, let's try to get some work done today," he would plead. Since he was also from Lewiston, a recent graduate of the school there and vaguely knew some of us, even calling us by name, we'd get up for him.

By then the army must have lost a dozen to twenty men each day to desertion. Those that were caught, and many were, ran the gauntlet. Men would be lined up, fifty on each side, each ordered to cut a switch. Then two corporals with musket and bayonet would walk the deserter through the line, making certain he didn't run in either direction, and the men struck. The deserters were flayed bloody when they reached the end.

It became a horrible daily ritual, and men whose backs were stripped to bloody meat and bandaged would be back on the drilling field that afternoon. Our morning ritual in the summer was breakfast at dawn, then out to fight with the officers until about nine, when we began to drill. By September it had changed; we breakfasted, then collected our switches, set up the gauntlet almost without being ordered to, and beat our brothers. Then we would drill, helping up the punished.

"Why'd you do it?" I asked one fellow younger than I on the drill field, letting him lean against me for a moment's rest, "I'm homesick too, but look at you."

"We ain't fighting," he said, "what's the point?" He hung his head in misery. "I just want to go home."

In late September the general ordered ten repeat offenders executed. The first time I ever saw a human life taken was as punishment for desertion. I didn't know the men. They came from near Syracuse, and were trying to return to their families. They'd left prosperous homes, and were eating spoiled food they wouldn't throw to their pigs. Still, it was made very clear to us that there would be just two punishments for desertion. Running the gauntlet was the gentler one.

The youngest was a drummer boy of thirteen, the eldest had the gray beard of middle age. All of them had tried three times or more to desert, each time returned and run through the gauntlet. That morning we were called to the drill field, but instead of marching, or the gauntlet, we saw that a simple gallows had been set up under an elm tree. Three ropes were hung over a bough ten feet off the ground. Camp stools were set under each rope. A drum roll began, and that put a chill in my blood and bowels.

General Van Rensselaer rode onto the drill field, but remained mounted. "I need a volunteer," he said to his aide, and his aide turned to Lieutenant Dawes and repeated the order.

Dawes saluted. "It would be my pleasure, sir."

"Bastard," rose from some voices, just loud enough to make Dawes glance in our direction. He took his place behind the condemned. "Mount the stool," he ordered, and the first three stepped up. The drummers began a roll. Dawes fitted the ropes around their necks.

"Drummers," ordered Van Rensselaer, and the drummers stopped. "These men are guilty of desertion, third offense." He spoke tersely.

I expect nothing in his life had prepared him for the task of ordering men hung in his presence. "Mercy has been extended. Each has run the gauntlet. They have deserted again, and again, and only one punishment remains."

The entire army was dead silent. "Proceed," the general ordered. A minister from Lewiston village spoke briefly to each of the three, the drummers rolled their sticks again, and then Dawes kicked the stool out from under the feet of the first, then the second. The first dangled wildly. Dawes was forced to grab his legs, suffer a kick, and pull down. The first man finally hung limp, and then the lieutenant kicked out the third stool. And then they repeated it.

I felt bile rising and found a private space to vomit. Lucas helped me up, scowling at the hangings. "A damn waste," he said, "damn waste." He wouldn't criticize the officers, nor the deserters. "They knew what they were signing up for," he said, "but it's an awful thing when the truth of it becomes clear and you know what you've gotten yourself into."

It was Old Shultz again, driving the wagon into camp, and when he saw me waiting, he laughed. "If you didn't like the pork, you don't wanna look at what I brung ya." When we had the first heavy wooden crate on the ground, I opened it to see a tangle of muskets. I saw rust everywhere, mud on the barrels, wooden stocks split, some without stocks.

"Do you expect me to issue these?" I asked, looking at him in shock.

"I don't expect you to wipe your ass without complaining," joked Schultz. "But I hear you and the Judge had a talk."

I nodded. "These are the muskets the Judge is sending us?"

"Yessir," the old man grinned, revealing pink gums, and he fished out the bill of lading. "Your signature, please?" he asked in mock courtesy.

We had been led to expect Springfield muskets, the regular army issue, .70 caliber, which still shot a lighter load than the .75 caliber British army musket. The muskets we got were of varying make and varying caliber, none as powerful as the British muskets and in universally poor shape. I held an ancient musket with French writing, from the days of George Washington's army, .65 caliber or lighter. "Did you see these?" I asked Old Shultz, but he shook his head.

"I just brung 'em," he said. "Could have been firewood in them crates for all I knew."

"Tell him, tell the Judge, that," I thought for a minute, then handed back the unsigned bill. "Just a moment," I said, and fished out an especially decrepit musket. It had half a stock, the hammer was firmly stuck halfway, and the gun maker's name was inscribed en Francaise. Running to Captain Williams' tent, where he was writing a letter, I stood at attention just outside the tent and said, "request a moment of the Captain's time."

Williams, who was hoping to gain some stature in this adventure and then study the law, was writing to his uncle in Canandaigua. "What is it, Cleary?" he asked, irritated, as he stepped out of his tent.

"We just got a wagon load of these, sir," I held out the musket, "most of them broken and barely any two alike, and I wanted you to see them before I signed."

Williams looked like someone had shit in his dinner. "A wagon load of these? All of them like this?" He took the musket, tried in vain to work the hammer, then shouldered it with the broken stock, then struggled to work the ramrod free. It was bent. "Deuced trash," he sighed. He looked around, hoping to see a superior officer, but the officers were usually at Van Rensselaer's headquarters. It was much more comfortable there. "How many of these are there?"

"About thirty per crate, or so. He has twenty crates out there now," I said. Williams left me standing there for twenty minutes while he tried to find someone of higher rank to make the decision. He came back, finally, looking furious. "Sign for them," he ordered me, and went back inside his tent.

"This is a joke," I told Old Shultz as I signed the bill.

"You ain't laughing," the wagoner chuckled as he drove off.

The less said about the day I had to issue the muskets, the better. We couldn't find more than ten cartridges for many of them. The officers blushed and complained among themselves, and the men ultimately laughed at what they'd been given. "Mine don't fire too far," Lucas told me after cleaning his musket for a day, "and the hammer, if I pull it back all the way it won't release. But if I pull it back just about three quarters she'll catch, and if I'm already aimed I can fire it." As for mine, I spent a week cleaning the action, and three times I pulled the trigger, and each time the hammer jammed halfway.

A new fellow, Joshua Neal, got assigned to our barracks when a skinny boy named Courtney died. One day, with Joshua's help, bound and determined to get it working, we managed to fire it; the barrel developed a hairline crack.

Most fired once, perhaps twice, before the hammers jammed or the barrels began cracking, a warning that a good charge of gunpowder would blow it part. "Best save what little it's got left," I overheard often, as the men worked their muskets, "got maybe two more shots from it, and I'll need it in Canada more than here. And I've only got a few cartridges for it anyway." There was no chance to learn marksmanship. We sorted out the good rifles to the marksmen among us, and planned to put them in front. We felt defenseless. An army, feeling defenseless.

After getting the muskets the desertions worsened, and there were two more executions the following week. Instead of hanging, the next five men were shot. Van Rensselaer sent a wagon to Fort Niagara to get proper Springfield muskets, and regular army to handle them, to be sure the damn things shot right. The deserters were crying for mercy when the soldiers fired and gun smoke rose and the deserters dropped, and didn't move.

I overheard a card game among the officers. "We are completely unprepared to fight," Lieutenant Dawes was saying while waiting for his cards, and none of the others challenged him. "That rabble couldn't spit in unison, much less march," he said. "They ignore every order. If we get stuck in battle with them, they'll be a danger to themselves. And those muskets!" They laughed; they were privately armed. "Good Christ, someone is making a handsome fortune off this business. I don't know what they expect us to do with these awful things they've issued. Certainly not fight."

I'd been called to fetch ale, and then they seemed to remember I was there.

"Cleary," Captain Williams called me over.

"Yes sir," I answered, standing at attention, resting the ale on the table. The others were suddenly dour, looking left and right.

"Private, we're in a state of armistice, and cannot attack Canada," he began, in a big-brotherly tone. "Now, we know the muskets that were issued are mostly not useable. And it doesn't matter, because a treaty will end the war and we will never need to fire them. In the meantime we must appear to prying eyes to be fully armed, and for that purpose a rusty musket is not only as useful, it is cheaper. Understand?" He was dealing his cards as he spoke, looking neither at his fellows nor at me, just at his cards. "Keep what you've heard to yourself."

Lucas was right, I remember thinking, *the officers are just cowards.*

The useless muskets were not so scary when we were told the peace treaty was imminent. Then, one September morning, the Sergeant got on the stump. "Dispatches. The armistice in effect between the United States and Great Britain will expire one week from today. Repeat, the armistice will expire in one week."

Some began to cheer. I panicked.

Shortly after that we saw the British setting up batteries. We saw men camping in Queenston, directly across the river, our presumed target. And I would look at the hairline cracks in my musket.

We awoke the first morning of October to a chilling wind out of the north, a reminder that in another month the cold winds would blow down from Canada and turn the war into an exercise in sentry-duty and frostbite. "Did you hear about Black Rock?" Stump asked me one afternoon as we drew rations. "There's another army, camped in Black Rock. They captured a prison ship at Fort Erie, full of American prisoners, bales of furs and barrels of pork. They brought back our boys and the food, and then they burned the ship."

It was like lightning struck the camp. Brock was not, we decided, invincible. The British were spread too thin, we'd heard, and this seemed to confirm it. That same week our camp filled with regular Army and their officers. I guess they prodded Van Rensselaer into action.

Next morning, Pitt read orders to us. "Our plan of invasion has been set. Men have been sent to collect at least thirty boats and crew experienced with the river. With these we will cross before dawn, tomorrow." The roar of the river churning out of the gorge would drown out the sounds of the boats. Batteries at Fort Gray and along the river would pound the British defenses into silence while the boats threw hundreds, even thousands of us at the thin British lines. The attack would move fast, first taking the heights overlooking Queenston. After that we would subdue Fort George at our leisure.

From my diary:

> *October 9th, 1812. The General has ordered an assault on the heights before sunrise. We have been issued extra rations, and some of us without proper boots are being shod, finally.*
>
> *October 10th: We're still here. We waited all night. Lieutenant Sims found only thirteen boats, not thirty. With just three men to help he towed them upriver in the dark, during a terrible rainstorm, he somehow missed the landing, continuing on upriver. I hear the dark and the noise panicked him and he beached the lead boat, in which he'd piled all the oars for the boats being towed behind, returning well after dawn, sheepish and wet. We have a new song in camp. "Sims lost the boats in the river, Sims lost the boats in the dark, the boats have run the gauntlet, and the lead one has been shot. . . " The General has postponed the battle, we fetched the boats back, and they've been turned over on shore to dry so Brock can count them. Now we know the General hasn't a brain in his head.*
>
> *We are being prepared for battle, again. More rations were issued, and my new boots issued on the 8th are broken in now. More men have arrived, some in regular uniforms with good muskets. We know ours will not be replaced before we attack. We hear the regular army lads with the good muskets will go over first and do all the shooting. That's good, as mine seems most likely to blow into pieces. This is assuming, of course, that the Dutchman's shirts are clean, and his tea leaves read well, his yellow fever has passed, and no other excuse cancels the attack. Captain Williams tells me that a spy of ours reports that Brock has led hundreds of his men to Detroit. Why, we haven't a clue, but it must be making our general a little more confident.*
>
> *October 11th: The folk hereabout have wisely hid all their boats. We couldn't find one nor buy one, and there's not enough time to make them.'*

Something like two thousand men were in camp by the evening of the twelfth. It certainly was crowded, and the regulars were pretty arrogant, free with insults and starting a few fights. Still, having them was good news to us, because they were properly armed and would certainly go over first. The bad news was there just weren't enough boats to get them over before dawn. So it would take twice as long, at least, to land the force. "That's the Dutchman's problem," Lucas reminded us, and we all smiled, talking about what the best vantage point would be from which to watch the battle.

The sunset on October 12th, was a gray, disappointing display. We knew the attack would probably take place that night because surrounding General Van Rensselaer were half a dozen regular army officers who knew what they were doing. But the plan of battle changed, it seemed, every hour. The first wave would be all regulars, then it changed to being all militia, changed again to half regulars, half militia. Just before I turned in for the night, we heard that Lieutenant Sims volunteered our company for the first wave, then was told that regulars would be sent first, militia in support. "Trying to recover his honor with our blood," grumbled Lucas.

That night was rainy and cold. The regulars wrote letters, then slept, knowing they might find little chance for rest in the ensuing days, but our boys were visible by their raucousness, behaving as though dawn would bring an election instead of a battle. Homemade spirits were passed around and the fires burned bright in spite of the rain. Our tent was quiet that night. Lucas told us, "Let the fools gamble and drink. They'll be begging for ten minutes of sleep this time tomorrow."

"Are you scared?" Joshua asked me that night. He was such a quiet fellow that I didn't realize he'd spoken, then I didn't realize he'd spoken to me. He was a tall, lean fellow, with a nose like the sail on a clipper ship, a lad you'd call homely but with a gentle, God-fearing, kindly soul. "You scared? I'm scared," he repeated.

Outside some drunks were singing a bit of doggerel that somehow rhymed with Van Rensselaer. "Well," I admitted, "I'm a little scared." My eyes fell on my rusted, useless musket and I pictured myself standing ten paces from a British soldier in a field somewhere, both of us aiming our muskets, me knowing mine wouldn't fire, and I barely kept some bile down. "I'm really scared," I said softly.

"I went against my Pa's orders coming here," Joshua said. "I've written to him twice but he hasn't written back." His eyes filled with tears. "I just," he folded a sheet of parchment and used the dripping of a stub of candle to seal it, "wrote him again. Told him I was sorry. Did your pa approve? Of you signing up?"

Someone fired a musket, and then two more fired muskets. That was surprising, as the regulars were better disciplined, and I didn't think any militia had muskets that could afford to be fired casually. "My pa is dead. Died years ago," I said. "My mother didn't want me coming, but she sort of gave me her permission."

Lucas had been cleaning his musket one last time by the light of a candle. "Lads," he spoke up, "it's late. Even with these morons carrying on, try to get some rest."

"Night, Lucas," I said. "Don't fret about your pa," I whispered to Joshua, "when this is over he'll be proud of you." Lucas pinched the candle out, and we tried to sleep, listening to the rain.

I got a letter a month ago from Mother that I hadn't answered, and it nagged me that night, that I might never be able to answer her. I rose in the night, stepped out of the tent, and wrote by the light of a nearby fire.

Mother, I will be in battle when you read this. Please forgive me for not responding earlier. I know you didn't want me to join, and I am sorry for enlisting, for the pain I know you suffered. If I get through this, I'll come home as soon as I can and ease the burden I've been in your life. I stretched out on my blanket and tried to sleep.

And then it was time. Still in darkness, Lucas roused us. That was how I knew I'd slept, when I woke. Then the order came down to form up. I couldn't stop trembling as I rolled up my blanket, pulled on my boots, and hung my shot and powder around my neck. While we lined up, Lieutenant Sims collected our letters. Stepping outside into the rain and the muddy ground, a crowd was growing; we formed up in the rainy darkness. I marched behind Lucas, down to the river. When I smelled the water my stomach turned. Running into the bushes, I saw Joshua join me. "I guess this is it," said Joshua. Embarrassed, I turned my face up to catch a few drops of rainwater. It refreshed my mouth, as the cool wind behind the rain chilled me.

We got back to the line and Lucas gave us a taste of whiskey. "Put a warm spot in your belly."

Stumbling like drunks in the dark, we marched down to the landing. The sloping pathway was full of hurdles, slimy mud and rocks and tree roots tripping us up. Laughter bubbled up as we slipped and slid, crashing into trees and each other. "Quiet!" hissed the officers, the ones that weren't also laughing. And we laughed. Until we got to the river, and saw the boats, and saw Queenston.

In the darkness the order of battle was confused. Regular army Colonel Chrystie was at the front of the line, but, calling in hoarse whispers for his officers and not hearing sufficient replies, he knew what had happened. His three hundred regulars were the men we counted on going first. They were in the back of the line. "Shit," cursed Joshua. It was the only time I heard him curse. Either they went last, or the battle would begin in daylight by the time they got to the front of the line. And if we went first we were certain we'd be cut down like wheat. "They're mad," I said to Joshua, "they aren't thinking of sending us first, are they?"

"All right, lads," ordered Pitt, rain water dripping from his hat, gripping his own musket, "let's load up this boat."

"Our Father, who art in heaven, hallowed be thy name," Joshua prayed. I concentrated on keeping my powder dry, out of habit, and Lucas took some more swallows of whiskey.

"Stop loading the boats," someone in an army uniform ordered. A messenger climbed up the slope to update Van Rensselaer. If there was anything worse than heading into that battle it was waiting for it. So we waited, Lucas and Joshua and I bobbing in a boat, others on land with less than two feet of ground to move in, and darkness and mud to contend with.

Finally, word came down from the general: "Proceed."

"Lord God Almighty," Joshua prayed in a breathless voice, his eyes huge in the moonlight, "I'm going to die today." He was hushed, but he was beyond caring. "I'm a dead man. A dead man." He sniffed back tears.

"Buck up," I whispered. "You're scaring the hell out of me."

Colonel Solomon was in the next boat. He'd led us in drill a few times and allowed us to openly question him about war. "Hardest part is waiting for the battle," he told us. "Once it starts, you just do what you're trained to do. It comes naturally." He had insisted on leading the militia, for reasons known best to him. He looked brave to me; I saw his face in a burst of moonlight and he looked charged with energy. "Away all the boats," was whispered down the slope. Men on the bank pushed us off.

As we rowed out into the river, the current swept us downstream, past Queenston. "We're drifting too far," said Lucas. The plan was for experienced boatmen to row, but just as the boats disappeared, so did the rowers. I had an oar, as did Lucas, and Joshua sat between us holding our muskets. We had to pull hard to get back upstream. The boat was only a couple inches clear of the river, so we shipped some water. "Easy, easy," said Lucas, and directed Joshua to bail with his cupped hands, "let's die on dry land." We finally got the bow aimed towards the village. We could only see three or four other boats.

"We the only ones?" I asked, between pulls.

We didn't dare call out to find others. Apparently no one in Queenston heard us, heard our oars thump against the boats, heard us splash into the river when we landed. We landed at a ferry landing, at the bottom of the riverbank.

"We the only ones?" I asked again.

"No," said Lucas. "Now shut up." More boats landed; luckily one of them with Solomon Van Rensselaer. By that time it felt like an hour we'd been out there. It all took, I later learned, about eighteen minutes.

At Solomon's command we began climbing the bank, a good thirty feet up, as high up as the bank we'd slipped down on the Lewiston side. Lucas caught my eye and we let the regulars climb past us. We heard Solomon cry out, "This is it, boys! Attack!" We finished climbing, ducking at the volleys of musket fire, and saw that our men had nevertheless breached the battery. I was among the last in, and found my comrades in control; I was relieved at not being killed. Lying dead were several British regulars, and a few of our own. Then someone on the bank below called out, "help," and scrambled up to report, "the colonel's been hit, badly."

Good turned to bad. We were stuck on a sliver of beach, our commander was severely wounded and most of our officers were killed. "I knew this would happen!" Joshua said, more angry now than scared. A regular captain from the last boat, John Wool, took over. At about that time, American artillery fire from Fort Gray on Lewiston Heights, opposing Queenston's heights, finally began to shoot at the British, thundering in the dark.

Facing us on the shore was a small force of regulars and militia. Reinforcements arrived, a few at a time. The dueling cannons dropped cannonballs into the river and our few boatmen ran away. Some boats were swept past the beach by the current and landed further downstream, where they were captured. Still, more and more men landed and we regained confidence. Before being taken back to Lewiston, Solomon ordered us, "try for the heights. Everything depends on us taking the heights." Bullets whistled past, hitting the water with a hissing noise. Crashing booms echoed off the walls of the gorge, gave me an earache, and shook the ground as a British battery nearby dueled with the battery in Lewiston. Lucas nudged me and pointed at several others creeping away. "Follow them."

Captain Wool led us through brush and tall grass, and sometimes a slippery spot or two that got one a wet foot. "Where we going?" I asked Lucas, and he put his finger on his lips as the captain led us on a path up the steep climb to the heights. As we left the firing below, we realized we were undetected.

It was a hard climb on a narrow path. I remember pausing twice, panting for breath. Lucas was behind me. "Get moving," he whispered, prodding me with his stock.

"I'm catching my breath," I said.

"Catch it fast. You're holding up the line." I got up the hill, a little embarrassed at my hard breathing. "You spent too much time counting supplies."

Awaiting us on the height was one British cannon and eight gunners, exchanging volleys with the cannons on Lewiston Heights. Wool waited until we were together, just below the ridge, and we charged again. At least fifty of us charged the eight; they fired the cannon and a few musket shots, then ran, leaving us in control of the high ground.

Our men began moving up from the beach as well and the Queenston militia abandoned their positions for higher ground. Then Brock arrived with his men, the 49th of Foot, recently in my nightmares, their red coats visible in the dawn's light through the trees and the sound of their infernal drums rolling up the slope like thunder rumbling up from the ground. Brock, no doubt, knew the importance of holding the heights, and organized a charge up the slope. "They're coming!" I heard someone behind me yell.

On Captain Wool's command—"Fire!"—the regulars and the men with reliable muskets fired on the redcoats.

Someone put a bullet through Brock's wrist, making him drop his saber; the same volley killed several officers. The 49th faltered.

"My God, we've stopped them!" yelled Lucas.

Brock picked up his saber in his good hand. *What a fearless fellow,* I remembered thinking. Yelling to his men, waving his saber, flashing it in the dim light of a rainy dawn, he rallied them and they charged again, uphill through the trees, firing, dropping to one knee to reload, firing, reloading, returning fire in a show of well-trained, drill-field-perfect British firepower. I confess at the time they drew my respect. At the height of the charge, as the British were closing to fifty feet, Wool, nursing a wound in his buttocks, prepared us to send off one more volley before retreating south. "Make ready. Aim," he yelled through the noise of musketry, of drums, of cries of pain, "and fire!"

Our regulars fired a second volley and hit Brock again, and he fell again. We watched him a moment, but he lay still. His regiment faltered for the second time, but again the charge was renewed, this time under a lieutenant.

"They're damn good," Lucas said.

The British kept climbing, muskets gripped waist high now to bayonet as they closed.

"Retreat!" Wool yelled. He had seen Brock fall, then saw the redcoats continue the charge without him. As the bayonets flashed in our faces, we were already one foot higher up the slope and Wool's order followed us.

But he ran ahead of us and stopped us where we'd first charged from; panting for breath, we knelt for cover and those with working muskets returned fire; I threw a rock. And another one. Then I saw Wool point to our left, and saw some regulars scramble to out-flank the British and exploit our superior numbers. A few minutes later our men charged back down the bloody slope.

This was the moment we'd dreaded. Lucas caught my arm at the trench, letting the regulars run ahead of us down the slope. They yelled, fired their muskets, reloaded, then closed in to such close quarters that muskets need not be aimed. "We outnumber them," Lucas reminded me. "The regulars thought we were useless, let them do the fighting." We watched them fight, some with fists. "Looks like Pitt was right. Pike training wasn't a bad idea." I looked around and saw a dozen fellows, all militia, waiting. "We'll stop the next rout," Lucas yelled to keep us. So we stayed low and peeked over the edge of the shallow trench the British artillery had dug to look down at the fight.

The woods were filled with red and gray uniforms, and plainclothes of both sides, firing, slashing at each other. Blood jetted straight up not ten feet ahead of me. I couldn't tell whose. My ears ached from the noise.

Men fell. Men crawled away. Men ran, some down the slope, some off into the trees, disappearing. The fight dissolved like ice facing winter sunshine. Our superior numbers made the 49th falter. Retreating down the slope as one of the few officers left screamed, "withdraw," they recovered their fallen general, and their wounded and dead.

The sun at seven that morning shone on the Stars and Stripes flying over the Heights of Queenston.

The smell of gunpowder, like a fog blanketing the ground, made me cough, dried out my mouth and made me take drink after drink from Lucas' whiskey, the only liquid at hand. Stretcher parties moved through the wooded slope like spirits, taking away wounded. Lucas took a piece of ball straight through his hand during the first charge, "didn't even feel it until now," he said, "but it's a good omen. We'll all stop a musket ball in this mess sooner or later." He tied a scrap of linen around his hand. "This is a wound I can live with."

Captain Wool limped by and ordered us, "get to work on fresh trenches. They'll be back." We scooped the muddy soil with pieces of bark and our bare hands, chattering our brief, scrambled memories of the battle.

"Think I shit my britches. Maybe I'll throw them at the British."

"Thought I was shot, but it was the fellow next to me. I got blood all over me. His blood."

"I found a British musket, one that'll actually fire."

"I can't believe I ain't dead. Can't believe we're up here."

"I bet they don't even come back. We kilt their general." No one believed that.

"Same general we was told had moved to Detroit. Like to get my hands on the lying skunk that told that whopper."

We dragged some fallen logs into place, piled up rocks, and formed a ragged line. The lack of sleep caught up with us then and we tried to find resting places, backs against trees, flat out where the ground permitted, and slept in the drizzling rain.

It got quiet then. We could hear the river below, we heard musket fire, a cannon now and then, distant sounds from Lewiston and down the River Road. The air stank of gunpowder, and just beneath it was blood.

But it was quiet. And though I was staggering with weariness, the violence I'd been in wouldn't let me sleep.

Lucas lit his pipe, the smell of tobacco a relief. "Have I ever told you of my family?" I shook my head. I'd asked him once in camp and he'd changed the topic. "My mother's name was Madeline and my young sister was Jennie. She looked just like my mother. One day my father took me with him to trade at Canajoharie. We had slaughtered a couple pigs, more meat than we needed. We were going to talk to a man about buying some land my father wanted and my father was going to surprise my mother with a music box she wanted. I wish I remembered the tune it played. It doesn't matter." He drew on his pipe but it had gone out. "While we were gone, Butler swept through the valley with his Indians. When we heard we rode all night, but when we got there the cabin was a burned wreck. I found Jennie's body in the embers. She was just four. Mother was gone. Taken as a slave, most likely," Lucas said softly, and he re-lit his pipe. "My pa sent me to a blacksmith, Justin Hargreaves, and joined the Continental army. He wanted vengeance. I guess I got that from him, too. He died at Saratoga."

"Did you ever get married and have a family?"

He shook his head.

"I ran away from Hargreaves and joined the army. I started as a drummer boy, and mustered out after the war. I tried farming but I didn't care for it. I did some blacksmithing, which I was better at. But I haven't felt like I had my feet under me for years. Then this war comes by, I fell right back into it." He yawned deeply. "But the problem with vengeance is that you never feel the weights are quite balanced."

"Does this help?" I asked, looking down the hill at Queenston.

He looked down the slope at a pair of soldiers navigating the pathway with a wounded man in tow. "It helps a little." He blew his nose, shifted his powder horn and lay back on the ground.

I stood and stretched and yawned deeply, and took a look around. We faced north, overlooking the village and the road to Fort George, whence British reinforcements would come. "Are they going to come back? Will they try to push us off again?"

"More'n likely," Lucas answered, eyes closed, "but they lost their general the last time. I think they'll need fresh hands from Fort George. It's going to be a little while. Get some rest."

"Should we go down there," I looked down the slope, where the remains of battle were still fresh, "and see if we can't find a good musket?"

"Suit yourself," said Lucas, not moving. "I heard if they capture you and you're carrying one of their pieces, they won't give you parole."

I rolled up my coat for a pillow, closed my eyes and thought of turkey hunting last fall with Electa tagging along. Her brown hair was braided down her neck. She had my mother's face. "Do you have to shoot the turkeys?" she asked. "The musket is so loud."

"You like turkey stew, don't you?" I asked her. She nodded. "I'll warn you before I shoot, so you cover your ears, okay?" She followed me through the woods until I reached a meadow I'd found game in before. We waited a few minutes and, sure enough, two fat hens strolled calmly across the meadow. "Now," I whispered, and she stuck her fingers in her ears. I sighted, and fired.

Lucas prodded me awake. Through the bare trees we could see and hear, in the distance, British reinforcements. They made my mouth dry. "I'm thirsty," I said.

"Go, but be quick," Lucas said, and handed me his bottle. "Fill mine, too."

We'd crossed a shallow creek climbing the heights. Going back for water, I saw for the first time how thin our lines were. Just half of the army crossed over that day. The rest stayed on the New York shore.

The general rode amongst the militia gathered on the east bank of the river. This war that he thought wrong, he was in the middle of it now. And surgeons were tending his brother. Yet, a thousand men had successfully invaded. He'd begun to hope he might emerge from this miserable adventure with a military success to propel his political interests. But now it was falling apart. "You see your fellows across the river, holding the Heights. They cannot prevail without reinforcements!" He rode up and down the river, urging, scolding, begging the militia to get into the boats. "The battle is won! We must have more men to secure it! They need your help over there!"

Plead and demand as he might, the men from the Lewiston camp ignored his calls to cross over. Their enlistments bound them to defend New York, not invade Canada. They'd heard the shooting. They'd seen wounded men, their fellows, carried back. They looked at their weapons, and stayed put.

I reached the creek and filled our bottles. I knelt to take a drink but a shot showered my head with spray. Coughing water from my mouth and nose, I scrambled for cover and heard firing. Climbing back up the hill, I saw our men crouched behind our crude trenches, anxiously peeping over. "Down!" I heard several voices bark at me. I scrambled behind the trench with them.

"Lucas," I got out, "I was almost shot down by the creek. I was just—"

Lucas hushed me and pointed straight ahead.

Captain Wool had a field glass, and he could see some of the enemy through the trees, assembling on Queenston's commons. "British troops, some militia, and some Indians. They're coming down the River Road, this way."

"Indians?" Joshua asked, flinching, "where're our reinforcements?"

Wool looked around and tried to mask his anger. "We'll have to hold our ground without reinforcements."

We could hear the fifes and drums of the British. They made us wait. They must have known how scared we were. When it finally happened, instead of attacking up the slope straight at us, they flanked us on the west. When we realized what they were doing, we tried to shift our thin numbers. "They're hitting us on the flank!" cried a young, dirt-smeared, terrified regular, appearing suddenly, crashing through the woods. "They're coming!"

And suddenly they were there.

The British fired from a safe distance. They had the better weapons and their fire was deadly accurate. Half a dozen men near me fell dead before they could fire back. Lucas raised and fired his musket in the general direction of the sounds. He looked through the cloud of smoke, wondering perhaps if he'd hit anything, and what should then come running through the trees?

"Indians!"

They advanced from tree to rock to tree, staying behind cover, blending into the forest and moving like ghosts. I saw one a hundred feet away, then he was gone; there he was again, just fifty feet off. Then again, close enough that I could see his fur-trimmed earring. Lucas fired, reloaded and fired, and reloaded again; then he pulled his trigger and I heard, "goddamn it." They were all around us by then, whooping, screaming. Lucas threw his musket like a spear, then turned to run. "Come on!" he yelled at me.

I froze. I curled up behind a boulder. I saw Joshua, and we exchanged scared looks. Then an Indian appeared in front of him. He stood, raised his musket and fired, but the charging Indian did not clutch at his heart and fall. Instead, Joshua fell. The Indian raised his grisly steel hatchet high in the air, then swung down, and I heard the blade hit bone, and I heard Joshua's scream.

That got me moving. I ran, straight into a tree. My nose tingled and my face was sore and scraped. I braced myself to feel a hatchet hit me, to feel my scalp torn from my head. Musket balls whizzed by, thumped into the trees, and ripped straggling leaves off. "The Indians will scalp us. If you see a British officer, hold onto him for dear life," Lucas told me that afternoon. Coming through the woods, flashing a saber like he was Brock's protégé, I saw an officer. "Help me," I cried out. The officer made a path towards me. The Indian murdering Joshua had just shrieked in ecstasy and my cry for help caught his attention, and when the officer was as near as the Indian he stopped, caught his breath, and looked at the Indian, and I realized he was waiting to see me killed. "You bastard," I got out. I dropped my blankets, my bullets, and, like iron drawn to a magnet, I collided with every blessed tree and root trying to get down that hill.

There were five boats left at the shore. One had just pushed off half-full and was drifting, as the boat had just one oar. Men were throwing their kit aside, fighting to get a seat, and once in were punching and shoving to keep others out and to cast off. The last boats pushed off overloaded and likely to sink. I turned to face the woods, terrified of what I'd see. But the first face was Lucas; somehow I'd passed him on the way down.

"You move fast when you want to," he said.

I snorted some blood. "Ran into a tree. Couple of trees." The bullets flew at us again.

"We have to surrender to an officer," Lucas kept saying, studying the slope, searching for a red jacket, but we saw none.

"I already tried that. He was waiting for the Indian to scalp me."

"The hell you say?" Then he tugged on my sleeve and led me along the riverbank south, into the gorge. It was hard walking, dragging a musket through brush. I became fiercely hungry and looked around for wild carrots or anything I could eat, but it was no time for foraging. I stumbled and slid into the river several times, Lucas' strong arms pulling me out. As we neared the gorge we went into shadow. The sounds of fighting faded, replaced by the roaring of the rapids.

We hiked upriver in the dark, along a narrow stretch of shoreline. Above us were the layers of rock the river exposed. After an eternity, after I'd asked for the dozenth time, "can't we rest here?" we stopped in a glen of woods in the gorge called Foster's Flats. The ground was a soft bed of needles and leaves, and we found a spot sheltered from view behind huge boulders. As best we could tell, we were alone. We dropped to the ground and slept.

The storm was finally blown out, and the sky was clear when we woke, still tired. We could see where we were. The rapids there churn furiously. "There's no way across here," Lucas said. "Is there a trail out of here?"

"There might be, but I don't know where it is. Now what do we do?" I asked Lucas.

"You're from these parts. If we continue upriver do you know a spot where we can climb out or do we have to go back to Queenston?"

I studied the gorge walls, then shook my head.

"I guess it's back to Queenston." Lucas said. "But not today."

We built a fire, and my hunger returned, but our minds were back at Queenston. "Did you see if Joshua made it?" Lucas asked.

As much as I didn't want to, I remembered the axe cleaving Joshua's skull, and I heard his scream. I shook my head.

"Damn."

"How about Pitt? Did you see Pitt anywhere?"

"No. He was in the second boat but I didn't see him after we went up the hill. Hope he made it."

"Yea, Pitt was a good fellow. I liked Pitt." I looked at what I'd held onto; my water bottle, my useless musket, two cartridges I'd made for my useless musket, but not a piece of bread. "I'm starving."

"Me too."

"I had half a loaf of bread back at the camp. Why didn't I bring it?"

Lucas yawned deeply. "Probably isn't there anymore."

"So what happened back there? Why didn't we get reinforcements? Did our boys abandon us? Even those regulars who thought they were too smart for us?"

"At the rate we lost boats I wonder how many could have made it across by noon. Hell, it was a miracle as many of us got over as did," Lucas said, "it was a botched plan."

"Why didn't they cross? We already did the hard part. Why wouldn't they cross?" I asked. Lucas stared into the fire, shaking his head. He nodded off.

It was like we couldn't sleep enough. I lay back and dozed. I heard a sound, opened my eyes, and saw Joshua standing over me. *How did you get here?* I asked. His face was blasted, destroyed. His jaw was just red meat and bone and dried blood. His eyes were gone, and that's when I knew he was dead. He knelt before me, holding his musket. The stock was splintered and the barrel burst near the action. He tried to say something to me but I couldn't understand him, and he leaned closer. He tried to shape words in what remained of his mouth, leaning closer to me each time, and I recoiled in disgust. Then he leaned over so close to me that I could see a bit of gunmetal lodged in his jawbone, and I heard his voice croak 'Remember'.

Please, I begged, *go away*. Part of his tongue still moved, and on his last try a gush of blood flowed from his eye sockets. Then he limped down to the boulders and waved good-bye to me. I waved back. I wanted him gone. He dove in.

Lucas woke me. "Nehemiah, wake up."

"It was Joshua. He looked awful. His hair was bloody, sticking to his face, and his right arm was dangling. Like a shot-dead animal. And he dove into the rapids."

"It's no wonder you having bad dreams," Lucas tried to comfort me, "but you can't be shouting at Joshua's spirit or you'll give us away to any Indians hunting for us."

"I don't think it was a dream." I was shaking, looking around for Joshua, and felt warmth. That was when I discovered Lucas had built a fire. "This feels so good," I said. "Is it safe?"

Lucas sighed. "No, but I was sick of being wet and cold. Guess I'd rather get shot than die of pneumonia."

I curled up close to our fire, Lucas put more sticks on the flames and my shakes gradually stilled. I was weak with hunger. He got up to fetch more wood. "Don't leave," I begged.

"I'll be just a minute," he promised. I studied the fire, kept my eyes on a flame growing from the top of a burning stick until I heard his footsteps.

"I'm here." He sat, and let a pile of sticks fall next to the fire. "It was an awful day," said Lucas. "You need to get beyond it."

"He asked me to remember."

"Remember what?"

"Him, I suppose. Everything. Our muskets."

He sighed deeply. "I doubt I'll ever forget." He sat, his legs crossed before him, staring into the fire. "Y'know, we might have held the heights if our muskets weren't useless. The others might have crossed if they could have held their own in battle." He stirred up a half-burned stick. "How many of us held off firing in camp to be sure our muskets could hold one more charge, and to save that for the battle? What kind of army is that?"

What he didn't say, perhaps was ashamed to say, what I remembered, was Lucas holding us back during the charge, letting the regulars take the heat of the battle. What kind of army, indeed.

A twig cracked and we both jumped. "We can't stay here," I said.

"I think we're safe for another night," decided Lucas, "we'll move in the morning."

I heard the voice of my father, and that calmed me. "Back to Queenston?"

"You said it yourself. Don't think there's another way out. We'll pass ourselves off as good Loyalists." Lucas smiled, "I find myself more in sympathy with them now. Still hungry?"

"Starving."

He offered a dirt-stained root. "Wild carrot growing over there. Not much, but it's better than nothing."

"Barely." Still hoping one of our coat pockets would mysteriously sprout corn meal, a chunk of pork, a crust of bread, I ate the wild carrot. Even the dirt stuck to it tasted good. "So tomorrow we walk back to Queenston. Then where? If we return to Lewiston we're back in the militia."

"Where do you want to go?" asked Lucas like an indulgent father, laying back, his eyes closed.

"Where do you want to go?"

Lucas sighed in exasperation; the mantle of fatherhood was an unaccustomed burden. He answered softly, his eyes still closed. "I've given it some thought. We've got a musket that might fire once, and if we can lay hands on some supplies, I've a hankering to head out west. There's open land out there, so fresh you throw seeds on it and it grows corn. What do you say?"

"Let's be gone early."

I slept deeply. Shortly after dawn we started back. Lucas stopped to study the river rapids several times and I remembered that he was from Cherry Valley. "I'll take you to see the falls if we get out of this intact," I promised. His face wrinkled in a smile.

We reached the end of the gorge near noon. A stench hung thick in the trees. It made me gag; made Lucas pale. The pathway took us to a clearing where we found twenty or so Americans. They lay in a heap, thrown like trash, all dead, some from musket-shots, most with arrows or bloody axe gashes. Each one had been scalped. It made mine tingle. Lucas studied one a moment, then another, rolling them over with his foot. "This one hardly even bled," he said. "Looks like they scalped them well after they were already dead." He looked at another. "That's mutilation," he said in a hushed tone. Looking at me, he spoke as if in church, "see what running away saved us from?" Flies were buzzing amid the gore, maggots squirming in the scalp wounds; I heaved, dry heaves, thin strings of bile. Lucas led me on down the path, away from the dead.

Watching always for sentries, when we reached Queenston we turned west, inland.

The horror of the scalped men passed and we were starving again, and late that day we traded Lucas' last tobacco to an innkeeper in St. David's for bread and cheese. We lived off barter for two more days, ranging west, then south towards Chippewa, moving cautiously, an eye out for soldiers. But by the fifth day after Queenston we had traded away most of our possessions for food. Lucas spoke glowingly of the west, but with each day I grew more homesick for Niagara.

"I need to get home," I said, knowing how childish that would sound and trying hard to make it sound like a necessary errand.

"And how will you avoid the militia?"

"I'll take my mother and sister and go to Pennsylvania."

"The last regular troops we got came from Pennsylvania. You go to Pennsylvania to hide from the militia and you'll end up coming back as a regular."

Weary and chilled, we risked a fire in a dense woods well off the road, and the warmth put us to sleep. The smoke attracted another party of four deserters. They surrounded us, and one nudged Lucas in the gut with the toe of his boot. "Don't reach for your musket," he heard as he awoke, "you'll get four balls in you." Lucas blinked a couple of times, then nudged me, but I was already awake. They all carried muskets. Lucas started reaching for his knife and that same voice, behind him, said, "don't."

One was a regular soldier, in uniform with a good musket. The other three were dressed like Lucas and I, in broadcloth and deerskin leggings, one with a knife drawn. We were all unshaven and dirty, dark shadows under our eyes. The one who'd warned Lucas appeared behind me and took my musket away. "You can have it," I said. "You from Van Rensselaer's army?"

"Yep. Who are you?"

Lucas being the elder, he spoke. "I'm Lucas Ames. This is Nehemiah Cleary. And you?"

The one who'd taken my musket examined it, spit in the firelock and set it down. "I'm called Birch. Joe Birch."

"Samuel Camden," said the oldest one.

"Thomas Lee," said another.

The regular spoke last, hesitantly. "Private. David Longfellow, United States Army."

"Well, we're all in the wrong place, aren't we?" Lucas tried to joke. He looked warily at Birch, who had a face like a fox.

"That's a fact," said Camden, who was close to Lucas in age, and he relaxed, set down his musket and got warm by the fire. All of us now in the same boat, the others followed suit. "Thomas and I joined the battle just after dawn. We got captured early in the afternoon by some militia but we got away." He yawned and sniffed. "We've been trying to find a way back but the damn British are watching the river like hawks."

"Can hardly blame them," Lucas said. "Nehemiah and I were in the first wave," he said quietly. "First wave." He raised his bandaged hand to show them his wound. Camden and Lee nodded respectfully. He hadn't so much as mentioned it while we were running.

"British do that?" asked Birch with a dark look. Lucas nodded. "Like to get revenge for that?" Birch asked, his eyes filled with excitement.

Lucas was looking at Birch like a fight was headed their way. "I decide when I want revenge, and for what. We invaded their country. This," he held out his hand, "is healing up. A shot fired in self-defense is no reason to seek revenge."

"That's true enough," said Camden.

Birch spat by the fire. "You men join the army or the church?" He sounded like a petty thief, though, not a patriot. "We get no spoils of war if we don't win."

"So you're in it for the spoils?" I asked; Birch was scary, and older than me, but I was bigger.

"I'm trapped in their damn country," he said, changing his tone, trying perhaps for pity after he failed to arouse vengeance or greed. "I'm hungry, got no dry place to sleep, and anyone sees me I'll end up in the stockade in Fort George," he complained as though he alone were hunted.

"At least there you'd have a dry place to sleep and some food," Lucas joked. The others smiled. They were getting warm now, and, Birch aside, they looked like a nice enough group for strangers.

"You're quite the funny one," Birch smiled in an ugly way, and Lucas looked ready for trouble with him when Private Longfellow raised his hand for quiet.

We held our breath. Someone was coming. Birch having fouled my musket, I reached for my knife, knowing I wouldn't use it.

Longfellow and Birch disappeared for a few minutes. They were both skilled at keeping quiet, moving like phantoms as they disappeared into the underbrush. With the fire almost dead, we kicked the embers apart. Then the spies returned. "British soldiers," Longfellow whispered, holding up five fingers.

"One on horseback. Carrying something heavy," hissed Birch. "We can take 'em." He waved us after him as he crept back towards the road.

"Take 'em?" I whispered to Lucas, my eyes wide. "Take 'em where?"

The road wove through the woods, and Birch led us to a slight rise just above it. Coming our way were four British soldiers on foot and a captain on horseback. Lucas spotted full canvas sacks slung over the saddle. "Pork. Think they've got pork? Bread, anyway. I'd kill for some bread." The others readied their muskets. Like at Queenston, Lucas and I stayed back a few feet; I was less ashamed this time.

I'm sure a band of deserters was the last obstacle those British expected to meet. I think Private Longfellow fired first. It was a small, quick skirmish. Four shots were followed by three more. One came close to me, though my face was buried in the dirt so I couldn't duck any lower. Angry yells mingled with men running, another shot, then metal cutting into gut and a groan. I primed my musket again and ran down the hill, but the fighting was over.

Longfellow laid near death in the River Road, coughing up blood, his lips moving but saying nothing, his hand on a wound in his neck, blood seeping between his fingers. "He took two of them with him," Birch said, by way of benediction. Two British soldiers lay by him; one was bleeding badly from a bayonet stab in his gut, the other lay quite still, shot dead. Camden was dead too, as was a third British soldier. The officer was on the ground, Birch and Lee were holding him and the fourth soldier, both disarmed. Birch stuck his face into the officer's, and spit. "You redcoated bastard. I'm gonna blow your bloody arse back to England." He pulled a pistol from the officer's belt and pushed it into the officer's mouth.

We paled at Birch's savagery. "What's in the bag?" Lucas asked Birch, partly to distract him.

"You can't kill in cold blood," I said, and without thinking about it I aimed my musket at Birch. I looked at Lucas. "Can he?"

Birch looked at my musket, and at me, like I was a curious new animal he'd found.

"We're at war," Lucas said tersely, not liking it. "Drop your musket, Nehemiah."

"On the battlefield," I insisted. "Not like this."

"Drop the musket, lad," Lucas repeated gently. I eased the hammer down and set the butt on the ground.

Lee asked the officer, "Where were you headed?"

"Take the pistol out of his mouth and he might answer," Lucas suggested.

Birch pulled the pistol out. The officer, blinking his eyes as though that might help maintain his dignity, answered, "I am on the King's business."

Birch screamed like an Indian and fired, blowing off part of the officer's right ear. The officer held his right hand to his ear, mouth contorted in pain. "You can't seem to hear anyway," Birch said. He pulled his knife out and tucked the blade under the officer's chin. "You want to try answering again?"

"I hear something," said Lucas. Perhaps he did; perhaps he just wanted to distract Birch.

We listened, and Birch reloaded the officer's pistol. A moment of silence, broken only by the officer groaning, a trickle of blood traveling through his fingers as he nursed his damaged ear. There was a distant crashing sound that could have been almost anything. "Let's get out of here," Lee suggested.

"Aye," said Birch, and without another word he stood, aimed the officer's pistol and fired into the officer's head. His brains splashed onto the dirt. He sprawled in the roadway, blood spurting from his scalp, then trickling out, dark and thick and puddling in the road, soaking into the soil. Birch, spattered with his victim's blood, nodded to Lee. Lee shook his head. "Do it," Birch ordered, glaring until Lee used his knife and cut the other soldier's throat. "Get those," Birch ordered Lucas and I, indicating the bags, even as he primed the pistol again.

I looked around quickly, wondering if someone else was coming, wondering if we shouldn't have tried to escape this scene ourselves. "Get them," Birch ordered, the pistol already reloaded and aimed not quite at us. Birch was handy with firearms. We hefted the bags.

"This ain't meat, or bread," Lucas grunted as he hefted a sack.

"We shouldn't just leave them here," I said, looking at the dead. But the others were already hiking back into the woods, so I followed. We went back to the dying embers of the fire and set the bags down.

With Birch at his elbow, Lucas tore open the first canvas sack. Still hoping for corn meal or bread, maybe salt pork, he discovered gold crowns. "God in heaven," he said, picking up a gold coin and studied it. "Looky here," he said to Birch.

"Toss one here," Birch ordered.

Even as he did, with the same motion, it seemed, Lucas pulled out his knife and surprised Birch in a headlock, the knife at his throat. "Listen to me," he said to the renegade, glancing at Lee, "my mate and I want nothing to do with this. But since you've dragged us into it, we'll just take one of these for our troubles, and we'll go our own way."

Lucas took Birch's pistol and discharged it into the air, then threw it into the woods. "You happy with half?" he asked Lee, who nodded quickly. "Nehemiah, get his musket."

"No," said Lee, "I'll come with you, if it's all the same. He's a madman," he indicated Birch. "Go ahead and kill him."

Birch was struggling, but he was slight of build and Lucas held him easily. "Prime your musket," he told Lee.

"Lucas? You aren't going to kill him, are you?" I asked. He said nothing, but when Lee had primed his musket and was shouldering it, Lucas directed him, "aim at his knee." Lee fired, and Birch fell to the ground, screaming, rolling and gripping his smashed kneecap.

"You bastards," he hissed. "I'll find you. I'll cut your throats. I'll cut off your balls. This is the biggest mistake you ever made."

"You shut your mouth or the next one will go between your eyes," said Lee. "You think I'm fooling?"

Birch whined in pain and curled up, rocking gently.

We found the officer where he'd been left, quite dead now, and Lucas searched his pouch. He unfolded a paper and read. "This is the British payroll for Queenston and Fort George."

"What happened to mine?" Lee asked, looking up and down the road. "The man whose throat I cut. He's missing," Lee said, and started looking for him.

"Leave him," Lucas argued, "he's bleeding to death. We have to get away, too."

We tried.

My breath frosted and my toes were numb with cold. It was a day later. We huddled at the tree line, studying the beach ahead of us. "What's that?" Lucas asked, pointing to a mound on the beach, "is that a boat? Upside down? What else could it be?"

"A boulder," I suggested.

"It's nothing," said Lee.

"No, I think it's a boat." Lucas was sounding feverish. His hand was greenish and had begun seeping. I think he was getting blood poisoning. "Nehemiah," he looked at me, "keep watch. I'm going to check it out." Then he stepped out onto the sand and began trudging through it. As he approached it, he turned east, distracted by something. Then he spun around and ran back towards me, running as hard as he could through the sand.

I heard a musket fire. "Shit, shit, shit," I swore. I felt air move next to me and saw Lee scramble into the woods. I could have run into the woods, too, let the patrol take Lucas. Lucas was a loyal friend, he would have lied and claimed to be alone.

But that's the problem with a loyal friend. You can't run away and let them fall into trouble alone. So I froze as Lucas slogged his way towards me, and coming around the bend in the lake, on horses, were two British soldiers. Lucas fell into the sand just ten feet from me. "Go, go!" he wasted breath on me. "Get out!" And I did get the gumption to stand, though that probably just made me more visible, because a moment later a musket ball clipped the branch just above my head. And one of the soldiers knew the marks of a third set of footprints enough to hunt down Lee without much trouble.

We were marched to Fort Erie where we were put in chains.

Our cell was a just-emptied powder room, still fresh with the smell, a door of boards bound in iron bands and bolts. The three of us slept heavily from the minute we were shoved through the door. I didn't think of it at the time but it was the first we'd slept under a real roof in months. There being no window, nothing woke us until the next day, when they opened the door.

We were led out and chained to each other in an orderly room. Nobody had spoken to us, beyond gruff orders. The soldier Lee had cut, who had somehow reached help, was brought in, his neck thickly bandaged. "Corporal Mews, can you speak?" asked an officer. The corporal coughed, cleared his throat a couple times, and managed a whisper. "Very good. I don't want you to strain your throat, but can you tell me if these are the men who attacked your party?"

"Yes sir," Mews croaked. The officer left the room. The orderly room, rough-hewn timbers with gaps in need of fresh mud to caulk them, was chilly. A fire burned and Mews and two others huddled around it and we were left chilled. One seemed to notice our trembling. "Not to worry," he said with an awful chuckle, "you'll be warm soon enough."

They had cooked some bacon and corn bread, and the officer and another officer came in and ate some breakfast and drank some tea to chase it. The smell of their food almost reduced me to tears. When they were done, they seemed to remember us. "Let's have a trial, then," said the first officer. "I'll be judge, Lieutenant Sinclair will be barrister. On the double." Dragging in a table and producing the bag of gold coins seized, along with the letter declaring it the payroll, the lieutenant seated himself behind the table. "You first," he indicated Lee. "Are the facts of this case clear?"

"They are, Sir," Sinclair answered. He had an obsequious tone to his voice. "This coward from the Yankee army took part in the ambush of a payroll party. All the participants save Corporal Mews were killed and the payroll stolen." He set his hand on the payroll money on the table. "This is the evidence."

"Thank you, Lieutenant," said the Captain. "The witnesses have identified you," he nodded at Lee, "as the guilty party. While you could have stayed with your regiment and been safe in Fort George, you have chosen to wander the countryside like a highwayman. You shall be punished appropriately. Sergeant?" Before Lee could utter a word in self-defense, two British soldiers dragged him out of the courtroom. A few minutes later a volley of musket fire echoed in the blockhouse.

Lucas was next. "This is the man who shot Captain Rudner," croaked Mews.

"I am not," Lucas answered, glaring at the soldier. "The man who shot your captain we left in the woods. I'm a thief, but I'm no killer."

They didn't listen, didn't care. Lucas was found guilty of theft and murder and was marched to the doorway. He turned at that point and nodded good-bye to me, his eyes brimming. He waved, and I saw the ragged bit of bandage on his hand. Then he was gone. A minute later another volley of musket fire filled the air. Then I was brought to the table.

"I didn't kill anyone," I said to the lieutenant, then to the captain. "I didn't kill anyone." My mouth was cotton-dry, my knees felt weak, and I slumped against the table.

As they began their brief deliberations ". . . this man was with the party that killed Captain Rudner—"

"I didn't kill anyone. I didn't. I swear I didn't." I fell to my knees then, the chains on my wrists clanking, looking up at them, tears streaming down my cheeks. "Nobody, I swear. I tried to keep Birch from killing Captain Rudner." I looked at Mews and begged him, "tell them."

"He's telling the truth," croaked Mews, who decided to speak. "The worst of them was the one he calls Birch."

Mews' testimonial held up the trial. "So while his fellows were ambushing our fellows, this one tried to save Captain Rudner?" asked the captain, somewhat dismayed at the testimonial.

"Yes, sir," croaked Mews. They looked disappointed, as though there had been a bug in their biscuit. I could tell then that they probably weren't going to shoot me, and I stopped crying. Wiping my face with my sleeve, a sense of dignity returned, and I stood silently, at attention, smelling the gunpowder drifting in from the executions. My stomach grumbled loudly.

My verdict was guilty of theft, of course, but my sentence was lenient: "I think twenty years at hard labor in Dartmoor should teach this thieving bastard a lesson, don't you, Lieutenant?" asked the Captain. The Lieutenant agreed.

A young man near my age, dressed in broadcloth, was called and received the order to, "march this bloody deserter to Dartmoor," followed by two deep chuckles. Armed with a clean, sturdy musket, he took me to a small room that actually had a barred window, a proper cell.

"Here's Dartmoor," he said, opening the cell door. He looked sorry for me. "Captain thinks it's a good joke. You've got a slop bucket over there, and a pile of clean hay. I've slept in worse places." After locking me in, he left, but came back a few minutes later. Opening the door, he set a wooden plate with a quarter loaf and some hard cheese and a mug of water inside the door. "Here's your supper."

The bread and cheese disappeared. I could have eaten twice that.

Calming down, my stomach happy, I listened. The fort was alive with noise. Perhaps it had been before as well, but that's when I noticed it. Through the walls I heard cart wheels squeaking, voices giving and receiving orders to set the watch, footsteps down the passageway, footsteps outside on the boards. Later I heard musket fire during what must have been a bet, which ended with a bottle shattering and claps and laughter. The cell was chilly, but before night fell the door opened, and the guard stepped in. "You," he said to me, "you cold?"

"Yes," I said, my voice sounding much softer than I'd intended, sounding cowed, "it's chilly. It's October."

"This'll help," he said, dropping a heavy horse blanket on the pine plank floor. "It smells a little, but it's good and heavy. I'll bring in a hot stone from the fireplace before I'm off duty. That'll keep you from freezing to death."

"Thank you," I said, my fears thawing in the presence of a measure of kindness. I hadn't realized it, but I'd had a knot of fear in my gut for two days. "What's going to happen to me?"

He stepped out of the cell, pulled the door shut, and I heard the bar snugged in place. I saw him glance around, then he said, "I doubt your hide is worth the expense of a trip to England. There's a supply boat due tomorrow or the next day. They'll put you in that, take you up to York. What they'll do to you there I don't know. Probably parole you, maybe trade you for one of ours, if you've any value." He took up his post again and I sensed the conversation was over.

With a huge feeling of relief I dozed off, but woke when the door opened again. The guard, as promised, brought a stone heated from the kitchen fire in a small metal pot, and he set it next to where I lay on the floor. He also brought in a bucket of water with a cup, so that I could drink at my leisure. "Thank you," I said.

"You from around here? You sound like you're from around here," he said, standing.

"I'm from Manchester, by the falls," I said. "You?"

"From Pelham." Pelham was a day's ride west from the falls. "I'm Thomas Bartlett."

"Nehemiah Cleary." My shackled hands prevented the normal exchange of handshakes.

"You got land?" Bartlett asked.

I'd never thought in those terms. Our farm included twenty acres, little of which was under cultivation anymore. "Well, my father's dead, but I guess I inherit twenty acres from him."

"You got family?"

I nodded. "My mother and sister are still in Manchester."

He studied me, perhaps the first Yankee he'd seen up close since war erupted, since this ugly side of America had shown itself. "So you got land, you got a home. Why'd you join up?"

I looked at the cup in my hands. 'To smell scented handkerchiefs' was the correct answer. "I can only tell you that I wish I hadn't."

"My mother tells me that if we let your army take our homes, we'll be back under mob rule again. We'll lose our land, just like my grandfather lost his."

I nodded. If there was a worse feeling than being sent into battle with a musket that wouldn't fire, it had to be being taken captive and asked to justify the war itself. "Between you and me," I told Thomas Bartlett, "I won't be fighting for America anymore. I just want to go home." *And, if necessary, live without smelling a scented handkerchief.*

At dawn an explosion shook the fort and woke me. Fort Erie was under bombardment. I could hear the artillery teams at work, the grunts of the crew shoving the powder charge home, the eruption of the cannon, the hissing of the blanket to cool the barrel, and the whole building shaking when Buffalo's cannon balls hit. After what seemed a hundred bone rattling hits, I smelled wood smoke. A few minutes later I saw it drifting in through the walls. It grew thicker and I began coughing. I tried to breathe through the blanket, my eyes tearing. "Here!" I couldn't see my guard, but the door opened and I felt his hands on my collar, pulling me from the smoky jail.

Coughing, blinking to clear my eyes, I followed him to the orderly room where I'd been tried. Thomas was struggling with the lock on my chains when a red-hot ball of iron came crashing through the roof over our heads. And my guard took the full weight of it, and I thank God he was killed immediately.

And I was unguarded. Thomas had freed me with his last breath. Around me, the bombardment raged. The ball of fear in my gut returned.

Smelling fresh air, I followed a hallway past my cell to a entry way. The bombardment continued, the fire burned and smoke blinded me, the confusion of battle kept the fort in a state of frenzied noise and activity. I passed an open door and saw a musket leaning against the wall. Grabbing it in one hand, a leather belt with ball and powder in the other, I ran down a hallway and reached daylight.

Blinded a moment by the bright light, a ball almost took off my right ear lobe and spun me around. I saw soldiers, all of them too busy working on cannons facing America to notice me. I scrambled out the gate, falling down a dirt rampart. *I'm so sick of dodging musket balls,* I thought as I escaped. The tree line was close by and I ran into the woods without even thinking of stopping.

When I was deep enough into the woods that I couldn't see the fort at all, I glanced at the musket I'd grabbed. It was my own. "Damnation. Damnation! I'm in a fort surrounded by fine British muskets and I grab this?" And the balls were for British muskets. "So they won't fit." I threw away the balls, kept the powder, and kept my musket anyway. "We're a fine pair," I told the musket. "Neither of us has it in us to kill."

Benign as the woods felt, I reminded myself I was deep in British territory. I hid, and as my panic ebbed and calm returned, the whole vile episode came back. I saw Birch holding the pistol to the officer's head, one knee bent to get close, a smile he might have used to flirt with a barmaid, then his hand and arm recoiling with the force of the shot, and the spray of blood that hit us all. The back of the officer's head splattering against a sapling, his body dropping on the leafy ground. I kept seeing his hand land in a puddle, and saw tremors on the puddle's surface.

I remembered the stubborn, shocked look on Lucas' face as they dragged him out to be shot, and felt a tearing pain at losing a father again.

And I expected Joshua to appear at every turn.

For two long, frightened days I hid in the woods, digging for roots and picking berries that left my stomach aching. On the third day, hungrier, I decided to try stealing. I looked for a remote farmhouse where I could steal a loaf of bread, a chicken, a few potatoes. Twice I scouted barns, saw chickens and once saw eggs, and tried to grab and run, but much as I couldn't run when Lucas was discovered, I couldn't lunge after food I wasn't entitled to. "Mother, you raised me well," I said when

I found a stream and filled my stomach with cold water. "Taught me not to steal. Maybe you should have said, if ever you are trapped behind enemy lines and starving, you are entitled to steal a little?" I decided then to follow the road to the next village and take my chances.

Just past sunset on October 21st, 1812, eight days after Queenston, I entered Pelham. I needed new clothes, a bath, and a shave wouldn't hurt. There were a few people on the Main Street, all of whom gave me a wide berth and long stares. The only open doorway was at the Pelham Inn. It was empty and quiet when I stepped over the threshold.

Claire Teal was nearly finished with her day. She was closing on her eighteenth birthday, but looked older. Brushing a strand of long black hair behind her ear, she had an apron tied over her housedress. She had already blown out the lamp shining in the front window, hoping to sweep up the public room without interruption, but had left the door open to sweep the dirt out. Her broom firmly pushed the dirt from every nook in the public room, from beneath the chairs beside the pot-bellied stove. Humming, "there is a ship. . . and it sails the sea," she didn't hear me. "It's loaded deep, as deep can be. . ." She pulled her pile of dirt to the front, turned, and with a firm thrust pushed the sweepings on me.

Her hand flew to her mouth in shock. "Oh my goodness. Sir, I am so sorry. I didn't see you."

A casual glance at her would see a woman worn with labor, still enough of a girl to be clumsy and embarrassed. She tried to dust me off, and the sight of her, and the smell of her, and feeling her touching me, was wonderful. She quickly realized that I was already dirty, and gracefully retreated. "What can I get for you, now?" she asked, a little weary from her long day.

Her figure beneath the dress and apron, and her deep brown eyes in her lovely young face swamped everything else in my mind. *Is this where all the pretty girls are?* I asked myself. I drank in the details of her face for far longer than was comfortable, and she blushed. With an effort I looked away.

I smelled something hot in the iron pot hung over the fire. Then I smelled some rum, from a mostly empty mug left on the counter. And then I saw the storeroom with its Dutch door, and saw the shelves of goods. "Oh," I groaned in hunger, "could you give me some of that?" I pointed at a soda bread loaf and she'd just set it on the counter when

I tore off a handful and chewed it down. "Is that cheddar cheese?" I pointed, and she cut off a thick wedge and set it before me and I bit off a huge mouthful and probably chewed with my mouth open, for she glanced away, blushing as crumbs fell to the floor she'd just swept. Another big bite of bread and the loaf was half-gone.

"You probably need something to wash that down," she suggested, and poured me a mug of cider, which I gulped down thirstily. Then I burped, and blushed, and she giggled.

My stomach gurgled when the cider hit it, and then I noticed the candy. "Some of that ginger candy," I asked, "one scoop. And the horehound." While she was scribbling the sums on a piece of paper, the warmth of the nearby stove dropped a wave of exhaustion like a blanket on me. I reached for a chair by the stove, set down and fell deeply asleep.

As she told me later, she wanted to smack me. "Oh, blast it," she said, softly. She finished tying up my order, half-eaten as it was, finished her sweeping, and when I still wasn't awake, she gently nudged my shoulder. The nudge did no good; she tried to tickle the back of my hand. Still I slept. So she did smack me on the head. Hard.

Half awake, I looked around. "Sorry, Ma'am, I guess I dozed off."

"Yes, you must have had a long day. Could I ask your name?" she asked with the utmost in courtesy, "and where you come from? Your face isn't familiar. I'm Claire Teal."

"Nehemiah Cleary," I said. "I'm from. . . Amherstburg."

Claire arched her eyebrows. "What brings you so far?"

Still a bit foggy, I made it up as I went along. "I came to join the fighting."

"How noble of you," she said, though she was obviously not convinced.

I stood, stretched and yawned deeply. "Beg your pardon. I'm so sleepy."

She was terribly lonely. Her husband had gone to Queenston. The first, unconfirmed, reports put Gordon Teal among the missing. A woman awaiting her soldier husband was expected to be chaste and patriotic, but Claire felt less ennobled by her husband's status than victimized. Married at fifteen to a thirty-four year old innkeeper, her parents and friends thought it a lucky match for her. "He's hard-working, he doesn't drink, and he's prosperous," her mother had summed him up. "You'll learn to love him. Sometimes it takes a little time."

He had been faithful, probably, but his absence was not as painful as it should have been. It was almost not painful at all. She was faithful because she'd been told to, because she didn't want to hurt Gordon's feelings, because she did respect him, but mostly because she'd found no one to lead her astray. She'd been told to marry for respect and security, that love would follow. In three years it hadn't shown itself. Tonight, maybe for the first time she was aware of, there was opportunity. *Who had seen Mr. Cleary step in, and who would notice if he stayed?* The sun had set, but twilight was no protection.

She looked, again, at this dirty, exhausted stranger, a young man her age. She could justify aid and comfort to a soldier. He needed a hot bath, some clothes, and a proper meal. And she needed to hear someone's voice at her dinner table, someone to hear her voice. "Mr. Cleary, may I offer you a meal and a room for the night?"

A night under the same roof as her? "That would be very kind. Thank you."

The inn was otherwise empty. "Normally we would have two or three guests, but the war has been bad for business," Claire was saying. I followed her as she locked up and led me through the kitchen. "Would you like to wash up?" she asked, and showed me, in her pantry, a true luxury, a tub. I'd never used one before. "Just take off your clothes," Claire said, "and lie down in it. I'll heat up some water."

I could smell her even after she'd left the room, nothing flowery but much nicer than what I'd been smelling the past five months. The cotton of her dress was like a scented handkerchief.

As I began working on unbuttoning clothing I'd worn and slept in for days, Claire heated and poured two pots of boiling hot water and three of cold into the washtub. I paused at my undressing when I heard her coming with more hot water. "Are you ready?" she called out.

"More or less," I mumbled, and she came in and poured more hot water into the tub. She left, and I finished stripping and settled into the tub.

As clouds of steam rose around me, a protective fog, Claire stepped into the pantry to scrub me. I opened my mouth to remind her I was naked in the tub, but said nothing, just lay there and watched her. British women were proving to be a wonderful discovery.

Gordon had preferred Claire to scrub him. She soon realized that her hand on a washrag on his back was the closest Gordon could come to seduction, with hot water, lye soap, and a stiff brush, and it was her job to seduce him. Gordon usually penetrated her in bed after a bath; she neither loved it nor looked forward to it, but lumped it with bathing Gordon as one of her chores.

Tonight she came into the pantry, bringing the washcloth and brush and the bar of soap. Her heart was pounding as she prepared to leave her marriage behind. *He's a stranger*, she thought. *You know nothing about him, except that he's not from around here. That*, she thought, *is why he's perfect*. With a hollow gourd she scooped water up and drenched my scalp. She saw my dark, matted hair, my shoulders and arms firmer with muscle, and remembered it was not Gordon in the tub.

"Perhaps I should handle this," I said, gently.

Blushing, she saw my aroused condition. It was my turn to blush. "I guess so," she said. She backed out.

"Your clothes are a ruin," she said through the door. Briefly, she examined them, holding them between two fingers, then tossed them into the stable for rubbing down the horse. Upstairs she had a closet filled with Gordon's shirts and pants, and she picked out a pair of new pants and a shirt. She left them by the entrance to the pantry and called in; "I've brought you some clothes. I fear your old ones were beyond the help of soap."

"Thank you," I called out after a moment's hesitation, uncertain what else to say.

Gordon Teal's pants were the right length, but he was stouter, so I was clean but baggy. I tucked in the shirt, but it still billowed. When I'd done my best, I presented myself to Claire in the parlor.

He cleans up nicely, was her first thought, and she felt a sensation she'd not felt since anticipating her marriage, a powerful desire for a man.

"Your husband's clothes are a bit bigger than I am," I explained to her critical eye. She circled me, trying to pin up the slack, and I felt my arousal return as she touched me. I remember how the light shone on her dark hair. *She's beautiful*, I thought, *why would a man leave a woman like her to fight in this stupid war?* A single gray hair was visible but it enhanced the sensual brown of her hair and eyes.

Claire's thoughts were now far from maternal. She continued to smooth the shirt down my arm, to measure my inseam, and turn up the bottom hem. She finally caught herself and made herself stop. "You look better," she said, smiling, "that shirt left room on Gordon." She spoke of him in the past tense. "I'll adjust it later. The stew is ready," she said with a smile.

It was chicken stew and I emptied my bowl before she'd finished filling her own. "It's good to see a man with an appetite," she said with a beautiful smile.

I tried hard not to shovel the second bowlful in but Claire seemed pleased at my taste for her cooking.

"I've made a full pot, so eat your fill." She was still cooking for herself and Gordon. It rivaled—perhaps was even better than—my mother's chicken stew, which reminded me of her. And with real food in my stomach I wondered for the first time in days about how Mother and Electa were faring.

Over the years Claire has made it clear, in thought and word, that her first marriage was not a happy one. Gordon worked hard and his inn prospered. When she met him he impressed her with his industry. But she had hoped there would be another side to this man, a gentler, happier side, a Gordon who could respond to something besides his prosperity. If Gordon had come through the doorway that night, she told me once, she knew that night, for the first time, that she would leave him. Not, I know, because I was such a wonderful prospect, but because that night she realized how lonely she was.

That night she praised him. "Pelham sent two drafts of young men in the summer," she said, "and again in September. Gordon left with the last draft. His family came to Canada as dispossessed farmers from Pennsylvania," Claire explained. "My family too." Driven from their homes, the terms of the peace treaty that called for fair treatment of them and their property ignored, the Loyalists had been forced to trek. Some walked to Ontario. They starved, they labored, they sacrificed to build new homes in the Ontario wilderness. Then, when communities had grown up, as churches were being built, as children grew out of their traumas and time had given the adults some distance from their anger, then the Americans cast their greedy eyes north. "So they want Canada now, to add to their roll call of anarchy and disloyalty?" Claire asked, shaking her head in disbelief. "Let them wallow in hell as traitors," she said angrily, echoing the church meetings and town gatherings across the thinly held land, "but they will not dispossess us again." Her eyes lit up with anger and tears. "Gordon heeded that call in the final hours."

I said, "You must be proud of him."

She caught herself. The day Gordon reluctantly untied his apron, kissed Claire good-bye, and left with the others was the last she had seen of him. *God forgive me for this thought, and for voicing it to a stranger*, she prayed. "Proud? Gordon went to war, as near as I can tell, to protect his prosperity."

"I see." *And me? Scented handkerchiefs.* The fact was just registering that I had finally found one, and it was making my head swim. But I wasn't sitting in a kitchen in Baltimore, or even Buffalo. I was in enemy territory. As badly as I wanted to stay forever, I realized for the first time since I'd fled the Queenston battlefield that I had to go back. I had to let Mother know I was alive, to chop more wood for her and Electa, to help them through the coming winter. I decided, then, to go home, and sit out the rest of this war. And then return to this beautiful woman.

Claire collected the bowls and set them in the pantry to clean later. "Would you care for a hot toddy, Mr. Cleary?" I blushed at being addressed as 'Mr.', and hot whiskey sounded wonderful. Mother had never seen me as an adult and wouldn't tolerate anything stronger than cider.

She poured the whiskey, heated it with a hot poker from the fire, and brought it to me in a mug. Then she sat with a cup of tea in a chair by the fire, facing me as I enjoyed the rocking chair. My heart began pounding, for I was in a sitting room with her, as an equal, sipping hot liquor, and though my war experiences were a passage of sorts, this was my first intimate moment with a woman. We sipped in silence, letting the dance of the flames relax us. Gradually Claire indulged her curiosity. "You're from Amherstburg?" I downed a mouthful of whiskey, its burning warmth so relaxing, and nodded. "Were you in the battle there?"

"No," I said, remembering to lie, "my father's farm is a good distance out from the settlement. But we did see the soldiers marching, and when the cannons fired we could hear a little." I took a drink of whisky; *little lies should be kept from growing up.*

"I see," Claire said quietly, "Gordon wasn't going to go at first." She looked up at the mantle over the fireplace, where their wedding cup sat. "He said he wasn't a young man anymore," she said, smiling, "so he waved good-bye to the first draft after giving each of them a taste of rum for the road." Her face was empty of emotion then. "But then the recruiting officers came back through, and we heard that the Yankees had mustered a thousand men to attack, and then a lot of the men in town who thought they were too old put on their coats and went." She sipped her drink. "The first time they said, we'll take the single lads, as they're champing at the bit to go anyway. Discouraged a few of the older, married men who said they had scores to settle with the Americans, said they could best serve by keeping the towns going. Then they came back and said to come after all, that every man would be needed." She spoke their deepest fear. "We thought we'd lose our homes again."

Her story, and my guilt over deceiving her, and more than passing anxiety over the possibility of Gordon Teal's return to find this American in his pants, sipping hot whiskey with his wife, worried me.

"I've heard rumors," she said then, "that he may have been killed." She looked distant. "And all I can think, selfish me, is at least he stopped them from seizing our land." She spoke as though she were reading from a letter, unemotional, reporting the facts.

When they weren't predicting an armistice, our officers and the newspaper writers had insisted that the settlers of Upper Canada were happily awaiting our arrival and their opportunity to join the United States. I had had my suspicions, but it made the invasion more acceptable. If these people didn't want to become Americans, that made Queenston impossible to explain.

"Why?" she asked me, suddenly, tears welling in her lovely, sad eyes, "why do they want our land? They've plenty of their own. What could they need ours for?"

I said nothing. "Where are my manners?" she asked, and she poured me another drink.

I took a long swallow and remembered that terrible day, and said, "We couldn't even get most of them to cross the river."

She glanced at me curiously. "Who to cross the river?"

"My Uncle Nathan was at Queenston, and," I conjured desperately, "he told me of how the Americans had thousands on their side of the river but only some few hundreds crossed. Most refused to invade." I didn't even believe myself.

Claire filled my mug a third time, sat down and said, "Mr. Cleary, you're a poor liar."

Nodding, "I am."

My musket leaned against a corner in the kitchen, and she rose and picked it up.

"Oh, Ma'am, you needn't do that, just let me leave," I asked, getting to my feet and moving towards the door.

"Please enjoy your drink, Mr. Cleary," she said, studying the musket, "I want to inspect your musket, not fire it."

She brought it back into the parlor, struggling with the hammer, sighting down the barrel, and scrubbing mud from an engraved signature on the barrel. "This musket, if you can call it that, was made by a Frenchman," she read. "Mr. Cleary, on whose side have you carried this musket?"

Quietly I said, "New York's."

She nodded, her mouth tight. "So you are a spy?"

"No," I said quickly; I knew what they did to deserters and I knew what they did to spies. "I'm no spy," I insisted, raising my hands in surrender.

"A deserter." She spoke matter-of-factly.

"Yes, Ma'am. If you'd allow me, I'll leave you now." Would she? I took a step towards the door, eyes on her. She still held the musket, and there was no accounting for a passing rush of patriotism. I was just a step from the door, when she called out, "aren't you forgetting your musket?"

I stopped and turned towards her.

She held the musket like she'd held my ruined clothes. "Tell me, Mr. Cleary," she asked, as much amused as anything else, "this musket of yours, it's quite a piece of junk. Is this how it was issued to you?"

"Yes," I answered, knowing now she was not my enemy. "I was only able to fire it once, for practice, a month ago."

She nodded, and then held it out to me. I took it, and between the whiskey and my exhaustion, I set it against the wall, then dropped to my knees and sat on the floor, staring into the fire. I would have fallen asleep again, but the shadows shifted erratically over the ceiling and walls, and the ghosts of Queenston filled the room.

"Did you really see the war?" she asked.

"Part of it."

"Tell me about what you saw," she said, softly.

"My mate Lucas and I, we sat up on the heights most of the day. We finally gave up on the rest of our men, back on the Lewiston side. They wouldn't cross. They left us to be captured. Or to die. Then the British beat their drums and sent the Indians in after us." It was pouring out of me, incoherently, in a rush. "Then we hid, and thought of heading out west. Then we met other deserters, and they attacked the payroll party, and we got captured and they shot Lucas." I began to cry. It was the first moment I'd felt safe to mourn Lucas. "They dragged him out and shot him for something he didn't do. I saw his face before they shot him and I never saw a man look so surprised, so scared," I whispered through my tears. Then she was at my side, comforting me. I buried my face in her shoulder and sobbed deeply, remembering the names of the dead. For a while as the fire burned down she held me.

A clock, a tall, grandfather clock made by an Ottawa clockmaker, chimed in echoing tones. A log broke and fire was released, and the shadows marched away. In the shadows I saw their faces from camp and from the battle, and only after I watched them awhile did they begin to mercifully fade away. The grandfather clock chimed again, in clear, minor tones.

When the clock chimed the tenth hour, she rose and carried our bowls and spoons to the kitchen, setting them in a deep wooden sink. I followed her and she smiled when I hoisted the black kettle from the fireplace and poured hot water over the dishes. Claire rubbed the dishes with a linen rag, and when they were clean she reached for a clean towel on a drying rack to wipe with. I reached it first and she smiled and handed me the dish to dry. I took it, but set it back in the water and held her hand a moment.

It was the first intense emotion I'd ever felt for a woman. For a moment we held hands.

"Mr. Cleary," she whispered, and we closed and kissed and held each other in the dim light of the kitchen.

I caressed her, awkwardly, and kissed her again, long and hard. My body was well ahead of my mind, breathing fast, and my heart pounded as my groin throbbed. She seemed excited at my arousal, and then I gently pressed her against the wooden sink. "Claire," I almost said 'I love you' but she kissed me. I was pressing hard against her, and my hands roamed her dress in search of her buttons. Then I touched her breasts, and my mouth couldn't leave hers.

Gordon had never approached her outside the bedroom. She was halfway to climax just on the novelty of the experience. But when she felt her breasts swelling free, her propriety returned in small portion. Gently, sighing with reluctance, she caught my hands and put them to my side, and shifted her waist so my excited state was less pointed.

I hesitated for a moment, but then pulled back, embarrassed. I started to apologize but she held my face and kissed me lovingly.

"I'm sorry," she whispered, "I can't." I nodded, and we pulled apart, breathless and embarrassed.

"Perhaps a good night's sleep is in order," she suggested. "I'll go pre-pare a bed for you. . . in the parlor." She left me alone in the kitchen, my imagination still thunderstruck with its first experience in passion, and my body gradually accepting disappointment.

When my heart and crotch were calmer, I went into the parlor and found one oil lamp flickering, illuminating a goose down comforter and pillow neatly set on the sofa. From the staircase at the far end of the room I heard her footsteps, her door closing, and a door latch fall shut. I listened in the silent house a few moments longer, while she walked to her night table, and I tried to picture her unbuttoning those damn buttons, and her smooth arm and the soft breast I'd not actually seen but had felt, as she washed before sleep. And when I thought I heard her climbing, alone, into bed, I reluctantly lay beneath the comforter.

I awoke at dawn, stretched, and appreciated the deep sleep I'd had. Opening the door and looking out I saw it was a good day for travel, a few wispy clouds and a wind that blew down the open street from a cool, clear autumn sky.

She hadn't gotten around to taking in Gordon's clothing, but it fit well enough and kept me warm. With all my thoughts of her, if Claire had come down that moment I'd be tongue-tied. With a coal I scrawled my name in the stone of the fireplace; if Gordon returned alive she'd have some explaining to do, but I wanted her to remember my name. Then I hefted my musket; it was wartime, and it did have perhaps one shot left in it, and set out into the morning.

The streets of Pelham were still quiet and I met no one as I walked out of town and set out on the road east. The day was a cool one, especially in the open when the wind blew, but the walking left me quite warm and I was only a day's travel from the river. There was reason to smile now. Mother would be happy to see me, and I occupied myself for hours in heroic scenarios of returning home. We would all go somewhere else until the war was done. And then I would come back here.

As I got closer to the river, closer to the fighting, the countryside seemed deserted. I saw some soldiers in a wagon riding north before they saw me, and I hid in some trees until they were past. A few villages I passed through were shuttered up.

It was dark when I reached the river. I found a boat tied up. I couldn't steal food when I was hungry, but to get home, I thought, I'd steal a horse, and certainly a boat. I hid and watched from the woods, and when no one appeared at dusk, I launched it, stumbling and drenching my legs. My rowing seemed to send the boat flying across the main current, coming up on the American shore in good time. I landed a short distance upriver from Fort Schlosser, and stepped ashore, shoving the boat back into the stream. I passed the fort, following a little used path, and so avoided the sentries I knew were on watch.

I moved quietly through the familiar paths, listening for the sounds I'd grown up with. Then I reached a cluster of birch trees by a flat outcropping of limestone that told me home was near. I heard and gave wide berth to a group of soldiers returning from dinner at Broughton's Tavern. Waiting in the brush for them to pass, I thought of my great adventure in the army. I had become a man since leaving the Judge's employ. I had drunk heavily, I had nearly killed a man—as I remembered it. I had loved a beautiful woman. God permit the war ended soon, I would return to tell her how I had loved her.

As I crossed the meadow and saw the silhouette of home against the sun-touched horizon, I called, "Mother!" but heard no answer. I reached the house and pushed open the door, and heard the emptiness of the house. "Mother. Electa?" Searching, I saw that her hairbrushes were gone. They had gone to the Porters, I knew, if they were still in Niagara. Facing my old employer after my experiences as clerk in the camp was not a pleasant thought, but I had no choice.

The last of the moonlight flooded the meadow before the house. I wanted to find my family before sunrise. I grabbed my musket and headed out the door for the Porters'. Across the meadow, through the woods, and just briefly down the Portage Road. "Mother," I rehearsed, "I'm alive, and I've returned for—"

"Halt! Friend or foe!" Militia, younger than I was. I stopped, then continued to run. The sentry had clearly not reached that dubious rite of passage called killing a man. He chased, yelling, "Stop! I'm just making. . . certain. . . you're not. . . a spy."

I ran hard, trying to lose him, leaping over boulders, turning sharp corners in the woods, using every twist in the trail I knew. But the sentry stayed close behind. I ran down a narrow, rocky, twisting path that led back to the portage. A regular sentry would have abandoned the chase early on, but this one followed, pleading with me, "stop, I order you." *What is he*, I thought, *trying for corporal?* We'd run for a few minutes and I was slowing down, the sentry was catching up and I knew I had to stop him.

When I reached the Portage Road and could still hear the sentry's pounding footsteps in pursuit, I backed away from the pathway and put my musket to my shoulder. *I'll aim at him, but then I'll fire straight up*, I planned, *well over his head, not to hit him but make him jump, scramble for cover. Then I can get away.* The sentry was thrashing tree branches with his musket, and he apparently stumbled once for he cursed, and paused in his pursuit, and then he appeared on the road, limping slightly.

"Stop there," I ordered.

"Oh Lord," he said, hands up to protect himself, staring at the musket barrel.

The flash and explosion was sharp and clear in the quiet woods. On the dirt road, carpeted in fallen leaves, I lay, bleeding horribly but feeling nothing. I'd aimed for heaven, but that's not where the ball went. Bits of my flesh and bone and pools of my blood mingled with the shattered remains of the musket barrel, and the splintered bits of the stock. Birds had flown at the shot. "Mother. . . Electa. . . Claire. . ." and then I fell asleep.

The sentry ran off to find an officer.

And the war raged on. Fighting burst out like a sudden infection along the Niagara where Black Rock faced Fort Erie, but in the end there was nothing gained, and nothing changed. Cold weather moved in and the armies settled into their camps, where disease, boredom, and cold would do to their ranks what neither could do to the other.

"You're awake. Thank God." My mother seemed older, grayer, than when I'd left. "It's been four days. Can you eat some stew? I just made it." She brought the steaming bowl to the table by the bed. Already on the table was a wooden bowl for hot water, a pair of scissors for cutting bandages, and the ruin of an old linen shirt that would be my next change of bandages. Linen bandages covered my face, neck, and right arm. My head was propped up on pillows.

I tried speaking. "How did you find me?" My voice was more or less normal, a little hoarse.

"The guards from Schlosser brought you to Lavinia's," Mother answered. "I was staying there. I had them carry you back home."

"So I'm not in jail?" I asked, my voice weak but suspicious.

She frowned as she prepared to feed me, "you did fire at a sentry, but probably because he startled you. In any case, they let me bring you home."

Blinking to clear the vision in my working eye, blinking like I was wiping a dirty window with a rag, I looked over the familiar walls, the boards in the ceiling, and at the bandages on the table. Mother, a wooden spoonful of stew at the ready, said, "Eat some of this, Nehemiah."

"I'm not hungry." I couldn't feel much, other than shock.

"If you don't eat soon you won't get your strength back and you'll die."

"I'll die, then."

She held the spoon to my mouth, her lined face creased with fresh worry. "You haven't eaten since you were hurt."

I had awakened once before, just enough to convince my mother that I still lived, and for me to learn where I was hurt. "How long have I been asleep?"

"Four days," she said, pushing the spoon at me, "now eat. Four days you've slept and no nourishment." She spooned up a fresh, hot spoonful and held it to my mouth. I looked at her, and her worry saddened me. I tried to eat.

She'd bandaged my face where the flesh had been torn away, but she'd left an opening for my mouth and I slowly pulled back my hurt lips and fit the spoon in. I could still taste a little, and I almost smiled with the taste of her cooking. She guided another spoonful in, and again until the bowl was empty. "That's much better, son," she said, relieved, and she tucked my blanket in after she rose. "Do you hurt?"

Did I hurt? First, there was the shock of waking up alive. Then there was the tentative testing of senses; however I moved my mouth I felt sharp, tearing pains. My right eye was covered with a thick bandage. My right hand tingled, and it seemed to be lying out there, distant. I thought my right arm was gone but if I could feel my hand, how could my arm be gone? When I tried to smile to please my mother, the stiff, damaged flesh was immobile as stone. "Everything hurts," I mumbled.

"Well, save your strength," she said.

"Mother," I asked, fighting off tears, "what's left of me?"

She stood by the bed, quiet at first as though pretending I hadn't spoken, then began reluctantly reciting the grisly inventory. "Your left eye suffered a bad powder burn. The surgeon from Schlosser doesn't know what kind of vision you have left there. Your right arm is badly hurt, but I don't think you'll lose it."

"I can't move it."

She nodded. "You have a wound from the corner of your eye down to here," she touched her jaw line. "There were other cuts, but not so deep. You've been badly hurt. I," she overcame her own despair. "You are alive, and that is the most important fact. You are alive."

I was alive.

As my convalescence passed, I learned my boundaries. The first week was the worst. I couldn't hold a spoon or pencil, couldn't write my name, couldn't feed myself, and couldn't clean myself or empty my bowels. My arm survived, though I wished it gone at times, when I forgot it was wounded and lifted it. I had no feeling on the inside of my upper arm, that being the part that took the worst of the blast, and the nerves were damaged. The forearm had feeling and when I jolted it, I was rewarded with a fresh reminder of how it felt to be wounded by a burst musket barrel.

When Mother eased a spoonful of her broth past my lips it broke open scabs and I tasted my blood in the broth. And when she changed my bandages, as was necessary every few days, dampening the bandage to loosen it, pain tore through me. I tried to bear it silently, but it always overwhelmed me, and I trembled and screamed and cried like a newborn.

I woke up giggling one morning. "What in heaven?" I asked, looking down at my bare feet. Electa had pulled back the blankets and was tickling my feet with a turkey feather, giggling. "I haven't heard you laugh since you came back," she smiled mischievously. "Mommy, did you hear Nehemiah laugh?"

Mother had come to the doorway of the bedroom. "I sure did. I should've thought of that," she said, smiling. "I'm glad you're smiling. We need to change that bandage."

Around the second week my face and forearm were sufficiently healed to spare me the daily change of bandage. One evening, at my insistence, Mother and Electa went to the Porter home for a meal. It was also my first privacy since being wounded.

I got up and walked, cautiously, my sense of distance still unsure. I was supposed to wait for the surgeon's visit to remove the bandage from my right eye, but that was my motivation for being alone. I unwound the wrapping, carefully peeled back the patch and felt fresh air on my eyelid. I couldn't open it. With the rag and warm water used for softening bandage, I dabbed at my eyelid, and it opened suddenly like a shade rising from a window.

Gasping, I blinked furiously and watched an opaque picture of the world appear. I looked in Mother's looking glass and saw a milky caste on my eye. *Like an old man with cataracts.* And then I knew that my tear ducts both worked.

Moving through the kitchen, with a slightly better sense of distance now, finding the meal of bread and cold venison Mother had left for me, I decided to test my vision further and try cutting a slice off the loaf with my left hand, injured but increasingly useable. On my first try I almost lopped off my thumb with the knife. Looking closer, like an old man with cataracts, I sawed with the knife. I couldn't hold the knife normally. I changed my grip to that used in slashing down, and in that awkward faction cut a slice. Feeling better, I knocked over a mug I was trying to fill with water. *I can sort of tell distance*, I told myself, encouraging myself, *but it's not much good for guiding my hand. I have to almost touch it with my nose to be sure.* I explored my scars with my good hand, something I'd done often in bed, my mind trying to map my new body. Then I touched my still-bandaged right arm, gently, for parts of it throbbed with the fever of healing.

All I wanted was to see something besides Manchester, a pretty face, I said. Mother had reared us as rudimentary Christians, and I always expected God to show his anger by hurling lightning bolts. I'd lived my life with a few close calls but no direct displays of disapproval. *I guess this was one of your smaller bolts,* I said. *Too bad. Your biggest might have killed me.*

That night I remembered Birch, Lee, Camden, and the gold we stole so briefly. I wanted to tell Mother, but telling about the gold would lead to telling about the theft, about the murder of the soldiers and the officer, and so many more stories I did not want to tell. I had never held so much back from her.

That night I dreamt of the woods, a muddy, dripping, foggy woods, and instead of four British soldiers there were ten, maybe more. Lucas was nowhere to be found, and they were all coming for me, their muskets tipped with sabers that tingled with sharpness, dripped blood, charging at me. In the dream I threw up my arms in self-defense, and in real life I jolted my bandaged arm, and broke scabs, and woke myself from the pain.

I lay awake, waiting for dawn to light the room. I remembered Claire, and for the first time since being wounded, something lifted my heart. I got up and found a sharp knife. In the light of dawn, with my left hand, I began to cut her name into the wood of the door. I had to rest my hand more with each cut, and I almost didn't get past the 'r', which looked a lot like the 'i', but I finished, my left hand throbbing afterwards. The letters were large enough for me to see from my bed, and made her seem near. If Mother ever noticed it she said nothing. I dozed off.

The wounds hurt badly that first week; when they began to heal and hurt less the headaches began. Like rolls of thunder inside my skull, changing tempo until I was crying, Mother tried some herbs and teas, but nothing helped. The nearest to a cure was fresh air.

Exercise helped. One day I heard my mother cry out, and she came in and I saw a smear of blood on her cheek. "What happened?" I asked.

"Splinter of wood hit me," she said. "It's nothing."

I felt my old responsibilities come back to prod me. I got up, said, "I need to visit the little house," our euphemism for the privy. I'd been able to attend to my own needs for a couple weeks at that point. I pulled on a shirt and kept my lame right arm out of the sleeve; it still hurt if it got wrenched. But instead of the privy, I went to the woodpile and the axe.

I could only lift the axe with my left arm, and I struggled just to set up a length of wood to split. My left hand was completely unbandaged then and my muscles strained at a task I once did easily. Sweat trickled down my face, dampening my bandage and making my scabs very ticklish. I hefted the axe in my left hand and found, with practice, I could sight it better. Of course my left arm by itself had little strength; my first, ineffective, blows amounted to raising the blade over the wood and letting it fall. Picking out a piece of soft pine, I held the axe and let it fall. It sank into the wood, and I managed to lift the axe and, slowly, persistently, pound it through the wood. In about ten minutes, with me pausing to rest my arm and hand, the piece was split.

"Take it slow, son," I heard my mother, who had watched from a distance.

"At this rate it'll only take me twelve hours to split enough wood for the day," I said, catching my breath.

"Just take it slow," she said, smiling more happily than in recent memory.

The next day I split a few more pieces, and the day after I tried playing a little 'tag' with Electa, but that went poorly when I realized I couldn't catch her. But I got out of bed every day after that.

One night late in November the headache woke me. Mother and Electa were in bed. After hours of half-sleep disturbed by pain I rose, cautiously, my two-dimensional world and balance making me wobbly, and struggled into my boots. My modest wood chopping had improved my stamina but my right arm still hurt so pulling a coat on was out of the question. I pulled my blanket tight around me instead. Taking care not to bump into walls or doors or knock anything over, I left Mother and sister still sleeping when I stepped outside.

It was a cold night and a breeze whistled in the trees; the chill helped numb me. I looked into the night sky for the first time since the accident, and saw stars, but they looked dull, without their natural twinkle. I was discovering how life looked to a one-eyed man, and I fought against the despair and doggedly followed the Portage Road. Leaves rattled, pushed by light gusts, branches shifted, and the moon threw a dim shadow on the road. I wanted to see the falls that night so I walked slowly but steadily, my muscles coming back, sweat forming on my skin.

My lungs tingled from the frosty air, and I felt tired before I was out of sight of my house. My foot caught a tree root and turned but I stayed up. If I fell I would break open the scabs on my face and arm and lose a week of healing. So I plodded carefully down the road; it wasn't far.

I reached the river and followed it, enjoying its fresh smell. There was an oak tree near the crest of the falls where I wanted to rest. I was pushing myself; I tripped again on a tree root, but my good arm grabbed the tree to keep me up. My headache was gone.

As I got my wind back I saw a stick of driftwood head for the falls. It submerged, then burst free of the river for a moment, shining and smooth, then spun clockwise around a boulder. I turned to follow it and watch its dive at the brink, and my foot wedged between two rocks, and I bumped into the damn tree and my good arm clutched at air and I fell full and hard on the pitted limestone. "Oh God," I got out, hitting the side of my head and rolling on my bandaged arm.

Oh God, how my arm hurt that night. Worse than the morning I was wounded. That was when I wanted to die. I felt light-headed and I asked heaven, *am I ever going to feel whole?* I was aware of the falls roaring beside me. The pain ebbed, and I drew a ragged breath and the sweat sheathing my body turned cold. Still alive. Would I ever feel whole again? I doubted it.

I had considered killing myself the day Mother took the bandages off my face and I saw the monster I expected I was. Having stolen an awful peek, I was ready. The river flowed past, just a few feet away. I sat up and nursed my arm into the last painful position, and watched the falls under moonlight.

The cataracts roared and the mist blew over me, chilling me, and then the pain faded, leaving me feeling drained. Crawling to the oak tree, I leaned against it and closed my eyes and remembered the Lewiston camp and the muskets, and I remembered the tickling, burning sensation when mine exploded. Judge Porter's wagons of supplies rolled down the dirt pathway from the end of the Portage. Barrel tops were pulled off to reveal maggots crawling on the pork, and on dead bodies, and I saw the rows of fresh graves just outside the camp, some from desertion, most from disease. I remember forcing a pledge from Lucas that if I died he would take my body back to my Mother. I saw greyish-white gunpowder smoke rise through the canopy of tree branches at Queenston. I saw us hang back at the charge, letting the regulars and the better-armed militia face the British. *Was I a coward that morning?* Lucas had already faced divine judgment. *What awaited me?*

And then I remembered my young jailer Bartlett, and Claire. And what my mother had confessed of my father's British sympathies. And I realized that I'd been on the wrong side. *I might redeem myself,* I thought, *if I knew where I belonged.*

For the first time since my wounding I felt a faint desire to live. My arm felt blissfully numbed by the cold. Then a deep, restful sleep swallowed me. I woke before dawn, stiff and aching. It was challenging, but I got to my feet on the uneven ground in the chilly light of the sunrise and walked home, to fall asleep in my own bed.

In the wake of Queenston the United States was left reeling. Its largest army had collapsed from within. Three thousand men had been under arms October 13th. Approximately nine hundred crossed, two thousand refused. The nine hundred were taken prisoner by the British, held in a semi-guarded condition at Fort George, to be eventually paroled back to New York.

In the wake of such a colossal failure the accusations flew. Van Rensselaer was accused of cowardice, of incompetence, and of conspiracy to defraud the government. Cowardice was a charge he could respond to, and did. Incompetence? Solomon, the trained military man ennobled by his wounds, wrote his brother's defense and pointed sufficient fingers to remind all concerned that commissions were a matter more of patronage than of merit. Meanwhile, stories from those at Lewiston told of rusted, useless muskets, of rotten food, of rotted kit. Invoices, ledgers and promissory notes were gathered. The Senate finally decided that full price had been paid, but inferior goods were delivered. A court of inquiry was called for in November.

Van Rensselaer, already shamed by the collapse of his Queenston attack, was more annoyed than worried when he was called before the court. "An objective assessment of my present fortune, gentlemen," he poisoned the honorific as he addressed the shopkeepers sitting in judgment on him, "and you can appreciate that the sums I am alleged to have pilfered by purchasing inferior goods would not salary my lowest servant. Would I exchange my family name for such a modest sum?" In fact the precise pilferage was never so clearly assessed as to know the value of Van Rensselaer's humblest servant. The court was, in the end, looking less for a thief than a scapegoat.

"Ignore my military record," the Dutchman finally conceded, throwing them the bone of his humility, "and consider my personal and political fortunes. What did I stand to gain?" He conceded his failure and they were embarrassed into looking elsewhere for culprits. They dismissed him, and summoned Judge Augustus Porter from Niagara.

Porter arrived in Albany, but did not speak to the convened court. He spoke privately with the three senior senators, and two days later left Albany to return to his duties as commissary agent, all charges dismissed.

The court then summoned me.

One evening a knock on the front door made us all freeze. Friends do not travel at night on a warring frontier. Mother paused on her way to the door to find Father's old pistol, kept loaded since I'd left. I waited at the kitchen entrance, my good left hand tightly gripping our sharpest knife. She pulled the door open a crack, saw her visitors, and opened the door. Two soldiers stepped inside. "Evening, Ma'am," said the first. He was bearded, in his twenties. "I'm Sergeant McLaughlin, this is Private Sears. This is the Cleary home, isn't it?" She nodded politely. "We're sorry to come barging in at this hour, but I've got orders to locate Private Nehemiah Cleary. Would you know where he is?"

I showed myself, the knife behind my back. "I'm Nehemiah Cleary, Sergeant."

McLaughlin looked me over. Reading from a paper, he said, "Private Cleary, I have orders from Albany to take you into custody, pursuant to transporting you under guard to Albany."

"Who is summoning me?"

"The state senate," McLaughlin answered in clipped tones, uncomfortable in my presence, "they have convened a Court of Inquiry."

"Sergeant, I haven't been reading many papers lately," I said, smiling, "can you tell me what they're looking for?"

"Well," the officer looked at me, then, "I hear they're looking into the accounts from last summer's encampment at Queenston."

Mother, confused, stared at the officer, then at me.

"Sergeant," I asked, "has Judge Porter testified?"

"As a matter of fact, the Judge did go to Albany. From what I hear he answered some questions," McLaughlin stressed, "then they let him go about his business."

I knew I was doomed; they'd had the right man and let him go because they could more easily hang me. "What are the terms of my arrest, Sergeant? Must I be held under guard at Schlosser, or can I remain under my mother's care?"

McLaughlin studied the floor a moment, glanced at the soldier behind him again, then looked at my bandages. "Well, you'd normally have to return with me, but I guess you can stay here."

"I do have to take walks as part of my convalescence. Do I need to be guarded?"

"I don't expect that'd be necessary," McLaughlin capitulated, then said, "I'll return to take you into custody in three days, when the next coach leaves for Albany." They bade us good night and Mother shut, then barred the door.

I knew then I had to leave. First I sat with Mother in front of the fire and drank cider. "I never told you about the battle, did I?" She shook her head, obviously not keen on hearing it. But I needed to tell her. "It was. . . " I struggled for a word to begin with, "wasted. It was all just wasted." I told her about the camp and Queenston, concluding with the failure of the rest of the army to cross in support. "I've wondered, lately, if I would have crossed if I'd been assigned to the fiftieth boatload instead of the first. If I'd had hours to think about it, like the others did. I probably would have taken one look at my musket, heard all the shooting, realized I didn't have much chance in a real fight, and not crossed."

"What do you mean," she asked, "'in a real fight'?"

"Captain Williams told me that we'd never have to cross," I said, smirking now at the memory, "that's why they didn't make a fuss when the Judge delivered those muskets. Captain Williams told me that we didn't need to be really prepared, that it was just a show. They would be signing a peace treaty, he said. We weren't going to actually fight." I took a drink of cider. "Then the British mustered. That's when we knew we'd be fighting. And then they told us, don't be worried, because the settlers over there were actually waiting to rise in revolt against Britain, and," I blushed at Mother's incredulous stare, "I know, I know. But I think the first time I really thought of just running away was when I was sitting in the boat. And then it was too late."

Sighing, I rested my head in her lap like a small boy, and she stroked my hair. She hummed a lullaby a little while, then asked, "the Judge delivered the muskets himself?"

"He delivered some spoiled pork, when I complained. Old Shultz delivered most of it."

"Well, they let him go after questioning," she said, "I expect they'll probably just ask you some questions. After all, you just checked in the supplies. They'll end up pursuing the merchants who sold the guns to the Judge."

"They won't pursue anyone after I show," I predicted, "I think they're just waiting for my hanging." I didn't want to tell her more than she needed to know, to burden her with truth. "I won't be going to Albany, Mother. I'm not going to let them hang me to ease their consciences."

"They'll question you and let you come back," she argued, "you've done nothing." She began to cry in frustration. "You don't need to leave again, do you?" I kissed her cheek. She was still weeping softly when I went to bed. That was the last time I saw her.

Since being wounded I had not strayed beyond the stone house in daylight. The night after I was arrested I went to the front door and took my winter coat off the peg on the wall.

Most of Manchester was deserted. If King George wanted the Portage back, Schlosser's modest contingent was not going to keep him from it.

I was grateful for the quiet. I'd come to grips with my scars, but I didn't know how others would react. From the river I followed the path to Broughton's Tavern. Fort Schlosser was visible through the trees, only a few hundred yards away. Broughton's front door was heavy against my shoulder. Inside, I smelled beer and tobacco for the first time since camp. The soldiers were on duty at the fort as another invasion scare shook the frontier so I was alone at the bar and realized the only money I had was a dollar left from my muster bounty. I fished it out and let it fall and ring on the wooden counter. Broughton, a short, stocky man, came out from behind a blanket tacked over the storage room where resided the best—and only—dice game between Lewiston and Black Rock. His eyes narrowed in vague recognition. "Cleary?" he asked.

I nodded. "What the devil happened to you? I heard you was killed."

"Not killed. Wounded." Apparently he hadn't heard of my arrest, which was good.

"What can I get for you?"

"Ale," I said. I'd never bought ale in Broughton's, in part because Mother thought Broughton a low sort of fellow, with his dice games, and forbade me from entering. I'd entered a few times anyway, but I'd never drunk there.

Broughton took a large clay mug from a shelf, pressed the stopcock on the barrel set on the counter, and let the foamy ale fill the mug. Settling it gently before me, he pushed the dollar back to me. "For your service." I nodded my thanks. "Anything else? Bread 'n cheese?" I took a long, cool, wonderful swallow. Broughton was still buying British ale, somehow.

"Perhaps," I asked, "you could tell me who's still running boats?"

"Nothing regular these days," said Broughton, rinsing another mug in a basin of water. "The war's kept things quiet. You might be able to hire a boat." He indicated the only other patron, a large bearded man hunched over a mug at a bench. "Remember him? Business has been real slow lately," he said softly, "I'm sure he'll give you a reasonable price."

I smiled when I recognized Elias Kravit, a burly giant of a man, face almost hidden by a bushy black beard, and one of a few I felt capable of handling tonight's work. "Evening," I greeted him, "I understand you own a boat. I'd like to hire it."

Setting down his mug, Elias looked up. "Do I know you?" I shrugged. "You used to be the portage clerk?" I nodded. "I heard you joined up." He looked at me like I was slow-witted, my enlistment evidence of my youth and stupidity. "You get wounded at Queenston?" I nodded again.

"About your boat?" I asked again. "I hear you might be available for hire."

"You're right about the boat. Business has been terrible. I'll take you wherever you want to go, so long as it's on water."

"So what's your rate for wounded soldiers?" I asked, smiling.

"I used to earn seventy-five cents for a full load to Black Rock. I'll take you for fifty."

I sat down on the bench opposite Elias. "I'm not going to Black Rock. You've crossed the river in your boat, haven't you?" Most of the boatmen were smugglers.

Elias answered, after a moment, in a lower voice. "You mean the British side?" I barely nodded. Elias frowned. "I can get across. But my rates go up. What business you got over there?"

I turned and looked for Broughton. With no one buying ale the old man had retired to the dice game in the back, which was still lively, rumors or not. The tavern was otherwise empty, the fire in the hearth crackling loudly in the quiet. "I'm going to the British side. I'm in trouble."

Elias leaned closer. "What sort of trouble?"

I told him of my pending arrest, and that Judge Porter had sent the Army after me because of the bad supplies at Lewiston.

"Is that the God's truth?" Elias asked, eyes narrowed with outrage. "We heard some of what was going on down there. How were you involved?" He was a good man, illiterate and likely to drink his wages, like many, but honest.

I explained, in as few words as possible. By sprinkling Porter's name in liberally I brought Elias to my side. He had a general dislike for the Judge, dating back to what the Judge termed 'a business misunderstanding'.

"I see," said Kravit. "So he's trying to make you the scapegoat. Bastard." He swallowed some more ale. "I'll help you."

"Thank you. One more detail," I said, and Elias nodded, "we leave tonight."

"Cross the river at night?" he asked, angry and scared. "That's awfully dangerous. We can cross at dawn and see where we're going and the patrols will still miss us."

"I want to land near Chippewa. Our patrols may not go to work until they've had their breakfast, but the British patrol their shore at sun-up," I said, "but only as far as Strawberry Island. Past that they know the current is too dangerous and they don't bother."

"Since you know so much about why they don't guard it, why are you going in there?" Elias asked angrily.

"I have to assume the armed guard will arrive at sunrise." The bearded giant sullenly nodded. "Care for a mug of ale before we go?"

"I'll take a double shot of rum before I go into the Niagara at night!" growled the boatman. I went to fetch Elias' priming fluid. He downed it in two gulps, growled to me to come to the docks in a few minutes, and left.

I finished my ale, and stepped outside. The fort was performing drills, the barked commands of officers carrying over the wooden walls of the fortress. *So,* I thought, *Judge Porter sent the army after me to explain the muskets.* My heart began hardening.

Elias' boat was wide and flat-bottomed, squared at the bow, built for cargo. Two boats were forlornly tied up to the dock. *Guess Van Rensselaer's men missed these when he was hunting for boats*, I said to myself. Elias had just finished hammering a board crosswise into the ribs for him to brace himself against the river when I arrived. Since the boat carried only cargo, there was just one seat, for Elias. One could easily hear the falls downriver; my nerves began to fail as I got in. *Perhaps going upriver a ways and then crossing wouldn't be too risky*, I remember thinking. *No,* I decided, *if Elias couldn't make the crossing he would have told me.*

I almost fell out the other side when I climbed in. Elias chuckled, "find your seat in the bow." I crept to the bow, leaning heavily on my left arm, feeling the boat roll under me, and knelt on the bottom. My bad arm was pinched, and a board cut into my back. "This isn't very comfortable," I complained.

"And I'm going to be pulling against the falls," he said as he fit the oars into improvised oarlocks, "we got thirty minutes of light and there's no time to put in a seat now unless you want to try crossing in the dark, which will all but guarantee we go over the falls. So," he said, reaching for the bowline, "I suggest you keep a look out for British patrols when we get to mid-channel." With that, Elias let the boat free of the dock, and it immediately moved downstream. "Now you'll see me earn my rum," he grunted as he dropped into position, planted his feet against the brace, seized the oars, and swung them out.

The mist of the falls was much closer than before, as the sunset lit it from behind. The river was smooth, and there was no breeze, so the surface was calm. If Elias hadn't begun huffing so at the oars one would have thought the river was still. Schlosser's dock receded in the distance as the boat nosed out into the main current of the Niagara. Elias favored his left oar to point the bow upriver, then threw himself into his work with both oars. He dipped them deeply into the water, pulled smoothly until they nearly touched the side of the boat, then quickly swung them to the bow and dipped them for another hard, rapid pull. The bow broke the water, but the river's speed was too great for a wake.

For all his powerful rowing and the angle he compensated with, the passage was slow and slightly downstream, where the shallower, white water was. I knew well the force of nature he was fighting. From the channel I could see the mist of the falls and my mouth was instantly dry. I cupped my hands to dip river water to drink. Elias sacrificed precious breath to gasp, "don't drink the Niagara! Bad luck!"

I had forgotten that bit of river lore and jerked my hands out of the cold waters. "That might explain things. I used to swim in here everyday."

We reached mid-channel, Chippewa as far away on the bow as was Schlosser on the stern, when a soft grinding rubbed through the boards. Elias doubled his pace, favoring his left oar again, and pulled hard, the flex of his muscles showing through his thick shirt. The grinding went away.

Chippewa's shoreline grew near, and I studied the shore for British patrols, though what we would do if I sighted one I didn't know, certainly not turn back. But there was no one on the river road as night fell, and a wind began to kick up behind us as we passed the mid-way point. It must have helped a bit, for Elias' rowing seemed a little less frantic. The boat began to make almost measurable headway between dips of the oars.

Elias pulled hard, glancing once over his shoulder, aiming the boat for a bushy willow whose long strands would provide perfect cover, when the grinding noise returned, sending soft shudders through the boat's ribs. I looked towards the approaching falls, and even in battle, never felt as helplessly terrified as I did that moment. Elias pulled hard on the left oar for one, two, three mighty pulls, but the grinding shook the boat and held us. "Jesus!" he cursed, and threw his muscles fully into battle, the oars dipping and scraping on the rocky bottom. Then my feet got wet; I looked down and saw why. "Elias!"

He didn't respond, he already knew.

"We're taking on water." The boat was grounding in the shallows. A board had broken and water was streaming in, adding to the weight Elias tried to move. Sweat dripped off the giant as he pulled and moved the boat a few inches, scraping hard on the rocks, more boards breaking, more water flooding in. The boat's keel was stuck in the rocks and the force of the current tipped us. The rapids suddenly surrounded us. I looked over the side and saw the craggy river bottom. We were drifting into Little Niagara, a shallow three-foot drop that would probably shatter the boat, and the water, very fast now, would sweep us to our deaths over the falls.

The shore seemed so tantalizingly close: the willow seemed just a little out of reach. "We're almost there," I said, the water pouring over the side, soaking me.

Still at his oars, Elias pulled, but the battle was lost. Then he tore an oarlock free and the river pulled the oar from his hand. "God help us," he cried hoarsely into the dusky sky. The boat slid off a ledge, wallowing badly in a stretch of deeper water, and I tried to stand, only to fall over the side, face-first. "Swim!" Elias yelled.

The cold water took my breath away, but I kicked off my shoes and let go that wonderful coat Mother had patched, freeing my hand and feet to claw for life. My right arm being useless, at least it felt nothing. My feet brushed the rocky bed and I tried in vain to find footing, but I was swept several feet downstream for my trouble. My right hand finally caught a handhold on the bottom, which tore my index fingernail off.

The roar of Niagara that I'd grown up with was now very close. The shoreline was barely twenty feet away now, so close I thought I could almost reach it, but I lost a yard to the current for every inch I pulled towards shore. The next hold would be too smooth to grasp, I knew, the current would sweep me too quickly to catch another hold until I felt my legs kick free and the bottom drop out, and then I was on the brink of the Horseshoe.

Instead, the water became shallow, and I collided with a rock that parted the water, and then my good hand grasped a thorny bush and I pulled myself up onto dry land and collapsed onto grass. I lay there, trembling and gasping for breath, and then thought to look for Elias.

Straining to see in the dark, I saw the wrecked boat sliding steadily downstream, plop over Little Niagara and break apart. And, holding to the stern, with one arm still holding an oar like a walking stick, was

Elias. "Let go of the boat. Let go!" I screamed, but I knew my voice could not reach him. The rapids had him now; the man was still in the stern half of the boat, trying to jam his oar into the crevice-lined riverbed but he couldn't make it work. The stern up-ended, and then Elias was on his own in the water. He almost stood up for a moment, above the rolling, splashing water, as though he might walk to safety. Then he fell, disappearing into the froth, then I saw him wave the broken stump of the oar, and then he was at the brink.

And he found a moment's grip there, on a boulder that rose above the water, where a wretched bush somehow had rooted. He was trapped there. There was no escape from that point. No sound rises above the river's own roar, but I knew he was screaming when I saw him disappear.

The War with the States II

At the time I was due to ride under arrest to Albany, Claire learned officially, courtesy of a chaplain, that she had been widowed, and she began her period of mourning. Two nights later, a surprisingly warm November evening brought out more people than usual. The inn was filled with her neighbors, gossiping and joking, in part to comfort the young widow. The failure of the Queenston attack had left everyone relieved and in high spirits.

Job Wilson, the blacksmith next door, told a joke that had gone the rounds. "I was told by a friend in His Majesty's Army of the new maneuver the Americans tried at Queenston. They call it charging backwards!" He roared, slapping his thigh and bellowing with delighted laughter. The others, mostly women, politely smiled at the joke that had already gone the rounds. The men chuckled agreeably, but none as loudly as Wilson himself.

"I hear they're going to release all the American prisoners from Fort George before Thanksgiving," announced Mrs. Cohoe, always seated nearest the stove. A few heads turned towards her; Mrs. Cohoe usually came up with the most provocative news.

"There's nine hundred in Fort George," said Caroline Moore, a teenager sent for sugar and deliberately lingering and trying to not look at young George Sinclair, "they can't let that many go. That's a whole army." A fresh taste of invasion anxiety swept the room.

"Oh, I expect they'll keep them under control," said young Sinclair, trying to impress Caroline with his courage. "I'd go and guard them myself, but with my father gone with the militia my mother can't bear for me to leave," he added softly for Caroline's benefit. He got the blush he was hoping for.

Claire's neighbors were being very kind to her. She wasn't naturally outgoing, not comfortable in a crowd, and as a young woman so ill at ease with men it was a miracle one had married her. But as proprietress of the Pelham Inn, and what passed for a store, she was something of a public figure, and she had eased into her own role, first as Gordon's wife, now filling her own role. Her woodpile never ran low and she was embarrassed with gratitude at frequently finding warm pies and fresh loaves on her counter. She planned to finish her mourning period, sell the inn, and return to her family in York, but she would take fond memories of Pelham when she went.

Finishing her last task, she yawned slightly, a gracious reminder of the hour. "Well, folks," said Wilson, "I think Mrs. Teal has been saddled with our company enough this evening. Time to be getting home, eh?" It was late, and whether or not George would have liked to linger in the inn, taking the opportunity to chat with Caroline and the young widowed Mrs. Teal, they were all farm laborers or the sons of farmers and had early chores ahead of them. The party gradually collected coats and left, only Wilson lingering.

"Mrs. Teal," he began, not too comfortable himself around the shy woman, "I understand you've been given formal notice of Gordon's heroic demise." He paused a moment, then asked, "I wanted to express my sympathy. I've known Gordon since we were young roustabouts, and he was a hard worker, a God fearing man. We've lost a good soul."

She nodded, and whispered thanks. She didn't know how best to mourn her husband. It was a new experience and she sensed that to do so in an accomplished fashion one needed, God help her, experience with dead husbands, experience she didn't have. *Should one summon tears at every mention of Gordon?* It wasn't possible. Should she simply purse her lips, a slight smile, her eyebrows arched in supplication that

Gordon be among the angels? She settled for simply listening as though Wilson was discussing the prices of nails and seed corn, looking at her hands and thanking him.

His next words surprised her. "Have you given any thought to your future here?"

"My future?" she asked, not sure what the middle-aged bachelor was suggesting. Out of habit her hands touched her hair to search for strays.

"I am referring to your business," said Wilson, blushing. "The inn." Even if he wanted her, it was too soon to even suggest a courtship. "Gordon was a hard worker, and while I know you are also not afraid of hard work, this enterprise requires more than you alone can give it."

She nodded, thinking again of her family in York; Wilson was right. A single woman could not keep an inn. The business dealings all but demanded a male presence. The trade goods were also more work than she could handle; the inn had, in fact, required hard work from both of them. She suspected on occasion, helping her husband in manual labors that a young male clerk would be more suited for, that her late husband had sized her up based less on her figure and her face than on her family's financial standing and rumored physical stamina.

"Once you've had time to absorb your loss, please let me know if," he meant 'when', "you plan to sell. I'll give you a fair price." He wished her good night and left. She had just shut the door when someone rapped on it.

I stood in the dark, scared of rejection and frightened of what lay beyond. She answered the door with a candle for light. The first detail she saw was my eye patch. "Can I help you, Sir?" she asked, politely but cautiously.

Claire didn't recognize me; my heart broke; I wished I'd followed Elias over the falls.

She asked again, more impatiently, "I'm closing, Sir. Can I help you with something?"

Preparing to walk away, I whispered, "it's me, Claire. Nehemiah Cleary." She hesitated. "The Yankee deserter," I reminded her, stepping into the dim light of her candle, "you cooked me dinner. Then, you gave me some of Gordon's clothing. I left before you were up but I scratched my name on the hearth. Do you remember me?" She stared at my scarred face and the eye patch, then touched her own face, nodded dumbly, then let me in and closed the door. My hair had been shoulder-length in October; now it was cut unevenly, just growing out of a shaved scalp on one side. My eye patch just made her tremble.

You hideous cripple, I thought, *spare this woman your presence and run into the night.* Instead, slowly, still stiff, I stepped inside and pulled off my jacket and then she saw as well that my arm hung limp. Then she began crying, taking my lame hand in hers, leading me to a chair by the stove. "What in God's name have they done to you?" she asked.

I sat down, still studying her face like a beautiful painting, an image I'd almost lost. "When I left you I made my way to Erie, found a boat, and crossed the river. When I reached Schlosser, I found my mother gone. While I was searching for her a sentry discovered me. I fired my musket, into the sky, just to scare him off. But you remember how rusted it was?" She nodded. "Well, it burst. In my face." My voice had a detached sound, that of the witness at the scene, not the victim. She was gently stroking the side of my face, and her touch reminded me of that night and why I'd returned. "As you can see," I briefly lifted the eye patch, "my eye is damaged. I can't see very well out of it. I can judge distances, roughly, but I'm hoping it gets better." I looked at my arm. "My right arm also took a lot of the blast. There are probably still pieces of the damn gun in me."

"When did all of this happen?"

"The dawn after I left here." She pulled up a chair and sat next to me. "My mother cared for me. In fact, I left home only a day ago." She rose suddenly when she thought someone was coming in, and thought to bolt the front door.

Then, fetching a kerosene lamp, she studied my wounds more closely, wincing. "This must have hurt so badly," she murmured in a sweet, sympathetic voice, and took my limp right hand in hers, "can you make a fist?" I could barely close that hand. "You still need a doctor's care. I'll fetch Doctor Crabtree tomorrow. Tell me how you got here. There's a war out there, still, isn't there?" she asked, trying to get a smile from me.

She isn't ready for this, I thought, but I told her. "We were most of the way across the river when the current took us into the rapids. The boat broke up, and I jumped." Her eyes narrowed in dim appreciation of a trip down the Upper Rapids. "I got to shore. Elias stayed with the boat."

"Why?"

"Maybe he couldn't swim, not that anyone can in that water." She closed her eyes as if to shut out the image. "The story gets much less exciting after that."

"Thank God."

"I stole a horse at Chippewa this morning and some shoes and a coat. I lost mine in the water"— she almost smiled at the petty loss — "and I rode straight here."

She gripped my right hand gently, protectively, and studied the scar on my arm, then my hand, then my face again. After a silence that lasted through the chime of nine she said, "I don't know how this must sound, given your wounds, but the Lord must not be willing to see you dead yet." She laughed, and when she laughed I laughed. We only stopped when we were speechless and crying.

"I'm so glad you came back," she said then, and kissed me.

"I think, with time, your eye will regain full use." Doctor Crabtree, Pelham's octogenarian doctor, peered closely. "For a musket to explode and not take the user with it is rare. Must have been a light powder charge. Count yourself lucky." He reached for his bag by the bed and pulled out a wrapped array of probes, unrolling the packet on the side of the bed. Pinching and gently probing, the doctor examined my right arm. "It will heal, it will eventually be fully useful, I think," he said, "and if you find yourself financially able, you might consider a trip to Montreal. There are skilled surgeons there who have done amazing things with scars," he touched the one from the corner of my eye to my jaw, "to make them less. . . ghastly." He stood, after an hour's examination. "For now, just get as much sunlight as you can arrange. The flesh needs a healthy diet."

"Go outside?" I asked. The trip to Pelham had been hard enough, avoiding the few strangers I met.

"I understand," said the doctor, his gruff voice laced with fatherly affection, "but the eye must be allowed to properly heal. And the arm will heal best with exercise."

After Crabtree left, Claire returned to my bedside. "I told him you were my cousin," she said. "I don't think he believed me, but he's a very kind man, and minds his own business."

"Claire," I asked, "how long can I stay with you?"

"As long as you like," she answered, puzzled. "Did you think otherwise?"

I was afraid to broach the new truth, but love was making demands on me. "I . . . this," I indicated my wounds, "isn't the way I intended it to be. When I first met you I thought, there's the prettiest girl I've ever seen. I'm in love." She blushed. "I remember the night I was here." She blushed deeper. "I'll never forget it. That night I dreamed of coming back to you, of taking you away with me." She looked down and smiled. "Then, this." I struggled, unsuccessfully, to not cry. "I would have asked for your hand that night, but I was also afraid you'd turn me in. Today, I'm here, and you know your husband's fate, and," I realized I was proposing. "I would like your hand in marriage," I finally said, looking up at her.

She held my hand in both of hers. "That's a very kind proposition," she said, "for a spinster widow." She let go of my hand and stood and went to the window, looking out at Pelham. It was a prosperous village, but it was an anxious one, still a frontier community, war on the near horizon; it was a time for a community to join and survive. There were rules, codes of behavior, for women to follow when their men were gone to war, and other rules for mourning. If she violated the rules of propriety they would shun her, leave her isolated. Widow or no, she could not fly in the face of community judgment without fear of retribution. To love me she should marry me.

But she had had a few weeks to herself, the first time in her life alone. She'd found herself enjoying it. To be her own person, not a wife, not a devoted servant, was an experience few women knew. Diving back into marriage felt stifling. She wanted to explore it further. "Nehemiah," she finally said, "I insist you stay with me. I don't care what my neighbors say. I shall do what I wish. As for your kind proposition," she looked away, "I won't say no, but I can't say yes, either."

I nodded, disappointed but also grateful she hadn't turned me down.

Instead, she would risk the stigma of cohabitation without marriage. "Let me have some time to consider your kind offer. For now, I think you still need some rest." She kissed my forehead, and when I reached for her mouth, she kissed me. When we separated, she smoothed my hair back, set my head back on the pillow, then rose and left, saying, "get some rest, my love."

Claire introduced me to her neighbors as her cousin. Then she insisted we both begin regular attendance at the Anglican Church, a building she'd seen little of herself. Together we worshipped amongst the townsfolk, sitting on rough wooden benches and singing *a cappella*. "This is like gold and silver for the gossips," Claire told me as I drove us home in the wagon the second Sunday in a light rain. "They can whisper among themselves all they want, but they will keep it to themselves so long as we maintain ourselves." With the able-bodied men gone to war, the dowagers had been starved of gossip until my arrival. But the situation was, in fact, quite delicate. On one hand there Claire was, respectably widowed but sharing. . . whatever with me. On the other hand I was a war hero from Queenston, or so ran the story Claire had circulated, and I obviously bore the scars for such a tale, and maimed war heroes were not to be idly gossiped about. And, in the worst circles, the worst question was hinted at; did she find my condition somehow appealing? Were we sharing a room? "No," growled the elderly Crabtree as his wife nagged him for details. But not to worry—one need not be in the fields to be at play, so the gossips chattered on, the subject remaining alive and deliciously unresolved.

Claire's inn had four spare rooms. I slept in the room next to her my first night, yelling at my nightmares. I moved the second night to the end of the hall, four doors away, a storeroom. "Sorry about the noise," I said.

"I can learn to sleep through it," she offered.

"If I can't, how can you?" I asked, and got her to laugh.

"What are you seeing in your dreams?" she asked.

"I keep going back into battle. And I never have a weapon, or if I do it's a knife without a handle, or a musket that won't fire. And everyone, everyone is coming after me. Sometimes New Yorkers, sometimes British. Sometimes they're people from this village, some from mine. But the good news is last night was a little less awful than the night before."

Some nights I slept four or five hours, my dreams following me into the blank reality of my room. Other nights, exhausted, I slept twelve hours, moaning but staying asleep. Claire brewed me teas mixed to calm nerves. I tried an occasional sip of whiskey. In the end, nothing really worked except time.

We learned through the papers that the British were to parole the prisoners they held at Fort George. They were delivered in boatloads across the river before hard freezing hit. I took a copy of the *Pelham Courier* with me on a ride that day. It would have been my first day of freedom if I'd been captured. I rode down the frozen muddy trail to the east. To cover my wounds I wound a scarf snugly around my face showing just my eye and my patch; strangers stared at my eye patch but not so much as when they saw my scar. At a crossroads an hour's ride east I rested in the saddle, steam puffing from the horse's nostrils, and pulled out a flask of whiskey. The smell reminded me of Lucas.

I read the paper. 'We can only look at the incompetent behavior of the American Army, with its superior numbers, and how thoroughly British forces fought them back, and conclude that America's proud revolution has not produced much of a nation. Godless anarchy has produced a nation of greed. Claiming to pursue life, liberty and personal freedoms, they have taken their first opportunity to try to steal the land of their former brothers. We have, for now, defeated them. We mourn the loss of General Brock, and stand proudly defending our borders.' "That pretty much says it," I agreed.

I thought about Judge Porter. I considered his corruption. Being young I was outraged, and in the quiet safety of that crossroads outside Pelham I looked east towards Niagara and wondered what I could do. I wanted to kill him but I couldn't, and I couldn't quite stand to forget it, much less forgive. The ghosts that haunted me had to be mollified, if I was ever going have a good night's sleep, and that day I understood for the first time that the pursuit of justice might take away my nightmares. I rode back to the inn feeling better, stronger, but without a plan, no idea of what to do next. Surviving seemed the highest priority.

A farmer's wife had brought in a large basket of eggs, which Claire traded for some yards of flannel and some nails. She was busy boiling the eggs when I came in. "Getting some sun?" she asked, without taking her eyes off her carefully counted piles. I smiled and nodded. "What's the news?" she asked, seeing the folded newspaper sticking from my coat.

"It says the captured American prisoners at Fort George were to be released today, paroled back to New York," I said. "If I'd been captured, today would have been my first day of freedom." She had penciled her count on a scrap of paper.

"Remember my musket?" She nodded, glancing up at me. "Did I ever tell you about Judge Porter?"

"He was your employer before the war?" she asked.

"Yes. And he was the quartermaster for the militia," I said, "he bought the supplies for the army."

"Oh," she responded, her dipper holding an egg over the steaming pot for a moment. "Oh my."

I sat at the table, collecting her boiled eggs in a wooden bowl, and told her about the deliveries and the invoices I was compelled to sign. "Did you report this to your superior?" she asked, her indignation leaving her face flushed. I nodded and told that story. The cowbells nailed over the door clanked, announcing visitors: Mrs. Hill and her young son, so I was silent, leaving Claire to shift from outrage to solicitude. Mrs. Hill and son Tom had harvested potatoes, two bushels, which they exchanged for a pound of tea, a bolt of cotton, some thread, candles, and a ginger twist for Tom. With the chat of goings on, and hearing the Hills' adventures with a hive of wasps in their eaves, it was a half-hour later before we were alone again.

She hadn't forgotten. "Judge Porter has done you a serious injustice. I wouldn't blame you if you hate him," she said.

I looked at the paper. "I'm glad it's not just me. I'm not sure I knew what hate really was until now. I had no one to hate. I miss that." I helped her carry the potatoes into the cellar, where they'd keep longer. "I'm trying to turn the other cheek, but it's hard."

"That's asking a lot." She pulled the last of the dirty spuds out of the basket and into the bin, and we shut the cellar door.

"I know it sounds over-simple to say good guns would have made the difference at Queenston, but I think they might have. And I want," this was where I stalled. Anger without direction. Hatred without an outlet. "How does one satisfy a lust for revenge?" I asked her.

She shook her head. "I've never lusted for revenge." She looked at me and asked, "are you plotting a way to kill the judge?"

"It crossed my mind. But it didn't get far."

She took my hands in hers, smiling. "Good. There's got to be a better way. Let's think on it."

As I got my strength back I helped Claire as much as possible. Honest labor was good for me physically and spiritually. The inn usually had a boarder or two in peacetime; it had been empty since September. The trading of goods made the inn more of a general store as autumn passed.

The air went down to freezing for a week, followed by a summer sun. "Nehemiah?" I heard her voice the third day of the warm-up. I'd been tossing in a bad dream, in the gorge this time, and the Indians were chasing me as far as the flats, and I was climbing up the rocks, trying to scale the gorge wall, and then an arrow shot through me. It hurt like hell. Some of my nightmares had replayed so often I recognized them as such. Then I'd get one like this, where waking up was a relief. "Nehemiah?" and that time she woke me. She was already dressed in her cape and heavy boots for mud. "Another nightmare?"

I nodded. "You going somewhere?"

"Mrs. Webster isn't feeling well, so I've heard. I'm going to pay her a call. She lives a few miles south. I'm taking her some sweets while the warm weather lasts."

"Sweets?" I asked, "for a sick person?"

"Her illness is loneliness," Claire answered. She brushed my hair back to examine the changing color of my scar. "I know you feel uncomfortable in public, but would you mind the inn today? It'll be quiet. I'll be back before sunset." I really didn't want to but I loved her too much to say no. She kissed me good-bye and then she was out the door.

Despite the calendar, it was another warm morning. I rose as she rode off, and set coffee to boil on the stove. Then I pumped water into a basin, bent over the basin, and scrubbed my face. Damn, it was cold. If the flies buzzing thought it was still summer, the well surely knew winter was coming. Pulling on my cleanest shirt, I tried to flex my right arm. The nerves were still too damaged for my sense of touch, but the muscles were responding to daily exercises. I could grip with the hand, so getting through the day was easier. Crabtree had suggested bathing the arm to stimulate nerve growth and I thought I felt new tingling.

I studied myself in a small mirror. I looked sullen. *You are going to handle business today*, I lectured my reflection, *and you will be pleasant, smile at everyone, and when Claire comes home tonight you'll be able to show her that you aren't a useless cripple.* I splashed some more cold water on my face, toweled dry, and opened the half-door joining the larder to the public room of the inn.

After building up the fire in the fireplace of the public room, I retreated to the storeroom, among the sacks of flour and beans and the shelves stocked with everything else Pelham used. I warmly greeted the oak barrel of whiskey with a hug. "I'll not re-order more spirits," Claire had insisted when I discovered it, "but it having long since been paid for I'd be foolish to throw it out." I tapped a pint now and then for my rides, and remembered that a taste of it from Lucas' flask had helped me cross the river at Queenston. The bells over the door rang and I saw Mrs. Cohoe come in and I wanted a stiff one. No, that would be foolish. Mrs. Cohoe, who was quite familiar with the smell of spirits, would smell it on my breath, and if she knew, the world would soon know, and Claire and I were trying to be above reproach.

Mrs. Cohoe, thirty years a farmer's wife and ten years his widow, had set by the fireplace, though it was a warm morning. I gingerly came to serve her. "Is Mrs. Teal feeling ill today?" asked the old gossip.

"No, Ma'am," I answered, avoiding eye contact, "she's visiting Mrs. Webster for the day. Can I help you?"

"Mrs. Webster," noted the widow, fishing in her pocket for a slip of paper folded precisely down the middle, "will keep Mrs. Teal until the spring planting if she can." I smiled politely. "I just need a few things today," she paused, looking and wincing for the dozenth time at my scarred face, "Mr. Cleary, isn't it?" Her order was short. Mrs. Cohoe came in twice a week with short lists, spending an hour each visit bending Claire's ear. That she could shop once a week and have the goods delivered to her home all of two doors away was explained to her, but one learned nothing about one's neighbors if one only shopped once a week via delivery boy.

She followed me into the storeroom — I hated that—where I set up the scale and began to dip sugar from the wooden barrel. The scale read correctly to the tenth of an ounce. "That's a pound of sugar?" Mrs. Cohoe looked hard at me. I double-checked the weights for her. "Oh dear," Mrs. Cohoe sighed as she acknowledged the even measure, "Mrs. Teal always gives me a pinch more," she looked down, "my condition," and said no more. Knowing Claire's policy of keeping Mrs. Cohoe happy, I managed a thin smile and poured one more heaping scoop, until the paper parcel would barely tie shut, and set it before the beaming Mrs. Cohoe. "Thank you, Mr. Cleary."

The next item on her list: medicinal brandy. Brandy, whiskey, any alcohol, all meant the whiskey barrel. I found a clean flask and a tight fitting cork and drew the flask nearly full. It being brandy, I added some maple syrup for color and taste. For proper brandy she'd have to travel to York; she seemed to like the substitute well enough. I shook it a minute, held it to the light, liked the color and brought it out for her to see, then set it discreetly behind the bulging sugar bag. Mrs. Cohoe became radiant.

"So you are her. . . cousin?" I nodded. She'd been told the story at least three times. "And you're from York?"

"Yes Ma'am," I said politely, pouring some flour.

"And you were at Queenston?"

She was testing me, again. Had she heard something, or was this what passed in her life for entertainment? My left hand trembled between the flour barrel and the scale and spilled some onto the floor. "That's right, ma'am."

"Strange," she said, and paused, and I scooped nuts with both hands trembling, "about you not knowing her husband, Gordon. Had you ever met Gordon?" I shook my head. "He was at Queenston, you know."

"There were a lot of us, Ma'am."

"Are you related to Mrs. Teal by marriage or blood?"

Mrs. Cohoe had missed her calling. She should have been a constable. "Blood. Her mother's second brother is my pa." It took me two tries to tie up the sack of flour, snagging my finger in the string and missing the loop. I blushed and had to get close to the sack: *damn eye, damn nerve damage.* Maybe Mrs. Cohoe had heard something? The Pelham militia was starting to head back in ones and twos—maybe some names had been exchanged? "And I thought I heard Mrs. Teal say once that her family came from York."

"That's right," I said, carefully piling her purchases together on the table, hoping it would speed her exit, "my father was brother to Claire's mother." I had been tested in school and in battle, but Mrs. Cohoe still made me tremble. "My Pa left York to set up a trading post up north. He got killed by Hurons a few years past. Mother raised me, and when the war broke out I signed up."

"Of course," she responded with a smile, "I'm so forgetful. Please put this on my account." She began the slow trip to the front door, pausing to glance over the copy of the *Pelham Courier* sitting by the stove. I pulled out the ledger book and found Mrs. Cohoe's name. She was special, Claire permitting her a credit ceiling well above other customers. "The price of peace," she called it every time Mrs. Cohoe visited. Besides, Mrs. Cohoe was that rare customer who, when she paid, paid in cash.

Another customer stepped into the inn, a rough looking stranger. "Tobacco?" he asked in a gruff, tired voice, "and whiskey if you have it." He had a bearded face, hard to see under his wide-brimmed hat. His shirt was dirty but there was a touch of military about him, a regulation bullet pouch slung over his shoulder. He rested his musket against the stone hearth. I studied my first soldier since returning to Canada. "Whiskey?" the soldier asked again.

Nodding, I stepped into the backroom, found another flask, filled it to the top and brought it out. Setting it before the soldier, I apologized, "sorry, no tobacco."

"What do I owe you for this?" asked the man, removing his hat to show gray hair.

"You with the militia?"

His eyes narrowed slightly, "yup, the York militia."

Mrs. Cohoe, who was almost gone, paused at the door.

"No charge. I was with the militia myself."

"Which unit?" he asked. Mrs. Cohoe continued to hover.

Seeing her there I remembered one of the little lies I'd prepared, knowing the militia would return. "I was the assistant artillerist. I signed up in York, but when we got to Queenston we were assigned to another unit guarding the shore batteries." If there was a God, Brock had not assigned the York militia to the shore batteries.

"We were assigned to the upper village. Your unit took the first wave. That where you were hurt?"

Mrs. Cohoe was turning again, on her way out, my story having held up under its most severe test. "Yep."

The soldier offered his flask to me with a wink when Mrs. Cohoe had finally left. "Here's to the death of Madison and the other damn Americans."

We drank, and then the solider saw me looked enviously at the musket. "It's been a while since I held a musket," I said.

The soldier hefted it and handed it to me. It was well made, clean, a proper weapon. "See much of the Americans at Queenston?" I asked.

"Sorry to say I didn't. Time we got near 'em, General Sheaffe was calling the regulars to drive them out. We just stayed in reserve the whole day," he said, sounding both disappointed and a little relieved.

"Well," I said, my mouth running off again, "they had the sorriest looking muskets you ever laid eyes on. They were rusted so badly some of their triggers wouldn't pull. We didn't even bother ducking low because half their shots never fired."

"You do say," said the soldier, taking another sip of whiskey, "now I do recall hearing something about that." As I admired the musket I listened. "One or two of our boys went across the river one night after the battle, as a prank. They set off some firecrackers by a battery, and laughed when the Yanks went running for Fort Niagara." We both chuckled, myself less heartily. "What I heard was that there's a barn over there in Lewiston, close by the river, and it's full of them muskets they had at Queenston. Y'know the whole bloody army up and quit. What with most of the Yanks being too cowardly to cross, they just dropped them pieces and walked away. Or, that's what I heard," said the soldier. "Just before they let us leave for the holidays I heard the governor in New York announced amnesty on all deserters, just so's they could put the army back together. What a pitiful mess, eh?"

"To the York militia."

"To the militia." We drank another toast and the soldier was on his way. That warm glow was back in my gut, reminding me of Queenston. I watched him leave, thinking about what he'd said. An amnesty for deserters? It would have been a nice idea a couple of weeks earlier, but since then I had changed sides. I guess I became a traitor that day. And then I got to thinking about the barn filled with cast-off muskets in Lewiston.

When I stepped to the door to watch the soldier leave town I saw that it had begun to rain. Lead colored clouds had rolled up from the south and the rain was coming down in large drops. A bitterly cold breeze was pushing it.

Not having swept the public room out yet, I got to work. The wind grew stronger, and the temperature dropped. I stirred up the coals in the stove, then stepped outside to fetch more wood, and snowflakes blew in my face. I pulled three pieces from the woodpile and, just in my shirt, hurried back in. When I looked out again the air was thick with snow flurries. "Damn." I knew how suddenly and intensely snow blew up around the lakes. I pushed the door shut as the cold air sucked the heat out of the room. *Claire*, I vowed, *if you aren't two minutes ride away I'll know soon enough and. . .*

Winter arrived with a vengeance. No one else came in. I finished sweeping, then read the paper again. The clock gonged noon; the wind howled outside and the neighboring homes disappeared from time to time in the swirling blizzard that had developed. Lunching on some crackers and cheese, I watched snow pile up. Every few minutes I opened the door, looked out, got a face full of snow driven by ever-colder wind, and pushed the door shut again. I paced, circled the room, stirred up the coals in the fireplace, dusted, swept the clean boards, checked the temperature outside and pushed the door shut against winter's rampaging arrival, sinking deeper and deeper into anxiety. When the clock gonged the half-hour after one I pictured her lost in the snows. *If you're not back by two*, I decided, *I'll saddle up the second horse and head out.* Then the wind picked up, howling and blowing snow hard against the windows, and I pulled the shutters close, bolted the door, and pulled on my heavy coat.

The horse had been Gordon's and Gordon had known horses. A glossy brown coat and strong, she accepted the bridle, took the bit, and was saddled in seconds. I pulled a heavy sweater on, my coat over it, then tied a blanket around me with twine. And still the wind cut through me with its first blast. There was already at least six inches on the ground. I climbed into the saddle and pointed Gordon—my name for him—south down Main Street.

God in heaven it was cold. Before I cleared the village my hands were numb inside my gloves. I tucked one in my pocket to keep warm, holding the reins in the other, alternating them when one hurt too much. The snow blew into white-outs, then cleared for maybe ten feet, but when the road left the protection of Pelham's houses there was nothing to stop the wind and nothing but my memory for guidance.

The horse was sure-footed and traveled slowly but steadily. The Webster farm was five long miles out. Claire had left at seven-thirty that morning, probably reached the farm by nine. If she started back early, dressed as she was, she was in a bad storm with a spring cape. If she had stayed put, I'd look romantic but foolish, frozen out on the road. A whiteout blinded me then, Gordon stopped, and I had to get off and walk him a short distance. It let up, and I saw that we'd reached a crossroads and I was less than a half-mile from Pelham. "We need to move faster than this," I ordered the horse. I climbed back in the saddle, leaning down close to his mane for his warmth. The horse's hooves made crunching noises in the snow. My blanket was soon stiff with ice and breathing was hard; my face and hands were numb.

Ten minutes slow ride beyond the crossroads and another blinding flurry enveloped us. I was trembling with cold by then, and the horse stopped. "Go, Gordon, go!" I begged the horse on with gentle kicks to the ribs. Guided by instinct, the horse refused. "I won't freeze to death out here," I prodded him. Then a contrary gust blew the whiteness away and the horse responded when we saw Claire's wagon ahead. As we approached I saw that the wagon was down in front; the axle had broken and the wagon was abandoned. "Claire!" I called for her in the wind, and rode towards a line of trees. Again a whiteout smothered us and Gordon stopped. I pulled on his reins to turn him around and return: I couldn't take any more cold. Claire could have wandered a long distance from the wagon. Maybe she'd reached a farmhouse. Then the wind calmed a moment and at the edge of the swirling snow I saw her, half buried in a drift, lying by a tree. "Claire!"

She was lying face down and I turned her over. She was very cold but when I pinched her cheek she showed color. I couldn't lift her; instead I got both of my arms under hers, grasped my right with my left, and dragged her to Gordon. Then I had to treat her like a sack of potatoes to get her over the saddle, pushing her rump and tugging her from the other side. Her flimsy spring cape was frozen tightly to her, and I somehow worked the knot in the twine, pulled off my blanket and tied it around her. Turning Gordon around, leading him by the reins, I began the return trek, walking back over the freezing landscape, looking for his hoof prints in the snow. Three more times we were surrounded by mad howling winds, and once we were lost and I chanced turning when I saw a familiar tree. I was clenching my teeth tightly to avoid biting my tongue. When he saw the outline of Pelham's buildings his gait picked up and I wrapped his reins around my arms and let him tow me.

Getting Gordon into his stall wasn't hard. Getting Claire in her bed was a protracted, clumsy struggle; it was hell working the door's iron latch. I snagged it on the metal edge and sensed I was cutting myself, and my hand bled when it thawed. Bumping her a few times against the door and stairwell, I got her to her bed and built up the fire. She responded to the heat like a sleeper waking slowly. "Nehemiah?" she called for me softly and I realized I'd been holding my breath waiting to hear her voice again. "I thought I was dead," she said slowly, her lips still blue from the cold. I had gotten her outer garments off; her dress was frozen to her body. I hesitated from propriety, but her skin was blue so I undressed her, threw her wet clothes onto the brick threshold of the fireplace, and laid her under the quilt.

I sat by her fire and grunted in pain as my fingers and toes thawed. My own clothes were wet, but I didn't have the strength left to work the buttons. Claire lay deathly still and twice I hovered over her, once putting a mirror to her face to see her soft breath fog the mirror. A bruise emerged on her forehead, where I stumbled on the last step and her head collided with the bedroom door. I went downstairs and heated water to brew tea for her. I dozed in the chair, waking when the kettle whistled.

She was awake, but sleepy-eyed, in bed when I came back with strong hot tea. "How are you feeling?" I asked.

She was still trembling so I helped guide the cup to her mouth. The first hot mouthful caught her breath. "Oh." She sipped again, then made a face. "This is terrible."

"It's china black, your favorite. Just sip it. It'll warm you up."

She sipped a little, then I set the rest aside. Then, her arms still like lead, I held her close and felt her chilly body. She rested her head on my shoulder. Our trembling eased.

"I'm so tired," she said softly. "The fire feels good."

"So what happened?"

"I reached Webster's about ten o'clock," Claire said, "and Mrs. Webster was doing her 'I'm at death's door' performance. After she tasted the molasses twists, with a cup of the good tea I'd brought, she perked up a bit." She smiled. "I saw the rain start at noon," she continued, soberly, "and said good-bye. I was on the road when it turned to snow, and it just blinded me." She looked sadly at me. "I lost Bluebell out there. She's wandering out there. The wagon axle was old. I think it was cracked, and Gordon never got around to repairing it. When it broke, I tried to ride Bluebell without a saddle, but I couldn't stay on. So I set her loose and started to walk. I got lost." She closed her eyes, shivered, and cursed herself for the day's adventure, then sneezed. "I've gotten off lightly for this day's stupidity, that's for sure," she muttered.

The sun set, leaving winter to roam over the darkened country and the firelight to shine in Claire's eyes. I could feel that she was warm again, and the fact that she was undressed beneath the comforter was not forgotten. "My love," she whispered softly, "I think today we surpassed the bonds shared by mere 'cousins.'" She lifted the edge of the comforter and then I was beside her.

Whatever doubt she'd felt before, she seemed certain now. My virginity made our first attempt somewhat brief, but my embarrassment was hushed by her loving smile. Later, when the fire had burned low, we touched like we had no cares or concerns, satisfied each other, and then slept deeply.

More invasion rumors passed through the community but nobody took them seriously. Nobody expected invading armies when winter storms were sweeping the country with snow and bitter cold and high winds. Dr. Crabtree shared some cures he'd learned, and Claire sent for a book on healing my scars. The book called for roots and berries hard to gather in the winter, but the doctor's cure recommended warm baths and skin lotions, readily available and agreeable, and we spent some time every night gently treating my most hideous scar, from my right eye socket to my jaw. It seemed to help, or perhaps the lotions and bathing were just a pleasant way to pass time while nature did its work. One day in the storeroom, putting away some blankets, I caught my reflection in a mirror and I looked almost ordinary but for the eye-patch. I surprised myself by smiling.

Gordon needed new shoes, so I walked him across the road to Job Wilson's. I found him filing down a piece of iron to fit a hinge. "Mr. Wilson," I said, "this horse needs new shoes."

Job Wilson stood a foot taller than I. His muscles were impressive, and he seemed to enjoy flexing them. He nodded to me. "Mis-ter Cleary. Shoes, eh?" He set aside the hinge and walked around the horse, lifting the front right hoof and, using a ruler he pulled from a pocket of his leather apron, measured the width of the worn shoe. "I remember this one. Gordon talked me into a trade, free shoes for whiskey. I don't know what I was thinking. I don't even like whiskey." Job smiled at me; his face was not as blackened with soot as it sometimes was, but it was early in the day. "Did you know Gordon?" Job asked, walking back to the bin.

"No," I said. "We grew up a little too far apart for much visiting."

"So you'd never met Mrs. Teal?" Wilson asked, watching me this time for my reaction. I shook my head. It was a suspicious little town, after all. "Only reason I'm asking is how you manage to appear after so many years absent, just when she needs to have a man around. Coincidence." I licked my lips, finding that my mouth had dried up.

Wilson was well within the grounds I considered meddling, but I knew Claire would want me to answer any question about the 'legitimacy' of our living situation. "That's right. Just," I tried and failed to find a better word, "coincidence."

Wilson rummaged in a bin, holding his ruler to a couple likely candidates and found a shoe that fit. He went to work with his claw hammer, lifting the front hoof and prying out the nails holding the old, broken shoe. "Did Mrs. Teal tell you I'd asked about the inn?" he asked, his eyes on his work.

She hadn't. He picked up the horse's hind hoof. "Well, I'd say the two of you could make a handsome couple, if that's your intention," he continued, and I blushed, but he couldn't see me through the horse, "but if you've never run a business, and Mrs. Teal being just a young woman, I think she'd be wiser to sell." He turned the hammer around and vigorously pounded a nail. When the ringing of the hammer was gone, he asked, "I heard tell from some sources that some of the Americans who invaded at Queenston escaped capture. Might be still roaming around the countryside."

I waited. "I don't make other folks' lives my business, you understand," Job continued, letting the hoof down to see how comfortable the horse was. Straightening up, he looked at me. "Whatever a man has in his past is up to the Lord, not me. And I'm not the only man in town who knows this. But if you and Mrs. Teal want to find a new life somewhere where nobody knows anybody's business, I'll give you a fair price for the inn."

"That's good to know," I said. Job stood with his arms crossed, confident with his offer. He'd intruded a little far, a little closer to the bone than I was comfortable ignoring. So I tried asking a question. "Since we're not making other folks' lives our business, might I ask why you didn't go with the militia to Queenston?" It was a fact that Job was a rare creature, a single male in that village.

He was holding a hammer when I asked him, and he held it in a lethal manner for just a minute. "That's a pretty risky question," he said, in a lower tone. We held each other's gaze for a moment. "I stayed here because I was of more use here. The men who went were looking for a little adventure, I guess. I don't need no adventure. And they were good British subjects. I don't count myself a good British subject. And that's no secret around here, in case you thought you could make trouble."

"A Yankee sympathizer?" I asked, my own voice almost a whisper.

Wilson looked past me, into the street, to be sure we were alone. "No. I was raised near Black Rock. My father's family is from there. My mother's family is from Newark. We lived in Black Rock. But then my father went and died fighting for the American Revolution. My mother was still a British subject, so when he died we came back here." He threw a bent nail into the back of his shed a little harder than necessary." I don't think either side is worth getting killed for." He fished out another nail. "Four shoes is a dollar. Payable in advance."

I reached into my pouch and counted out the dollar for the four shoes. Job's arms still crossed, I set the coins on the broad ledge of his coal furnace.

"You think on my offer," he suggested, his face suggesting I think on it privately, "I'll have the horse done by noon. I'll need to work on the rest of the shoes, I don't have any more that size." I thanked him and walked back through the mud.

Near closing one Sunday evening in late January, a man in a captain's uniform, muddy from the road, stepped into the public room. I fetched him a mug of ale, for which he nodded as to a servant; I didn't like him. "What can I do for you, Captain?"

"I'm here to see Mrs. Gordon Teal." My heart froze. Dead men sometimes come back.

Claire had gone into the kitchen to start supper, but she heard her name and appeared in the doorway. When she appeared and saw the officer she didn't cry out "Gordon!" and swoon in his arms, and I remembered to breathe. She politely greeted the officer, "I am Claire Teal. What can I do for you?"

"Good day, Mrs. Teal," said the captain, and he reached into his tunic and retrieved a scrap of linen. "I am Captain Richard Lightfoot. I serve in the 49th of Foot. Your husband was a captain of militia, posted to my command at Queenston. We were friends." She maintained a placid demeanor, but for the white of her knuckles where she gripped the storeroom counter. "During the attack at Queenston your husband commanded a battery at the river."

A battery at the river? The same battery I'd charged? My face burned; I could still see the landing in the dark. *How could Gordon Teal have been behind the guns?* For the first time I knew who the enemy had been in the wonderfully anonymous dark, and I felt bile agitate in my gut. "That battery held its ground bravely under your husband's leadership," continued Lightfoot. "I wanted to offer you a comfort, aside from the fact that the battery slowed the assault by injuring or removing from action a high number of enemy officers."

That's for sure, I thought. Though Captain Lightfoot had glanced my way a couple of times, suggesting he'd like privacy with the widow, I leaned against the counter and listened openly.

"—he died of a musket ball that killed him instantly. He suffered no pain. On that I can give my word as an officer in his Majesty's Army." The captain laid a scrap of linen on the counter. "He was able to ask that I personally bring this to you." Claire picked up the scrap and opened it to find a gold ring. "His wedding ring, I believe. He said with this, you'd know."

She nodded, and I saw her eyes moisten with tears, and she silently stepped back into the kitchen. A few awkward minutes later she returned, her eyes a little red but otherwise composed. "Would you please join us for tea, Captain?" she asked, her voice softer, as though she'd just wept. It was closing time, and Captain Lightfoot accepted her invitation. I was jealous of the dead man, but reminded myself that even a poor marriage is a marriage, and the end of it carries an impact.

Lightfoot stood by the china cabinet, his eyes studying Claire as closely as he dared. I shut the storeroom door and joined them in the kitchen as she carried in her best imported china service. "Well, Captain," said Claire, pouring his tea, "I imagine you've seen some exciting times in this war."

As Lightfoot sat on the sofa, his eyes roamed from her to me. I, in turn, tried to keep watch on Lightfoot without him knowing. Claire was struggling to make eye contact with both of us, and her halting attempts at starting conversation stalled. When she caught Lightfoot's gaze he smiled at her as one does when courting.

I didn't trust him. His tale about Gordon's death was a lie. If the ball that killed Gordon did so instantly, then how had the mortally wounded innkeeper given instructions on the disposition of his wedding ring? In that wild, pre-dawn darkness the luxury of a last will and testament was impossible. I suspected Gordon Teal was mortally wounded during the initial exchange. He was probably carried by his men out of the line of fire, given a drink of water and left, bleeding and in terrible pain, until Lightfoot or some other regular officer deigned to examine why the militia was making such a ruckus.

Lightfoot admired Claire's collection of figurines, displayed in a corner hutch. "This one looks exquisite," he said, "may I?" He took the opportunity to run his hands over hers when Claire took it out for him. She blushed deeply.

"You served under General Brock, Captain?" I asked loudly, to ruin his moment.

Claire retreated to her seat and Lightfoot reluctantly turned to answer me. "Yes, same as Gordon," he said, speaking to her, using her late husband's first name as though they'd been close friends. "Just a bunch of bloody—excuse me, ma'am—bad luck that they shot Brock. And you?"

Claire said, "my cousin, Nehemiah, also served at Queenston."

Lightfoot looked at me, studied my face. "Mr. Cleary," he asked, "could you tell me where you were posted?"

"Artillerist's assistant. I manned a battery a quarter mile downriver from where the Americans landed."

"And your injuries?" Lightfoot asked intently.

"Cannon barrels sometimes have flaws," I said matter-of-factly; it was close to the truth.

"My sympathies," said Lightfoot, perhaps meaning it. On the other hand an officer in the military saw wounds frequently and his sympathies had probably run dry some time ago.

Claire, watching us lock glares, changed the subject. "It's late, Captain. Can I offer you a room for the night? Business is slow, with the war."

"Thank you," he answered. "I'll accept your offer." She gave him the room furthest down the hall. It hadn't been used in months, and I had to build a fire in the fireplace. Claire set out a quilt and said goodnight. I scooped up some hot coals from the public room and used them to start the fire. "So you were injured at Queenston?"

"Yes," I said, and made myself look busy building the fire. I resented the wood I had to burn on his behalf, but Claire had an innkeeper's sense of hospitality.

"And you are her relation?"

"Cousins." I blew on the coals, which were glowing fine without me. "By marriage."

"She's a very attractive young woman," said the captain. "And with her husband's demise, an attractive young woman of means."

I blew steadily on the coals. "What's your point?"

"If you're too stupid to see it, I'll thank you for the fire and say goodnight."

I got to my feet, having left him with the impression that I was a dullard, and pulled his door shut behind me.

"Get off me," I groaned in a nightmare. A British soldier was on me, pinning me to the ground, raising his musket, and preparing to gut me with his bayonet. The first cut went in and my ribs burned. I got to my feet and managed to run a few steps, then picked up a musket from the ground. I aimed at my attacker and pulled the trigger but squeezing the trigger was like squeezing bread, soft and crumbly. So I smacked it against the nearest tree and the damn thing went off and I woke, sweating, in bed.

And I had a thought, and it turned into a plan, and Lightfoot was a key part of it.

The next morning Claire made breakfast early and said good morning to Captain Lightfoot, then announced, "it's my day to visit the shut-ins. Captain, you are welcome to stay. Nehemiah, I won't be home until suppertime."

She's running away, I knew. At least for the day. And Lightfoot was visibly annoyed and disappointed. I was relieved, also anxious at having the captain on my hands. He sat down at the public table and began eating the porridge Claire had made.

"Can I speak with you?"

"About what?" He looked at me like a creditor pursuing a bad debt.

"I wanted to offer you an opportunity," I said.

Lightfoot glanced at the door, no doubt thinking of Claire. "Well, speak up," he said impatiently. "I do have to look in on my men."

"I've heard that the muskets used by the Americans at Queenston last fall are being stored in an old barn in Lewiston," I said, testing the accuracy of that rumor.

Lightfoot nodded absent-mindedly. "I've heard a similar tale. What of it?" He poured himself more tea.

"I propose stealing those weapons and selling them back to the Americans."

He set down his mug. "Steal their muskets and sell them back?" he repeated. "Are you as stupid as you make out to be?"

"The weapons are useless," I continued hastily, "they are rusty and old and most won't fire anymore. That's why the Americans failed to hold Queenston," I added, painting with a broad brush.

Lightfoot was piecing it together now. "Really?" he asked. I nodded. "That's why the Americans failed to hold Queenston? Cowardice was not a factor?" I needed him so I let it pass. "So why do you think the muskets are being stored?"

"They are evidence in an investigation by New York State."

"Why should I inconvenience the court of New York State?" he asked, saying the words like they were words to a children's song. *New York State. Three blind mice.*

"Purely to sell them back."

He was confused, but wanted to know the truth. "Why would they buy trash a second time? Presumably they'll look a bit closer this time?"

"Oh, they will," I said. "See, I'm not interested in the sale. I have a score to settle with the purchaser."

"Oh," said Lightfoot. I think the element of revenge made it all understandable to him. "And who is this enemy of yours?"

"Judge Augustus Porter. Commissary agent for the army."

"Why would you seek revenge on a Yankee arms trader?" he asked. His mind worked on the notion. "Of course," Lightfoot slapped the table, making his bowl jump. "You." He smiled. "I recognize you, Master Cleary. From the heights." He smiled and nodded. "You were crying to me for help, remember? To save you from the scalping Indian?"

I wasn't expecting that. I didn't remember any British faces from that morning. "That was you?"

"Why," Lightfoot asked, "shouldn't I take you into custody now as a prisoner of war?"

A cold stab of fear, like the one in my last nightmare, cut through me like a saber. My wonderful anonymity, my shield against my past in this little town, had just failed. "Why not take me into custody?" I asked, a little foolishly because I didn't have an answer myself. "Captain," I said with more certainty than I felt, "you'd be found dead from the steel of your saber."

He seemed to like that. "You'll pardon the slight, but I am the larger man, and I am not wounded."

"Shall we attempt the trip? Are you prepared for the praises you'll hear?" I asked, flexing my right hand. Capturing an enemy soldier carried the underlying assumption that the soldier was able-bodied and dangerous. Capturing me would produce more laughs than rewards. *Did you take him by yourself?* his brother officers would ask. *What's the official commendation for arresting a cripple?* Lightfoot thought it over a moment, then changed his mind. "I will take you at your word that you are no longer a combatant," he offered.

"Hardly," I agreed. "What about my plan?"

Lightfoot frowned. "I'll need to consider it. What would be my reward?"

"All the proceeds," I said. "About two hundred pounds. I'm only doing this for the revenge."

"A large risk on your part for simple revenge. And no interest in the gold? I don't understand that. But then, I haven't paid your price." He nodded. "Very interesting. I do have to return to my camp. I'll be in touch shortly."

He returned two days later, in time for tea.

There were two girls, Carolyn Moore and Dottie Sinclair, sitting near the window, reading a newspaper, enjoying a morning's errand to town from the farm and making it last by stopping by to see whom else they might see, and our calculating blacksmith stopped by for a mug of tea he could just as easily brew himself.

"Let me tell you about the Americans. I know Americans. They think they're the new chosen people," Wilson blathered on. He was offering opinions on the news to the ladies, and Carolyn and Dottie were hoping someone more interesting than he might show up. They brightened when Lightfoot appeared, but looked dismayed when he devoted his attention to Claire.

"If the Americans had to attack, I suppose we should be grateful they waited until the harvest was in," Claire tried to joke. Lightfoot was sitting with her at the largest table in the public room, almost as romantic as meeting in the privy, and I was struggling to bury my smile. Lightfoot wasn't especially comfortable, but Claire was.

"Mrs. Teal," he started, hoping for a more private meeting, then changed his tone, "so, what will become of you?" he asked, trying to sound gentle, perhaps charitable.

"Become of me?" Claire asked, smiling as though her choices were too many and luxurious to describe. "Oh, well, I may sell the inn, I may keep it. Perhaps my cousin, Nehemiah, can stay and help me," she teased, enjoying the effect it had on all concerned. "Perhaps I'll go back to York, which is where I'm from."

"If I might be so bold as to suggest, it would be a tragedy for this village if someone as lovely as yourself should have to leave," Lightfoot said, smiling, a toothy smile he seemed to brandish like a weapon made to slay the hearts of women. It started Claire giggling, to Lightfoot's confusion. Job glanced at the sound of giggling, as did the girls.

I burst in, asking Claire, "didn't little Frank Archer bring in a rabbit? I'm going to roast it on the spit."

"It's in the storeroom," Claire directed. I left, and Lightfoot got her attention again, and tried his smile again, and then I came back, knocking as I came in.

"Are we out of pepper?" I asked, drawing a murderous glare from Lightfoot.

"Oh no," Claire said, trying to suppress her smile, "it's in the storeroom. It's with the spices."

"I was just in there," I said.

Sighing, Claire got up, "let me show you."

"Perhaps you could draw him a diagram of the storeroom?" Lightfoot suggested.

Together in the storeroom, behind the door, Claire surprised me with a long, romantic kiss. When she drew back I asked, "how did I earn that?"

"You know," she said, giggling for a moment, then composing herself. "When will he leave?"

"I'm doing my best. What should I ask for the next time?"

"Surprise me," she said.

Lightfoot surprised us by appearing in the doorway of the storeroom. "Mrs. Teal," he said, "thank you for your company today. I actually need to speak to Mr. Cleary, if that would be possible?"

She'd been hoping for at least one more interruption. "Oh, all right," she said, disappointed. She bowed politely and went back to the kitchen.

When she was gone, Lightfoot turned to me. "So you really want revenge on that trader?"

I nodded.

"In your convalescence are you finding Canadian hospitality to your liking?" he asked, "or are you, in fact, just cousins?"

"I find it quite to my liking," I said, "and in what port does your wife wait with child, Captain?"

"Mr. . . . is it really Cleary?" asked Lightfoot.

"It is."

"As it happens I'm engaged to an exceptionally beautiful woman. We may settle here when I'm wed. But about your little plot, I confess I'm intrigued. I want more details of your plan, and the reward I can expect."

"Well, it requires two or three of your men to go to Lewiston and bring back some of those muskets, and your help in contacting Augustus Porter of Manchester."

"How are my men to cross the river?"

"It's choked with ice in the late winter," I explained, feeling my throat tighten with excitement, "and can be crossed on foot. Your men can cross anytime until late March, take the weapons, and hide them in a gully called Foster's Flats."

Lightfoot nodded. "And how do I contact your Judge Porter?"

"Send a letter across via one of the many spies your army employs. Call yourself an arms merchant. He's in no position to question it. Claim to be a secret patriot. The price is what he'll be looking for."

"And what price do you place on these muskets?"

"Sell them for," I paused to calculate, "forty pounds per."

Lightfoot set his cup down. "They don't fetch that price in this country."

"Precisely," I said, "everyone is gouging the Congress. If the price is exorbitant, he'll be convinced it's a real offer."

He nodded slowly as he reviewed the plan and finally smiled. "I'll write Judge Porter and keep you informed."

MARCH, 1813—NIAGARA FALLS, NEW YORK
Augustus Porter was up at dawn, a peacetime habit of his, back when his business demanded every waking hour. Besides managing the Portage he owned a healthy share of it. He also owned a rope making shop and a carding machine, part of the contract with the state to maintain a private merchant marine on the Inland Sea. Since the war, however, it was all idled under continuous threats of invasion, and when Augustus rose at dawn those days he was often idle. With only his job as commissary agent, and the idleness winter imposed on the war, he had time to plan his next big step.

The islands at the crest of the falls were his latest goal, the only tract of land on the river he had been denied. They divided the cataracts, Goat Island the centerpiece, and around it a cluster of smaller islands. Water power turned the wheels of human progress, and water power on Niagara's scale was an empire waiting to be built. The man who could get Goat Island had an empire for the building, and Porter was determined to be that man. His vision covered the Upper River with every known application of waterpower.

He would venture down the pathway to the river on mornings when the wind wasn't too bitter, the ice crust on the snow at once beautiful, blinding, and treacherous, and study the foaming rapids and the ever-present mist of the falls. He was there that March morning when the messenger arrived from Schlosser with a letter for him.

The Honorable Augustus Porter
Fort Schlosser, New York

Sir.

I am in receipt of your response to my offer and am pleased to supply you with the details you requested. The regulation

British army muskets you inquired about are in my possession. I propose a sale as soon as you can assure me your satisfaction with these terms. Price per musket shall be forty pounds. I can supply as many as you like, requesting only that you reply with an order prior to the transaction, as the actual procurement requires advance notice. I can only deliver these pieces during the winter months for reasons of my own and humbly request that you keep in mind this time limit.

With warmest Regards,
Richard Lightfoot

"Forty English pounds," Augustus read, pursing his lips. "Forty damn pounds." He didn't feel the cold anymore. Albany was angry with him for his purchases last summer. Purchasing these muskets, the British army's Brown Bess, the best in the world, would placate the senate. Moreover, Augustus' ultimate goal of getting Goat Island from the state would be advanced both by the price—which would put the state heavily into debt with him—and in improved relations for having found such superior pieces. There was really only one reason not to buy the muskets: he didn't have the money.

He wrote promissory notes when possible, paid out cash when necessary. Most of his suppliers had insisted on cash, leaving Porter rich with bills to Congress but painfully short of liquid assets. Congress was very slow financing the war. And the price Merchant Lightfoot wanted was exorbitant. To buy enough to clear his name, Augustus had to request a personal loan, for which the cost would be dear. He hesitated only a moment; visionaries must take chances.

Returning to his office, in the foundation of his house, he found a clean sheet of paper and wrote a short note to a business associate in Canandaigua. Two thousand pounds, or eight thousand American dollars, would buy fifty muskets. He'd order more, but prudence dictated starting conservatively. '*I need eight thousand dollars and have no avenue available other than to request a loan, with my own properties and my contracts with the government to secure the debt. Reimbursement will be forthcoming from Congress but it may take some time. My reasons are both prudent business judgment and to advance our nation's cause. More I cannot tell you.*'

MARCH 21ST, 1813

Claire had taken the musket in exchange from a discharged officer of the Ottawa militia headed home who had traded it for flour and beans. She had no use for the musket and tried to give the man the food, but he had respectfully declined. "No need for charity, ma'am. Not when I've still got a strong back. It was my brother's musket. He died beside me in the battle. It's a good musket. The action is clean," he handed over the musket, "you can tell folks that it killed Van Rensselaer if it'll help."

"Did it?" she asked in a mix of disgust and delight.

"No ma'am," said the weary soldier with a grin, "only fired twice, to tell you the truth, once at a deer, once at a pigeon."

She laughed, then gave him a generous drink of whiskey and waved to him as he left, "Godspeed."

When I discovered it, I dropped a bag of salt. "Look at you," I said, like it was a puppy. I picked the musket up fondly. The barrel showed stains from weather, but nothing a good cleaning wouldn't fix. The stock was quite capable of taking the recoil of a shot. "If only mine had been like this," I said, and put it to my shoulder. "I wouldn't have held back on the ridge, with the others. I would have charged them, firing as often as I could reload." If only I could do it over again.

I drew aim on the whisky barrel, and spun quickly as if detecting attack—and sighted in the quiet Captain Lightfoot. "I didn't hear you knock," I said, embarrassed, resting the stock on the floor.

"I didn't," he responded, then pulled a paper from his tunic. "I thought you'd want to know that Judge Porter has replied, promptly and enthusiastically. Are all you Americans so gullible?"

"What's he say?" I asked. "When do we proceed?"

Lightfoot held out the letter with a flourish and read; "I agree to your terms. Given a favorable performance of this contract I hope we can pursue further transactions, etc.," Lightfoot chuckled smugly, then folded the letter, put it back in his tunic, and glanced around. "Can we speak privately?"

"For a minute," I said, not happy. "Claire's gone visiting shut-ins."

Lightfoot set his gaze on me, like two poker players with lots of money on the table. "I have further conditions to our contract." I said nothing. "It seems to me I'm taking all the risks in return for very little reward."

"I wouldn't say so," I said. "The money is all yours."

"Yes, I know," Lightfoot said impatiently, "and all you want is vengeance. I understand that. Let me make myself clearer. I want different payment."

"Different payment?"

Lightfoot divided his gaze between the musket and me. "I fancy the social life you enjoy with the Widow Teal," he said, "I suspect your intimacy is greater than that ordinarily enjoyed by cousins."

"I don't rule Mrs. Teal's life," I said, knowing how flat my words were. "She chooses her companions as she wishes."

Lightfoot smiled again, a patronizing air to his voice. "Of course she does." He took a deep breath, as though savoring a fine meal. "Still, if you. . ." I took a half-step towards the musket and saw Lightfoot's fingers tighten around the handle of his saber. *Was the musket loaded?* "If you left," he continued, "she would be helpless to stop you. And without your interference I could pursue her without risk of her being distracted."

"She's not a commodity to buy or barter. This contract is limited to muskets and gold." I took a step towards the musket. Lightfoot shifted his feet slightly, to be able to quickly draw his sword.

"Without an assurance that you leave Pelham, indeed, leave Upper Canada, your silly plan is history. I'll march you to the Regimental Commander's quarters and turn you in as a spy with our little plan as proof."

"And your involvement in it?" I was inches away.

"Simply drawing a spy into a trap by pretending to abet him." Lightfoot smiled with the assurance that the prize was his. "I'll accommodate your travel needs. But you must let your revenge carry you out of Mrs. Teal's life."

How much damage could Lightfoot do to me with a saber before I aimed and blew him to Kingdom Come? His upper lip was accustomed to showing contempt, and there was a darkness around his eyes that could be alluring or dangerous, potentially sensual. He might worm his way, temporarily, into Claire's bed. If he did, he would only stay as long as his blood quickened at her form. When she was no longer a novelty, he would leave her. She was a conquest, a step up, perhaps, for an officer who satisfied himself with barmaids and whores. Pray God he bore no diseases.

"Alright," I said, to get rid of him. "I'll leave." To sound more believable I added, "and I expect a very comfortable travel allowance."

Lightfoot nodded, and then left Porter's letter. "I presumed you'd see reason. The final arrangements are underway," he added at the doorway with a victorious air. "I will see you in a few days. My country calls."

Arrangements underway? It was happening faster than I expected. That night was rough. The nightscape of Queenston was familiar, though Queenston in hell was overrun with scalping Indians and British bayonets and not a friendly face anywhere. I was in the midst of gunfire, of bayonets gutting fallen soldiers. I was wounded this time, shot in the side, painful but apparently not serious. A knife sang in the air and I narrowly escaped scalping. Someone was screaming in my ear. My musket was a good one, but I'd left it leaning against a tree, just out of reach when, from out of nowhere, a British grenadier charged. He was enormous. First he fired and put a big hole in my chest. Then he aimed his bayonet at me, squarely in the mouth. I could almost taste the blood smeared on the tip. The morning sun woke me. I closed my eyes against the light. *I have to try one of Claire's teas,* I decided. *Something good for the nerves.*

Sun filled the room. I opened the window a crack, the first warm morning of the year. Claire lay beside me, still asleep. Her long brown hair was curled around her neck and half covered her face. She was twisted up in her flannel robe, outlining her stomach and bust. I put the nightmare behind me, alongside the others, and was admiring the curve of her breast when she awoke. "I'm guarding you," I said.

"Guarding me?" she asked with a sleepy smile, "against what?"

"Evil spirits. Indians. Renegade Americans."

"You've failed," she smiled, touching my chest, tracing a scar, "this one's almost gone. So is the one on your arm." She touched my eyebrow, saw my red eyes. "Did you have another nightmare?"

I nodded. She kissed me. Then she asked, "what are you up to with Captain Lightfoot?"

That woke me up more. "Just a business transaction," I lied. I wanted to kiss her breast with her awake, or at least touch it, but I settled for the safer option of her neck; Claire was unnerved by foreplay. She liked to kiss, and then preferred to just begin.

"What sort of business?" She rose on one elbow, fully awake, looking at me.

I began to toy with a lock of her hair. "He and I are simply taking advantage of an opportunity."

She didn't like secrets. "Are you sure you're in no danger?" she pressed.

"None." She brushed my hands away from the ribbons that tied her neckline, but then let them be. "Why don't we go somewhere to get away from the war?" she asked as I began to pull her nightgown open.

"Where?" I asked, somewhat breathlessly, ribbons entangled in my fingers.

"Anywhere," she sighed, "you risk arrest the minute a British officer walks through the door. I risk," she looked at me sadly, "losing you."

"After we've completed this business transaction, we can leave," I said. I toyed with her ribbon again, trying to pull her gown open. She was feeling patronized, though, and angrily pushed my hands away. "Claire," I whined, laying back on the pillow in defeat, "why do we make love when you want to but not when I want to?"

"Would you prefer not at all?" she snapped. Seeing my frown, she changed her tone. "We can," she said, "but on a condition."

I waited expectantly.

"I know you are planning something dangerous with Lightfoot," she said, "when you leave to finish your business, not before but when you are leaving, tell me everything. Everything," she emphasized, "and you must promise to return, and we will leave this town together." I nodded.

I kissed her and climbed onto her. She guided me into her. We pulled tightly together, and pleasure left us breathless as we kissed and touched and moved together. After the second climax, as we lay beside each other and rested, I whispered, "isn't there a second way to couple? Our passion has smoothed the passage. I took twice as long as necessary this last time."

Her eyes were closed in rest when she answered, politely but a bit aloof. "We are good Christian folk. Only savages, the Indians, or the Africans, copulate like monkeys or dogs. Civilized people are given a dignified posture to use. I'm not going to risk injuring myself behaving like a savage."

I lay quietly for a while, embarrassed. "I'm sorry," I whispered, "I've only been with you, never anyone else. I've never been... told. Can we... as civilized people?" And we finished, with greater exertion but no complaints.

MARCH 30, 1813

The final arrangements between Porter and Lightfoot were made and on the evening of March 30th the next stage was put into motion.

Chunks of ice from Lake Erie pass over the falls and pile up in the Lower River. The ice chunks freeze together into a solid span. Four of Lightfoot's men crossed, stole fifty muskets from the unguarded barn, dragged them back to Canada and hid them. Working hard through the night, they finished just as the sky was lighting in the east. Cutting pine boughs to make a crude camouflage, they covered their plunder and climbed back up the Canadian side of the gorge to ride back to Pelham.

5:40 A.M.

If my dreams were an omen, I was being warned not to go. I awakened several times in the dark, each time panicked and short of breath. Every time I fell back asleep, I returned to the Ice Bridge. I struggled across chunks of ice in the gorge, ice as tall as the tallest pines. The ice would open without warning beneath my feet, exposing the rushing river beneath which sucking me into the dark, suffocating torrent. Next, I would slip and slide, unable to get a handhold or dig my bare feet into the icy crevices, and somehow the ice would slide me upriver, and I would still be scratching in the ice for a grip when I slid into the falls. Finally, I would cross the ice and face Judge Porter and the Judge would shoot me, point blank, in the face.

When exhaustion began overwhelming fear, I slept longer and stayed longer in the land of nightmares. The Judge chased me across the ice, and before that dream played itself out I found a deeper sleep. But I woke before dawn, groggy and exhausted.

And then, just like the morning of Queenston, it was dark and it was time. Sleeping, she turned towards me when I rose from the bed. I wanted to kiss her; I wanted to make love to her, but I let her sleep. I had made a promise to her I couldn't keep.

Even placing my feet at the edge of the top step made the step groan, so I took them two at a time. While saddling the horse in the stable I heard the iron hinges on the door creak and there she was, hair still wild from the bed, the quilt pulled tight around her. She hadn't slept well either. "You are off to finish your business," she accused.

I saddled the horse. "Yep."

"You promised to tell me," she said, angry and hurt.

"I know." Reaching beneath the belly I caught the strap for the girth.

"Why did you lie to me?" She was crying.

"I didn't know I would until now," I answered. "I didn't think I could do it." Pulling up tightly, I held the belt with my left and buckled with my right. "I'll come back when this is done and we will leave."

She watched me. "You know," she said, picking her path through clods of dirt to me, "he offered to take me to Montreal."

I glanced at her. "I'd have thought he'd offer Ottawa. I hear he has a fiancée in Montreal."

"Perhaps he was women in both cities," she said angrily, "I made my own inquiries about him. He's not widely trusted among his brother officers. He's not good to his men. He's a drunk, and a gambler and he doesn't pay his debts in a timely manner, and he tries to be a womanizer. Very few women trust him in their beds." She pulled the quilt tighter around her. "And I don't want you going off with him."

"For all the reasons you have recited, he is the only one I can work with."

"I don't understand."

I shielded my eyes as the sun rose; I'd hoped to be out of Pelham by sunrise. It seemed only the truth would do. "I intend to draw Judge Porter into a sale of muskets. I need the help of a corrupt man who can command labor. There are probably other corrupt officers in the British army," I said, "but Lightfoot's the first to happen along."

Sunlight gradually turned the landscape from twilight gray to browns. Pelham was quiet. It was a prosperous town, only in its men had the town paid a price for the war. In another season's campaigning the town would burn, but for now it was still quiet, still peaceful, a cut glass awaiting the rampage of the bull.

I swung the horse around and paused before riding off to turn and look at her. "I'll be back," I promised, "not tonight. Probably tomorrow night, and definitely by the night after."

"Or not at all."

Why did she have to say that? I looked at her again, but I didn't want to die with my last memory of her face being one streaked with tears, so I dug my heels into the horse and trotted off, flinging up bits of mud.

7:03 A.M.

"Be careful, my love. Be careful with the profiteers when they plot, for men who shed others' blood for money care nothing for life. Be careful with them. Do what you must do, and earn a measure of peace.

And come back to me."

11:02 A.M.

He studied the letter again. He'd read it obsessively since getting it a week ago.

> *The Honorable Augustus Porter*
>
> *Sir.*
>
> *The purchase will be completed in the following manner. The muskets will be delivered to a point in the middle of the ice in the Lower Niagara River, near Foster's Flats, one hour past sunset on March 30th. Signal your presence on the ice with a lantern, covering it thrice and then letting it shine. You may bring two assistants to help in handling the muskets but all must be unarmed. These are unfortunate precautions in wartime. We shall come out when you signal.*
>
> *Richard Lightfoot*

Last night two men arrived on horseback with the money from Canandaigua and a collection of sidearms that made Augustus' expert eye light up. He locked the money in his office safe and sent the two to a quiet room in the other part of his basement with a bottle of rum apiece; he intended to use them for the final transaction. Being strangers they were perfect to use and then send back to Canandaigua.

7:00 A.M.

On the road from Pelham I passed a wagon and at the reins was a boy who looked like — Joshua! He was bleeding, no, flowing with blood. The war cries, the shrieking terrible cries of the Hurons, filled the woods. On the front line, hunched down in the wet leaves and mud, peering over the rotten logs we dragged into place for cover. Our bladders and bowels lost control when we saw brown faces smeared with paint, muscled arms wielding steel axes compliments of the British, axes decorate with animal fur, and bits of human before the day was done. They leapt over logs, roots, moving through the woods as though they could pass right through the trees.

Get up. Get up now. Aim your musket, you damn coward. Fire at the heathen son of a bitch. Fire. Take AIM! Sight down the musket barrel as though the Apocalypse itself is coming at you, an ax raised by a powerful brown arm aiming to split your head. But your eyes can't blink, your finger can't pull the trigger, you can't even pee anymore. A shot on the left, another, then Lynde turning and running. He got grabbed by a Huron. The Indian threw him to the ground like an empty shirt. He's screaming as that heathen sinks his ax into his chest, then raises that ax to strike again and cleave his skull in two, then pulls his knife and in one terribly swift, smooth movement takes a lock of scalp. Fire at him. Fire at both of 'em—kill the Indian and put the guy out of his misery! Fire!

Off to the left. Joshua is standing. He's aiming, and a moment later there's smoke puffing from the barrel of his musket. Good for you, Joshua. You got off a shot. Duck down, Joshua. Reload!

Look to your own danger, Cleary. In front of you! Twenty yards off— a ten foot tall painted devil swinging a bloody ax, coming to rip your head off! They can run right through the trees! They can run through rock! They're in front, they're beside you, they're behind you! Run! Run, you idiot! RUN!

Standing, turning, running. I see Joshua again. He's falling down, crumbling to the earth, and he's been shot. His musket looks busted up. A half step towards him, looking over the arm he threw up against death—

The Pelham Road took a turn by a flowing brook and I stopped to splash ice-cold water on my face to chase the ghosts away.

7:03 A.M.

A warm breeze of all things. Where in heaven's name did a warm breeze come from? Where could it have warmed itself today? It's March, after all. The lakes? Frozen over. The sun? Bright but not warm. There was no source of warmth for the wind. But that wind, that little pocket of breeze right there, in the middle of that road and the middle of nowhere, it was warm and gentle. A warm breeze like that could only come from God. The fields were brown stubble, with shallow pools of snowmelt, and the road was hard mud. The breeze continued to warm me for several moments, like a warm hug, then I touched the horse's sides and rode a few feet on and the air was cold again.

Lucas. The echo of the volley outside the log wall of Fort Erie.

"Jesus Christ," cursed Lucas. He was shaking a little in weakness, watching his stool emerge in a flow as he squatted with me and the young boy, Courtney, from some farm down near Black Rock. "I think I'm bleeding down there," he said. We were twenty minutes past breakfast, which had been coffee and pork and barley stew from yesterday's supper. "Can't hold drill for another thirty minutes, Lieutenant," went the joke, "the boys have gotten it down and as soon as they do it runs out." The trench flowed with an obscene current of diarrhea. After crouching over it for a while one could look elsewhere and almost forget the stench. "Watch what you're doing. Don't get that on me."

A week before Queenston, Courtney collapsed during drill. Lucas pulled him to his feet but the frail boy crumbled again. With the lieutenant's permission, Lucas carried Courtney over his shoulder a quarter mile back to the doctor's tent. "What's his trouble," asked the doctor, a stout alcoholic with a pale complexion. He stooped and took Courtney's thin limp wrist in his own chubby hand, pushed up one of Courtney's eyelids, and surveyed him like a week old lump of salt pork. "Camp fever," he diagnosed, and Lucas grunted under the boy's dead weight and set him on the nearest cot. "Good God no! That's my bed. I don't want to catch the fever, you idiot. Take him," the doctor paused, stepped out of the tent to survey the line of tents stretching down the field, "take him to the fifth tent down this side." Lucas nodded, shouldered Courtney, and carried him down the row of tents. Each of the first three was filled with the sick, up until the fourth. Inside the fourth were no groans, only a stench, and the bodies weren't moving. The fifth tent was the same.

"Doc?" The doctor stepped out of his tent. "These men in here are all dead!"

"So's your friend. Throw him in. Burial detail's falling behind but they'll get to him." The doctor disappeared back into his tent. The sun's warmth suddenly burned through Lucas' shirt, or maybe it was the sight of the death tent, for he was sweating hard when he gently laid Courtney's slim, still body on some fresh grass next to the tent. It seemed improper to lay the still-warm boy amongst the dead. For just a moment he held his ear to the boy's mouth, yearning for the sound of a breath. Then he looked at Courtney's eyes, but they were rolled up white.

"Sorry, lad." He left Courtney on the ground, stood, said a simple prayer. Then he backed away from the death tent and Courtney's body and trudged back to drill.

3:00 P.M.

I got hungry and pulled a chunk of Claire's bread and a wedge of cheese from my coat pocket, one of Gordon's. The memories were almost overwhelming and the taste of her bread and cheese helped erase them. Comfortably warm with the heat of the horse through the saddle, I bit off a mouth full and wondered, *how many could I name from camp?* There was Courtney, and Joshua. And Lucas, of course. We shared a tent. Then there was Lieutenant Sims, who ran into the woods as far as he could to find unsoiled ground to soil. Stump McCartney who told crude jokes that just weren't funny. Lieutenant Sims was probably shot somewhere during the morning at Queenston because during the day Colonel Scott had had to promote a man from Pennsylvania named Daniels to take Sims' place, and Sims was so wildly patriotic he'd have had to be dead if he weren't on the heights.

Beyond them, the others were not strangers but not friends. You shared a tent, you shared a cooking pot, but because every army inducts liars and thieves you didn't share friendship with just anyone because they were in camp with you. If you had reason, one day on the drilling field, you might share a drink of water and make a friend, but strangers were to be watched first, befriended slowly.

I couldn't name many others, just parts of others. Lynde, Wilson, Jack with the French last name no one could pronounce. Tom Panche, who played the fife, believed passionately in the war right up to the last, and was shot through the throat crying for a charge when we were struggling on the beach that awful morning.

I saw no one on the road, no one in the fields, no trails of smoke rising into the sky, no sign of human life. And for just a moment I thought, everyone else is dead. I've been left alone. I tried, but I couldn't recall a face that had survived Queenston. Had I been living among ghosts since? Did I survive Queenston or has all of this just been the start of my afterlife? All along the road, for as far as I could see in any direction, it was just the ghosts and myself. Lucas was still with me when the others finally faded; I wasn't scared then, just deeply sad and tired. "I'm on my way," I said to the sky and the fields. "I'm doing it, Lucas. You didn't think I'd do it, did you?"

No lad, I didn't think you would. You had reason, God knows, even before your face got blew up, but I didn't think you had it in you. Knew you didn't really have it in you to soldier.

"I didn't, did I?" I confessed, "never even shot at anyone."

Going to tonight?

"I might. But I've got another idea. You remember that day in the gorge?"

How could I forget?

"Do you remember what you said about Porter?"

Do you plan to shoot Porter? Lucas' voice sounded excited—who says the dead feel nothing?

"Do you want me to?" I teased the sky and the fields.

Not just so. Don't kill him outright. Shoot him, but in the guts. That won't kill him fast but it'll hurt like hell. Then, as he's bleeding away, tell him we've not received our shipment of bandages and we've never gotten the medicines we needed either. He's going to have to heal himself as best he can. And when he's weak and wants nourishment, fetch him a bowl of camp stew and watch it run through him. Make it rain and put him in a leaky tent. Make it cold at night so he shivers so his teeth rattle, then give him one thin blanket, tell him he's lucky to get that. And then watch him waste away and die.

"A good plan, Lucas, but that could take days. Maybe weeks. I've only got tonight."

You'll think of something, lad.

I had.

Lightfoot's camp was on the north bank of the Chippewa at its juncture with the Niagara, near to where I'd landed the night I crossed the river. The creek was flowing smooth, chunks of ice drifting; cooking fires had been stirred up and the stew boiled. A sergeant greeted me at the camp's periphery, a line of willow trees. "State your name and business," the ruddy-faced Sergeant ordered. He was strongly built, balding on top and old in his eyes.

"Nehemiah Cleary. Captain Lightfoot is expecting me."

The Sergeant knew enough about it to admit me, have my horse tended to, and to offer a meal from the nearest pot. Suddenly hungry, and nostalgic now at the smell of pork boiling with vegetables—very good ingredients this time— I took a wooden bowl of stew and found a dry seat on some canvas.

"So, Mr. Cleary," said the Sergeant, having set down for a bite himself, "what about tonight's business? I've seen the muskets. Helped fetch them. But I don't understand it. Seeing as you aren't an officer," he said softly, with a conspiratorial wink, "maybe you could give us some idea of what to expect?"

"We're going to sell those rusting pieces you helped steal, Sergeant."

"We stole the pieces to sell them back?" his well-campaigned face wrinkled with confusion. "Is his Majesty short of money again?" he quipped.

I choked on my food laughing. "No, his Majesty won't be needing the money. Won't get any, either."

"Well," continued the Sergeant, rummaging in his kit now and finding a pipe, "why did we bother stealing worthless muskets?"

I liked him; there was something of Lucas in him; another touch of my father. The Sergeant lit his pipe and sucked on the stem, plumes of smoke curling from the bowl. At the nearest fire some soldiers muttered loudly about "smelling an old woman round somewhere," and the Sergeant tossed the burning twig he'd used at them. "I can't explain my own interests," I said, "but it will cost the Crown nothing, and gain you a few pounds." I added, "I'll pay you and any who help a bonus for your help tonight."

"Fair enough. Will there be any Americans?"

"Should only be a couple, but you won't need to shoot at them."

The Sergeant nodded, sucked on his pipe. "That's what I'm normally paid to do," he said smiling, "but we've spent a lot of time in this war not shooting at them."

I changed the topic. "Where are you from, Sergeant?"

"Near Fort Erie. I farm there, on a Crown grant of my father's. I lived in Pennsylvania when I was a lad."

"What brought you here?" I asked, knowing what brought most of them.

"Damned rebels," said the Sergeant, rattling off the curse as a single word. His face tensed at the memories and he stared at his scuffed boots. "You're probably too young to know. Where're your folks from?"

"Pelham."

A nod. "They'd know." Another puff, the gray curl of smoke rose, twisting and turning until it disappeared in the darkness above the branches of the overhanging tree. "We came up from near Lancaster. Bucks County. I was eight. We had over two hundred acres, and cattle and horses. The Lord was good to us." He paused to re-light his pipe with another burning twig, then continued; "when the war came the old man insisted the rebels leave us be. They came by for supplies a number of times but my old man said 'not one hen'. Then a bunch of them came, at least twenty, armed and smeared with coal black to pretend they were disguised, and they banged on the door just after dark. George Davies! You Tory bastard! Come open this door or we'll smash it to kindling!" Another deep puff. "Hated they way they cursed like that. So the old man, he'd got his old squirrel gun by the door, he hefts it, pulls open the door and he points it at the lead rebel, his name was Nate Williams. Ugly bugger, used to run a tavern, nasty place, fighting all the time. And my father yells at Nate, 'what business have you got with me under cover of the night, painted black as a Negro, Nate Williams?'"

The Sergeant grinned broadly at the memory. "The old man had fight in him. Nate Williams turned pale." He chuckled. "Yea, Williams starts ducking around the end of the barrel and my old man just follows him with it," the Sergeant mimicked the ducking left and right, "and Williams starts sputtering about the Continental army needing supplies and it being determined by the local Committee that we had more than what we needed, " the Sergeant wasn't smiling anymore, "we should supply the Army of George Washington with fifty head of cattle and so many sacks of corn, and such other nonsense, he had a list he was reading from." The Sergeant tapped his pipe on a rock, knocked the ashes out, tucked the pipe back into his kit, and pulled out a small flask. "Chase the chill away." I took a swallow, the Sergeant drank an inch, and continued.

"Well, they took the cattle that night. Took every head, no matter how many Washington wanted and didn't want. Had a good seventy head. They took them all, and the same with everything else. They tore through the house and took everything that wasn't tied down. Just common thieves. Cleaned us out. We came up here the next spring with nothing. Started over."

Lightfoot's voice called out when the sentry called him. "Mister Cleary?" His speech was slurred, and his voice was too loud. He rode up to the fire. "Oh good, you're here. Are we all ready, Sergeant Davies?" His face was flushed. "We have an appointment to keep." He pulled a flask from his coat and took a drink.

We mounted up and rode in silence, at a gentle pace in the dark. We passed the falls, the roar greeting us in advance, and slowly fading behind us. The ride was quiet and chilly, each of us keeping our thoughts to ourselves and Lightfoot quietly sobering up with each puff of frosting breath. Finally we were along the Lower Niagara above Foster's Flats. "Sergeant Davies, lead us down the pathway you used last time."

"Yessir."

"There's a pathway down?" I asked. The Sergeant nodded. *That would have been handy to know*, I thought.

Across the river, Augustus Porter set out on the ice.

"Mister Porter?" called out one of the guards, "this is damn soft ice. I don't like this."

"The river gives a warning before the ice breaks," Porter answered, "we'll know in plenty of time if it goes."

The ice's frozen peaks and jagged plateaus had smoothed off in the past few days of warm sunshine. The bergs were slushy and the melt was like a lake they crossed, jumping from islands of slush. They slipped and slid into the ice water, and their fear grew as they put the shoreline further behind them. "This is craziness. If it breaks we're dead men. This wasn't part of the deal." The bigger one stopped, looking back at the land, and dared the smaller one to go back. "You scared?" he taunted him. Reaching for a handful of slush, the smaller one threw it at the other. "Feel like solid ice to you? I'm not taking another step."

Porter came back for them. "Do you realize how thick this ice is?" he argued with them, "it's measured in yards. It'll take another week or two of sunshine to melt this." He convinced them, and himself, and they were sodden and cold when they'd crossed it. When they climbed the next slope they found they were in the middle of the river.

"By God, that bastard better be right about this ice," the first complained to the other.

"If he's wrong, you'll be able to tell God about it soon enough," his friend answered.

They could see the Canadian side. Sweat was streaming off them, they coughed up phlegm, even as their feet froze. "Now," huffed Porter when his breath returned, "I must make a confession to you gentlemen." They looked at him warily. "You must have wondered why I ordered all your weapons left at my house. We're going to be buying some muskets with this money. You've been brought along to help me take them back." He felt in his pocket for the derringer he'd been careful to keep dry, and watched the men stare dumbly.

"Muskets?" asked the first, "are you mad?" He pointed back across the soggy obstacle course they'd just passed through. "We damn near drowned getting ourselves out here and you plan to drag muskets back?"

"You'll be well paid," the Judge answered, ignoring their looks. Pulling a lantern from the sack he'd carried with him, he lit the wick and set the lantern on the ice. Using the sack he shrouded the lantern, then let it shine towards Canada, repeating the signal twice more. They watched him and when he left it shining they looked across the ice to the opposite side, looked up at the inky void of the night above them, pulled their coats tighter and stamped their wet feet to keep circulation going.

"I'm freezing," mumbled the bigger one.

The Sergeant led them straight to the muskets and they pulled the pine boughs off them. They loaded some canvas sacks. "I got about fifteen in mine, Thomas?"

"I got ten. It's a smaller sack."

"And ten in that one," said the Sergeant. "I can carry ten myself. There's five left. Who'll be taking that, Captain?"

"I can handle it, Sergeant," I said. I was glad now that my right arm still didn't feel much; I pulled my right arm from the sleeve and tied the sack to it. A flicker of light on the ice caught his eye. "Look!" he pointed. From mid-river flashed Porter's signal. "They're out there. Let's go."

"There they are," Porter said softly as five dark figures stepped out onto the ice. "Almost on time."

The first puddle was much deeper than I expected; how thick was the ice? I sank in knee-deep. *I waited too long*, I realized. I let the others get ahead and asked myself, *how badly did I want this? Why not climb back up the walls of the gorge, and just ride back for Claire?* The idea felt good, but it left me feeling like a scared creature, one who would ever after run from the light. I looked out and knew Porter was near. I looked at the load of muskets I carried, looked up into the dark night, and my anger swallowed me whole. "Go on," I directed the Sergeant, who was watching me with concern, "I'll be along."

My legs were trembling, my face was tingling, my feet were freezing. My breath shrouded my head in a gauzy halo. I searched my load of muskets and found the best one, its stock cracked but a good trigger; I pulled back the hammer; it would fire. Calming myself enough to pour powder from a horn, I loaded it. Taking a leather sling from another musket, I hung it over my back. Then I shoved the rest into a puddle and kept going.

The others were now almost at the meeting place. I circled around, slipping in slush and soaking myself for the third time. The others met on the plateau in the middle, not a hundred yards away. Just outside their circle of light I paused to double-check the musket's charge, adding a pinch of dry powder just in case. I climbed up to the ice sheet they stood on and held my musket waist-high and aimed at them as I stepped into the light. They faced Canada as I came up behind them from the American side, and I heard Lightfoot complain, "he is a cripple, perhaps I should have taken his load."

"Gentlemen," I surprised them all, "I'm pleased that everyone else has obeyed the order to come without loaded weapons. I'm sorry to be the one to break it." Nodding to the Sergeant, "Sergeant, please leave your muskets and yours," I indicated the other soldiers, "and wait for us on shore." The Sergeant glanced at Lightfoot, who was clearly confused, but nodded to his men. They started back.

Turning to Porter. "Augustus," I had never addressed my former employer in familiar terms, "remember me?"

Porter knew me in an instant, but pretended otherwise. "You?"

"I was in your employ on the Portage," I hinted.

He dropped the pretense. "Nehemiah Cleary." He noted the eye patch.

"I'd heard you were wounded."

"You'd heard correctly. Before we go further," I said, "I want to be certain you've come unarmed. Captain, search them." Lightfoot hesitated, so I aimed at him. "Search them."

"I will not."

I drew a bead on his crotch. Lightfoot was furious, either because he was being ordered about or because of my chosen target. He brusquely searched Porter's helpers, then stopped in front of Porter. "As a gentleman, I will spare you the indignity of a search if you can swear that you are unarmed."

"I am," Porter answered.

Lightfoot turned to me and said, "they are unarmed."

"Search him," I said. Lightfoot didn't move, even after I pointed the musket at his face. "Fine," I said, irritated. I stepped behind the Judge, rested the barrel on his head, and patted him. "Open the pouch."

Porter reluctantly opened his pouch. I reached in and felt the derringer. "Gentlemen's honor? Looky here, Captain." I let the musket barrel hang, using the derringer now for control. "And now," I said, trying to disguise my trembling hands, "Judge, send your men back."

"Won't I need them to retrieve the muskets?"

"Send them back. You won't be inconvenienced." The Canandaigua men didn't need to be told twice and could be heard slipping and splashing and cursing their way back to the United States. "And now it's just us." With just the two I felt calmer; my hands stopped trembling. "Captain Lightfoot, I have another confession to make. I came out here to deal with Porter." Augustus looked at Lightfoot, then at me, confused, scared. "In the process I had to deal with you." Extending my good arm, aiming quickly, the pistol trembling, I closed my eyes and fired. Lightfoot took it in the head and the impact threw him back, spilling his body almost out of the circle of light.

I looked at my work, and my stomach churned up, and like that morning on the river waiting to assault Queenston, I vomited.

Porter, wide-eyed, tried to run. He slipped and fell, and I managed to fire a warning shot from the derringer's second load well over his head. "Don't. Don't run, Mr. Porter." I knelt, scooped a handful of slush from the ice at my feet, and put it in my mouth. My teeth tingled but the melt cleared the taste of vomit from my mouth.

Porter stood, turned, and faced me. "What's your business tonight, besides murder?"

I glanced at Lightfoot's body. "That's the first person I've actually shot in this war." The awful power that washes over you when you've taken a life almost froze me in my thoughts. Perhaps that's how we're supposed to respond, to keep us from killing again. With a powerful effort, aided by thoughts of Claire, I concentrated on Porter.

I'd rehearsed a speech, but it was all jumbled in my mind now. "Augustus," and it's silly but even under those circumstances I wasn't comfortable addressing a senior by his first name, "I think you're confused about which side you're on. That's the problem here." I lost my place then. "War isn't just deliveries and profits." I couldn't remember any of the phrases I'd been so pleased with on the ride from Pelham. Instead, when I was face to face with Porter I pulled off my eye patch and showed him my eye. "Look at me." Porter flinched. "Looks scary, doesn't it? It's terrifying the first day the bandages come off. It might get better with time, but I'm not counting on it." I felt myself starting to cry, which I didn't want to do. "And I don't know why, but there's actually someone beautiful in this world who doesn't turn away when I enter a room, or I'd have killed myself by now."

Spitting on the ice at his feet, I asked, "did you ever think this could happen when you and your brother planned this damn war?"

Porter, still a half-head taller, tried to extend a hand in friendship. "I'm sorry, Nehemiah, but I'm not to blame for the war. Or your unhappy fortune. They started this war," he pointed at Lightfoot's dead body.

"I've heard all that," I said, shrugging off his arm, "I know how people around here feel. Half of us were as loyal to King George as to King Washington. So I don't know why we're still fighting, except that people are getting rich." I knelt down on the ice. "Do you know how I got wounded?" Porter shook his head. "It's a good story, one you should hear. The musket you purchased for the militia that was issued to me," my anger was welling up into more tears and I struggled to keep my voice clear, "it exploded in my face the first time I fired it." Porter closed his eyes, shaking his head in denial. "All those muskets, you must tell me where you found them. Did you dig them up from somewhere?" I glanced downriver towards Lewiston. "Y'know we cleaned them and cleaned them just to get them to fire. Some had rusty barrels, some were muddy, like they'd been buried. The triggers? Hah. You pull back on the hammer, and half of them would freeze. So we greased them, rubbed them with fat, worked them, tried to repair them." I looked into Porter's eyes then, and they were filled with fear, so I knew I was reaching him.

"And once we got them to fire, the barrels began to crack. We were sent into battle with muskets that might fire once, and the Devil only knew who'd get hurt worse, the shooter or the target. And I won't bother with my memories of the medicines you didn't send. I guess I have to let God have ultimate vengeance." He perked up a bit, just a bit. I stood. "But those muskets? You will pay me back tonight for that."

I took a deep breath, and watched it frost in the night air. I felt stronger. "Open that sack," I said. "Pull out a musket. Any musket. Here's powder and shot." I handed him my pouches. "Load it." I stepped behind him and, as he fished in the sack for a good, clean musket, ordered him, "test-fire it, as you should have test fired such a dubious musket in the first place."

Porter's hands were trembling as he pulled a musket out. The wooden stock was broken, half of it missing. The trigger wouldn't move. He shoved it back in, pulled out another equally bad. "Where did you get these atrocious pieces?"

"Stolen from a warehouse in Lewiston, abandoned on the riverbank after the attack on Queenston. Property of the New York Militia. Supplied by Augustus Porter, Quartermaster. Tell me, how did you buy these?"

"I bought most of them by mail," he said, distracted as he looked at the muskets, "offers from merchant, reasonably priced for muskets that were desperately needed. Most I had shipped directly to the Portage for delivery to the camp. Oh God." He looked at me. "You've gone to some pains to arrange this, haven't you?"

"Select one, load it, and fire it." Porter pulled another one out, checked the hammer, and set it aside. He pulled another. It had a cracked barrel and he dropped it. "Select one, load it, and fire it," I repeated.

"I'm trying," he said. He emptied the first sack and left twelve muskets in the ice. He reached into a second sack and continued.

"The others are pretty much the same," I said. I felt my anger lessen. With each musket he pulled out, looked at, held up to the light of the moon to examine, then tossed aside, I felt redemption. I felt vindication, the end of my own suspicion that perhaps I'd exaggerated the condition of the muskets. That my memories weren't trustworthy. That I exaggerated their condition to hide my shame, that perhaps it was pure cowardice that day that made Lucas and me and others duck and run. Ghosts were walking the river that night, and for the first time in months they were heading away from me, perhaps towards him.

He all but stuck his head in the sack, digging around inside. He finally retrieved one. "Let's see it," I said, and he held it out. I worked the trigger; it was stiff but functional. The barrel had tiny cracks around the breech. The wooden stock was solid. "Ah," I said, pretending to admire its fine lines, "this one would have been the envy of its entire company. This one we would have given to the best shot. Good choice. Please load and fire it."

He wiped sweat from his forehead and he was panting, his breath frosting and shrouding his head. His shoulders sagged and he seemed smaller. Taking his powder horn in trembling hands, he poured some onto the ice before getting it into the barrel. It was a very light charge. The ramrod was bent. He struggled with it, sweat trailing down his face, then put in the ball, again with the bent rod, and then it was ready to fire.

I backed away. "Fire your musket," I ordered, and waited. Porter was giving the musket one last examination. He pulled back the hammer, then held the musket with an outstretched arm, trying his best to keep the action away from his face, and pulled the trigger; it was less a blast than a firecracker's snap. I instinctively dropped to my knees to avoid the shrapnel.

When the powder smoke cleared, the Judge was bleeding from his hand and from a cut in his neck, but neither seemed mortal. "Damn it to hell," he said, gritting his teeth in pain and pulling a kerchief from his pocket to wrap around his bleeding right hand. Perhaps he didn't know he was bleeding far worse from his neck.

Crack. It was faint, but clear. It came from the south, from the direction of the falls, and had come down the gorge, and it was followed by a crack from a nearer point. "The ice," hissed Porter, and he looked expectantly at me. "The ice," he repeated, "it's breaking up, Nehemiah. If we don't get off we'll both be dead. You weren't counting on that, were you?" I listened for more evidence of the breakup. "You've had your revenge. Let me go."

I heard another loud crack and knew Porter was right: time to flee. "I can't come back, I'm a wanted man," I told Porter, "unless you tell the

Senate the truth. Meanwhile, do the right thing in the eyes of God. Take care of my mother and sister. Tell them I'm alive." Then I turned and dove over the edge of the ice, down a melting slope, out of the lamplight and into the inky blackness.

The ice beneath crackled loudly, and shifted beneath me. The new few minutes were a dance, leaping after moving targets as cracks broke the ice apart, larger chunks riding up and forcing smaller ones beneath the surface. The roar of the river, released from its prison, drowned the cracking, and filled the gorge with the unmistakable final sign of spring. In my dash back I was almost crushed under a chunk of ice pushed into the sky. But I made a wild, standing leap, and fell hard on a piece that got me to shore. I slipped and slid down its incline to rest abruptly against a bruising but solidly earthbound boulder.

I hurt almost as much when I reached dry land as I had the first morning I woke after being wounded. Bruised everywhere, one ankle twisted, drenched in ice water, I was proud that I could just walk with a limp when I reached the men. "Captain Lightfoot is dead." Sergeant Davies and his men took the news without sorrow and they all smiled when I counted out their gold. Davies, God bless him, had a blanket and put it around me.

"Heard some shooting out there," said Davies as we hiked back up to the horses, "you have any trouble with them Americans?"

"Believe it or not, they were angry about the quality of our goods," I said, smiling, "and they made trouble. I had my musket on them, and Lightfoot killed one of them with his saber. I shot the other two, but one of them shot Lightfoot first." The story didn't quite knit with what they'd witnessed from the shore, but the soldiers had their gold, and Lightfoot's brother officers did not pursue the matter.

As for Augustus, after the War the United States sought to fix its national and regional boundaries. In the muddle, a lawyer named Samuel Sherwood bought title to lands that New York, to its embarrassment, found it did not own. To compensate Sherwood, the state issued him what amounted to an open title, good for any two hundred acres the state did possess. Porter purchased the title from Sherwood and made claim to Goat Island and the other islands of the river. The claim was reluctantly accepted by the state. Augustus had the beginnings of his empire.

Claire had mourned my imminent death before opening the public room, and she was relieved that the day was quiet. Two farmers, Lane Goodson and Earl Shelden, came in and had mugs of tea and brandy and sat by the fire and talked privately. She spent the morning finalizing her plans. First, she would approach Job Wilson and offer to sell the inn. Five hundred pounds was the price she settled on, not based on her assessment of its value in these odd times, but her own decision to go to Europe. She would send half of the money to Gordon's family. Her family lived in York, but she was one of twelve and the last burden her father needed was a spinster daughter. No, she would visit York with presents, explain Gordon's honorable death, and then leave for Europe. What she would do there she didn't know, but she was angry at America, angry at England, suspecting both of wanting this return of hostilities. She could be a maid in a fine hall in France. She'd heard the French enjoyed Englishwomen as servants.

And then I walked into the public room. I saw two men enjoying an early brandy and said good morning. "Claire?" I called.

She was in the back, doing an inventory of the dried goods to be sure her price was fair. "Oh-thanks-be-to-God," she whispered, and I led her behind the doorway of the storeroom, shut it tight, and kissed her. "You came back," she said, crying, "you didn't die. You came back." She gasped a little as her heart pounded. "Did you kill anyone?"

I nodded. "Porter?" I shook my head. She seemed relieved. "Lightfoot." It was a statement. I nodded. "Is there any trouble following you?" I shook my head. "And are you done now?"

"Let's sell this place. Where would you like to go?"

In truth she didn't want to go to Europe. She despised the French. "I want to see my family again. Take me back to York."

Within a few weeks time we sold the inn. Our last day in Pelham we visited the parsonage and said our wedding vows in the presence of Reverend Arbuthnot and his wife. Claire blushed deeply through the entire ceremony. "I'm sure it's what Gordon would have wanted," the Reverend assured her, and she hugged him.

The next day we packed her belongings in the repaired wagon, hitched Bluebell and Gordon to it and prepared to drive to her family's home in York. It was arguably the worst time of year to travel over land.

It was a crisp April day. The roads were frigid mud. We set out near dawn and before an hour had passed I'd gotten out twice to turn wheels sunk in mire. "Aim for the frozen patches, please."

"I'm doing my best," she said.

Being married was another new experience for me. Claire was quiet about it but she was feeling embarrassed. "I should have mourned Gordon for longer than this," she said. "It'll appear as if you've been in the wings. My saving grace is your wound," she said, half-smiling with a crassness she rarely showed. "If I had to hurry into wedlock, at least you're honorably wounded."

"Hurry into wedlock?" I asked.

"Hurry into wedlock."

"And why," I asked, getting back into the wagon, taking the reins, "did we hurry into wedlock?"

Claire smiled in a shy, knowing way, her bedroom smile. "You're going to be a father before autumn."

The war raged another year before sputtering to its undignified conclusion. We somehow reached York, where we spent a week. Henry and Abigail Burns were not sure what to make of me, but hearing the word 'grandchild' made the difference. Henry ran a mill, which had to be the dullest work of which I could conceive, after clerking on the Portage. He was preoccupied with the price of grain, speaking of little else all the time we were there. I guess that's how he became wealthy, but I could see why Gordon Drummond seemed dynamic to Claire.

Since the proceeds of the inn were a handsome dowry of sorts, I didn't need immediate employment. Claire and I bought a cabin in Burlington, so that she might be near her family in York, and I might have a little distance from them. We farmed a little, partly so I'd have reason to exercise my arm, which was starting to feel like a useful limb again. Claire knew this all along, but I was just biding time until the war concluded and I could return to Manchester.

When Claire went into labor in the winter of 1813, a storm was raging that came in off the lake the day before. The rain fell in inches, making a muddy river of a nearby creek. The creek flooded the best road to Burlington so I had the choice of slogging to the village to find a midwife, or calling on a neighbor, Maria.

Maria was a Chippewa, living in a bark and pole cabin that seemed to hold up and keep her dry no matter what fell from the sky. She was in her sixties or seventies, small and wizened, and walked only with difficulty and the aid of a stick she'd cut for herself. We usually stopped on our way to the village to see her. Claire was a little scared of her. "She smells odd, like she's using animal grease for soap." Since Claire was very polite, but still found Maria hard to be close to, it usually fell to me to climb off our wagon and call through the bearskin that was her doorway. "We're heading into town, Maria. Do you need anything?"

Her voice was a deep whisper. "Some candles and some pipe tobacco," she always said. She rarely asked for food. On a few occasions she called me inside. She sat on a stool near her fireplace, slept on a bed of pine boughs barely off the ground, covered with animal furs. I wouldn't take her money, and she customarily took a moment to cast a good spell on me.

When Claire began labor, winter thrashing the land, the only nearby help I could think of was Maria. She lived barely five minutes ride away, and when I called for her at her door she was there, wrapped in a snug fur, in an instant. "It's Claire, she's in labor."

"He'p me up," she asked, frozen to the ground, and I realized she'd never ridden in my wagon. We made a quick ride of it back to the cabin, where Maria directed me, in her minimal English, to boil water and expertly took over the job of guiding Lucas into light. By the dawn, we were a family and Claire had suffered minimally, resting and in good health, no awful hemorrhaging.

"You have to let me pay you," I said.

She was collecting our bloody sheets, and at her direction I followed her outside. She opened up the folds of one sheet to show me a mass of bloody tissue. "I keep this. It has power, for my spells." It was, I soon learned, the afterbirth. I almost threw up.

"Are you sure?" I asked.

"It has power, for my spells," she repeated. She looked up at my weak eye, the one that had taken the gunpowder blast. It had improved slightly over the year, but my vision was clouded and I'd become resigned to it. "Let me have it, and I will make a spell to let you see again," she indicated my eye.

"Not necessary," I said. She nodded, but why I didn't know. I took her home and thanked her again. She dismounted without help, raised her hand in goodbye, and disappeared into her hut with her bloody payment.

A while later, while Claire and I were remembering the birthing, she asked me if I'd paid Maria and I told her how. "So what was it that I gave her?" I asked in innocent curiosity.

She looked at me as though wondering how I could be so dense. "The afterbirth," she said in a voice just above a whisper. She stared straight ahead, her face gone pale. "Let's not speak of it again."

A month later, I was heading into town to get more blankets for our son and a treat for my wife. I stopped, as usual, at Maria's cabin. "Maria, it's Nehemiah Cleary. I'm headed into town. Can I get you anything?"

"Come in."

Claire had a point, the air in that cabin was not fresh. But I stepped inside.

Maria was on her bed, the first time I'd seen her that way. "I not good today, but I make you a spell for your eye." She guided me to a poultice she'd made of a broadleaf containing something dried.

"What's in this?" I asked, and hoped it wasn't what I thought.

"For your eye," she repeated, touching her own right eye. "Put it on and leave on for the time it takes the sun to move a foot across the ground."

"All right," I said, prepared to examine the contents outside, meanwhile nodding my thanks to her. "Can I get you some water?" She shook her head. She was sipping something from a wooden cup. "I'll check on you on my way back." Opening up the leaf outside, I found crushed leaves, berries, some grass, and a very sweet smell I couldn't identify.

Maria was beyond waking when I returned two hours later. Several of the townsfolk who'd known Maria over the years helped me bury her in our burial ground. Her hut was examined by Doctor Hirth, from the town, who promptly lit a torch and burned it. "Pestilence. She probably died of it. There's nothing in there safe to use."

I forgot about the poultice for a couple days, until I found it in my coat pocket. Out of respect for Maria, I took an hour's rest each day and held the poultice on my eye. "What in God's name is that?" Claire asked. I explained. "I hope you examined it first."

"Just nuts and berries and some kind of mint."

"Throw it out when you're done with it," she said. "Don't let Lucas get to it."

To my delight and amazement, within a week the cataract in my eye had entirely faded and my vision was almost normal. Claire kept the poultice in a high drawer. "I'm going to get Doctor Hirth to look at it, and see what the secret of it is." Hirth did examine it one day, and almost dropped it in his carelessness. "Nothing here but roots and berries. If your eye healed, it did so because you rested it," he decided. Doctor Hirth always was a fool.

With normal vision I found myself in the militia again, defending my new home when the American army invaded in 1813. After seizing Fort George in April they began marching towards York. Against superior numbers, the British militia could do little but fight delaying tactics while reinforcements were gathered. Our militia was well armed, well trained and we knew what we were fighting for. Superior numbers or not, we stopped them just outside Burlington.

One morning, a steaming June morning, reminiscent of my days on the Portage, I was one of three sentries guarding our lines. I had a field glass and periodically swept the slope of the escarpment. That morning I saw smoke coming from a cabin that was impudently flying the Stars and Stripes. "Captain Graves," I reported to our captain, "I think the Americans are looting again."

Graves, a few years my senior, took a brief look. "And they've raised that flag of theirs," he said, "take Grouse and Cassidy, send the looters back to their lines with a taste of justice."

I had a good musket, a sturdy .75 musket that had bruised my shoulder solidly when I practiced with it. I still had a periodic dream with a taste of Queenston in it, and the best cure was to fire the musket a few times. Fully charged, and taking the precaution of fixing my bayonet, I led the boys down the pathway. We could see more smoke through the trees. "Hurry up lads," I urged them, and we broke into a run.

As we crossed the open land surrounding the cabin, the smoke was confined to the back corner. It appeared to have been lit from inside. In front of the cabin the owners had stripped a pine for a crude flagpole. Our flag was lying in a pile on the ground and the American flag was tied off. "Cut that down," I ordered Grouse. My heart was pounding, my mouth was dry, but I was exhilarated. *This*, I kept thinking, *was what I wanted at Queenston. A fight I could be part of, a good cause.*

Grouse cut down the American flag but, seeing Cassidy and I approaching the cabin, he followed without tying off our colors. As we approached the entry a man came out, limping. I knew Simon Birch immediately. He was dragging a bed sheet filled with whatever he'd stolen from the house.

"You son of a bitch," I said, addressing him loudly. Seeing my musket leveled at him, caught with his hands filled with plunder, he stopped in the entry.

His right leg didn't bend. He had to swing it wide, using it like a crutch. Behind him, another came out with a smaller bundle. Bumping into Birch, he dropped his package and I heard glass breaking.

"Stealing from civilians?" I asked. Covered by the boys, I approached them. "Drop your sack, Birch."

"You know me?" Birch asked, scared. "How do you know me?" He took off his hat, a wide brimmed hat normally seen on the heads of wealthy gentlemen. He dropped the bedsheet.

I moved around him to see inside the cabin. "Anyone else inside?"

"We're just looking for food," said the other looter. "That ain't a crime, is it?"

I stepped forward and pulled a pistol from his belt. Birch appeared unarmed. I used the pistol to guard them and Grouse opened the bundles. "Dishes, a little pewter, and," he hefted a book, "a Bible."

"A Bible?" I asked. "Which part were you planning to eat?"

He riffled through the pages and we saw pound notes flutter to the ground. "A Bible for a bank," Grouse smiled. "If you hadn't set the fire you'd've had more time."

"Fire was an accident," said Birch. "This lout," he nodded to his companion, "is a bull in the china shop." He wiped his forehead of sweat. "We'll just leave this behind and go back to our lines, alright?" He looked at each of us, but mostly at me. "No need to spill blood over this, is there?"

Talking to your enemy is the surest way I know of disarming both parties. A faceless, voiceless adversary one can pull a trigger on, gut with a bayonet, and kill with little difficulty. But talk to your enemy and you recognize another human, and you might as well have spit in your powder. However much I despised Birch, I also saw fear in his eyes, and somehow his worried voice touched my sorely strained sense of pity. But before I let him go, he opened his mouth.

"I know you," Birch said then, and his worry was replaced by surprise. And then I heard contempt. "You're that scared youngster from Queenston. I forget your name but you're an American. What in hell are you doing with the British?"

Grouse and Cassidy kept their weapons aimed at the looters, but Cassidy asked, "Mr. Cleary, what's this looting bastard talking about?"

I was recognized by Captain Lightfoot at the Pelham Inn. Recognized again by Joe Birch in the Canadian wilderness. Thousands of men under arms on both sides, and I kept running into people who recognized me. Scarred by a misfire and people who barely knew me recognized me. My head suddenly pounded. I let a sigh of despair escape.

"They don't know, do they?" Birch asked, smiling. He looked at his friend, then beamed at the young Canadians. "Yea, lads, this proud man was part of the American army that stormed Queenston." He chuckled, a deep, revolting sound. "I recollect him telling me how he fired a shot himself at General Brock. Killed several British that day, or so he boasted. Guess he decided to pretend he was British. Wonder why?"

Cassidy looked at me. "Is he a damn liar, Mr. Cleary? You want me to put a ball through his lying mouth?" Cassidy was just fifteen, and behaved towards me like I was a father, not just his commander. I was just six years older.

They waited for me to say something. The cabin's fire spread. I felt its heat and waved away some burning sparks the breeze sent our way. The morning dew kept the sparks from igniting the grass, but the breeze fanned the flames and the roof caught. "Well, you didn't save the cabin," Birch said, chuckling. "Some poor loyal British subject is out of a home and possessions. Didn't suspect he'd left his home to be guarded by some American turncoat. Let's go," he ordered his compatriot, and he bent to heft his bag of loot. He spit on the ground in front of me. "Give my regards to the King."

"Stop," I said. I'd meant to say more but my voice was trembling. From the look in Cassidy and Grouse' eyes I had a little explaining to do, one way or the other. Letting the American looters walk back to their lines with their plunder was not possible. "What are you doing here,

Birch? You have a bad leg. No conscription wagon would force you to carry arms. Are you here for the plunder?"

"Of course," he sneered. "What the hell are you here for? Love of country?"

And then Joe Birch gave me a gift. Apparently he had concealed a second pistol. When I saw him turning, I knew he had no reason to turn, no good reason. His right arm bent as if to reach in his clothes, and I knew instantly he had a weapon. I held my musket on him and fired without thinking about it.

He took the ball in his throat, went to his knees, coughed blood twice, then fell face forward. The other looter dropped his sack and started to run. Twin bursts, from both Grouse and Cassidy's muskets, dropped him.

I walked up to Birch. "You should have stayed home," I said.

He looked up at me. He was scared of death just then, but still had so much anger he raised his pistol and pulled the hammer back. "Traitor," he got out. I kicked the pistol from his hand, gripped my musket tightly, and sank my bayonet as close to his heart as I could guess.

"Go home, now," I said. He spit up blood. He thought he was raising a pistol, and pulled his trigger finger as though he was shooting, but his hand rose just above his side, and then it fell, and he died, sneering his contempt at the sky.

We left the stolen goods by the burning embers of the cabin. "Sir," Cassidy asked, and with 'sir' in place of 'Mr. Cleary' I knew he no longer saw me as a loving father figure, "what did that man mean by calling you American?" I looked at him, and saw the same troubled look in Grouse's face.

"He was lying," I said. And I started walking back to our lines. They followed, a few steps behind me. They didn't speak much to me after that.

Two days later we counterattacked and gradually chased the Americans back all the way to Fort George. I stayed with the fighting until I was within sight of the Niagara River. It was about ten days after I'd killed Birch. Cassidy and I had stopped by the river to rest, savoring our victory. "We're winning," he said, smiling broadly, a solidly built man with long, curly blond hair. "I knew we would."

I hadn't seen the river in months and I missed it. It smelled fresh in my nostrils, flushing out the stink of gunpowder. "This is where I'm from, originally," I told Cassidy.

"You mean Newark?" he asked.

"No," I said, and pointed across the river. "Over there."

"So the looter was telling the truth?" Cassidy said. No longer smiling, he asked, "why'd you switch sides?"

"Somewhat by accident. There are winners, losers, and then there are survivors. I count myself in the last group. Over there I'm a deserter. I've started a family over here, and that's given me something to fight for over here." I remembered a sunny day last year, across the river, listening to an American army recruiter. *There's nothing over there but some starved Americans married to British, and the ones that don't join us as soon as we arrive, they'll run away for the second time when they see our flag.*

"So that's how it happened," I said to Cassidy. "And let me say, speaking from a point of experience, the English Army is far better equipped than the American."

Cassidy smiled, but I was still a mystery to him and I wasn't going to try changing that. "You take care of yourself, Cassidy. You're a good boy."

"Will I see you after the war, back in Burlington?" he asked.

"Maybe. Do me a favor. Tell Grouse the truth, and if you can, keep it to yourselves." Since I never heard another word about it, I expect those boys did as I asked. Two days later I rode back with a few other militia to our homes in Burlington, under a pass signed by our commanding officer, Major Butler.

In December, the Americans abandoned Fort George and Newark by putting it all to the torch, in a howling snow storm. It was the worst act of terror seen in the war. A week later our forces took Fort Niagara, and swept down the Niagara River bank to Buffalo, burning everything in their path, retribution for the atrocity at Newark. I wondered what still stood in Manchester, and didn't sleep well while news of the fight filtered back, but I stayed in Burlington and watched Lucas learn to walk.

I returned to Manchester in 1815, with Claire and Lucas. A general amnesty erased the blurred loyalties of the war, the ulterior motives and the inconclusive ending. When we rode into Manchester in the spring, I saw that my father's inn and the few other homes of Manchester had burned. Being constructed of stone, the walls of the inn still stood. With help from some of the soldiers from Schlosser, I repaired the roof and floors and moved my family in. I was home. Since Claire had experience running an inn, I let her take charge. I just tried to follow orders.

On a warm day with the feel of summer, I was trying, with a mule borrowed from the fort, to break the soil in a spot we'd never farmed just off the kitchen door. "My mother has a magnificent herb garden," Claire mentioned at dinner the night before, "and if you could break up the soil in that spot near the kitchen door, I know she would visit us with some seeds."

So I was struggling to keep the plow blade anchored in the soil, pulled by a mule that didn't want the work, when I heard, "never took you to be a farmer."

Angry anyway, I wasn't feeling talkative but the voice sounded familiar and when I turned to see the speaker my jaw fell. "John Sims! Hello, lieutenant." I gave him a mock salute. I felt a rush of joy almost embarrassing to experience.

"Please don't call me that," he said softly, getting off his horse.

John was the first survivor of Queenston I'd seen. "I thought you were dead," I said.

"Likewise." He limped as he came to shake my hand. "Shot in the leg at Queenston. I thought I'd lose it, and if we'd had any surgeons I probably would have. I heard you lost an eye."

I smiled. "It got better." Our new world, of peace and small children and gardens to be planted, paused as we took a moment to live in the past. "So what happened to you after Queenston?"

He looked at the single row of soil I'd turned. "I was wounded near the village, got back across the river, and was brought back here," he said. "The missus got me well. I heard about you coming back, and being wounded." Visible near the river were a few burned upright timbers of a warehouse. "We ran when the British burned this side of the river," he continued. "We've been staying with family near Chautauqua, but I wanted to come back when it was over, so here I am."

"You know, you're the first man I've seen that survived Queenston," I said. He looked around, but we were alone. It would always be that way, a bit shamefaced to admit we'd been at Queenston.

"You spent the rest of the war in Canada?"

I nodded.

He smiled in an understanding way. "The camp broke up in a couple of days. Some went down to join up in Buffalo. Some just left. What happened to that older fellow in your tent? Lucas?"

"He didn't make it."

Sims nodded sadly, as we'd both done and would always do.

"Your boat got burned," I said, apologetically.

He shaded his eyes as he looked towards the river. "I figured on that. And I see I've got a cabin to rebuild."

"Stay here tonight, John," I offered. "Tomorrow we'll get your new cabin started."

"That would be much appreciated. What about your new farm?" he asked, grinning.

"Oh, that can wait." We shook hands and I felt a warmth I didn't know I'd missed. The return of neighbors, of friendship.

A month after we reopened the inn, Judge Porter returned. I was in the yard, trying to discover why my newest horse was limping, suspicious that the trader had cheated me. I had his left hind hoof up, looking for an injury. I looked up at the sound of wheels going by and saw the Judge. I think he saw me, but neither of us acknowledged the other.

He began building a mansion with his profits from the war, as well as the money he badgered Congress for in compensation for his torched homestead. When the building was finished, his wife Lavinia and their children returned. Though the village was still small, I stuck to my business and he stuck to his. We had few occasions to speak and we mutually avoided doing so. But I wondered where my Mother was, and three months after Porter returned I wrote a letter to the Postmaster in Canandaigua asking him to make inquiries. Reluctantly, I found Judge Porter, who was also our Postmaster. At his mill, his hired man directed me to the riverbank, where Augustus was supervising the building of a rope bridge across to his new prize, Goat Island.

A strong swimmer had managed to cross the stream from well upriver, with a rope for safety around his waist. Now he was anchoring that rope and pulling heavier ones over with it. I found Augustus sorting through loops of hemp, selecting the ones to be used. "Judge?"

He looked up impatiently, saw me and reacted as he would towards a debtor. "Yes, Nehemiah? What can I do for you?"

I pulled the letter from my pocket. "Well, as you are our Postmaster, I wanted to see that this letter was mailed. It's to Canandaigua."

"Yes," he took the letter, reading the address. "Addressed to the Postmaster. Might I be so bold as to ask why?"

I hesitated, but couldn't think of a reason not to answer. "I'm asking for him to make inquiries about my mother and sister. They should have returned, but they may not know I'm here, and that my father's house has been repaired."

Augustus looked a little troubled, and walked me away from the ropes and the working men. When we were further downstream, where our voices were masked to others by the roar of the falls, he said, "I have some sad news to tell you. I'm sorry I didn't tell you sooner, but," he paused, looking away, "your Mother died of fever in the summer of 1813. She's buried in Canandaigua in a churchyard. I can give you directions if you want to visit."

I felt the tears well up in my eyes. "And my sister?" I whispered.

He looked at the letter in his hand. "She was adopted by a family named Peck, and they left the region for opportunities in Ohio. I don't know where, exactly, they are."

I closed my eyes a moment. My chest ached. I felt tears warm on my cheek. Ashamed to be crying in front of Porter, I turned away. Augustus stood silently, looking at the ground. "I asked you to look after them," I said, my voice a whisper.

"I'm sorry. Lavinia nursed your mother. It was a terrible fever. Twenty people or so died from it. It couldn't be helped."

"And Electa?"

He blushed. "After your mother died. The Peck family lived next door, and they befriended your mother and sister. I was away, Lavinia had too much to do. Electa was very fond of them. They have a daughter her age. It seemed the logical thing to do."

I took the letter back. I returned to the stone house, and fed the letter to the fireplace.

Claire found me sitting on the hearth, crying. "What's happened?" When I told her, she held me for a long time. "So I'll never know the look of a happy mother-in-law." She held my face to hers. "Would I have made her happy? Or would she have looked at me and said, 'Nehemiah, where'd you get that skinny, bow-legged English cow? Is that how I raised you?'"

I laughed through a gush of tears. Lucas wondered what we were doing. "She would have loved you," I said, brushing my infant son's hair.

Claire put her determined smile on. "You're a good man. The Judge," she glanced away, as though he was already just a spirit, "will die someday and go to hell. You have a son to raise."

We lifted him between us. I saw my mother's nose, and I remembered when Electa was learning to walk. I had my family.

The Judge built his rope walkway to Goat Island, and prepared us all for new neighbors, new projects, new money. Perhaps God exercises his judgment too rarely. Perhaps he likes to save it for moments when his flock will know it unmistakably for what it is.

No one came. Oh, a few small businesses set up, but the pioneers were moving west, to Ohio, the Northwest Territory. And the Erie Canal finished his dreams off. The falls did provide a modest stream of visitors every summer and fall, so the inn had business, but nobody shared the Judge's vision of Niagara's great power. Around 1840, in his final years, he was so desperate he wrote an advertisement for several New York papers, touting our great village, reminding the Easterners of the falls, offering them the most generous terms to come and build.

No one came. Some nights I had a little too much rum and laughed myself sick.

One other thing. He has never said a word of apology about the war, nor do I expect him to. After learning of the dispersal of my family I have not spoken to him or his family. I have the joy of Claire and my boy Lucas, and that is enough for me. And every morning in good weather I go out and walk around the wild, unspoiled falls, and look across to empty Goat Island.

In the end, I did learn one lesson. One should never go to war over reasons too embarrassing to mention. Silk handkerchiefs? The only reason to go to war is to protect your home.

Honeymoon Capital

"It's the sight you've traveled to see and one you'll never forget! The mighty Niagara! Three million gallons of wet fury pouring over yonder precipice! A cloud that never disperses and a roar that has never been silenced! Below is the *Maid of the Mist*, the hearty little steamer that hourly challenges the thundering cataracts with its cargo of thrill seekers, taking them through the tumult and into the very face of Niagara! Behind the water is the Cave of the Winds that you've read so much about! These fantastic sights are only part of the day of thrills you'll enjoy with Sawyer's Guided Tour!"

Pausing to catch his breath, Sawyer set his red tin megaphone on the ground. It was humid today and his gray linen suit was holding the heat and making him sweat by the gallon. Wiping sweat from his forehead, he licked his dry lips. *Looks like it might be slow today,* he thought, seeing a smaller crowd than usual milling about the train station. Appearances being less critical than they would be with a good crowd, he took off his cap, lifted the dipper from the wooden bucket and poured cool river water over his head. He panted as the water cooled him off. He let the trickles run dry, and drank the second dipper; he could hawk the crowd as well as any, but today he felt the insistent tickling again and he needed cool water from time to time.

Sawyer Jackson's guided tour booth was a simple little stand, brightly painted with a large sign. Sawyer was his own boss, his best employee, and his only salary. Behind his stand was his carriage, a black buggy with gold painted letters on both sides, two passenger benches and a worn bench up front for Sawyer to sit on as he took the tourists around. His booth was set up today on a site he'd eyed all last summer, between the Central Depot where the trains pulled in every half-hour, and a restaurant with a large sign—CLEAN WASHROOMS. When the people stumbled off the train they wanted something wet for their whistles and then they wanted washrooms, and then they wanted tours. So this morning at dawn, Sawyer drove his buggy to this spot, unhooked his little stand from the two hooks it hung on behind his buggy, and proceeded to fish the waters. After filling a short tour on the eight-thirty train, and following suit on the eleven-thirty train, he had returned to try his luck on the three-thirty.

Some rough characters worked the crowds, practically dragging away the travelers. There was a notorious fellow named Water Bill, a huge, muscle-bound brawler, who had been known to raise the price of the tour while on Goat Island and once held a small fellow over the railing, dangling him above the rapids. His tour price had suddenly doubled and the customer objected. Sawyer didn't always charge the same price for a tour himself. If he saw good clothing, or jewels, or other signs of wealth, the tour doubled, maybe tripled. But he never threatened the lives of his customers; he had ethics.

As he raised the dipper for a second drink he saw the cop on the beat making his way towards him. "Sawyer," Officer Knox hailed him, and Sawyer dropped the dipper back in the bucket. "Don't you usually make your noise down on River Road?" Knox ran this block of Falls Street, and Sawyer had expected a shakedown sometime today. The cop was patting his well-worn nightstick in the palm of his hand. He had no family, and only one flaw, in Sawyer's eyes—he seemed to enjoy stopping fights by using his nightstick on all brawlers, whether there was a clear instigator or not. He'd no doubt seen Sawyer's tours today and could guess within five cents how much he had earned.

"You're right, Sergeant," Sawyer flattered the flunky with the single stripe, "but I was barely keeping my horse in oats working down there, and here I figured with the traffic I'd be able to earn a proper living." His hands tightened nervously on the megaphone; the next train could be heard down the tracks, fast approaching. "Is there something wrong, Sergeant?" he urged; *let's get this over with.*

Knox glanced in the direction of the train station. "Must be doing a good business here, Sawyer, smack between the train and," he turned to look at the modest, slightly tilted shack that looked like a stiff wind would flatten it, "this fine restaurant." He strolled over to the carriage, which was backed into the alleyway and called out to the fidgeting tour guide, "course I don't expect you know about the sanitary permit, do you?"

Jesus, Mary and Joseph, thought the tour guide, thumbing the bulge of paper and coin in his purse, *let's get this business done with.* "No, Sergeant," he answered, impatient but still deferential, "I quite completely never heard about no permit." Steam was hissing from the engine as the train slowed into the station.

"Well, what with that horse doing his business back there, the street cleaner has more work to do, and the taxpayer shouldn't be footing the bill for your business, if you get my drift," went on Knox, circling the little stand and noting the train was now pulling into the far end of the platform with bells clanging.

"Could you do me the service of telling me the price of the permit?" Sawyer took the initiative, one eye on the cop, the other on the slowing train.

Knox held out until the train was stopped and the conductors had jumped off to help the passengers down. He'd seen Sawyer do two trips today, added in the one he'd make before sunset, and did his own figuring. "An even five dollars should cover it."

Sawyer visibly flinched. "That's for the week, and there's nobody else going to collect?" Knox nodded his agreement, and palmed the bills just in time for the passengers to get on the street, as the train whistle blew again.

"You'll make this up in two minutes time," the cop yelled over the train whistle, "by the way, Sawyer, you've got more overhead here than down at River Road, you charge a full dollar a head. It's the going rate on Falls Street." And he was off.

Sadie, Sawyer's horse, promptly had a bowel movement. "You can say that again," said Sawyer; he took another dipper of water, gripped his megaphone, and took a deep breath. As the first passengers hesitantly crossed the traffic of Falls Street he let loose. "Ladies-and-gentlemen! The Mighty Niagara!" He had a crowd around him in seconds, and he signed up the ones closest even as hawkers for other tours converged on his crowd.

With his carriage full he climbed onto the bench and touched Sadie with the reins. "As you may know," he began his sing-song to his passengers, "there are two falls at Niagara, the American and the Canadian, also known as the Horseshoe Falls. Of the two the American is taller but the Canadian is wider and carries more of the water."

"We should've kept both falls when we whipped the British in 1812," said the father, an elderly gent in a black suit, wearing a permanent scowl, introduced as Emmett Logan.

"Couldn't agree with you more," continued Sawyer, the customer always being right even when unbelievably wrong, "we will begin our tour of the mighty Niagara at Prospect Point." He drove his carriage expertly through the traffic, carriages, those on horseback and pedestrians, skirting around other carriages with other tourists, using his carriage's size to dominate anything smaller, all the while conducting his reins with light tosses and jerks that guided Sadie through gaps in the traffic, finally pulling up in a small lot next to the entrance for the Incline Railway. He changed his pitch to a suggestive one, "this is the famous Incline Railway that carries folks down to the base of the falls, known as the 'Shadow of the Rock'. It's only fifty cents a ride and we will pause for twenty minutes to accommodate any who will dare the falls." Only twenty yards further ahead the Niagara roared and fell, and Sawyer leaped out and stayed one step ahead of his four passengers.

They were a family from somewhere in Ohio and the old man had haggled with Sawyer over the price, and he finally agreed to knock twenty-five cents off the price—for which they'd lose half the tour. "Can you believe the majesty!" he bellowed to remind them of his presence. He led them first to the fence that kept the curious a few yards from the water, then led them through a passing cloud of mist, then walked carefully past the entrance to the Incline Railway.

"How much is that ride again?" asked the wife, a younger woman only Sawyer's age, introduced as Angeline.

"It's only five cents, Daddy!" shrieked the youngest, Gabriel, a boy of eight, and the old man—he must have married Angeline when she was half his age—looked sour.

"It's fifty, Gabriel," he corrected sternly. "I thought the price was part of our tour," he challenged Sawyer, who was calculating how much shorter he could cut the tour and get the hayseed out of his hair.

"The tour gets you the carriage, my experience, and the stops I listed. I simply make these opportunities convenient," Sawyer said, officiously, diplomatically.

"Come on, Dad," whined Gabriel, and Angeline chimed in, sounding more child than mother; these aren't her kids, Sawyer was certain. Emma, the daughter, an attractive dark-haired girl who looked just a handful of years younger than Angeline, didn't seem too happy at being on vacation with her family, and said nothing.

Emmett was scowling as he dug out the money and let his family through the turnstile. "Hurry up, Emma. You're keeping your mother and us waitin'."

"I'm coming!"

They were ushered into a line of people waiting as a car was hauled up the rail. When they were seated and on their way down, Sawyer stepped to the ticket window. "How's the day, Turnbull?"

"Doing okay," answered the ticket seller, "that family of hillbillies your bunch?"

"Afraid so. The three-thirty came in a little light. I'm on Falls Street now," he let drop his new business location.

"Oh yeah, I heard about that. Better than the River Road?"

Sawyer shrugged.

"Knox take his piece yet?"

Sawyer scowled. Turnbull chuckled mildly, then pushed fifty cents across the counter. "Maybe this'll ease the sting of your 'sanitary fee.'"

"It helps," he said with a half-smile as he pocketed the kickback, and strolled over to the fence to wait for his charges.

Without a wind the mist was rising in a cloud a good three hundred feet high, casting a perfect rainbow in the gorge. "Very pretty," he heard another guide exhorting his group, "Niagara's eternal rainbow!" The Maid was bucking its way through the current and passed through the rainbow. Sawyer sniffed the air, fresh and cool. He strolled upriver from the crowd at the brink, and when he'd escaped them, he climbed through the fence. Kneeling by the river, he cupped his hands in the water and bathed his face and sweaty brow. Then he gulped another two handfuls.

His hair was straight brown, gray at the temples, not bad for thirty-nine. In his name at the Niagara Falls Savings and Trust was an account with forty dollars. The bankbook was stuffed into his mattress, in his room in the boarding house on 3rd and Falls. The money was his savings since April, when the touring season got off to its annual tepid start. Before September, when the season dropped with the temperature, he needed to have two hundred dollars saved. Some years a hundred was enough, some years only seventy-five, but this year he'd be getting an operation, so he needed more.

There was this nagging tickle in his throat. It started with what he thought was a cold in May, a dry cough he couldn't shake. "Maybe it's the fresh flowers, they make me sneeze," a friend suggested. Swallowing seemed to trigger the irritation, a tickle that, as he coughed to clear his throat would become tender, like a mosquito bite scratched until it bled. He never hawked up phlegm. By June, breathing hard, like after a run, triggered the cough, until it was raw and sore.

Today as he thought of it he took another swallow of river water to ease it. As bad as it was, he'd ignored it until the day last month when his constant coughing produced a little blood. The doctor had peered down his throat, almost gagging him with a probe tipped with a mirror, had him cough, looked some more until he did gag, then had him cough again, looked a considerable long time, over and over again for what seemed an hour. "You have a cancer in your throat," the doc finally said. "I can just see it. It isn't very big, and I think it can be removed and you should be fine. I'm afraid it will be painful, and since you'll need some hospital rest it's not inexpensive."

It meant saving more money. To improve his take he'd abandoned the spot he'd worked a quarter mile up the river, the other side of the railroad station, next to a lemonade and souvenir stand on River Road. The traffic up there wasn't half of what he saw at Falls Street, but the vast majority of tourists who walked up River Road that far were too footsore to continue. Sometimes he just earned the cabby's fare, sometimes he talked them into a tour. He shared the traffic with Black Joe and Calvin, and a few of the part-timers, those who showed up to make extra money around holidays. They were a friendly, sharing bunch, good for passing the time of day and a bottle when the day was slow. In the humid, moist August mornings, when the tourists didn't stir until at least noon, the guides fished off the old pier and fried what they caught. If any of them were still young they'd have gone swimming; instead, they pulled off their boots and dangled their feet. It was a nice life, a quiet life.

But this year he needed that extra money. And tonight, when he saw the boys, he could show them his take, minus the five, and tell them tours were worth a full dollar per head on Falls Street, and the part they'd swallow hardest was three booked tours in a day.

Here came the old man, so he took another mouthful to get him through the next stretch, and climbed back to the sidewalk. "Well, now, wasn't that exciting?" he beamed, leading them to the carriage. He saw that the daughter, Emma, had lagged behind and his protective instincts kicked in, too late.

"Hey! Little lady, I bet you never saw no picture better than this," hissed a man who appeared and blocked her path, holding some tattered prints of the falls. He had a few days' bristle on his chin, and wore a dirty collar on a sweat-stained shirt, with bits of his hay bed still clinging to it. "What's wrong with you?" he barked as Emma retreated, "these beautiful pictures, just twenty-five cents apiece. Give you five for a dollar!"

Sawyer recognized him—these types preyed on the crowds, and if Emma didn't hand over some change quickly he might get physical. "These folks are with me, Jed, got it?"

"And I'm just making a living," snarled Jed. Jed had no teeth left, and up close he smelled of the stable. And Sawyer could tell Jed had had a few drinks of spirits already today. "Fly-specked, dried-up old piece of trash!" he yelled at Emma, "get the hell out of my way," and he vanished into the crowd.

Emma was pale and was now hugging her stepmother's arm.

"Couple of men, just as we got off the train," the old man was saying, "grabbed my arm, said 'I'm takin' you to the best hotel in town!' I would've flattened him ten years ago. Caught him trying for my wallet."

Sawyer nodded ruefully as he herded them back to the wagon. "If someone flashes a picture machine at you, don't make eye contact. They'll tell you 'thought you wanted your picture taken', and then they'll give you the bill and it's for glass plates and chemicals and a dozen other things. It'll be enough to buy a hundred pictures." He looked across the rapids to the shore. "I'm afraid Niagara has collected more than its fair share of thieves." Between the dance halls, and the taverns, with their card games and prostitutes and thieves, and the number of strangers who would appear behind you on a moonless night and leave you broke and bleeding, it wasn't such a safe place.

"It's so pretty," marveled Angeline, blissfully forgetting the incident and Sawyer's warning, still drinking in the natural wonder, "have you ever seen the falls from up close, Mr. Sawyer?"

It did change the topic nicely. "Don't be daft, Angeline," said the coot, "he's a tour guide. Course he's seen it." He climbed up to the seat. "Probably got to see it for free, too."

Ignoring him, Sawyer helped Emma up; after his rescue she was giving him a modest smile, which he returned. "Oh yes, I've seen it. And nothing can beat it!" He had never bothered to see the falls from the bottom because Turnbull wouldn't let him in free. Black Joe said he'd seen it once, but his ticket had been bought by an old woman he was taking around, and Black Joe said it was nice, but not fifty cents worth. "From here we will cross over the Rapids and visit Goat Island," he continued, touching Sadie with the reins. A gentle jolt, a soft ringing of the shiny bells on her bridge, and the carriage rolled up the dirt path to Porter's Bridge. On either side of the road were souvenirs and cold drinks and hot snacks for sale. In the shade some tourists in their suits and dresses were trying to carefully eat powdered sugared waffles without powdering their lapels or bosoms. The line for a glass of lemonade or ginger beer was long, as the afternoon sun seemed to make the layer of dust cloying. Sawyer checked the shadows. He had to clear the bridge, show these folks Luna Island, then squeeze in the Horseshoe Falls, all in daylight. After that he dropped them at Tugby's to buy souvenirs until they ran out of money. Barely moving his hand, he rippled the reins and Sadie picked up her pace.

All was going pretty well when the daughter, Emma, asked, "I heard that years ago some men bought a ship and filled it with animals and sent it over the falls." *Was she trying to ruin the trip*, Sawyer wondered?

"Emma!" Angeline snapped, "that's insane."

Emma didn't pay attention. "Did that really happen?" she asked Sawyer in a daring tone.

Sawyer nodded, "yes ma'am, it did. It was the *Michigan*. It happened back when I was a small child, and some folks thought it was entertaining." *So are cockfights*, he thought, *but it was hard to think about such a sight being entertaining if you harbored any affection for the animals.* But the entrepreneurs of Niagara had always had much more imagination than taste. "Look at the rainbow!" he called out to change the topic.

Perkins, the boy taking tolls, touched his cap as Sawyer drove through; a small badge on the side of Sawyer's seat indicated that he'd bought a tour guide's season pass for three dollars in April. For that fee, Sawyer also promised to visit Tugby's, and Porter's kickback on souvenirs made him a tidy sum; even as Sawyer rode onto the bridge he passed by the great souvenir emporium perched on the river's edge. The boy lit up at the sight of Tugby's cigar Indian. "We going in there?"

"On the way back," he promised, spying just then a carriage coming up on the right, driven by McCrory. Frank McCrory, about ten years older than Sawyer, talked constantly and drove slowly and would never get his people through the tour in daylight. "We'll stop in on the way back."

"Go ahead," grumbled the old man, ignoring the churning rapids they were passing over, "I wouldn't give a penny for their damn trinkets. Nothing but paper and glue." He settled back in his seat, showing his contempt for these highwaymen by looking straight ahead and ignoring the mighty wonder he'd brought his family to see; his family was all but out of the carriage, leaning far over the side as Sawyer carefully rode by the railing, having edged out McCrory to give them the window view of the churning rapids below. "It's magnificent!" "It's frightening!" "I can't look!" "So get out of the way and let me look!" They were silenced by Angeline, who seemed to be inhaling the water and the mist, the great maple trees that lined the bank and the cluster of willows down to the left by Bath Island.

She didn't seem to mind the pulp mill whose smoking chimney shrouded Bath Island, or the buildings crowding the riverbank. The river bank was covered with small hotels and laundries, with the day's washing hanging out, a couple of 'bath houses' that were presumed to be houses of ill repute, a big stable that used the fast water as a horse toilet, a carpentry shop —*why*, Sawyer wondered, *did the carpenter need his shop there of all places*—and, to top it off, large painted ads on the backs of most of the buildings. It spoiled the image many had of the falls, as seen in a popular daguerreotype, looking wild and free. *Some still saw it that way*, thought Sawyer, watching Angeline; *she's waited her entire life for this*. He tickled the reins for Sadie to slow down. The mother was silent, didn't even blink, but started intently at the mad river as it rushed to the falls. She probably never saw, heard, or smelled the tacky, the tawdry, or the stench.

When they reached Goat Island, McCrory caught up, and, without obviously racing, each guide tapped the reins over their horses' backs, alternately edging each other out as they rushed to get to the hitching bar first: a time honored competition between any two guides from the bridge to the Luna Island hitching bar. Sawyer won; *that's a carrot for you tonight, Sadie*. McCrory gave him a good-natured touch of the cap, which Sawyer returned with a smile. "Off to the right, folks, this is Luna Island."

He led them down the stone steps hewn into the slope of Goat Island, leading to the bridge to the tiny island, pointing out en route, "the point where Sam Patch dove, twice, into the basin below."

"Amazing," said Angeline.

"Ridiculous," snorted the coot. Sawyer smiled, wondered how much he was worth, and led them over the footbridge connecting Goat and Luna. Standing still on the bridge, he pointed down, "below us is a tiny Niagara, a narrow torrent, called the Bridal Veil Falls. The name is well deserved. Newly wed brides at Niagara often toss their veils into this cataract as a wish for a happy marriage." Sawyer had never seen a newlywed bride toss her veil in, but that didn't mean anything. Smiling, always smiling, he led them onto Luna, where they ran to the railing to see the falls again.

In the end that was the bottom line of successful tours. Let them see enough of the falls. Anything else you slide in that's profitable, fine, just so long as they got to see their fill of the falls.

"We were just over there, right?" asked the boy, pointing across the crest of the falls to Prospect Point. Sawyer nodded.

"What are those people doing down there?" asked the daughter, pointing to the base of the island. In yellow oil slickers, tourists visiting the Cave of the Winds were carefully walking on the wooden stairway over the boulders at the foot of the island and streams running from the Bridal Veil, heading towards the base of the American falls.

"That's the Cave of the Winds," said Sawyer offhandedly.

"We going there?" asked the boy excitedly.

"Sure, if you like," Sawyer offered, "it's extra, but it's well worth it." Flexibility was key here; the minute someone looked interested you got them to the ticket-window before they lost interest.

"Seems like everything interesting is extra," Emmett complained darkly, and Sawyer anticipated some strained diplomacy.

"I'm having a wonderful time, George," snapped Angeline, momentarily distracted from her meditation, "so just hush up."

A silent thanks, then Sawyer cleared his throat and led them back up to the carriage. "Next stop is the Horseshoe Falls."

The livery stable Sadie called home was directly behind Sawyer's room, and he remembered the promised carrot. He unhitched the carriage and the lad who mucked out the stables helped him push it around the side.

The air was cooling off. It was evening. The crowds at the brink of the falls had thinned out. Lamps hung here and there, but the mosquitoes were out early and the air by the falls was thick with them. Several days of heavy rain had left some standing puddles on the rocky point and therein bred the pests. Sawyer had tried to sign up folks for tomorrow, but the mosquitoes were dispersing most of the people, including himself. A few of the taverns were burning tar or citronella to drive away the pests, but the smell was as bad a deterrent as the mosquitoes.

He opened the front door to the stone house, pulled off his suit coat and hung it on a peg. A lamp was burning and Sawyer saw a copy of the *Courier*, but he'd save it for later. The broad pine boards of the old house creaked under his boots as he went into the kitchen and sat at the kitchen table, his feet aching from the day's labor. It wasn't proper to pull off his boots outside his room, but he was sorely tempted. He could almost stand to be idle tomorrow after today's business. Uncorking a bottle of ginger beer, he swallowed slowly and let the liquid soothe the tickle his throat. With the irritating tickle eased, the yen to be among people that made him a successful guide drew him out again and he headed back out, leaving his suit coat behind. From the street he heard voices of joy and decided that he wanted a beer.

Leona's was a quiet tavern on Whirlpool Street, cozy and filled with the mementos of tour guides. Leona's was the guides' evening watering hole and had been since Sawyer had been a guide and some time before. Tour guides heard noise all day. They heard tourists shrieking over what had become commonplace to them, and they smirked, and they heard tourists complain over prices they'd become accustomed to, and they smirked. What they wanted at night was some quiet, a little conversation, friends and cheap beer. That was Leona's.

She only hung a small sign out front and then patrons had to climb down some basement steps that were rotting, suggesting an uninteresting, even threatening place to tourists. That was just right. The last thing they wanted with their evening beer was some hick from Saginaw stumbling in and asking directions for "a good hotel where two-bits gets me a decent room and a meal." They got that question all day, as though there were such things as good hotels and meals for a quarter in Niagara Falls; the meal itself cost a quarter. "Problem is," the guides would try to explain when the tourists complained too much, "is that Niagara is only open for business three months of the year. We have to make up for the rest of the year." The truth never helped. But, anyway, Leona's was nicely off the beaten track.

The walls were a chronology of the changing times. The first tour guide license ever issued—to Samuel Hooker—was framed up over the mirror behind the bar, and the license issued to the oldest guide—also Samuel Hooker—was framed next to the doorway. Hooker had also built the bathing facility on Green Island, thereafter changing the name to Bath Island. A picture of an old house where Leona had set up her first home for thirsty guides was hung over the door to the room with the big drain that passed for a urinal, and next to it a picture of the blasting out of Port Day—which was what replaced Leona's first bar. Some kid, probably just learning the ropes in his new shirt and jacket, was in the corner where a box of papers and handbills lay, reading a pamphlet on the Maid of the Mist. Leona's was the best place to catch up on the newest happenings in town. The tour guide's bread and butter depended on being a source for the tourists of what was hot in the city, and Leona made it her business to get a copy of any new guidebooks or handbills on new hotels or upcoming entertainment. Some of the smarter hotel owners made a point of sending copies of their latest announcements to Leona's to make sure the guides were alert. The bar was a school, a rest home, and a museum.

On the far wall hung a photograph of a crowd of men in suits. The suits were a bit frayed but the camera missed that detail. They were all smiling, some with their hands on others' shoulders and some shaking hands. They were the tour guides of 1857, an infamously slow year after the Panic of 1856. Sawyer still shuddered a bit at the memory. The picture on the wall was the best part of that year. One slow day, of the many they had endured that summer, they got the idea and in a few hours they'd spread the word and everyone showed up in their best to stand before the falls for the camera. Nice bunch of guys; Sawyer had found himself in the middle, next to John Bruce, a generous bloke from Scotland who died the next winter, broke, coughing out his lungs with TB. He raised his mug tonight to John, as he did whenever he thought to look at the picture.

Jesus that was a bad year! Sitting idle most of the time, they'd watch the train puff in and let out a few rich people who rode in carriages to the Imperial House and booked a tour with Sir Richard, the fop with the white carriage who paid some other cop thirty dollars a week for the right to park in front of the finest hotel in Niagara. He had cooked up a phony English accent and claimed he'd attended a fine school in England when five guides swore in church that Sir Richard was Richard Mole of Black Rock. Everyone went hungry that year except Sir Richard, who wouldn't share his turf, which made him the only guide Leona wouldn't let through the door. That year Sawyer ran his savings dry in January, a full four months before even the early-bird tourists showed.

The biggest company in town then was the Bath Island paper mill; it harnessed the river through a water wheel and produced paper from wood pulp. After the crash the town was terribly short of jobs, but if anyone in town could pay a guy to push on a broom for a few days it was one of the Porters, who owned the island and the mill. On the frozen morning that Sawyer paid the cursed toll to cross the bridge to the island, six other tour guides were already waiting. It was still dark so they found some sticks of wood and made a fire to keep warm. Someone had a bottle and someone else said something about "it ain't even dawn yet," but then a viciously cold gust blew through everyone's coats and the bottle went the rounds quickly.

At six the day shift showed up and the doors swung open. Huddling around their fire, the guides stayed off the main path as the regular workers filed in, some waving hello. Normally these guides considered mill work the worst job in town, but the mill had survived the panic and now the mill workers were the most secure in town. Sawyer's coat was very old, but had been top quality at one time and kept its appearance. Under the coat he wore his worst shirt, stained linen with buttons missing. He couldn't wear it on tour; he found this morning it also wasn't much for standing in January cold.

Finally the workers clocked in and Whitney, the portly, mustached foreman, came out. "Three men to sweep up and three to work the floor!" he called out.

The guides looked at each other; the wind blew the loose snow around their legs. "There's seven here," someone called out, "can you find another job?"

Whitney frowned, another frigid gust blew coats against cold bodies, and he waved them all inside.

Alongside the inside walls of the two story wooden building, a barn filled with a rhythmic roar, four great grinding machines were running. First, wood was chewed into pulp. The chipper was powered by a belt that was turned by a cam beneath the mill floor; the cam was turned directly by the great water wheel turned by the river. The pulped wood flowed onto flat pans where a small crew picked out any big chunks that had slipped through, then a man with powerful arms carried the tray of pulp to the final stage. A press so large its wheel couldn't be moved by less than three men would press the sheet of pulp for five minutes. It was a sight in itself, and if the mill weren't so infernally noisy, and a bit hazardous with wood splinters filling the air like mosquitoes, it could draw in tourists during summer.

Splinters flew off and piled up, and Sawyer's job was to keep sweeping up the bits of wood and bark. As he took his broom and began sweeping, it being his first time actually inside the mill, he realized that the chippers were the center of the operation. The cam had a gear that pounded a rhythm into the air. Each press worked on the same swing or half-swing of the gear with the other two, and when the process stopped, even for just a few minutes, the pace of work in the mill slowed, became irregular as the workers lost their cadence. Some would have been working to the rhythm of the first press and would have to adjust a half-beat to the other; some took the opportunity to relieve themselves of breakfast.

Sunlight never made it to the floor. Hooded gaslights dimly lit the interior. The air was thick with splinters and bits of woody paper. Soggy chunks of pulp collected on every nail head, every bolt, and Sawyer pushed his broom through inches of it on the floor. He worked slowly and carefully, worried that a good fast sweeping would only mean an hour or two of work. After clearing a path between two looms he took a few minutes pulling the junk out from under a table. When it was nicely piled up he glanced at the swept aisle.

It was thicker than when he'd swept. He pushed his broom back through it and swept another aisle, and saw that the little bits settled faster than snow fell in a blizzard. He swept faster, covering more ground with less care and managed to do another aisle and still clean the main path again. There were three sweepers hired this morning; Whitney could keep a dozen full time without fear of idling them.

He didn't hear the lunch whistle; he heard the chipper stop, heard the presses shut down and then he met the other guides at the door. They were all covered with bits of woody pulp and exhausted from chasing piles of it around the wooden floor. "How do they work were, day-in and day-out?" Sawyer asked McCrory, who looked like Father Christmas rendered in pulp. While they only had a few minutes to appreciate the relative quiet, eat some bread and cheese for lunch and sip some hot tea someone had brewed, another guide showed up. "Did you hear? The Ice Bridge formed last night." The Ice Bridge was the only respite from winter's quiet. They could afford to quit at the end of the day.

"Thank God," said Sawyer. "I don't know how they work in here all day."

"They probably got families," said McCrory, pulling on a piece of pulp snagged in his bristled chin.

"Good for them," said Sawyer. A family wasn't something he'd grown up with and wasn't something he'd ever sought.

Some Canadians were already on the ice, dragging down scrap lumber, when Sawyer and his mates descended the gorge walls. They brought their own tools and wood: scrap lumber, four stools, scavenged nails, two hammers, and a homemade distillery. It only took a few hours and they were set up. Hammer the boards into a drafty lean-to and prop it up on a flat ledge of ice, set down some flat rocks to build a fire to keep the still cooking. On either side of the ice were the rocky cliffs and before them was the falls, half-shrouded in ice. On pathways, the customers came when the mill changed shifts. By nightfall a half dozen lean-tos had set up temporary shop on the ice covered river. Blankets hung for doors, to contain the heat of the cooking fires.

Somewhere in the middle of the ice was an invisible line that separated the U.S. from Canada, and all the lean-tos were situated well out in the middle. If Officer Knox or his Canadian counterpart tried to arrest them they'd delay their court date until spring, when the thaw came and the ice broke up and swallowed the evidence. In court they always swore they had been on the other side of the border, and so were in the wrong court; whichever court they were in was always the wrong court.

So the guides, and the owner of the souvenir shop on Falls and 2nd, and some shady guys who always seemed to be into something other than work, set up Ice City and the rest of the drinking public watched their money go twice as far by the glow of the kerosene lamps. And what a view to enjoy moonshine with!

Sawyer worked with Calvin, Black Sam, Old Al and McCrory that first crisp afternoon to nail their shack together. Calvin had scavenged boards from a fence, with nails still in them. "This is better than last year," McCrory said loudly, the roar of the falls making them all talk like they were back in the pulp factory. "Sam you got the fixins cooking?"

"I seen the ice forming a couple days ago and got the corn and sugar. Even got some brewer's yeast this year. It's supposed to make the juice in a day or so. Should have some by the time I get back there." Sam had the advantage of living over a stable, which gave him easy access to corn, if not of the highest quality. He was gone for two hours, and returned with a burlap sack in a bucket. They untied the top of the sack and saw the pungent mash fermenting in the bottom. It was already watery on top. "We got the juice alright," Old Al crowed with glee. "Not it's time to heat it up."

Sam also owned the still, found in a junk pile with burst seams. He'd repaired it lovingly. It was copper, made by an unknown craftsman. Sam carefully cleaned it after each use and its output was liquid gold. McCrory's fire had burned down to a nice bed of coals and they set up the still, squat in the fire. "This should start giving us corn whiskey by sunset," Sam judged after the still had absorbed some heat and he could hear the contents bubbling and popping. "I put a lot of sugar and yeast in it. It'll go down hot. Meanwhile we need to get another batch of fixins going."

It was McCrory's turn to steal the corn and sugar. He returned an hour later. "Knox saw me coming out of the livery stable with the corn," he said, a little breathlessly. "He followed me a little ways, but I guess he found someone else to badger."

"He don't usually care about this," said Sam.

"Must be bucking for promotion," Old Al dismissed him. "But keep an eye out whoever's turn it is next. I saw Knox bust a guy's head open once with that stick of his."

"Sam and I'll shuck this and get it started," said McCrory, "Sawyer and Al, and Calvin, set up the stools and melt some ice. If I remember from last year, we're going to want to cut this by half."

"We could try aging it a little this time," said Sawyer. "I got so sick last year from this stuff."

"That's your mistake," joked Sam, "you see how we make it. Why would you drink it?"

Next to Leona's photograph of the tour guides of '56 was a photograph of Queen Victoria, half-covered with a dusty brown derby. The hat belonged to Willy Wabash, a singer who played the bill at the Cataract Theater as the 'Young Irish Tenor', then came down to Ice City after the show. Willy was barely twenty, but he'd learned to drink. Sawyer was pouring that night with McCrory and Willy was knocking back their swill twice as fast as any man on the ice that night. "You could kill yourself, sucking down this stuff like that," said McCrory, pouring three more shots as requested. The moonshine had a pinkish tint to it—too much sugar in the fixins—and McCrory had pronounced the first jar, "only drinkable for he who already has a snootful."

"I consider it my duty to leave this shop dry!" announced Wabash, who tried to make this statement standing on top of his stool but ended up slipping off and spilling his glass.

"You wanna be careful, Mr. Wabash," said Sawyer, helping him up, "aside from hurting yourself, that rotgut will eat right through the ice."

"Gentlemen," Wabash announced, "You've been very kind. Everyone in this town has been very kind. In repayment, let me share a little secret." He waited a long minute, until McCrory and Sawyer and a mill worker named Peters gave him their attention. "I'm... not really Irish." He smiled, smug with his own cleverness. "My mother was German, and I'm told my father's name was Waldek, whatever that makes him, I never met the gentleman. I was raised in Boston, where many Irish live. And the first time I sang, the manager of the establishment said to me," Willy took a sip, "you sound a little Irish, no doubt from being around them so much, and if you want to sing for your supper, you'll do better if you tell folks you're Irish. The fellow even thought up a good name for me. Willy Wabash." He finished his glass. "Only you, my dear friends, know the truth. Drinks for everyone!"

He fell again, and Sawyer struggled with his own slippery footing helping him up. He poured a shot for the mill worker who then headed home laughing a little. "Let's give him a few straight from the still," he whispered to McCrory, "so we can get home tonight."

"Gentlemen," Wabash was back on his feet, standing at the opening to the shack, one hand holding back the horse blanket they'd nailed up, the other holding a glass of pure corn alcohol, "I am offering a wager." His voice barely carried over the falls. "I am wearing a derby tonight, the finest made anywhere." He waved the hat in one wildly swinging hand and set his glass on the counter with the other. "I stake this fine hat, given to me by Queen Victoria herself, on the occasion of my debut before her Majesty, for having the sweetest voice ever heard in the British Isles," he paused to down more and Sawyer topped it off immediately. "Thank you, barkeep," Willy said in a softer tone, "and thanks for your silence." Speaking again to the entire gorge, "I am wagering this fine hat that I'm the last man standing on the ice tonight!"

A few men came over to Sawyer's bar so they went back to pouring the watered stuff, and they tried to match Willy shot for shot. And, true to his wager, Willy sent them all home, some over a friendly shoulder. As midnight approached, the mill workers headed back to get enough sleep for a sick day of work. Soon only Willy was left on the ice with Sawyer and McCrory, both of whom were anxious to get back on solid land and get warm. "Gentlemen," said Wabash, now back on the pure stock, "I salute the United States of America!" and he knocked it back. He didn't show the effects; he didn't slur his speech, and his eyes weren't glassy; he just couldn't keep both feet on the ice too well. "To the birthplace of liberty."

"It'll be dawn soon," sighed McCrory, and Willy upended his drink and himself, and when he slipped this time his head bounced off the ice and he lay still and quiet on the ice. McCrory and Sawyer looked at each other. Dead? Before celebrating the end of the night they felt obligated to check his pulse. It was there, and they felt his breath; neither wanted to smell it. "What's his tab?"

McCrory went behind the bar and counted empty mason jars. "Well, he personally drained a jar of straight corn, three jars watered, a half jar all water."

Sawyer searched the singer's pockets and found two ten dollar gold pieces. "Well, he's welcome to the river. And this nicely covers the rest, with compensation for the cold I've caught waiting all night for him to pass out." He tossed the other gold piece to McCrory. They set him on the bar to wake up and were on their way back when McCrory recalled the wager. "I say the hat belongs to you or me."

"You can have it," said Sawyer, yawning and feeling the gold piece in his pocket.

And so McCrory wore the derby—Queen Victoria's own—for a year, until Leona staked him to whiskey and became the third—no, fourth—owner. It was proudly hung on the wall by a print of the Queen, acquired especially for the purpose.

On quiet nights, late at night, that was when the pulse of the village calmed and all was quiet. Taverns were dark and silent. Shops were shuttered or their windows were dark silhouettes of CLOSED signs. No clattering horses hooves on the paved street, no rumble and hiss and whistle of trains, no sounds but from a few night birds in the trees.

Sawyer woke at this time of night more frequently, his throat sore. It had gotten worse since the summer came. Rising from his bed, trying to minimize the squeak of the iron springs from a craving for privacy in a boarding house, he pulled out his top dresser drawer and got out the paper envelope from the doctor. He sprinkled a little of the powder into a glass of water, mixed it up, held the glass to the dim light of the window, and watched the milky solution swirl. It would usually soothe his throat enough to let him sleep, but not so soon that he couldn't look out the window, see the signs on the buildings too dimly lit in the flickering gas lights to read. The rush of the river and the roar of the falls were a backdrop to the nighttime carousing of stray dogs, or the night cop checking front doors, or the screeching of an owl. The sound of the falls would fill his room and fill his mind, and that was when he knew he was on his way to sleep.

The house was a quiet one, sounds didn't travel, so quiet that Elizabeth Purdy, the ex-schoolteacher from Corning who had come to Niagara and played piano at the Cataract Theater, could practice downstairs and not disturb the upstairs. She owned the stone house at 3rd and Falls and let out rooms to boarders.

The other boarders were mill workers. Two of them shared one room, working different shifts, neither one spending any time in the house. Sawyer had talked to them a few times and learned they came from Eastern Europe and were saving up to head out west. They had let the room last spring; now it was this spring; Sawyer also knew that they drank most of their pay more often than not, and had been good customers of his last winter on the ice. Armand the Dutchman—as he was known in the house - was the other boarder, and while he wasn't too bright, nor spoke English well, he was friendly. He was also pretty deaf from working in the mill.

"Jesus," groaned Sawyer one summer evening, pulling off his boots while sitting on the narrow front stoop with Liz, who'd made a pitcher of lemonade, "I'm doing well but I'm going to die in my carriage. Three tours today and all of them full up. I think Sadie wants to quit." He was proud of his business decision. The Falls Street spot was very lucrative. Knox was right; even five dollars a week didn't hurt. Sawyer barely used his megaphone; people off the train piled into the restaurants, then thronged his booth. He raised his price by a dollar when Knox collected his bribe, and three weeks later by twenty-five cents more, and he still turned business away.

"How about a bath?" she asked, smiling.

Sawyer bathed as business demanded it, which meant weekly during the winter and almost daily during the summer. Elizabeth had once charged him an extra nickel for hot baths, until one delightfully cold winter day. It had been the fourth day in a row that Niagara lay smothered beneath a blizzard that stopped all business and shut everyone indoors. On that day the tour guide and his landlady had shared a bottle of claret. Ms. Purdy took to spirits like a babe to walking, clumsily but enthusiastically, and they began to see each other in a different light.

He first met Liz when he moved into her house a year after she'd been at the Cataract, but he suspected she looked moth-eaten when she first arrived. The first thirty-five years of dowdiness still showed in her wardrobe, but the last three in a dance hall had put a spark into her blue-gray eyes, a spark that Sawyer saw that winter day. They dimmed the kerosene lamp and danced to her gramophone, and Liz sang snatches of the songs. Her voice had a sensuous edge Nature had otherwise denied her. When they began to dance close, the week since Sawyer's last bath made him too odiferous for Liz, who was more refined in that area. So they pursued the mutual seduction by preparing his bath.

That first time it was very dark and chilly in the basement where the great enameled bathtub sat, but there was quiet and privacy. As they stoked up the fire in the basement to heat the water, they sipped more claret, Liz softly sang the love ballads that young lovers asked for at the theater, and the wind howled, somewhat lovingly, outside. Sawyer carried two great iron kettles of steaming water from the fireplace and poured them into the tub. Clouds of steam rose, a shroud of warmth in the cold dark. When they had half-filled the tub they began adding cold water from the pump until Liz's hand could accept the temperature.

"Ohhh," Sawyer began undressing and when modesty was face to face with seduction, Liz proceeded to undress herself and share the bath. Thereafter Liz Purdy had a special relationship with her favorite boarder; they were bathing partners.

This hot August night a bath was tempting, but he feared he'd fall asleep in the tub, and he lovingly, reluctantly, declined. She went into bed, after giving him a lingering kiss.

'Sawyer', began the note slipped beneath his door a few days later, 'I am going to buy a larger tub and need the old one moved to the front of the cellar. The delivery man will remove it from there. Could you move the tub for me? We might find a chance to use it Saturday night.' It was signed with her stylish 'E'.

He had just set a personal record of twenty-one people in one day, and this was not how he'd planned to end the day. Sadie moved mighty slowly on the homeward stretch. His feet were burning and his voice was gone. The last activity he needed after busting his feet all day was to drag an iron tub across the cellar floor, but he was obliging. He changed into an old shirt, keeping his working wardrobe intact; shirts were expensive and he was saving his money. By the stairs a pile of tools sat, some shovels and a rusted hoe; Sawyer dug out an iron pry bar he remembered seeing there. He had it in mind to somehow lever the tub, rather than try dragging it.

The cellar stairs were in the northeast corner of the basement, and the tub was in the southwest corner. There was also a wall of planks most of the way across the basement, in part for separate storage areas, and in part because it provided Liz and Sawyer with some advance notice of visitors. Today it meant the tub was in the farthest possible corner.

The tub was two and a half feet high, sitting on curved iron legs. He tried to lift it, but the legs were jammed into the floor. Pulling up, putting his back into it, he gave it his best shot and it wasn't enough. "What the hell?" He slid the bar beneath one end, and tried to tip it. The tub held, and he braced himself to throw his weight against the tub and pull hard on the bar.

It rose an inch, then settled heavily with a 'clunk'. "What's holding it?" He rested a moment, and gave a hard push; the tub rose again but there was definitely something besides dirt beneath it. He knelt and peered under and saw that one of the legs was jammed into some sort of crevice he'd never seen before, but then, he'd never tried to lift the tub before. He slid the rod as close to the mystery crevice as he could, levered it in as deeply as he could, then, grunting under the strain, used the tub and the rod to open the crevice. A floor stone moved another smidgen; there was something under that stone.

Someone, probably the builder, had cut a hole in the basement floor, but covered it so well that it was hard to see it unless one knew to look for it. Thirty minutes of hard, grunting struggle later he tipped the tub on its side, and was able, with the iron bar, to lever that stone and expose a hole. Someone, and he doubted it was Liz, had left a small, moldy book in the hole. With a modest amount of grunting and cursing he worked the tub to the stairs.

Floorboards overhead creaked. Putting the stone back over the hole, he went up to his room, leaving the book on his nightstand. He wasn't much for reading, much less someone's handwriting. When he heard Liz returning, he took the book downstairs and showed her his find.

"A hole in the basement?" Liz said, resting on a love seat in her room. He handed her the book. "And you found this in the cellar?"

"In an old hole in the basement," he said.

"It's a diary," she read. "By someone named Cleary." Her lover yawned. She held the book under her arm. "I'll take it up to my room."

In December, a quiet time for both of them, they went to Buffalo for the operation. Because it was winter and the ride to Niagara was long, they rented a nice room in a modest hotel near the hospital. Sawyer's doctor, Dr. Bergman, trained in Boston and only as old as Sawyer, had given him the most hopeful diagnosis of the three doctors he'd visited. "I think I can remove the growth," he'd suggested last March. That December day he took a fresh look at Sawyer's throat. With Liz sitting watching, knotting a silk kerchief in her nervous hands, using that mirror probe and forcing Sawyer's head back until the patient gasped in pain, Bergman looked for several minutes as Sawyer's eyes teared with the pain of his aching neck. "Do you still have an irritating tickle?" He backed out of Sawyer's mouth, and his patient nodded.

"I sure do," he croaked, "the powder you gave me helps, but it don't ever go away."

Bergman nodded. "Well, the bad news you've already heard." He set down his probe. Dressed in his suit, he leaned against his desk, a sturdy mahogany structure with ornately carved legs. "There're two ways I've read of getting rid of cancers. The first one is to go in with a scalpel and cut away." Sawyer and Liz paled; her hand found his and squeezed. "That's easily done with cancer in the mouth, or cancer of the skin." Bergman took off his glasses and used his handkerchief to clean his lenses as he explained. "Your cancer is on the edge of what one can do with a scalpel." Sawyer's jaw dropped a moment. Liz's face paled. "It'll take a while and it'll be painful, and the likelihood you'll have a voice again is poor." Sawyer, who had counted on going back to his old calling, lost that little bit of hope. "The other way, and it's a newer way, is to use a mild form of lye. You swallow a solution first, a milky solution, that helps coat your throat and stomach. Then I go in with a probe, but instead of cutting, I have a small sponge on the tip of the probe, and the sponge is soaked in lye, and I dab at the tumor with the lye. It burns the tumor off."

"You have much luck with that?" Sawyer asked, failing to mask his fear.

Bergman scratched his chin. "I've read of it in medical journals. The good part of it is that the lye is milder than the scalpel. I'll go in and apply the lye as frequently as it can be tolerated," Sawyer winced, "for as long as we see any growth. Since the lye is very diluted I shouldn't hurt your vocal cords, but it will probably take days, perhaps a week or two, to get rid of the tumor."

Liz cleared her throat. "Doctor, which method do you feel is the best?

Bergman put his glasses back on. "Well, any sawbones can go in with a scalpel and cut. But I would feel more like a butcher than a doctor. And I would assume you'll lose some or all of your voice that way. The lye treatment is new, rather experimental, and I've never done it before, but its beauty is its simplicity. I believe I can do it and it will leave you with as strong a voice as you've got now. It is, however, a prolonged treatment," Bergman swallowed, "it could take weeks, and multiple applications, and is therefore more costly."

"We're prepared to pay for the care," Liz said, breaking the silence. Then native caution intervened. "How expensive?"

Liz had savings, and they tapped them. Christmas was a quiet holiday for the two in Buffalo. They wrote to their friends back in Niagara, sent some gifts to Liz's mother who still lived in Corning. Sawyer having been an orphan he had no parents to give presents to, but he found a risqué postcard and mailed it to Calvin. On Christmas Eve they ate a simple meal of vegetable soup in their room. It was chilly, even with the fire burning. "I miss our house," Liz said, but smiled to show she wasn't sad. She had found a sprig of juniper, then made some popcorn they strung on cotton thread.

"Sing for me," he asked in his scratchy voice.

"Sing what?" she asked.

"A Christmas song. 'Silent Night,'" he whispered.

He managed to give his fiancé the slip and found a goldsmith. With the last of his savings, he bought a ring with an opal, Liz's favorite stone. "You probably could do better," he proposed with his scratchy voice, "but I'm grateful you haven't. Soon as we're done here, I'd like to be your husband." The day after New Years' was greeted, Sawyer was admitted to Sisters Hospital; Bergman wanted to keep him in the hospital for the first week of treatments.

Blinded by a bright light shining from behind the doctor's head, Sawyer lay flat on a couch with his head hanging off the edge of the cushion, as far back as he could tolerate. "I want as clear a passage to your throat as possible," Bergman explained as he tried to turn Sawyer's head. "If I touch your throat, it'll burn your throat just as much as the tumor." His throat was raw and he closed his eyes when he heard

Bergman directing his assistant, a young man dressed in a shirt, tie, and butcher's smock, studying under Bergman, "carefully, carefully. There. Just a few drops at first." Then Bergman came towards him and Sawyer closed his eyes. His mouth was filled by his doctor's fist, and then he smelled the lye.

"AAAOOUUUWWWW—" Sawyer choked off his own scream. The acid must have dripped off the sponge and seared a pathway clear to his bowels. A hot burning sensation in his throat pulsed for five minutes, his eyes teared, his bladder released.

"That was a good start," Bergman tried to calm his patient, letting him raise his head. "I put three drops of lye right on the growth. I know it hurts like blazes, but from the way it burned away the growth I'm very confident this treatment will be successful." Sawyer nodded slightly. "Would you like some morphine for the pain?"

Sawyer shook his head. "Maybe some whiskey," he whispered.

After the pain eased, and he drank another cup of milk, he assumed the position again and felt Bergman going back in. He knew what to expect this time, and braced himself, and then the white-hot pain hit again. Again a scream tore out of him, but as soon as Bergman's hand was out he closed his mouth and cut it off.

On the fifth pass Bergman's hand was a little tired, a little shaky, and he touched the wall of Sawyer's throat and then had to back out and go in quickly with a water swab to dilute it. "I'm sorry, Sawyer, that's going to take a little while to heal. I'll try to be more careful." Bergman paused after that last one. He wiped his forehead and let himself sit and rest for half an hour, sipping a cup of tea. "I think one more application should do it for today," he announced. "From what I can see the progress is remarkable. I've already burned off half the growth. We might not need to do this for more than another day or two."

It was excellent news, but just then, his eyes streaming tears and his throat on fire, Sawyer choked off another scream.

Liz fretted in a waiting room as a January blizzard howled outside. Twisting and turning and holding tight to the new ring on her finger, kissing it twice for luck, she made at least seven promises to God, looking out the windows at the city streets disappearing under the snow, wind whipping it into whirlwinds. "Still nothing compared to last year," she smiled wryly. Then, as she had been doing constantly, she looked up at the hands of the clock.

At three o'clock Bergman came out to see her. "The node has been almost completely burned off," he said, looking drained but sounding pleased. "I think at this rate maybe just tomorrow will finish the job. I see no other growths, and I see no reason why he shouldn't make a complete recovery."

"How is his voice?" she asked.

"Well," Bergman almost smiled, "this treatment is painful and Sawyer has given me several good, loud screams. I think his voice will be just fine."

Liz nodded, and then began to cry, from relief that he would live, relief that the operation was successful. A nurse came out to sit with Liz and got her some hot tea. Liz struggled to keep her eyes dry. "I'm just so relieved," she finally got out.

"Sure you are," said the nurse in labored English, her accent perhaps German, perhaps Polish. "Doc-tor Bergman is the very best. Your husband's gotten the best care available. You be having arguments with Mr. Jackson in no time." Liz finally dozed for an hour in the waiting room, and the nurse gently draped a blanket over her.

She saw him that evening in the private room, their other indulgence. "Hi... I'm alive," he whispered as she came in. She kissed him seventeen times and they both began to cry uncontrollably. His voice was a whisper and he was drinking milk by the gallon to coat his stomach and throat, though it was giving him some flatulence. "Doc says I'm in good shape," Sawyer whispered. "But it feels like the world's worst sore throat."

"That's wonderful. Too bad it's winter out there, dear," said Liz, blinking, "or we might open a window."

Bergman was a good prognosticator; the next day he peered a long while into the narrow passage and finally pulled his fist out of Sawyer's throat and said softly, "I don't see any more cancer and I know your throat hurts like hell, but the inflammation will go down in a few days and you should have your normal voice back before then." The doctor was drained but beaming. "I'm very pleased we could save your voice." Sawyer held out his hand and shook Bergman's firmly, nodding his thanks.

That night, as he slept in the hospital, Liz returned to their room and remembered the diary they'd found. She had carried it with her on this trip intending to read it, but couldn't think of anything but Sawyer's illness, until now. She sat by a reading lamp and opened it, cautiously, for the pages were old and moldy. She read enough of it to understand the writer's story, but found his story sad, depressing, rather uninteresting, and the handwriting a strain on her eyes. She put it back in her suitcase and didn't pick it up again.

When Sawyer was released they traveled to Corning to see Liz's mother, where they stood before a minister and Sawyer put a gold band on Liz's finger, and then, at Liz's insistence, to New York to see a few shows. They returned to Niagara Falls in March, the worst of the winter passed and Sawyer carried Liz over the threshold of the stone house.

"I guess it's fitting," he said, "that we end our honeymoon in Niagara."

The touring business didn't get started until warm weather, usually late April at best. The last two winters Sawyer had had to work at Whitney's mill to keep him in bread and beer until the gorge froze over for moonshining, but this year he was idle for his first time in memory. When they'd left for Buffalo they'd closed up the house and the boarders had moved out. "We're using up your savings," he said.

"And what did I save for? A rainy day," she said. "And now the sun is coming out. Besides, I like having the house to ourselves." Of course, the changes meant greater privacy but less income. Sawyer had had years of practice being idle in the winter. "Right," his wife explained, "when you were my boarder, I had to clean up after you and the others. Now that it's you and me, unless we want to hire some stupid girl to help clean, why don't you help with some of the chores?" It was a reasonable request, which didn't make it any more palatable for Sawyer.

"Washing and scrubbing up?" he said, in the whisper that was still the loudest he could be. "That's woman's work."

"Yes, but you've got a month before you can go out and earn us a living. If you don't help me with the woman's work, I'll have to hire a stupid girl, and we'll soon be poor."

He sighed and acquiesced.

"I've done up a list of chores," she said, "starting with Fabio's old room, especially the cigar smoke in the back privy."

Not surprisingly, he had no burning desire to scrub the walls in the indoor privy. He had a good head for reading, and he found the diary.

"Oh, look at you," he said in delight when he found it stuffed in a cupboard he was cleaning. It was the perfect reason to stop. Liz had mentioned reading part of it while he was in the hospital. She hadn't cared for it, something about the old war with the British. Nothing wrong with a good war story, he decided, and picked it up. "Nehemiah Cleary," he read aloud in his whisper, "and this was his house." He set the diary down a minute and looked at the papered walls, the old wooden beams stretching across the ceiling. "Thought this was just an old stone house." He read some more. "Fort Schlosser?" He knew where Fort Schlosser used to be. There was a dock near there, still called the Schlosser dock. He really hadn't appreciated what Fort Schlosser had been. And the Portage Road? Yep, he knew about it, but there was a lot of stuff here he hadn't known about. Sawyer liked to think he knew a bit of local history, being a guide and all, but he knew nothing. He was still reading it at ten that night when Liz came in late from playing at the Cataract Theater, just on Wednesday nights, 'because I don't want to forget how to play'.

"What're you reading, Sawyer?" she asked, shaking rain off her coat and poking the coals of the cook stone to heat up some water for tea.

"This diary that we found in the basement," he answered.

She curled her lip. "I thought I threw it out. I didn't care for it."

"I know. But it's about the fellow that grew up in this house. Son of the man who built it. And it's full of local history," he said, "and that's part of what I make my living off. There's a lot of stuff here I didn't know about. About the Porters, about the invasion of Queenston. I clean forgot we invaded Queenston. All you hear about is Lundy's Lane these days."

She made her tea, came into the parlor and sat down next to her husband. "Did you get a chance to scrub down the walls in the second story back?" she asked. He shook his head, his eyes locked on the diary. "You said you'd do that," she reminded him in that gentle whining voice she used before truly nagging.

"I'm reading, dear," he reminded her. "I'll do it tomorrow. There's only a few pages of this anyway."

She sipped her tea and looked for the dozenth time at a picture book of Boston she'd bought last winter in Buffalo. She wouldn't mind moving to Boston. She fell asleep next to him, and he noticed her only after he'd finished the diary and re-read parts of it. His imagination was filled with the dire tale of war and pain Cleary had recorded. Wouldn't the tourists eat this stuff up.

The next day was a warm one, so he saddled up Sadie and rode out to see his cronies. "Sawyer," he heard Black Sam call him, waving and smiling as he approached. The others looked up from their idleness and cheered his return. He'd like nothing better than to yell back, but his voice was still soft, still recuperating. Not until he was close enough for a regular conversation did he dare to speak. Shaking hands all around, he grinned; he'd missed these clowns.

"So how's it going to be this year?" he asked Black Sam.

"Slow, real slow," said Sam.

"You always say it'll be slow," said Calvin, "every year you say that."

"It could be good," Sam said, looking up as though forecasting the weather, "but. . . it feels like it'll be slow. How are you feeling? Guess the operation was successful?"

"Yea, it went well," he answered, "had a bitch of a sore throat for a couple of weeks, but I'm all better."

"Well, you missed a nasty winter," said Calvin.

"Hey," said Sawyer, "I was only in Buffalo. It snowed there more than it did here."

"Yea," said Al, like Sawyer hadn't spoken, "it was so cold, and with that wind, we couldn't even set up Ice City this year. No one could sit out there long enough to get their whistles wet."

"Calvin and me worked since the middle of January in Whitney's mill. Man would go deaf doing that too long. You picked a good winter to miss."

"Yea, and now he's a married man."

"Liz is a good lady. You best be good to her."

"So," Sam asked, "you going back to Falls Street and make the big money again? Or are you going to retire, live off your property? You don't need to horn in our peanuts, do you?" He added a too-hearty smile at the end.

Sawyer heard Sam's question, and knew then that he wasn't entirely welcome back here on River Road. They were chums, and they always worked here together, because they all needed the money. Not that they actually competed, no, they took turns pitching tours to whomever came by. Still, if there was one less guide they would all get a few more bucks in their pockets. This winter he'd pictured a lazy summer with his friends, just like the old days. But maybe he would move back to Falls Street.

Sam had picked up a sack of unshelled peanuts so they all occupied themselves breaking open the shells and snacking. "I'd be bored not doing the tours," Sawyer admitted. "And," he glanced at Sam with dismay, "with my operation, maybe Knox will give me a discount this year. I won't be able to yell like I used to." Sam seemed to smile more genuinely. "Hey, you guys get to work. I'll stop by later. Save me some of them peanuts."

He rode back down to the spot he'd rented last year, and watched the traffic. He parked his wagon so the TOURS sign was plainly visible to the travelers. It was quiet, of course, as it always was in early spring. He didn't even try to test his voice with his sales pitch, as the trains came in mostly empty. He just sat on the bench in front of the train station and watched the town. Knox came by later in the day to congratulate him on the successful operation. Sawyer nodded and half-smiled. "How's your voice?" Knox asked.

"Well, as you can tell, I don't have all my strength back, but the doctor said it should be fine with a little more rest."

"Coming back, then? To Falls Street?"

"Yea, I kind of like it here," Sawyer answered.

"Well, if you want to pay for your permit now, what with business being slow, I'll only have to charge you three dollars for the week," Knox offered. "Or you can get credit until the Fourth and it'll be the usual five."

Sawyer reached into his pocket and dug out the fee. "I'm ready to make an investment," he said, and the cop gave him a salute with the tip of his baton as he strolled off. So he was back in business, though he had no customers. "Just as well," he said to Sadie, "don't want to strain my money-maker." The train came in three times, and no more than ten people got off each time. They all walked off or took rides in the other direction and left town, locals returning home from somewhere.

Sawyer brought the diary with him, expecting it might be quiet. He started to read some favorite parts again and the hours rolled by. "This

Cleary fellow, he was a confused boy," Sawyer told Sadie. "Finds out his folks are Loyalists, but he joins the New York militia to meet women. This would all be a very sad joke except for the fact that he did." He lost himself in another passage. "And the British burned everything on the American side," he remembered some teacher in the orphanage telling the class. By early afternoon, with a cold wind coming from Canada, the streets were empty. "Well, I lost money today," Sawyer said to Sadie, "but I'll be busy down here sooner than those blokes up the road will be."

Then it rained for three days. Cold, driving rain, almost sleet, chilling to the bone. Winter charged back and nobody went outside except for necessities. Sawyer read, and reread, the diary. *I'm going to make my tour the best one in town*, he decided, *and it's all coming from this diary*. He even scribbled some of the tales on the backs of postcards, so he wouldn't forget the rich details. The first day of sunshine, a week later, he rode back up to see his friends. He wasn't very competitive, as he promptly started sharing the stories he'd read in the diary. "So what's the story with Schlosser's dock?" said McCrory.

"Well, Schlosser was the fort that guarded this end of the Portage," Sawyer warmed up.

"And that was what?" Sawyer had just explained the Portage. McCrory was a bit slow.

"The traders had to get out of their canoes and have this stuff carried around the falls. The road they used, it's the Portage Road."

"Yea, but what's there today?" Sam asked.

"No bazaars. No souvenir shops, right?" asked Calvin.

Sawyer was disappointed in his friends. Souvenirs, knicknacks, just more of the same garbage. "It's history, fellows," he said as loudly as he dared, "history." They looked unimpressed. "Then there's the Battle of Queenston," he added without much hope.

"Yea," Calvin said, "but I don't ever get down as far as Queenston. That's a half-day's ride and back. And besides, we lost that battle. I mean, maybe the Canadians'd like to see it, but they'll probably hire a Canadian to show 'em." The others nodded sour agreement. "Only place I get asked about is Lundy's Lane. And it's not much of a story. Americans fight the British all day, the British get their butts whipped but the Americans are too tired to hold the field and go home. Some story. And I'm sure not going up there with that sad story. It's not entertaining, you get no tip."

"What's it say about the falls? Anything good?" asked Al. He still fancied himself a retired guide.

Sawyer gently sifted through the now-familiar pages. "No, not about the falls. Except," he recalled, and added urgently, "that Augustus Porter owned Goat Island."

"Judge Porter?" asked Al. "That's not news. Porters still own it. Charge a buck to get to it, too, which is also not news."

"Did you guys know," Sawyer pressed on, "that during the War of 1812—"

"The what?" asked McCrory.

"The Second War with the British," he said, "that the army had a contract with the Porters. Judge Porter was supposed to supply the militia up here with food and guns and stuff. And this diary talks about how the Judge bought up these old rusty muskets, wouldn't even fire, most of 'em, and how the Judge bought biscuits that were rotten, and tents with big holes in 'em."

That caught a couple of ears. "Really? So the Judge was a crook?" Scandal was always welcome as a source of entertainment. "He get arrested?"

Sawyer back-pedaled, realizing he'd touched a nerve. "It wasn't like he was a crook. He wasn't ever charged with nothing. I think the army wasn't too happy with him," he saw their faces lose interest, "but that's what happened."

"So the Judge was a crook and got away with it?" asked Sam. That worked even better.

Sawyer saw how this was going and decided it would be better to not tell them the story about the Ice Bridge. "Yeah, so the man who wrote this diary, it was his father built the house Liz and I live in. The stone house. Says in the diary it's one of the oldest in the area."

"Well, I believe that," said Al. "My paw told me that old house has been around as long as anyone can remember. Does it get cold in there? Stone's kind of cold, compared to wood."

"Oh, no, you get a good fire in the oven and it's cozy as can be," Sawyer said.

"An' being a newlywed don't hurt either, does it?" Calvin joked. Sawyer took the kidding, and then left them again to try and scare up business, walking away smiling but feeling defeated. Did no one else take any interest in this history? He went back to the stone house and picked up the diary again. He had parts of it committed to memory.

In his former circumstances he'd still be out there, hoping to make money as a cabbie if tours were slow, but with no need to earn his room and board, he had decided he could afford to just be a tour guide. Trouble was, that was strictly a warm weather occupation. The damn weather stayed cold through May and into June. "I won't be giving a tour until the Fourth of July for sure," he complained.

"And you haven't done a thing on the list," Liz reminded him. Out of sheer boredom he picked it up.

Scrubbing gets things clean, with enough elbow grease. But getting the stink of bad cigars out of the indoor privy was going to take more than just lye and hot water and elbow grease. It was also taking a layer of skin off his hands, and his nose was suffering, too. There was a window, thank heaven, or he wouldn't be able to breathe. "I think the trick here might be another layer of paint on the walls," he decided after an afternoon of scrubbing. The plaster was thick and now it was very clean, but there was no fooling the nose. The little window, probably the smallest a window could be and still be called a window, was the reason the room smelled so. Shut the door and no air circulated at all. "And maybe we can burn something nicer smelling in here. Use one stink to chase away another. I think I'll just go ahead and not discuss it first with Her Majesty. I can do it before she's home. And I'm not wasting another day of my life up here with a bar of soap," Sawyer pronounced, adding more experience to the mantle of married life.

He went on his errand and was returning to the house with a tin bucket of whitewash and some sandalwood when Black Sam waved him down from his buggy. "Hey, Sawyer! Sawyer!"

"Hey, Sam," he waved. "So, how's business?"

Sam nodded agreeably. "Actually got five live ones yesterday. Listen, you remember the story you were telling us about Judge Porter selling rusty guns and bad tents and stuff to the army in 1812?"

Sawyer nodded. "Well," said Sam, "I included that in my tour, just a little piece on the Judge."

"How'd they like it?" Sawyer asked, the final assessment of any story.

"After paying a buck to get on Goat Island they believe it," Sam answered. "But Knox heard me telling it yesterday. And today, I'm not even giving a tour, just taking folks to a hotel, and Knox stops me in the street. Stands there, holds my horse's bridle. Says 'the Porter family is the cornerstone of this town and I shouldn't be libeling them with such made up stories.'"

Sawyer looked dumbfounded. "Knox said that?" This the same cop who collected 'sanitary fees'? "Since when are the Porters the cornerstone of Niagara? I just figured they got here first and bought it all up before the rest of us did. We call that luck."

Sam shrugged. "Well, someone didn't like hearing that story. Knox tells me 'I hear you tell folks that lie again and I'll tear up your license on the spot.' And he's telling me this right in front of customers!" That, clearly, had been the greatest insult. "Anyway, just wanted to tell you that you might want to be careful who you tell that story to."

"You okay, Sam?" Sawyer asked, "you in any trouble with Knox? Maybe I should try to talk to him?"

Sam shook his head vigorously. "No, the bastard gets his money and I don't tell no stories about the Porters and everything will be fine. Just wanted to tell you, you should be careful who you tell that story to. Gotta go, my friend." Sawyer waved as his friend tapped his horses with the reins and headed back to Falls Street.

So 'someone' had not liked hearing the story of the supplies scandal in the Second War with the British? Sawyer felt redeemed; so someone else around here did care about history.

Liz was very pleased with the paint and the sandalwood; another newlywed crises resolved. "Can you do the rest of the rooms like that?" Another newlywed crisis erupted.

If he wasn't home he couldn't be expected to paint. So he saddled up Sadie and took the diary with him and headed off one day to visit the places Nehemiah wrote about. First he rode up to Schlosser's Dock. It was still in use as a landing point for passenger boats as well as freight. It had also made history when the Canadians had their rebellion back in '37, being where the Caroline was docked. Sawyer had been a boy in the orphanage then and remembered very little. The rebels had boarded the old tub and cut her loose and set her aflame. It had burned to the water line in the upper rapids. But that was in 1837, that was just Mackenzie's

War, and that was Schlosser's Dock. It just looked like a dock today. Then Sawyer thought to look for the fort.

That was another story. He followed the road for a quarter mile, that being further inland than the fort should have been. The neighborhood there was a wealthy one. And when he found where Fort Schlosser once was, he was looking almost in the front window of Peter B. Porter's mansion. General Porter was dead now, but he'd built a beautiful house, two stories and looking very comfortable. "Help you?" someone asked. The questioner was an old man with a bucket in his right hand. "You have business with the Porters?"

"Good day, sir," Sawyer was surprised. "I was looking for Fort Schlosser."

The old man looked sour, as though his day was constantly interrupted with such requests. "Well, you're close. The front gate was right over where that apple tree is," the man pointed to a flowering apple tree near the road. "I remember seeing the burned logs." He looked at Sawyer as he bore witness. "They burned it, y'know, the British. Actually their heathen Indian allies."

Yep, burned everything on the American side, he knew that. "Follow me," said the old man. He led Sawyer around to the back of the mansion. From there, the man pointed at the house's big stone chimney, two stories tall. "That there is the only marker left of Schlosser, or of the tavern. Porter's built this wing to use it. That's a damn good chimney."

"Does anyone else know about this chimney?" Sawyer asked.

The old man shrugged. "Anyone old as me knows about it. Now you know about it." He seemed satisfied the historical record was safe.

"Well, thanks very much for your time," Sawyer said, his voice distant as he looked at the chimney, and then at the wing of the mansion using it. "God bless, them Porters don't miss a trick. Now they won't even build a chimney if there's one available." He looked around. Visitors wouldn't come here, there was no chance anyone would stumble on this chimney. Shouldn't there be a sign or something? Something to tell them this was all that remained of Fort Schlosser?

Yes, he decided, *there should*. And instead of buying some more whitewash and getting to work on the upstairs bedroom, Sawyer bought some black paint and set about making a sign to mark the site of Fort Schlosser and the neighboring chimney.

'This was Fort Schlosser,' Liz read his work that evening, 'and in the Second War with the British this fort guarded the Portage Road.' Shouldn't you say what the Portage Road was?" Liz asked. "Where did you say the fort was?"

"It's just a hundred feet or so from the chimney. As best I can tell, it's part of the Porter mansion."

"Did they give you permission to put up this sign?" Liz asked. In Sawyer's experience, signs were an exercise in free enterprise. Put it on the sidewalk and you've got business. "You didn't ask them, did you?" He frowned. She raised her left eyebrow; Sawyer now knew that to be a warning sign. "How many signs are you planning to make?"

Good question. He hadn't really thought this project through. "Well, there's Fort Schlosser. Should have a sign on the dock, but that's a pretty busy place, I don't know how well the sign would hold up there. Then, I guess the Portage Road gets a sign. Hmmm. . . this house, I guess, the stone house should get a sign."

"I don't want a sign in front of my house, dear," Liz said. "It's not a tourist stop, it's our home." He didn't know what to say. "History is a good cause, Sawyer, but this is our home and I don't want strangers stopping out front to read this. Besides, it's not historic, it's just a stone house. Houses made of stone do hold up better than wooden ones."

"It's practically the only house that survived," Sawyer pointed out. "The others were burned down in the War."

Liz smiled indulgently. "Dear, if you start putting up signs about what happened here during the Second War with the British, about the only thing you'll accomplish is getting people angry about the war again. You told me what happened when you got folks who wanted to see Lundy's Lane, and if they were British they got the version where the British win, and Americans got the version where the Americans win. It's still a tender topic. You start putting up these signs, you'll just upset folks."

She was right. There was still bad blood between the Americans and the British across the river. She was right. His idea deflated, but he still felt the calling of history. How to respond?

Next morning, before he went off for more whitewash, he opened the diary for the hundredth time and skimmed through. Then he looked at the walls. Stone houses last a good long while. Sawyer wouldn't have known any of this history if the stone house hadn't sheltered the diary so well. Others would come to live in this house after Sawyer and Liz were gone. He knew what to do, and he thumbed to the back and counted. The diary ended with twelve blank pages. *It's just asking me to write my own story*, he decided. *The Stone House Diary, chapter two, by Sawyer Jackson.*

> *I work as a tour guide around the American falls, driving tourists in my buggy. It's a wonderful job, I get to meet interesting people, some not so interesting, and I get to tell them stories. I'm a born storyteller, and the falls are a beauty to work around all summer. I just wish the job could carry me all year.' He started to write his favorite stories. 'The falls came to be called the Honeymoon Capitol when a nephew of the Emperor Napoleon came to visit on his honeymoon.*

He described the pulp mill on Bath Island, the story of how Goat Island got its name—from an ill-fated plan to raise goats on it, not appreciating the severe ice the island is covered in each winter—and some stories of the French trappers who discovered the falls. He gave a very brief summation of the story of the *Caroline*. There were other stories he'd learned. In two days he filled up the blank pages. *But I've got so many more stories*, he protested to the god of touring. Simple solution: he went around the corner and bought more paper and continued writing.

When he had filled eight new pages—to his amazement, as he'd never thought of himself as a scholar—he thought again of how one would locate Fort Schlosser today, or more pointedly, ten years' hence.

> *In order to find it, from Schlosser's dock, walk inland on the Portage Road a quarter mile, until one comes to the home of General Peter Porter. The chimney he's using was part of the mess hall for the soldiers guarding Fort Schlosser.*

And if that created a crowd of the curious out front of the Porter mansion that was just fine with Sawyer.

The Stone House.

> *The house was a boarding house that Liz owned when I met her. We were married this past winter. We kicked out the boarders*

when we got back from Buffalo, where I had my operation. I'm whitewashing now to get rid of the smell of cigars and other noxious smells. It's a cozy house.

Two days later, when the sun came out again, Sawyer rode Sadie down Portage Road to find the old Lewiston encampment. The spring plowing to open up the soil after the winter had commenced. *The Lewiston camp where Cleary and his comrades trained is farmland, which is probably for the best.* Canada remained Canada, the United States had begun expanding westward, not northerly. Leaves were budding on the trees. Sawyer found an old log, mostly rotten, and kicked it over with the toe of his boot. Was it a relic of the barracks? Probably not. Wood just didn't last. It had been forty-three years since this field had been a camp. Farms were more numerous now, the land fertile and the air smelling of the fresh land being turned for planting. Sawyer followed the road along the river, and paused at a spit of land with a good view of the river. This could have been one of the batteries, he guessed. He shaded his eyes and looked across the river at the enemy.

And as for Queenston? Sawyer spent a day whitewashing and the next day after that walked to Prospect Point, rode down the Incline Railway, and paid the drunken lout that rowed folks across to take him to the Canadian shore. He hired another ride and spent an hour getting to Queenston. From the height, he looked across at New York, and saw the point from which he'd viewed Canada.

The slope Nehemiah charged up is still wooded. There's a couple of places where you might guess some barricade had been set up, but you wouldn't know a battle had happened here if it hadn't been written down. The slope is a tough climb, and it must have been a fright to do with folks shooting at you from above. At the top is a marker where General Isaac Brock died. Queenston is still a small village. The river, where Nehemiah crossed, is still a trying boat trip. Must have been a bad trip going in the night.

With Liz accompanying him, Sawyer also made the pilgrimage to Fonthill, as the growing town of Pelham had been renamed. The town had burned during the war, and what had been the Teal's Inn had burned with it. It took an inquiry at the constabulary to find where it had stood. The cab driver stopped the horse and Mr. and Mrs. Jackson stepped out to see a two-story building that was a glass factory. "Missus Teal sold it to Job Wilson, but he only owned it a year before the Americans torched the town. After the war this fellow from York built the glass factory. They make windows, mostly," said the driver, "some bottles, and some drinking cups. Mostly windows. It's good glass. I got some of it in my place."

"Did you know of a woman named Claire Teal?" Sawyer asked.

"Claire Teal?" The cab driver was wizened, perhaps in his fifties. He'd have been a young boy in Claire Teal's time. "I barely remember the inn here, and I remember my mother sending me some times for a bit of sugar, flour, this and that. The woman who ran it was a real quiet, shy kind. Not the sort you'd think of as an innkeeper."

Sawyer felt his pulse pounding, as the story became life. "You wouldn't remember about a man that worked here. Had a bad scar?"

"Oh yeah!" the cabby chuckled. "I remember him. He was scary looking. Some of us kids used to scare each other, say Mister Cleary'll come and get you in the night!"

Liz turned in surprise to Sawyer. "That was his name, wasn't it?"

Sawyer smiled. "Yep. That was his name." To the cabby, "did you know that he and the shy woman, Mrs. Teal, went up to Ottawa and got married?"

The cabby thought a moment. "I thought she run off with some British officer."

Sawyer, remembering the fate of Captain Lightfoot, shook his head. "Nope, she went with Cleary. Did you know he was American?"

The cabby frowned. "How could that be? We was at war then, weren't we? No, I think you got your story wrong. I heard he was wounded at Queenston."

Sawyer nodded agreeably. It was too soon. The pains of that war still stung in the memories of the living. And Sawyer didn't want to offend the driver, not if he and Liz hoped to get back to Niagara, as the cabby could easily just drive off. Niagara was a long walk.

He wrote some notes down, and when he was sitting in his parlor with his pencil, he filled another twenty pages. He glued these new pages to the back of the diary. Then he tucked it into a cigar box and set it on the bottom shelf of the bookcase.

Liz came home one evening in a particularly foul mood. "We're at war."

Sawyer nodded. He'd picked up the paper and seen the headlines. The southern states were withdrawing from the union. South Carolinians fired on a fort in the harbor. "Shooting at our own people," Liz said, shaking her head. "And the people that are coming to the theatre," she complained, "now they all want to hear 'Dixie'. I played it four times tonight, and refused to play it again. I reminded them that they were still in the Union." She made her tea, brought it into the parlor and sat down next to her husband. She picked up the book on Boston. "Have you given any further thought to going to Boston, Sawyer?"

Sawyer had actually nodded off. "What? Boston? I hear it's nice. But I don't know anything about Boston. How would I give tours for a place I don't know? And I'd miss the falls." She said nothing, just leafed through the book again. "We need to get the roof re-shingled," he remembered. "There's a leak in the back bedroom ceiling."

She put the book back on the table. "New roof? And I noticed the plaster cracks are getting longer," she pointed them out on the ceiling. "House needs to be propped up. It's subsiding." She sighed. "Let's just move."

Sawyer frowned. "Move? We do all that work and the house'll be good for another thirty years."

"Why not move now? Let the next owner do all that work."

"What's a house in Boston cost?"

"I have no idea. The only way we can know is to go there."

That wasn't the only way, Sawyer knew well, but also knew when the discussion was at an end. They went to bed shortly after and didn't bring up the issue for a couple of days. Meanwhile, Sawyer went up a ladder and looked at the worn shingles. It was a little scary up there; he couldn't quite get the nerve to get off the ladder and negotiate the slope of the roof. *I don't know much about this*, he worried. *Fellow could fall to his death. Perhaps jacking up the main beam is easier?* With the help of a carpenter, Sawyer made a post and they wrestled it into place, jacking up the beam three inches. He was very pleased until he went upstairs; all the cracks were wider, and going in the other direction. "Went up a little high, did I?" he asked wearily. When Liz got home her jaw dropped a moment, then she shook her head in that way that meant 'pack for Boston'.

That evening, his back aching from the day's labor, he endured Liz's critical review of his work. "Dear, the ceiling now looks like a map of the Ganges delta," she said, unable to choke off a giggle. "I think we need to either get warm weather here faster to keep you out of trouble, or sell this house before you try repairing it anymore."

Sulking, he went out the next day to find his old friends. It was the coldest, foulest May anyone could remember. "Hey, Sawyer," two of them greeted him. "Calvin's gotten a job in that mill," said Black Sam, "he decided he wants regular money."

"I lay you fifty cents he's back out here in three days," said Sawyer, "soon as it warms up. Noise in that mill will deafen him. First peek of sunshine and he'll give notice."

They joked about how slow business was. "Y'know, you can always move down to Falls Street," Sawyer said. "I was making good money down there. There's still business down there."

They shrugged. "I like to do maybe two tours a day, with about ten people altogether," said Leroy, one of the part-timers, "I don't want to run my wagon into the ground." Sawyer understand that. But he felt ill at ease with his old friends now. He waved good-bye, heading 'home for lunch' when, in fact, he went down Falls Street to the train station. He set up his sign and waited for the train. The noon train pulled in and, joy of joys, at least thirty folks piled out. "Ladies and gentlemen!" he cut loose with his pitch, at full volume, with a broad smile, "welcome to Niagara Falls!"

Two young men in uniforms handed over cash and Sawyer jumped into his seat with the energy he'd had ten years ago. Sadie took the bit like it was an apple. Beaming, the tour guide fired up. "My name is Sawyer Jackson, and I've got a tour for you like none you'll get around here. Not only can I answer any and all questions you might have about the mighty Niagara, but I've been doing some scholarly reading on our town's history. . ."

"I start with the falls," he started out, but instead of hustling folks in and out of the souvenir shops and the other crap, he took them upriver to Schlosser's Dock. His customers were a young woman, the two young soldiers who both seemed to be competing for her, and an older woman, likely the chaperone. "During the hostilities of 1812," Sawyer started after driving them up the River Road, he told them all about the fort and the old Portage, how this little stretch of road made its mark on history.

"Excuse me," said one of the young men after learning about the Portage Road, looking out the back of the carriage towards the distant falls, "but why the hell aren't we looking at the falls? We've ridden in this carriage for over an hour and we've hardly seen the falls."

Sawyer looked pole-axed. "Well, sir, I can give you story after story about the falls—"

"Well why don't you?" asked the other man, more openly hostile. "I don't want to hear all this history stuff. We came to see the falls. Take us there, or we'll find someone who can."

Well, Sawyer thought, *so much for taking them to Lewiston*. And if they wanted to pay a little extra, I was prepared to tell them all about the storming of Queenston. It was a better story than Lundy's Lane, that's for sure. But the customer had to be pleased. "I'm sorry for distracting you good folks," he said, tapping Sadie with the reins to turn around. "We'll be back to the falls shortly." Sighing to himself, he felt the joy of the tour fading. They saw the falls, and Sawyer began his stock stories of the 'Mighty Cataracts' and they all seemed much happier. He even got a generous tip, adding insult to injury.

The next day was rainy and cold, which was fine with Sawyer; he was depressed. Someday, he hoped, people will want to know the history.

That night he woke from a sound sleep, coughing from a tickle in his throat. He felt the return of an old enemy. He got up, drank some water, then coughed harder. The tickle in his throat would not be eased. He remembered the powder the doctor had given him before, and found a little left, and mixed it into a cup and drank it. The tickle was eased, but he didn't sleep for the rest of the night. "It's back," he whispered to her through his raspy throat when she awoke the next morning. "I think it's back."

Two nights later a high wind ripped off more roof shingles and rainwater leaked down the back wall. "That's it, lover," Liz said with a determined look, "you need to get back to Doctor Bergman and I need to get the hell out of Niagara." They got the shingles replaced, put the house up for sale, and Liz and Sawyer said good-bye to Niagara. They went back to Buffalo and saw Doctor Bergman.

"Yes," he said sadly after a long examination in his offices, "I'm afraid I see fresh growth." He sighed with dismay. "I've begun writing up the procedure we used in eliminating your growth last winter. I think we broke some new ground. It's a damn shame it didn't stay that way." He didn't begin discussing surgery. "In other cases like this, it has proven to be more prudent to wait a little while and see what happens."

Sawyer didn't know what he meant. "Why wait? I want it out."

Bergman smiled, but it was a tired smile. "I'd like to wait a month. I need to observe a little more. I'll give you something a little stronger to ease the coughing."

"Observe?" Sawyer complained on the way to their rooms, "what's there to see? I'm wracked with this same scourge. He cut it out once, let's get it cut out again, get on with life."

"He wants to wait, so we wait," Liz comforted him.

So they went on a trip to Toronto, and for a couple of weeks Liz was happier than Sawyer had ever seen her. They took day trips around the city and dinner out, and concerts and everything that makes life grand, except the nights when he woke, coughing. When the coughing brought up phlegm streaked with blood it was back to the doctor.

"Okay," agreed Bergman, after he took barely a glance down Sawyer's throat, "let me schedule the procedure for a week from today. I have too many commitments. I can't do it any sooner, and I don't want to wait any longer."

They stayed in town this time as Sawyer was weakening, coughing like he had TB. It was a long, hot July week, Sawyer ill, Liz worrying more every day. He saw gray in her hair for the first time; *did she color it before, or is life getting harder*, he wondered. When they returned for the surgery, both of them looked haggard with lost sleep.

Bergman led him into his office, closed the door, and Liz prepared for another day-long vigil.

She was surprised to see Bergman emerge only an hour later. "Please stay seated," he asked her. "I looked into Sawyer's throat. There is more than one growth." Bergman hung his head in defeat. "And after listening to his breathing, I strongly suspect there are growths in his lungs as well." Liz's eyes began filling with tears. "That's where the bloody phlegm is coming from. If I burn the cancer out of his throat, there's more in his lungs. If I could even get to it there, I fear it'll end up somewhere else. There's. . . no further gain."

Bergman frowned with his own disappointment. "It would be painful to operate, and then there's the post-operation difficulties, all of it a struggle for a healthy soul. I don't think it would be worth the misery for him. Now it's just a matter of making him comfortable." Liz nodded slightly, tears spilling from her eyes, and Bergman returned to his office; she went to the ladies' private room, where she sat and let the crying come.

At Sawyer's insistence they went to Boston and found an apartment that would be comfortable for Liz, and he became resigned to using a wheelchair as his energy drained. Summer passed. Bergman had suggested morphine, and Sawyer resigned himself to it. He wrote some last postcards to his pals back in Niagara. 'Hope the season is going strong,' he wrote McCrory, 'is Knox still charging his sanitary fee?' By the end of September he wasn't getting much sleep, and every breath was a struggle. "It hurts, Liz," he whispered, "there's no goodness left in the powders. It's like breathing underwater."

One evening his coughing turned into a spasm that brought up a horrific amount of blood and phlegm. The next morning he couldn't get out of bed. "I don't know how much time is left to me," he told his wife, "but if I have to spend it this way I don't want it."

"What are you saying?" she asked, blinking away tears.

"I can't think of a better good-bye than here, with you, not in some hospital." That evening he and Liz had a bottle of champagne for the New Year two months away. "I want to have a smile on my face when I see Saint Peter," he suggested. He barely had the energy to make love, but they did, and when Sawyer was resting Liz rose, put on her robe, went to the kitchen and got out the brown bottle. With a hypodermic needle the doctor had given her, she carefully loaded more morphine than a human could shrug off. She returned to the bedroom and heard his labored breathing. "This'll do the trick, dear," she said softly, and carefully found a vein in his arm. It was very hard keeping her hand still for the injection but she persevered. She held him until he was still.

Sawyer was buried in Boston in the autumn of 1861. Liz presumably died in the Boston area some years later, but the date is unrecorded.

Power City

John Bruhn was the copy editor for the *Niagara Courier*, a daily, one of four papers in the village of Niagara Falls. Ten years at the paper had taken its toll; though he was just in his thirties he looked older. His face was lined, his brown hair was cut short with a generous splash of gray. It was a tough, competitive business. He had a broad desk with an 'in' box always filled with copy, a box labeled 'set', ten pencils scattered on his desk and always a sheet of copy he was editing. Office dress did not dictate collars, unless one was interviewing someone in one, and Bruhn rarely did.

At eleven Bruhn set his pencil down to interview a young woman. June Lockwood's application had been accompanied by a letter of reference from Mrs. Ada Lancaster, whose boarding school June had attended for ten years. In her application, June expressed her 'interest in being a creative writer'.

"We write every day," Bruhn occasionally lectured young reporters, "and not a word of it is creative."

When June arrived for her appointment he saw a mousy girl in clean hand-me-downs.

"Miss Lockwood, where does your family reside?"

She looked at her lap. "My mother died around the time I was born. My father lives out west, Chicago or St. Louis. He paid my tuition, but otherwise doesn't write much."

"And you've been a student at Mrs. Lancaster's school?"

"Yes sir," she said, her self-confidence returning. "For ten years. Where I excelled in music and rhetoric, and especially in writing." She suddenly smiled, as though Mrs. Lancaster had whispered in her ear.

She had given Bruhn a short essay for a writing sample, some tripe on nature probably assigned by Mrs. Lancaster that June felt was her best work. Her writing had some potential, if she could get away from Mrs. Lancaster.

He dreaded asking the next question, but it sometimes proved informative. "Who is your favorite writer?" *It's always Dickens*, he thought.

"I enjoy Dickens," she said promptly, perhaps another question she'd been coached on.

He tried a different tact. "What was the last book you read?" he asked, and smiled encouragingly.

She blinked, then gave him a mischievous smile. "I was able to borrow a copy of *Uncle Tom's Cabin*," she said. "I don't think I could write a novel, myself, I'm not comfortable working in fiction, but I admire how Miss Stowe put forth her arguments for abolition in such a," she paused, searching for a word, something Bruhn was pleased to see, "a creative manner. She wrote a novel that worked better than any pamphlet or broadside could."

Bruhn nodded thoughtfully. "What do you think of the new bridge?" he asked, changing topics.

"I expect the Village of Niagara and Suspension Bridge will end up as one big city eventually," she said. "It's been a great stimulus to growth. I hope to take the train up to Montreal someday. I haven't done much traveling." *Or any*, she thought.

"Do you have any questions for me?" Bruhn asked. Most applicants were too timid to ask any. Timidity was not a good quality in a reporter.

"What's today's lead story?" June asked, her eyebrows rising in curiosity.

Bruhn smiled and glanced at his 'set' box. "As of a week ago, May 11th, 1858, Minnesota is the newest state in the union."

June nodded approvingly. Softly, she said, "bully for Minnesota."

He liked her.

"Are you aware of how many female reporters work for this paper?" he asked her, his eyes narrowed as if he were grilling a politician.

June was taking it all in. Men were walking and running around, from desk to desk and out the door, the door itself banging shut so frequently she had to steel herself to stop glancing over her shoulder at it, and the pervasive smell of tobacco. "How many female reporters work for this paper?" she heard. She turned around in her chair and looked around. She didn't see any women, other than a secretary.

"I don't see any female reporters," she said, unfazed by her answer, speaking as though it were question twelve of twenty on the test.

Bruhn studied her face and allowed himself a half-smile. His office had a perfect view of the village. He glanced out. "Miss Lockwood, do you see that woman in front of the Cataract Hotel?" She looked out, followed his direction and nodded. "Describe what she's wearing, please."

She paled, clearly being tested. "She's wearing a... a yellow hoop skirt, with a brown, uh, satin jacket."

"Her hat?"

"It's ugly." A suppressed chuckle made his belly shake. "Uh, wide brim green hat with an ostrich feather."

He nodded. "Very good. Are you familiar with the Southern families who enjoy staying here in the summer?"

She'd heard some stories, so she nodded.

Bruhn liked her; he sensed that if he hired her, he would someday be proud of doing so. She seemed alert, unafraid, and very inquisitive. "The Southerners hold their debutante parties for their young ladies, usually in the hotel ballrooms. I would like you to attend these balls as our society reporter and write them up for me."

She left the paper with Bruhn's handshake still an impression on her hand, her first job to start tomorrow. Writing society news wasn't her dream job, but she was from humble origins and needed a job, and at least she was writing.

Sometimes, in episodes of excitement, June had a dream that took her back to her first distinct memory. It was the year so cold the falls almost froze. Some said it did, as the ice growing from each bank met in the middle, but it wasn't hard to hear water flowing under the ice. June remembered her father walking with her out onto the ice. It had ridges and slopes, a rapids ground to a halt by sub-zero winds, and she kept falling and her father had to carry her. She saw other adventurous souls out there on the ice. It was bitterly cold, with a wind that froze your lungs and made breathing painful, so they got out there and came right back, June getting carried back, tucked under her father's coat. He smelled of tobacco. "Well, little girl, you've walked on the falls," he said. That was her first distinct memory.

The dream she had more often was a memory from the spring of that year, of Mrs. Lancaster, the director of the girls' school to which her widowed father sent her. It was on Portage Road, in a large house that was also Mrs. Lancaster's home. June was seven. It was May, and she had just started at the school in April. She failed her first exam, on sums. With the other girls in the large drawing room that was their classroom, she had handed in her exam and stood before the teacher's desk as her test was graded. She saw Mrs. Lancaster's red pencil flash several times and feared the worst.

"June," Mrs. Lancaster stood and addressed her coldly, in front of the twelve other girls, "you don't seem too smart. That's unfortunate." She addressed them all, from eight year old Patty Joslin, her new best friend, to Miss Karen, seventeen and now assisting Mrs. Lancaster, "it's unfortunate because you don't look like you'll be growing up to be a great beauty."

June blushed, ashamed. Her hair was straight and brown, her features plain and probably homely. "If you aren't going to be pretty, you should try to be smart. Try, June." She handed the exam book back to June and let her sit down.

She wished she could forget it but the dream haunted her adolescence. Convinced of Mrs. Lancaster's assessment, noting that the widowed schoolmistress was not blessed herself with beauty but was smart enough to run a school, and so was in a position to pronounce accurate judgment, June buckled down. Her next exam was perfect. So were most of them in her years at Mrs. Lancaster's school. She finished when she was seventeen.

She had not, in fact, grown up to be a great beauty. She had grey eyes, a receding chin, and a nose that seemed meant for a larger face, and she faced the world on her best day with a half-smile, but she did become one of the brightest students Mrs. Lancaster ever taught. She enjoyed drawing, struggled with math, and loved to write. On her seventeenth birthday she wrote her letter of application to the *Niagara Courier*.

'Miss Adeline Plantagenet Carteret Simpson,' June scribbled on her notepad, 'whose mother is one of the Atlanta Carterets and who has recently graduated from the Finchley Finishing School of Charleston, turned sixteen at a party at the International Hotel. The party was attended by. . .' she would need to collect the guest list after the party. Also, she reminded herself, ask the mother for a formal description of the hideous orange puffball of a dress Miss Simpson was wearing.

Coming to Niagara was the fashion for the wealthy plantation Southerners. The falls' constant cooling breezes made it a summer resort for the Deep South and holding coming-out parties here was another cottage industry for the village. This was June's sixth deb party story in two weeks. Spending so much time with the debutantes in the luxury hotels, and in the fancy dress shops that had sprung up in the village, June heard herself back at the *Courier's* office speaking with a Southern inflection.

"Well, heaven's me," she lampooned for the others in the copy room, "Ah've been just worried sick that the gown's pearl buttons wouldn't get sewn on in tahm."

"Thank heavens they all leave in September," said Mr. Bruhn, smiling at June.

Yes, thought June. *When the debutantes leave, will I still have a job?*

A young man reached the top of the steps to the newsroom floor. "Oh, June," said Bruhn, without enthusiasm, "meet Ed Plater. Ed just started. His father is a friend of Abner Smythe, on our Board of Directors."

"Where else have you written, Mr. Plater?" June asked, politely but depressed, seeing in the cub another step she must climb over to get a real assignment.

"I just graduated from Black Rock Catholic Academy. I was the student editor of the school newspaper," said Plater. "I see you cover the society events," he said in a kindly, if condescending voice.

"For now," she said softly.

Plater then picked up her latest story from the 'set' box and began reading it. June blushed. After Bruhn read copy, it was sacrosanct. No changes were made, it was ready to be typeset. Yet Plater had plucked her story as though it cried for his touch. "What you might want to do," he furrowed his brow as though this were a weighty issue, "is start with a more sweeping sentence than 'Miss Adeline Dingdong from down south. Something with a hint of the great South, or of her proud family tradition."

Bruhn rose slightly from his seat, his stout torso framed by his suspenders, briskly pulled the copy from Plater's hand, and set it back in his 'set' box. "It's been edited, Mr. Plater, and it's off to typesetting. Why don't you see Miss Rappaport about getting a desk and pencils, then come by and we'll see what's worthy of your blistering prose?"

The next week a man calling himself Harry Colcord came to the paper's offices and made a great fuss out of ordering a full-page ad. "I represent the greatest high-wire artist in the world!" he announced to the secretary at the entrance, to the copy clerk she directed him to, and finally to the entire editorial floor, "and he will be coming to this wonderful falls to show you his skills in the most dangerous high-wire act ever performed."

"Who is this high-wire artist?" June asked, taking a break from writing her latest deb story.

"His name is Blondin," Colcord answered, again in his booming, theatrical voice. Though June was clearly the only one interested, being a woman he knew she wasn't the lead reporter he wanted to talk to. Still, she was an audience, "and we're going to string a cable from here to Canada, across the falls, and he'll go back and forth on it like a man strolling down a sidewalk on a summer's day."

"Is it rope or cable?" June questioned him further. "How thick is it? Where and how will it be tethered?" Unaware that Mr. Bruhn was listening, June interviewed Colcord for twenty minutes. Colcord took the opportunity to speak at length about his client and garner free publicity.

June took no notes but, when Colcord left, she composed a short piece. It didn't take long. With her interest piqued, she could write quickly and precisely. When she finished she picked up her deb piece as well and took both to her editor's desk. "Mr. Bruhn, here's the party piece you sent me on. And," she hesitated, though Bruhn had treated her like his own daughter, "could you just look at this and tell me what you think?"

She waited as Bruhn gave the deb story a three second glance, checking to see that guest names were included, the gown described, and measured it for column length, then set it in the bin to be typeset. Then he looked at her story on Blondin. For the first time, for June's writing, he actually read it. At the finish, he nodded slightly. "Nice piece of work, Miss Lockwood." He seemed to be thinking about something, then asked, "so now I'm guessing you want to cover this high-wire act for the paper?"

She blushed, but just a little. "Would that be possible?"

"It would." Bruhn said, indulging in a fatherly smile. "You've already collected the important facts. You should do the story."

She beamed. "Thank you!"

Years later as she recalled it, it was a wonderful moment, her big break. Another wonderful moment occurred the day Blondin began his act. Another spoiled little Southern girl was coming out, and Ed Plater was disgusted to learn that he was now covering the 'deb balls'.

Goat Island, and the land bordering the falls, was owned by the Porter family. The cable was originally planned to reach from Goat Island to Table Rock, but the Porters feared a catastrophe and refused permission. So it was stretched from a point three-quarters of a mile from the falls, across the basin to Table Rock. It added to the trip, running before the American falls as well, but Colcord didn't seem concerned. Half a dozen ropes were strung from points along the way out to the cable, to brace it and minimize its sway in the constant breeze. On the designated day, bands on both sides played as crowds gathered and the taverns did a roaring business in the early summer weather. People came by train, from Black Rock and Buffalo and from Rochester, and down from Toronto, and several newspapers, including one from Detroit and from Pittsburgh, sent reporters. The best seats, at the edge of the gorge, were roped off and sold for prices between a nickel and a dollar.

Blondin arrived four days before to supervise the anchoring of the cable. "Spend as much time around him as possible," Bruhn directed her. "And I'll send a boy from the printing room to get your dispatches." Bruhn himself would combine her pieces into a single story.

One of the first pieces of hard news she caught was his real name, Jean Francois Gravelet. "At least he's really French," Colcord pointed out with a sly grin. She didn't sleep much in those four days. Blondin was always in motion. 'He is physically very strong, but not brawny. He exercises vigorously each day. He does a hundred sit-ups, another hundred push-ups. He uses a jumping rope for half an hour, jumping very quickly at times. He has set up a practice cable, actually a long wooden pole, which is set on two chairs and on which he walks and tests different steps. When he practiced on the cable yesterday he used a long balancing pole. He has walked other high wires in France, and tries to minimize the dangers of walking through the mists of the falls, but clearly it is a new level of danger for him and he has, in the past two days, reinspected the cable and the guide ropes repeatedly. He has also changed his mind about which of his shoes to wear. One pair, brown leather with very thin leather soles, is his favorite, the most comfortable. But another pair, moccasins he purchased here two days ago, he experimented with and found they worked better than his shoes where the cable was wet. Since the cable will certainly be wet out in the middle, he would like the moccasins out there, but he has more faith in his old leather shoes.'

June thought her shoe story was the worst sort of tripe, but Blondin had spent the entire day before the walk being accessible to the press, doing interviews with all the papers, doing more inspections of the cables, being photographed inspecting the cables, meeting local dignitaries, getting photographed with the dignitaries, having breakfast, then lunch, then dinner, with each event taking hours as people came up for more photographs. Getting a personal interview with Blondin was impossible. She wrote, then scrapped, a detailed story of his first two meals of the day.

She managed to catch up to Colcord. "Mr. Colcord, I'm June Lockwood, from the *Courier*, I wrote the first story about Blondin?" Colcord graciously thanked her. "Could you get me inside Monsieur Blondin's suite? It's all for the story," she added. She was amazed and flattered when Colcord agreed to her request, wondering if her very understated womanly charms had swayed him, until she entered his suite. The rooms were overrun by others, reporters from New York, mostly men, and women in very fancy dresses, making her womanly charms even more understated and helping her to regain her journalistic objectivity. Blondin wasn't ogling the women anyway—leaving that to Colcord and some of the dignitaries. Instead, he was holding both pairs of footwear and debating their points with Colcord. Nobody else was paying attention. So the shoe story turned out to be the 'hard news' of the day. It made page one in the *Courier*. She was pleased at the day's end, but was concentrating and preparing for the real story, the walk.

JUNE 30TH, 1859

> *It is 4:45 in the afternoon. Looking into the sun, Blondin hefts his balancing pole. The crowd gathered around him is pushed back and he soon stands alone by the cable, which is tied off to a stout tree and reinforced with four stout stakes driven into the ground. If M. Blondin should fall to his death it will not be because the cable came loose.*

She debated that last sentence, then left it in. So did Mr. Bruhn.

> *He rests his right foot on the cable and the look on his face changes. It is as though walking on land is the difficult task, and walking on the cable more familiar. He hefts his balance pole, moving it a little back and forth between his hands, until he is comfortable with the balance. The only sign that he might be nervous is the quick wipe of his forehead with his sleeve. Then, with a brief wave to the rest of us, he steps onto the cable and heads off.*
>
> *The cable is not quite level. The Canadian side is higher than the American side, so Blondin is walking uphill. That appears to tire him out. But even as he stands above the roaring mists, he seems fearless.*

June's pencil hovered over her pad. She didn't like the word 'fearless'. It was a man's word. Still, her copy had to appeal to men, so she left it in. So did Bruhn.

She had purchased powerful opera glasses and they came in handy.

> *At a hundred and fifty feet out, Blondin pauses, and he appears to be drawing deep breaths. He actually sits on the cable for a minute. Then, perhaps to revive interest, he plunges face forward onto the cable, as if preparing to do a handstand. Instead, he stands and continues his journey to Canada. It takes another twenty minutes, and when he reaches Canada the bands begin to play, someone fires a pistol, and both sides cheer loudly.*

June thought the show would never end. Blondin crossed back and forth, tried to titillate the crowds by standing on one foot at times, by sitting again, and by bursts of running. She was told to expect 'a surprise' by Colcord, perhaps so she would stick around. As dangerous as this high-wire walk was, Blondin's skill made it look tame. Crowds began heading back to the taverns after the first hour; then Colcord's men in the crowd called out, 'look at the boat!'

The *Maid of the Mist* chugged its way to a standstill in the river below, right in front of the falls. Today the boat's deck was chock-full, as some folks paid to see Blondin from below. At about six, as the sun was casting most of the gorge in shadow beneath him, Blondin walked out in mid-wire and paused. He pulled a loop of twine from a pocket and began letting it down. The *Maid* was waiting. When the twine reached it, a helpful soul tied it to a bucket. Blondin hauled it up. From the bucket he retrieved a bottle. Opening it, he took a long swallow, saluted the crowds with the bottle, and then dropped it into the gorge. A few minutes later he came back to Prospect Point and stepped down. 'We will be doing another show on July 4th,' Colcord was hawking into a megaphone, 'be back here for the glorious fourth and watch this master of the wire again toy with death!'

June filled five pages of her notepad by the time Blondin stepped off the wire. She joined the throng gathering around him and elbowed her way—in a demure, feminine fashion—into crowds. She got close enough to see Blondin; he was streaming sweat. He was puffing hard. He had made it all look so simple. And now he was exhausted. "No questions, please," Colcord was bawling out, trying to clear a path for Blondin as they headed for his carriage. Stepping away from the crowd, June instead hurried up the pathway to the carriage.

"I'm feeling a little lightheaded," she said to the driver in that mock southern accent she'd cultivated. "Might I step in the carriage a moment? I'm with Monsieur Blondin?"

The driver glanced at her and smirked. What he thought she was he did not say, but he didn't order her out, so she got in the carriage. A few minutes later, the puff of a photographer's flash powder preceding them, Blondin and Colcord climbed up. They were still speaking to followers, their faces to the crowd. They were in the carriage before they discovered June. "I'm the reporter with the *Courier*," June reminded them. "I didn't mean to intrude, but I'd love to just chat with you a moment."

Blondin seemed pleased to see her. "The cable was very slippery," he said in his heavily accented English, "worse than I had expected. And I don't think anyone discovered my best trick," he smiled. "I had great trouble picking which shoes to wear -"

"I remember that," June interjected, "your regular shoes or the moccasins you bought?"

Blondin smiled. "Yes. You remembered." She blushed. "I wore my favorites out, but I had tucked the moccasins into my pockets. Between the American and the Horseshoe Falls the wind was blowing spray at me, and I felt my footing getting slippery. When I sat down out there the first time, I don't know if anyone appreciated it, but I was changing shoes."

June was locked in eye contact with her subject, storing away the details in her mind. She looked down and saw he was still wearing the moccasins; they were drenched and slightly torn. "The cable is very heavy," he said. "It started to tear the moccasins. Happily I had finished everything we'd planned."

"What happened to your other shoes?" June asked.

Blondin looked down, saddened. Colcord answered, "Monsieur Blondin had to abandon them as they wouldn't tuck into his pockets like the moccasins did."

The next day the story that cemented June's security at the *Courier* was known henceforth as the tale of Blondin's shoes, Part Deux.

JULY 4TH

This time the crowds were almost as large, but that was in part due to the holiday. Fireworks at sunset were scheduled, and the second cable walk by Blondin was simply further entertainment. The advertising was even heavier and more lavish. He walked the wire for an hour, doing his tricks again, and those in the crowd who had missed last week's show were properly impressed. Still, they began dispersing before Blondin returned to dry ground; they knew he'd make it. June covered the show, but wrote a more philosophical piece, noting that the crowds were becoming jaded. 'A man is risking his life, walking where man was not intended to go. Because he has shown his great skill, there is little expectation that he will fall to his death. Because of that, the crowds break up before he has finished.

There is something sad about us when we are only drawn to a spectacle to see death and destruction, not to celebrate someone's great skill.

Truth be told, even June was a little bored by the end of the second show. She made no attempt to sneak into Blondin's carriage. She walked back to the paper, wrote her story in just two drafts in a calm and clear-headed manner, then went back to her boarding house and had her dinner as she usually did, a cheese sandwich with a glass of milk.

Blondin returned August 17th, and to continue drawing crowds he carried Harry Colcord on his back. June covered that story too, and interviewed Harry beforehand. Harry had a few beers to help him go out. She didn't try to interview him when the show was done, as he had to piss like a race horse, then seemed desperate to get drunk again and forget it.

Her success with the Blondin stories earned her assignments to regular news reporting. She learned some unwritten rules. Business and businessmen were sacred. Better to miss a scoop than print a story that could hurt a local business without contacting them in advance for their response. Certain politicians were more easily found in bars and brothels than at City Hall. She went fearlessly into the bars, with indignance into the brothels and City Hall.

The summer after Blondin began the fad, June interviewed and wrote about another high-wire artist. Signor Farini also took out an ad in the *Courier*, and in the other two papers as well. He, too, intended to stretch a cable across the basin and walk across it. Unlike Blondin, whose credentials seemed honest and proved to be so, June heard too much of Signor Farini to believe he was Italian born. She had the chance to send a note to a compatriot in Lockport, where said Signor Farini was actually born Bill Hunt. After debating to herself, June spared Hunt the embarrassment of exposing him. The next day Ed Plater did it for her. But the stunts kept on, and the stakes got higher, and word eventually got out.

Farini-Hunt did his cable walk on the fifteenth of August. Cable-walking alone wasn't a draw anymore, so Farini belted a contraption to his back that was part wash-bucket and part squeezer and proceeded to wash the handkerchiefs of women from the crowd while he balanced above the torrent. June was shaking her head in disdain, but she didn't miss a detail. She also tracked down the women whose kerchiefs were cleaned. "The washing job wasn't bad." Two weeks later Blondin returned and he and Farini-Hunt both went out on wires. Then both carried their managers. "What began as an exciting dare is degenerating into a sideshow. . ." June wrote. In the end it was all about money anyway, and by the end of the summer of 1860 the excitement of high wire walking was fading, and so was the income.

In September the Prince of Wales visited, which was a welcome change of atmosphere. Before more foolishness could occur the next summer, the Civil War erupted and the border town quieted considerably.

In the fall of 1862 her father died in Colorado, leaving June a modest inheritance and no living relatives. With the money she decided to own her own home. Always drawn to the old stone house on Third Street, it came up for sale shortly after she received her inheritance. At her request Bruhn looked over the house, though he knew little of carpentry. "It appears someone knows even less about home repair than I do," he said, pointing out where the sagging main beam had been jacked up more than necessary. "Roof might need some repair," he pointed out from the front yard. It cost $2000, which took her inheritance and most of her savings, but she was happy with her buy.

Bruhn, Plater and three other reporters came by to visit shortly after she'd moved in. "Miss Lockwood," as Bruhn always addressed her, "this is an old inn. What on earth are you going to do with all the room?"

"Well, Mr. Bruhn," June said, a little goggle-eyed herself at what she'd bought into, "I've been sharing rooms with other girls my entire life. I decided I wanted a lot of space for myself."

"Well, you've managed that," said Plater. "Or are you considering giving up the life of journalism for that of running a boarding house?"

They'd become quiet competitors, she and Plater. He had better access to the men who made the news, while she was just a better writer. Bruhn was still her patron, so she felt safe, and she knew Plater was chafing. "No, Mr. Plater, I don't intend to run a boarding house. But if you'd like to manage it for me, I could hire you."

The others chuckled and Bruhn horse-laughed and Plater said little to her after that. Two weeks later he jumped to the *Power City News*.

June became copy editor when Bruhn moved up to managing editor in 1863. The carnage of the war was reaching every corner of the Union. The lists were the hardest part of her job, the casualty lists released by the War Department each week, identifying the dead. Adeline Crowther, a young woman from Ithaca with very poetic writing, was June's first opportunity to hire another woman as a reporter, and she gave Adeline the lists. "Try to give them a dignified flair," June asked. "The bodies may not make it back for burial. Think of this piece of paper as their funeral." Adeline stayed a year, wrote obituaries for local boys, and was hired away by the *Buffalo Messenger* to be a society reporter.

The lists were lengthy and June personally read each edition to find local boys. The county raised thirty companies, and with neighbors finding themselves together in the trenches, Niagara lost three men the same week. The first casualty was well known and a cause for public mourning. Peter Porter, a general in Grant's army, was killed in the Wilderness campaign. 'We are paying a terrible price for this war of unclear ideals. . . ' June wrote, probably the cause for a brick through the *Courier's* window.

The other two Niagara casualties were Willy Pinter and Daniel Kennedy, whom June knew as boys when she was a girl. Daniel had been a bully, and his death did not pain her terribly. But Willy Pinter had dared her to race along the upper river bank one summer, and he won easily, because she loved his deep blue eyes and his prize was to kiss her. He tasted of fresh sweat and something sweet she couldn't place, she still remembered, and he kissed her twice. 'Cpl. W. Pinter, d., Cold Harbor'. She had to excuse herself to the powder room for a few minutes.

There were lists of the wounded, too, and these were far longer. June made certain the returning wounded were interviewed; when she could she did the interview herself. "What battles were you in? Did you actually have occasion to shoot? Do you think Mr. Lincoln is preserving the Constitution or destroying it?" As the war dragged on, her sympathies were with the Copperheads, who risked treason with Horace Greeley when they met across the river in 1863 with Confederate diplomats in a failed bid to negotiate a peace treaty. She covered it, reported it objectively, and angry readers threw rocks through the *Courier's* windows.

And finally, in spring of 1865, the slaughter came to an end. When the telegram arrived the newsroom, like much of the nation, fell silent with weariness. "We have to put out an extra edition," June urged Bruhn.

Bruhn, who was thinking now of retirement, smiled at his protege. "I expect you're right. What headline would you write? Union Wins? That'll sell a lot of paper."

June was now fully confident in her work, comfortable with her flair for confrontation. It hadn't won her any friends in the editorial department, but John Bruhn, was her boss, her protector. "I would prefer something simple. 'Peace.'"

"That's so dull," complained Frank Shane, one of the three current newshounds, "nobody wants a piece of paper that says 'Peace'. I like 'Union Wins.'" Jock Tumbler and Albert Dent, both sons of wealthy families who'd paid for their replacements in the draft, chanted, "Union-Wins-Union-Wins-Union-", and June finished it a minute later with a single raised eyebrow.

Jock and Albert and Frank looked at Bruhn with exasperation. He smiled and said, "I think 'Peace' says it all."

"Horace," she called for Horace Pepper, her newest reporter. Horace limped, having taken a ball in the leg in the Wilderness Campaign. In truth, he could barely spell 'Niagara' but he'd asked for a job and he'd fought beside Willy Pinter, and June vowed she'd teach him to write if he'd stay long enough. He appeared from the hallway, where he'd been smoking and chatting with one of the secretaries. "Horace, tell the Print room to prepare for an extra edition. Our headline, 'Peace.'"

They groaned and she went to her large desk, sat down, and looked at them expectantly. "I can't edit copy if I have none to edit. We have an extra to put out. Let's get some copy. Frank, write me a lead story."

"What a limp-noodle title," mumbled Frank.

"What a 'what'?" asked June.

"Nothing," said Frank. He was already composing a stirring tale summarizing Niagara's contributions to the war, with a header of "Union Wins."

On the first of September, 1869, the stunters returned to Niagara. 'Professor Jenkins' crossed the falls on a cable. Showing more respect for human life than show-business, he rigged a bicycle that bolted securely onto the cable and was sturdy and safely balanced and that would've required crowds at either end cutting the cable before he'd be in the slightest danger. He was not applauded. Four years later, after June became the managing editor and no longer covered the foolish stories, Henry Bellini crossed on cable to mid-channel, then dove into the river. "Variety does little to excite the crowds anymore. . ." June wrote in an editorial. When Bellini's assistant, Stephen Peer, went out on the wire four years later and out-performed his boss, Bellini was caught trying to cut the cable. That edition, with a photograph of the cut cable, sold especially well. In the last wire-walking episode, Peer strung a cable between two railway bridges spanning the Lower River. He did his show successfully, but the next morning was found dead on the Canadian shore; it appeared he'd tried to do his cable walk drunk.

A month later Horace Pepper was hired away by a Lockport paper, to June's private sadness. They had become very discreet lovers, and while Horace was not the love of her life, she had come to realize her life probably would not have a great love.

The cable-walkers gave way to folks trying to swim the rapids in the Lower River. Now June protested every time the paper sent reporters to cover the stunters. "We're encouraging these fools to risk their lives," she argued. "Yes, but we have to sell papers," was Bruhn's response.

The summer of 1879 June decided her home needed a porch. The stone house had had almost nothing done to it by its various owners beyond necessary maintenance. It was still a two-story inn with a big public room, a dining room, an attic, a simple kitchen and seven small bedrooms. Each stone was original, the sturdy wooden beams unchanged. It sagged in the middle, but most homes sagged a little. June had grown fond of the house and expected to live in it until she died. So she thought about what would make the house more comfortable without touching the walls or otherwise changing the house itself. She thought of the porch.

It would be a wooden porch and looked like an afterthought. She had seen a painting of a country home and loved the idea of sitting on a country porch. What she'd failed to consider was her house's location, on Third Street, in the growing, bustling town of Niagara Falls.

"Miss Lockwood, this here's what you'd see on a farmhouse out in the country," said Felton Brewster, her carpenter. Felton was at least sixty and slowing down, but he was the only one of five men she'd contacted who'd do the job. "You're in the city, and you aren't going to want to sit out here and get covered in dust and what the horses leave behind. Why don't you let me convert one of those empty rooms into a nice sewing room, eh?"

"I don't sew," she said, looking at him as though he were the dumbest story she'd ever interviewed. "I asked for a porch, so build me a porch."

"It'll be noisy and dirty," Felton pressed. He wasn't trying to get out of a job, but he knew the porch wouldn't be any fun.

"A porch, please," she asked, and then left him out front, retreating into her kitchen to make tea. "I don't hear any sawing going on," she called out a minute later.

"You'll hear it soon enough," the man grumbled, then started measuring the ground for a porch. He built it slowly, expecting her to discover what a bad idea it was. He took a day off for every day he worked. What should have been a one week job he turned into three.

"You're being paid for the job, not by the day," she reminded him at the end of two weeks when even she realized he was dawdling. He gave up and got to work and the porch took shape.

Before it was finished, June realized it was a bad idea. But she wouldn't change her mind in front of a man, so the porch went up.

One evening after Felton did some finish work she came home from the paper and found an old, battered book on her kitchen table, with a short message on a scrap of paper. 'Found this.' The old book was a diary. She opened it, sat down to read, and the rest of the world disappeared. It began in 1812, when the town was barely a village. In pages attached by the home's previous owner she learned the beginnings of her hometown as a tourism shrine. She roamed from the front to the back, reading random passages, from Nehemiah to Sawyer, from Queenston to cooking moonshine. *This is wonderful*, she said to herself on almost every page.

She finished in early morning, took off her glasses and rose and touched the walls. The cool stones felt as they must have to Sawyer, as they would have to Nehemiah. She went down into the cellar. It was cluttered, dark and cob-webbed, mildewed and unwelcoming. She'd never been down there, as she recalled. On her knees she hunted, and the Indian hole was still there, and though she'd never noticed it before it wasn't hard to find when she knew to look for it. When she reached in, she held her breath but felt nothing; she laughed at herself. "I feel like a guest in an old hotel," she said, smiling. "Nehemiah Cleary," she said, smiling in delight. "I'm delighted to know you."

"I have an idea for a special story," June announced to Bruhn. She'd caught him right after his ten a.m. breakfast, his second of the day. He was always more accommodating on a full stomach, and June knew she was his favorite.

"What'd you have in mind, young lady?" he asked, and she delicately reached over his desk to flick a crumb of bread off his handlebar moustache. "How do you know I wasn't saving that for lunch?" he teased her. He liked to make her smile; if June had a flaw, it was her demeanor. She hadn't smiled since the gimp Horace Pepper had hobbled off to Lockport.

"I found a diary in my house," she began.

A meeting for a story would ordinarily take no more than two minutes, a little longer if the reporter was really green. The essential decisions might require senior minds to render opinions on, but a daily newspaper must make decisions on stories in minutes, if not seconds. That meeting with Bruhn, when June explained how she wanted to write about the Loyalists that had first populated the region, lasted most of an hour.

"They're the United Empire Loyalists," June continued. "They were the pioneers in this area. And the house I own was built by one, which is what suggested it to me. But I think we don't do enough feature stories, and this is one that's original."

"And a little controversial?" Bruhn asked. He hated the idea. He hated it within seconds of hearing his favorite reporter explain her idea. "Found a diary in your house, eh?" he asked, trying to redirect her thoughts. "I guess a story about local history is always good for filler," he said, "but why don't you skip the Loyalist and use the tour guide? It would be kind of a 'tales from the tour guide' story."

June was disappointed. She could tell he was dodging this story. He rarely did, only when a story would cause, to use his favorite phrase, more trouble than it was worth. "Do you think a story, an objective story on Loyalists, would cause the paper trouble?"

Bruhn smiled. "June, when you say 'objective story' like that I know it's going to mean 'a story all about the good points of being a Loyalist.'" He sighed. "I honestly don't know if anyone would get angry about Loyalists anymore. We've got British traffic through here on the railroad every day. They spend money here. But every local businessman, every American businessman that has competition from the British side will hate it. What I do suspect is that most of our readers either won't care, or it'll irritate them a little, and for both reasons they won't read it. That's how I'm looking at this story. Will anyone read it?"

Deflated, she shifted in the slightly padded chair, looking at her lap like Mrs. Lancaster had just failed her in a test. It was true, her concept of the story would focus on the nobility and sacrifices of the Loyalists, as she couldn't think of any negatives. "You don't think anyone will read it?" she asked, sounding to her own irritation like a little girl.

He was relieved to hear her voice, to see her showing signs of defeat. "I would read it, but only because you wrote it," he told her, smiling to get her to smile. "But do you have enough fans like me who would read it just because you wrote it?" She blushed and he regretted it instantly. He knew June had few friends among the reporting staff. Besides them mostly being male and seeing June as a misanthrope, she was a better writer than most of them and they knew it. "I meant out there," he indicated the town, "will people find it entertaining? 'Cause it isn't news."

She left his office a few minutes later. She might write the story, she said, and if she did, she'd like Bruhn to read it. He agreed to. And maybe, depending on how the story worked out, if they had space to fill, they might run it. She knew the chances of that happening were that of a snowball's chance in hell.

So she wrote the story. She took off a week to research it, a true sign to the rest of the editorial staff that she was Bruhn's favorite, and for some of the cruder fellows to suggest they were lovers, hence his indulgence. She arranged to interview civic leaders in the towns of the Ontario peninsula. It was a simple story for her to write. She wrote it, filling twenty pages, and she gave it to Bruhn to read when she returned. He told her it was wonderful work, and then it went into the bottom drawer of her desk, where it remained.

On Christmas Eve, 1880, Bruhn promoted June to managing editor. "You know the paper needs to keep the business community happy," Bruhn began their chat. "The paper has to pay its bills first. We get more money from ads than from subscriptions." June nodded; she knew that well. "You're tough enough for the job," Bruhn said, leaning back in his chair. "To survive in this place as long as you have, you've had to be tough. I know that. After your reporting and writing skills, that's what I most admire about you. And, this is hardly news, but I'll miss you."

June was bursting with excitement over her promotion, but losing her mentor made it a bittersweet decision. "Are you heading south, after all?" she asked. "To work with your brother?"

Bruhn had a brother who'd made a lot of money speculating in real estate in Florida. He loved the paper, but after thirty years of it he didn't have much to retire on. "I'm going down to visit. See what he's doing. Maybe I'll be able to make up my mind about it." He looked out the window, at winter. "I won't miss winter here. These snow storms have been something else."

"I've hired a new copy editor from a paper in Rochester. His name is Lester Davidson. He'll be here first of the year. He knows you're in charge." Bruhn had emptied his office of personal items. "There's one thing I wanted to give you," he said, and pulled open his bottom desk drawer. "Had a heck of a time finding it when I finally thought of it. Miss Peters had to help me find it in a very old issue." He pulled out a framed copy of June's story on Blondin's shoes. "I know you think you've done more important work, and you probably have, but I don't think I've ever had more fun on a story than stitching this prose into a piece. We made a good team." He gave her the gift in a polished mahogany frame, and June both smiled and cried. A few minutes later she helped her boss put on his mohair coat and watched him step out onto First Street, into a light snow fall.

And then, God forgive her, she went up and tried out the chair.

June loved to walk on Goat Island at dawn, weather permitting, and watch the sunrise. Her favorite spot was by the Moss Islands that broach the current above the Horseshoe. From there she viewed the sun rise from the rapids. A modest little falls between Goat Island and the first island was called the Hermit's Bath. There was a hermit who had lived on the island years ago. Whether or not he really bathed in this particular little stream was as important as knowing exactly where Brock fell on the Queenston slopes, but it was a nice spot, a little off the path and quiet at dawn, except for the roar of nature. There was a particular boulder she liked to sit on, about three feet out into the stream, further than good sense would have allowed.

In the warm months, when the water wasn't frigid, she would dare herself to jump to the boulder. The water splashing around it would be sufficient to drag her to more dangerous waters should she slip and fall. *It's a stupid little game I play with myself*, she told herself. And she did it every chance she could.

1881

"Explain it again," June asked Frank Shane. Frank was writing a story on electricity, the new form of power, and the installation of a new machine, a dynamo, at the facility built by local entrepreneur Jacob Schoellkopf. Schoellkopf bought the bankrupt canal that cut across the town, diverting water from the upper river over the high bank, spilling into the gorge. A few companies had built on the canal, using simple paddle wheels. But the paper was running a huge ad for 'Electrical lighting by the Brush Electrical Company, providing incandescent light for homes, offices, streets.' The ads were in all the papers, and June had seen a demonstration of the light at the International Hotel. "Explain how this electricity works again."

Frank nodded obediently. "Okay, Miss Lockwood. There's a magnetic field that surrounds the armature of the motor—Miss Lockwood, you've got that far-away look again."

She blinked. 'Magnetic field' was foreign. Armature was alien. It was Frank's fourth attempt to explain how the river's force was turning a turbine and producing electricity and she couldn't focus. "All right, okay," she said, looking down and blushing at her stupidity. "How does it create light?"

Frank rolled his eyes slightly. "There's a glass bulb, with no oxygen inside it, just a filament, and the electricity—"

She raised her hands in surrender. "All right. I don't need to understand it, I guess. Or maybe it's like the piano, you just pick it up."

"Yes, ma'am," Frank offered. "You'll just pick it up." Frank returned to his typewriter. 'The direct current generator can send electrical power to customers up to ten miles away. Incandescent light is being planned for the streets of our town, and in the most affluent homes. Good-bye to coal. Electricity is the newer, brighter power, and it's safer too.'

He looked at the last line critically. Would Miss Lockwood let it by? 'How do you know it's safer?' she'd ask him, and he wouldn't have a good answer. He dug out a gum eraser and scrubbed everything after 'newer, brighter power.' He dropped it in her 'in' box and it sailed through with no changes. *No changes*, Frank thought. *That's a first.* Miss Lockwood always changed something. She tightened up a sentence or added one, almost never sending a story to be typeset without her mark on it. *She felt stupid*, he realized, and was afraid to edit his copy. He could have written 'a whale was sighted going over the falls' and she probably would have passed it. Well, perhaps not a whale. He added 'safer too' to his next story on electrical power a few days later and it passed.

Three months later, workers were putting up wooden poles on First Street, then Niagara Street. Heavy cables slung from crosspiece to crosspiece, stretching up the street from the generator, adding a new look to the town's skyline, with porcelain knobs pointing to the stars. At night the incandescent lights were turned on and the city streets were bright with the yellow light. Everyone came out to wander the familiar blocks, seeing them new against the dark backdrop of the night sky and unfamiliar shadows from a sun just ten feet above.

"This is absolutely amazing," June said one evening from the Hermit's Bath. Moths swarmed around each bulb, drawn to the new light that illuminated but did not burn, and it was magical seeing ones shadow in twilight. And though she didn't trust what she didn't understand, she signed up to get the new lighting in her house.

A narrow copper wire swooped from the slender pine pole at the curb down to the corner of the house. A porcelain knob was nailed to the porch and the wire twisted tightly around it before it was run into the house. June watched in fascination as two men calling themselves 'electricians' brought in the delicate glass bulbs. "Where you like these?" asked one, a man with a strong accent she couldn't place.

"One in the parlor and one in the kitchen," she requested, "and one in my bedroom," she added with a blush. Most women might not want bright light in the romantic room of the house, where softer oil lamps set a more suitable mood, but all of her time in her bedroom was spent reading. She'd love to have the whole stone house lit up but it was an expensive frill.

When they finished running the wire through her house, mounting the light fixtures and grounding them, they showed her the switch at the porch, where she could stop the flow of power into her house. "If there's a fire, you want to turn this off," the same man said.

"I thought electricity was safer than oil," she said, then realized she'd read that somewhere. "Is it safe?"

"It's safe," he said. "But it does burn. If a piece of paper, or something that burns gets too close to the bulb, it might start a fire. Safest thing if that happens is to come out here and turn off the power."

She felt stupid then, as though she'd invited an intruder into her house. Electricity wasn't so safe, she realized. "Alright," she said.

The two electricians left, and June went in and sat in the late sunlight. It was Sunday, her day off, and she'd planned to celebrate the new light, but truth be told she was afraid now to turn it on.

Frank Shane stopped by. She let him in and he entered the dark front room after admiring the power line run to her house. "Miss Lockwood, you got yourself connected, just like you said you would."

She raised a faint smile. "Yes, I certainly did." She was studying the bulb from different angles, like it was a twitching catfish, fascinating but a little repulsive, and with a hint of danger from its tendrils.

Frank seemed comfortable with the hardware. He turned on the wall switch and the parlor light blazed on. Confined to her small room, the light filled it like the sun had just risen in the room. June flinched and shielded her eyes a moment. "Sorry, Miss Lockwood, did I scare you?"

"I wasn't expecting it to be," she swallowed, "so bright." She put her hand near the bulb. "It's hot, isn't it."

"Yea, it does get hot," Frank said. Then he explained, yet again, how the bulb had a filament, a piece of metal, burning inside the bulb. "The point is that it's burning. And it produces heat."

"Is it safe? Is it safe to read by? Can I sit next to it?" she asked, feeling vulnerable.

"Sure," he said. "If it feels too warm, move away."

She blushed. "Of course. That's sensible. Thanks, Frank."

He wished her good evening and left. When she was sure he was gone, she turned off the blazing light and lit an oil lamp to read by.

"There's a committee forming, by a lawyer in Buffalo, named Dorsheimer and Frederick Law Olmsted himself, to get the state to buy the falls and the land around it," June said, reading from the Buffalo Messenger. She was meeting with her reporters on a Monday afternoon, a daily session when they looked through the out-of-town papers for local interest stories.

"I saw something on that," Frank recalled, and rummaged through the stack of news sheets. "Rochester Daily. Here we go." He pulled the sheet free and, eyes narrowed, read the story. "Yes, the Governor opposes it."

"I love the idea. Why don't you take what we have and rewrite it for our audience," said June. "Talk to some of our businessmen, get their opinions." Lester Davidson, the new copy editor, joined them. "How do you like this headline," June asked Lester, "the Governor doesn't know beans."

Lester Davidson had proved a good copy editor, and he was faring reasonably well under June's leadership. "How about 'the Governor is mistaken'?" Lester suggested meekly.

June proceeded to indulge her first chance to be truly controversial as managing editor. 'As the citizens of this town we see every day the disappointment on the faces of visitors when they actually set eyes on the Niagara Falls of which they've read. They have been promised a roaring tumult, one of the Seven Wonders of the World. What we present them is little better than a huge latrine. There are tour guides, and pickpockets and worse, preying on the tourists the moment they step off the train. Stables and factories empty their dirt into the river, boarding houses hang lines of laundry over nature's wonder, and a pulp mill on an island in the middle of the Niagara is a blight on the landscape.'

'There are civic leaders proposing that the state raise the funds to buy out the businesses using the falls for commercial and industrial purposes. They would establish public land around the falls, thus eliminating the pulp mill in the midst of the river, erasing the business tailings and smokestacks, to say nothing of the toll that has forever existed on the bridge to Goat Island. What a wonder to see the falls as the first Europeans saw it, and not to have to pay a dollar for the privilege!'

"Miss Lockwood," Lester reminded her the next day, "this paper needs ads to survive. We've just had a cancellation from Tugby's and the promise," he caught his breath, "that they will organize an embargo against us if we persist."

"Good, they noticed it," she smiled.

"We also have a letter of encouragement from the Temperance Union," Lester added. "Signed by three ministers and a priest."

Why would they care? June wondered.

"If you look out there, you can easily count five or six taverns that almost certainly will be removed by this proposal," said Lester.

"I hadn't thought of that," June admitted.

In her mail a week later came a letter bearing the seal of the City of Buffalo. 'Miss Lockwood—I very much enjoyed your informed piece on creating a public park at Niagara Falls. It caused a sensation in City Hall. I will be traveling up there in a week and hope to call on you in your office at the *Courier*. Y'r humble servant, Grover Cleveland, Mayor of Buffalo.' Cleveland made good on his promise, and while in June's office asked her to go on the road and help him. "We've got some well-connected citizens pushing this. What we need now is to send a missionary out there to tell the people what could be. I think you could be that missionary." he suggested.

"Thank you," she said, a little perplexed that a man with the reputation as a barroom regular would ask her to be a missionary, but agreed to help. "I'm honored to join you." She wrote daily editorials and spoke to civic groups in the area, battling stage fright to speak, by request, at meetings across the state on what the falls was actually like with the 'rapacious tourist traps ready to strip the hapless visitors of their money in record time'.

"If you could come back with me, to Niagara," she spoke one evening in Albany, in a Mason's Hall lit by oil lamps, her voice a strong soprano that carried an air of urgency to an audience of the politically powerful, "I would show you pictures of what Niagara looked like in its natural splendor." It had been quite a stir getting her inside. She was the only woman. She took a sip of water, then said, "what you would see today, on the Maid of the Mist, with the falls before you, would be a hideous, unsightly stain on Nature. You would see the tailings of factories, laundries, stables and blacksmiths, spilling over the top of the gorge and pouring into the river, as if in a rude mockery of the falls. It is ugly," she paused, as she'd learned to in Syracuse, for dramatic effect, "it is dirty, and it is an embarrassment to every New Yorker!"

Her speech was honed on the stump, so to speak, with phrases that stirred applause adopted, some of her favorite passages, quite poetic, cut when she noticed people in the audience turning to chat with neighbors.

In November, 1882, Mayor Cleveland was elected Governor and the movement gained speed. A meeting was held in a private room of the International Hotel, to which June was invited. It was a small meeting, of whom June was the only woman. The room was bright, the hotel being a customer of the Schoellkopf station, proudly announcing its 'Incandescent Lighting' in its advertisements.

The invitation had come from Jeffrey Endicott, one of the governor's assistants in the state Treasury. June was in her late forties, Jeffrey was a rotund thirty-ish fellow. "Miss Lockwood, in your opinion how much of the Niagara should be saved?

Next to June was Lawyer Dorsheimer, whom June had written several times but never met. "Mr. Olmsted sends his regrets at being unable to attend," Dorsheimer said to Endicott. Also in the room was Abner Smythe, president of the Niagara Savings and Loan, a stocky, grand-fatherly figure of sorts, with his beefy build and white beard. June had written a few lines that went against his grain, but they agreed on this project and the bank was taking out more ads than usual in the paper. Abner was also the President of the board of directors for her paper.

Then there was Emmett Knox, once a cop checking storefronts in the village, now the leader of the town's Democratic Party and owner of a headstone carving concern. The men lit cigars. June would have tried one if they had offered, but they didn't. "Well," she said, smiling, "since you ask, I believe that it should go from the upper tip of Goat Island down to the Whirlpool in the Lower River."

Her suggestion pained the banker and the governor's man. Knox said nothing, just drew on his cigar. The mahogany paneling of the room and the smoke circling around it absorbed much of the light of the chandelier. June had come to the meeting straight from work, wearing her usual simple linen blouse and black cotton skirt. She always dressed plainly, and while she didn't socialize much with women who dressed well, in the company of these men and their suits and gold watch chains, she felt uncharacteristically embarrassed at her plain dress.

"That would cost millions, and the governor can't squeeze that much money free," Endicott finally said, sounding regretful.

June sensed defeat. She was very tired. It was November and she had spent the summer and fall traveling the state to drum up support. She hated neglecting her editorial duties—though she knew that Lester considered her travel to be his vacation. She'd just returned a few days ago, was gently scrapping with Lester over stories he'd run or hadn't run, and then she got a last-minute invitation to this meeting, which was turning literally into a small, smoke-filled room, where, she feared, a poor compromise would be forced down her very vocal throat.

"Can I have one of those?" she asked, nodding at Knox's cigar.

"One of what?" asked Smythe. "Oh," he realized, and with a snap of his fingers the waiter reappeared. "Please get a cigar for Miss Lockwood. I think she's feeling like one of the boys." Smythe looked amused as the cigar was presented and June looked at her prize with wonderment. "Snip off the end, Miss Lockwood." He reached across the table to help her. Knox struck a match and lit it for her. "Draw slowly, to get the end burning," he tutored her.

She coughed a little with the first pull, the smoke searing the back of her throat, but by the third pull she found she liked it. Drawing a mouthful of smoke, releasing it luxuriantly into the already gray air, she smiled. "What sort of cigar is this?" she asked.

"I don't know off-hand," Smythe said, "but, since you've developed a taste for it, I'll have a box sent to your office at the *Courier*. Or would you prefer I send it to your home?"

"No, the paper's fine, thanks." She smiled in anticipation of the reactions she'd get.

"Would you care for some bourbon?" asked Smythe, smiling. "I apologize for not offering earlier. I didn't realize how. . . cosmopolitan you were."

"Just the cigar, thanks."

"So, how much land can the state afford?" Knox asked. "Got a lot of local businesses that will be torn up by the roots."

Endicott nodded. "We're well aware of that. I think the problem has been, in part, how much those businesses are worth. Don't misunderstand," he said to Knox, "the governor wants this done. So it will be done. But the governor knows that we have to compensate the businesses. Still, the state's pockets aren't bottomless. We're thinking that some compromise price must be out there."

"Remember, gentlemen," June said, blowing a plume of smoke, "I was invited by our governor to be a voice in this campaign. I've spent a lot of my time speaking to crowds from Montauk to Black Rock. People believe we are saving the falls. They believe that if they make the trip up here they won't feel they've entered a den of thieves." She blew another mouthful of smoke through puckered lips.

Smythe knocked some ash from his cigar. "What are you saying?" he asked.

"My voice, and my paper, are a force behind saving the falls," June said, emboldened by the nicotine. "If we try too hard to keep everyone happy," she smiled at Knox, "my voice will just continue to call for reform. With louder and louder volume."

"And I will make certain her voice is heard beyond the roar of the falls," added Dorsheimer, smiling at June, amused by the sight of her puffing the cigar. By the time the meeting concluded, whether it was the forces already in play, or the sight of June enjoying her cigar, Smythe and Knox were in retreat and Endicott had some numbers to take back to the governor. June accepted a peck on the cheek from Dorsheimer. "I think the deal is done," he said, "I'm going to cable Olmstead. You have an editorial to write."

She got a cable from the governor a week later. 'New York State will purchase forty parcels for a total of over four hundred acres, three hundred of it under water. This is every acre of riverfront from which one can see the falls. Your efforts will be remembered by a grateful state.'

'A wise compromise. . .' June wrote, in the privacy of her office, enjoying a cigar. It cost almost a million and a half dollars. June wrote with gusto; 'Gone will be the factories whose slop defiled the gorge wall beside the falls, and the shops and the sleazy tourist traps'.

Well, 'gone' overstated it. Some of it disappeared. Some just rebuilt a thousand yards further inland, or upriver, out of sight, out of mind. Still, on July 4th of 1885, June joined in the cheer of the large crowd when the bridge to Goat Island dropped its dollar fare and became a public thoroughfare. Though it was pouring rain, there were throngs. Though she had seen plenty of the falls and of Goat Island, she wanted to be there as she saw people who had obviously come in from the surrounding country to see it for the first time.

'Imagine having lived alongside this falls and not having the financial means to actually see it. It was long overdue,' she wrote in the paper, 'but the state has finally stepped in to save us from ourselves. The beauty of the falls was being buried by the worst of business greed. Today Goat Island and the American falls are again the works of beauty many of us thought we'd never see again.'

That was her best year. Then the 20th century came to the falls early, and neither she nor the falls would ever be the same.

Perhaps she got tired. Perhaps it was all the science behind the forces that began changing the village into a town. She didn't like science, and what little she'd been taught was permeated with theology, and every day some new discovery discredited some of what she'd struggled as a child to memorize. She was left feeling especially ignorant whenever she saw a story about electricity, which was almost every day.

Lester came into her office one afternoon in February, 1886. The sky was dark and snow was falling, and she was wearing a shawl she hated because it made her look old, but it was the coziest garment she could type with. It was the only cosmetic concern she had. "June," Lester began, "what do you know about elec-tri-city?"

She frowned. "Well, I'm a customer. I work under electric lights and my home is lit with it. But I don't really know much about it."

"You might want to start learning. I just had lunch with some very important men," he said, and instantly regretted his choice of words as her irritation leaked out. "They have received grants from the state legislature to divert water for the purpose of producing electricity."

"So?" she asked. "We've been doing that for years."

"Electricity has been the subject of some experimentation recently," Lester went on, quoting from his lunch partners, "there's a story in Colliers about the different merits of direct current and alternating current."

Her eyes glazed over. "I have no idea what you're talking about."

"I don't fully understand it myself," Lester admitted. "But we need to learn it. I think electricity is going to be even bigger than the high-wire stunters."

She raised an eyebrow. "Really?" She looked up at the limelight. "It's brighter than oil, which is good. It's cleaner than coal, and oil. But it's just. . . light."

She got past her irritation that she, as managing editor, had not been invited to lunch but Lester, her subordinate, was. Being a man made him stronger. He'd steadily ingratiated himself with the business community in ways June would never. And now he was diving into the latest fad, this 'electricity'.

She joined a woman's group and took a trip with them to the Holy Land that year. She was gone for three months, and while she enjoyed herself, she learned she was a workaholic. On the trip back she hid in the ship's library to write out her columns. In the library she made a new friend, Alma White, the spinster daughter of a local judge. Alma had attended the University of Buffalo, studying theology and art history.

"You're so fortunate," Alma said on their last night on the ocean before landing. "You've made yourself into someone."

June finished her sentence, looked up at Alma, who was almost fifteen years younger, and smiled. "Yes, I guess I have. I'm a newspaper editor." Then, a little boastful, she said, "and I'm the only female editor that I know. And you see these gray hairs?" she held out a strand of her graying brown hair, a little longer than she usually wore it. "For every one of them I had to charm or outsmart or fight my way around a man. Mostly the latter two. That's what you have to do."

Alma looked dismayed. "I did have an offer to teach at a girl's school in Syracuse, but father didn't care for it."

"Why not?"

"He thinks I should concentrate on finding a husband," she dropped her voice almost to a whisper, "he says I'm not exactly the pick of the litter."

"That's damn flattering," June said. "Why don't you come to work for me?"

"I'm not a reporter," Alma said, blushing. "I couldn't do what you do. I couldn't ask people, ask men, difficult questions."

"Maybe you couldn't. Maybe you can, if you get some practice. But I can always use a society reporter. That doesn't involve men," June offered.

Alma smiled, her eyes wide with excitement. "Society reporter. That sounds delightful. I'd love to," she said, hesitantly. "If it isn't a bother for you."

"No bother. If you last a whole year you'll have lasted twice as long as usual. Here," she handed her latest column to Alma, "read that and see if you find any spelling errors. I'm writing about the trip, to be published by the paper when we return."

Her first day back, in early October, she learned that the front desk receptionist was now a Miss Hague, replacing Miss Rappaport, now the hastily married mother of one.

"Did you enjoy your trip?" Miss Hague asked June politely, a little cautiously, afraid perhaps that June would notice her. She'd heard stories about June. Cigar smoking, for one.

June intended to give Miss Hague, a pleasant looking girl with a mop of red hair, a general and positive paragraph about it, perhaps the first paragraph of the column she'd written, but she saw the day's headline, 'Niagara Falls Hydroelectric Power and Manufacturing Company offers prize to best design for transmission of electricity over great distance.' "Oh, this was that stuff Lester was so excited about," she remembered, forgetting Miss Hague's pleasantry. "I'll have to ask him about it."

"Uh, Miss Lockwood, Mr. Davidson told me to be sure to tell you when you first arrived that you will be wanted at a meeting," Miss Hague said meekly.

"You mean now?" she asked the receptionist, who nodded slightly.

June headed up the steps, pausing at step ten to catch her breath, to her surprise. She got to the top and saw her office door already open. "Isn't this a little rude?" she asked Lester when she found him in her office. "I've just stepped in the door, I haven't even had the opportunity to look at my piles of backed up correspondence, and you are in my office and I'm expected at a meeting?"

"Abner Smythe called it," Lester said by way of apology. "We're meeting here, in about five minutes."

"What's this about, Lester," she asked. "What couldn't wait?"

"Abner will be here shortly." Lester went out for a quick smoke.

Abner arrived five minutes later.

"June, you look tanned," said Abner, still a Father Christmas sort, but a little out of season. "I think the vacation agreed with you."

Her tan from the Holy Land had faded by that time. Her instincts were fully alerted; Abner almost never came by in his capacity as the president of the board, and he didn't compliment people much. "It was a very stimulating trip. But I missed this place terribly. What's the need for this meeting on my first day back?"

"I'm here in my role as president of the board. We need to see some changes." He took a seat, Lester returned from his smoke and took a seat by the door. He wouldn't make eye contact with her, instead looking at the framed story of Blondin on the wall behind her. "You've contributed a great deal to the paper over the years, so we want to be fair," Abner continued, and she felt the bottom of her world quaking. "In the past five years some important changes have happened in our little city, with the building of the Schoellkopf power plant, and the plans being made by Mr. Rankine and Mr. Adams. Niagara Falls is about to become a world leader in the commercial development of electricity. Lester has made it his business to follow it, and he's done well. Did you see today's headline?" She nodded. "We'd like to see Lester take on more responsibility for the editorial direction of the paper. For that to happen, he should be the managing editor."

She looked at Lester, who had been watching her. Her look was pure murder.

"Because we, Lester and I, agree that the paper wouldn't be the same without you," Abner was saying, "we've created a position of senior columnist. Your material would appear with a byline, as a column."

She took a deep breath, wished she had a cigar, then exhaled. "Would it be possible," she asked Abner, "for us to talk, without Lester?"

Abner nodded. "Lester? Would you excuse us?" Lester was gone in a heartbeat. "June, you're an institution around here, but—"

"What?" June asked. "What is this for? Have I irritated some local business?"

Abner failed to restrain a smile. "June, at one time or other you've irritated every local business. Sometimes with your opinions, sometimes with your piercing logic. I suspect you forget, sometimes, what a maverick you are."

"So this is what happens to mavericks? They suffer a coup d'etat?"

"That is what happens to political regimes," Abner corrected her. "You are not the president of a country, just the editor of a paper." She smoldered. "I talked with the rest of the board about this. We normally would have waited for you to retire. But you are already past forty, you show no inclination towards getting married and you're almost too old to have children." June blushed deeply. "The business community respected John Bruhn's opinion of you, and we've let you run the paper for a few years. And you certainly had fun with us when the governor decided to create a park where we had businesses. But our patience isn't endless." She gave Abner the same look she'd given Lester. It didn't seem to rattle Abner much. "You're a caretaker, not a captain. I think you never fully appreciated that. It's time the captain took control."

She went home and smashed some dishes. She went for a ride in the country and smoked some cigars. She had more claret than she could handle and stayed home sick for a day. Each day the *Courier* was headlined with stories on electricity. Each night she sat in the dim light of oil lamps, refusing to turn on her lights, refusing to sleep with the enemy. Realizing on the third day that she was running away, she returned to work. Her new office was a generous one, with a view of the street, but the door said 'Senior Columnist' and she never spoke a kind word to Abner Smythe again.

Alma White started as a proofreader.

At her home one September evening, June answered a knock on her door and saw Horace Pepper standing there with a bouquet of flowers, wild ones she suspected he'd gathered nearby. He was, as she recalled, gentle in temperament but not exactly romantic. "June, may I come in?" He was in a suit, hadn't added a pound to his gaunt five-foot-six, hundred-and-twenty frame, and had grown a beard that was specked with gray.

She smiled and let him in, invited him to sit and, without thinking about it, opened a bottle of claret. "Would you like a drink?" she asked, and marveled at the sudden leap in her mood. Horace nodded; always soft spoken, she wondered when he left for the Lockport paper how he'd cut it as a reporter. "How have you been?" she asked, handing him a glass of red wine and sitting with her own glass. "You look well," she said, and then shut up.

"I'm back here for good," he said, "I just got off the train, and the first place I thought to come was here."

They had been lovers, secret and discreet, like youngsters in their middle years, shy and easily embarrassed, each grateful to find the other. By lamp light after their first awkward lovemaking, Horace showed her the sunken skin in his left calf where a minie ball had gouged out muscle and a piece of bone, leaving him with a permanent limp. She took Horace to the Hermit's Bath one especially humid summer night and they'd bathed like the hermit once did, in the invigorating waters. Letting their toes feel the rush of the torrent, they enjoyed an hour of undiscovered carnal delight, their most daring act. It was the only sexual memory June had, and when Horace left she moped for weeks.

Now she couldn't help noticing that Horace's ring finger was wonderfully free of matrimonial gold.

"So what brings you back?" she asked, not expecting it was her. She thought of offering him a slot on the paper, before remembering her own dethroning.

"I've got a job working on the new electricity generating project. I'm to be a secretary to Mister Adams. I'm to help with the contest, handling correspondence," said Horace proudly. In his forties now, a few years younger than she, he wore glasses and stood just an inch taller than June. If they had children they would not be giants.

She smiled. "What contest? Oh, that contest. Two kinds of electricity?" *My lover returns, and he knows about the mystery of electricity,* she rejoiced. They drank claret, and joked about old times, and, two more glasses of wine later when June's clock chimed nine in the evening, they were embracing. "You should stay here tonight," June said insistently, her blouse unbuttoned but a corset and two other garments to go. "there's not a clean hotel worth the money in town anymore."

Horace nodded slightly, and they moved into June's bedroom for the rest of the evening.

"Teach me everything about electricity," June urged her lover the next morning over pancakes. "I mean, I've tried to learn it but I'm dense. I was bumped aside last week. They made Lester Davidson the managing editor."

"Who did you irritate this time?" Horace asked, smiling. "The Temperance Union or the brewery?"

"It's because I don't understand electricity," June said. "That's what Abner said. It's really because I'm a woman. And because I helped the Governor open Goat Island and Prospect Point to the public. So tell me about this contest."

Horace happily obliged. "Well, it's all part of our new company, the Niagara Falls Power Company. We contacted Thomas Edison, and members of the Royal Society in London, and I wrote letters to universities in this country, and in Europe. The contest is to figure out a way to generate power and send it long distances. There are, to keep it simple, two kinds of electricity."

"Direct and alternating, I know," she said, smiling, having exhausted her understanding of electricity.

"Direct can only flow about ten miles from its source. Then it just peters out. Mr. Edison has most of New York City lit up these days, but to do it there are generators every mile or so, and lots of wires in the air. And he has competitors and they add their wires. It's getting to be an eyesore. Or so I've heard," he said. "But alternating current can potentially travel long distances. We didn't have a way of using alternating current. So we have this competition, with prizes in the thousands, to see if someone can't think their way through this."

June nodded, soaking it all in. As a senior columnist, she only had to write a column, which left her with free time. She was also correcting copy and informally tutoring the new reporters. Frank Shane had written about the competition, and June barely touched his copy. She couldn't correct what she couldn't understand. "And what's happened? Did someone crack the mystery?"

"Possibly," said Horace. He lit a cigar and stared as his lover took it from his mouth and puffed away. After his astonishment faded with her giggle, he lit another for himself. "There's a young man from Eastern Europe named Nikola Tesla, and in the past year he's filed patents for an induction motor. It's a way of using alternating current. He's been awarded several patents now, and if they all work the way they're described, we have a way to generate electricity here and send it via cables to Buffalo, and I guess to anywhere."

"So what about the contest and the people in Europe and Mr. Edison? And the prizes? Shouldn't you just be talking to Mr. Tesla?"

"He's working now with a gentleman named Westinghouse, and they've declined to take part in the contest, so I don't know how we can use Tesla's ideas, that's up to Mr. Adams and Mr. Rankine. Mr. Edison doesn't want any part of alternating current. All his money is tied up in direct. But this alternating current could be really big. Some folks I've heard say it won't just be used to light up the night. It might become more powerful, cheaper even, than water power. Or coal."

"Really," June said, smiling. Was she smiling because she'd shocked her lover with her cigar, or because she knew perfectly well that there would never be a form of power cheaper at Niagara than water power. "That's silly. And there's going to be a second power company? How much demand for electricity could there be in this town?"

"Well, I can't help noticing you've got electric lights wired in here. Why aren't you using them?"

She blushed. "It's an experiment. That's why I don't see a big future for electricity. I find I prefer oil light. But tell me more about your business."

"We're going to generate current only, not be in the business of selling it. There'll be a second company to distribute it to customers. My supervisors are convinced it will be far more successful than the Schoellkopf station, if we can send power further than the city limits."

"Will it be as ugly as the one on the high bank?"

"No, actually, and that's thanks in part to you," Horace smiled in pride. "Having just spared the falls from desper- uh, despuh- uh—"

"Despoliation," June said.

"Right. They aren't keen on spoiling it again with a big electrical generating plant. The idea Mr. Evershed started with was to use underground tunnels. There's no need to put any of it up where people can see it. The turbines, the motors that convert water to power, can spin just as well a hundred feet below ground."

"But what difference does it make?" she asked. "We've got Carborundum and Pittsburgh Reduction here. They built their factories here to use the cheap power. There's no need to ship the power to Pittsburgh if they're willing to come here to use it."

Horace tapped the ash of his cigar into a plate. "You have to try and think more. . . broadly."

She butted out her cigar and they kissed.

They ate, bread and butter and cold chicken from the icebox and a bottle of milk. Horace was hungry. She was scribbling notes for a story on this new power plant.

Looking at her across the kitchen table, he looked at her proudly. "I read every piece you wrote".

June smiled. "Why didn't you ever write me?"

"I thought you were mad at me leaving."

"I was, a little," she said.

"You threw an inkpot at the wall when I told you," he reminded her.

"I remember," she said, smiling. "So if you leave again, I shouldn't waste my time standing by the post office." She set her pencil down. "Listen to this." She read aloud, "'Mess'rs Rankine and Adams are proposing a second power company for Niagara. Where the Niagara Falls Hydraulic and Power Company generates direct current to nearby customers on the High Bank, this facility will be mostly underground, and plans to generate current which can be shipped to Buffalo and beyond.'"

"You don't 'ship' electricity," Horace corrected her.

She frowned. "What do you do with it?"

"You transmit it. The lines it travels through, copper wires, are called transmission lines."

She scratched out 'shipped' and wrote in 'transmitted'. "Wait until I show this to Lester. We'll see who knows about electricity."

The city never seemed to rest. More companies built factories on the high bank, the gorge wall near the falls, close to Schoellkopf's growing direct-current company. On the other side of town, water intakes were being dug and blasted into the rock for the other power company.

June visited Horace for lunch, at his office, a neat wood frame building a little ways from the tunnels. "So how are you going to transmit the power to Buffalo?"

"Mr. Adams don't confide all the details in me," Horace said, slipping on his grammar as he had done as a struggling news writer. "The official answer is 'we don't know'. Unofficially, he and Mr. Dean are real interested in seeing what might happen with alternating current."

"Mr. Tesla's ideas?"

"Mr. Tesla's ideas."

They went for a walk to look at the hole in the ground. Looking down into the man-made crevice in the rock, June watched laborers travel in and out with donkey-drawn carts of lumber and others stacked with bricks. Deep underground the layers of limestone were being blasted. The stone was removed by hand, loaded in carts, and eleven men had died thus far, two when rock fell, the others from not handling nitro with the proper respect. She learned that three blasts of a steam whistle meant 'take cover'. About ten seconds after the blast, there was a muffled explosion. Sometimes it rattled window panes. Sometimes she felt it through the floor of her home, a mile away, just as she felt the trains. Then the laborers and wagons would be busy moving rock again.

"Today I spent the day writing letters to brick makers," Horace explained, "asking whether they could supply brick and how much. We line the tunnels with bricks. Two million of them so far. Our current supplier can't keep up."

She took off her new spectacles to wipe them free of dust. Electric lighting made for better reading, but age could not be helped. She got tired of holding type two feet from her eyes, and she rather liked how she looked in spectacles. "Two million bricks." She put them back on and watched the work and asked, "Horace, I know I'm the dullest of the dull in understanding electricity, but I know that all of the customers of the Schoellkopf plant build close to the plant because direct current can't travel far. We're publishing a story tomorrow that announces your company has acquired fifteen hundred acres here, specifically for tenants of your electrical company. Does that mean that Mr. Rankine and Mr. Adams have decided to throw in their lot with direct-current?"

Horace finished the sentence he was writing before answering. That was how he was. "No, that's not what that means, but I'm glad you mentioned it. You reminded me of the debate." Her eyebrows rose with interest. "I've received an invitation to attend a meeting to be held at the Mason's Hall. It'll be the day after tomorrow. It's going to be quite exciting," he said to his love, his own watery gray eyes wide with anticipation. "Remember Mr. Tesla?" June nodded. "And I know you're familiar with Thomas Edison?"

"Dear, five year olds know who Thomas Edison is," she jabbed.

"Then that's a 'yes'?" Horace said, and she lowered her eyelids at his riposte; it was the only sexy gesture she knew, and he was the only man she could use it on. But it was neither the time nor the place. "With the progress Mr. Tesla's made, Mr. Edison's gone traveling across the country in a very vigorous campaign against alternating current," he explained, a little brusquely.

"I believe I read something somewhere about that." She was miffed, but let it pass. An afternoon break for Cupid wrestling wasn't in the cards.

"Well," said Horace, as though he had the scoop of the week, "Mr. Edison and Mr. Tesla will be speaking together at the Mason's Hall. The whole thing is being organized rather hastily, organized by the American Institute for Electrical Engineers. It turns out Mr. Edison is in the area, as is Mr. Tesla. This could be the best night of science in the history of this town. Edison arguing the dangers of alternating current, Tesla arguing its benefits. It will certainly put us on the map."

"We've been on the map for some time," June said dismissively. A night of science, a night of men talking concepts she couldn't fully grasp. It seemed to reinforce their assessment of women, with minds unequal to men. As for the Mason's Hall, an institution where women were not welcome, it made her a little claustrophobic. But she'd fought these fears successfully for years. "You're right, Horace. It will be important. Can you get me in?"

Horace's zeal lost some shine. He knew telling her was a calculated risk, but then he liked the chance to be on top once in a while. "I thought you'd ask that." He thought a moment. Getting June Lockwood, the loudest female voice in town, into a Mason's Hall? "We'll arrange it somehow, I guess." He knew her figure well, but now he looked at her as would a tailor. "You wouldn't fit in one of my suits, would you?"

The Mason's Hall was filled. The auditorium, its walls draped in velvet, lit by electronic arc lights, the air already thick with cigar smoke. Above center stage, just above the curtains, hung the Masonic Symbol. On the stage was a table flanked by two podiums. Clamped to the table was a small generator with a hand-crank, two rubber-insulated cables, the power and ground respectively, and a lightbulb. A policeman was guarding the table, as men in suits, young mostly, were gathered around it pointing out details of the generator.

In front of the stage was another crowd, this one composed of reporters and photographers. At the center of this crowd was an old man with white hair, in a brown suit. "Mr. Edison, Thomas Monacre from the *Detroit News*," said a photographer. "Will you be demonstrating the dangers of direct current here the same way you did in Philadelphia?" Monacre waved two others clear and got a good exposure with the help of the theatre's cutting-edge illumination. He didn't wait for Edison's answer; the picture was his goal, the question just a way of getting Edison to look at him.

Sitting in their seats a few rows back, two gentlemen sat, one wearing his hat, the other holding his in his lap. The one wearing the hat asked the other carefully, mouth to ear, "what did he mean by 'the way you did in Philadelphia'?"

"Mr. Edison has been demonstrating the dangerous fluctuations in voltage possible from alternating current by touching the power cord to small animals. It never fails to electrocute them."

The first man's mouth hung open. He was unusual in the crowd in having neither sideburns, moustache nor beard. "You think he's really going to kill a defenseless animal?"

"He would consider it a sacrifice in the name of science," said the second man, clearly uncomfortable himself with the logic.

"I wish you'd told me that before."

A cheer from the back of the theatre rose in volume as a second group of reporters and men entered and came down the aisle. A tall man with curly black hair, younger than Edison, was the center of attention. "That would be Tesla. Nikola Tesla," said the second man.

"The genius from Europe. The one who invented alternating current," said the first man.

"He didn't invent it," the second corrected. "He invented a motor that could use it, which is almost as important."

The reporters took more pictures, but the cheers and some catcalls were growing in volume and asking either genius a question was almost impossible with the noise. A stout fellow in evening garb with mutton-chop whiskers Horace recognized as an engineer with the Adams project climbed the steps to the stage and used a wooden gavel at the left podium. The wooden raps gradually grew louder and clearer as people took notice.

Dimly at first, he called out, "we need order, we need your attention. Please take your seats and we can begin tonight's presentations. Quiet, please. Gentlemen, please take your seats."

Tesla was led to the stage and a seat behind the left podium. Edison ended up in a seat behind the right podium. The moderator continued. "Gentlemen, invited guests, members of the American Institute of Electrical Engineers, we have tonight a rare honor. As we all know, the power of electricity is the pathway to tomorrow." He paused to take a sip from a bottle. The audience was now almost silent. "Mr. Thomas Edison, holder of more patents than I can count," laughter and clapping briefly interrupted him, "is seated to my left. To my immediate right," and he bowed briefly to Tesla, "I have the honor of presenting Mister Nikola Tesla, who has recently patented an induction motor that runs off alternating current."

Another burst of applause, perhaps louder than the one after Edison, filled the air but ended quickly when the moderator raised his hand for silence. "We will begin with a statement from each scientist on their learned opinions on electricity and its potential, followed by a demonstration of his own, for which we have with us a small, hand-powered generator, which many of you saw. Without further ado, by mutual consent, Mr. Edison will speak first. Mr. Edison?"

Edison stood, went to his podium and scanned the crowd with a tight-lipped grin. "Gentlemen, it is indeed an honor to speak with you at Niagara, home of the greatest hydro-electrical generating facility in the world." The room was otherwise silent. "As you all know, direct current has been in use at Niagara Falls for the past eight years, at the Schoellkopf generating facility." A round of applause rose around Jacob Schoellkopf, in attendance in the third row, as he rose briefly and waved. Mr. Edison joined in the applause. "The Schoellkopf is a prime example of the use of direct current. Tenants can join in clusters within a mile of the generating facility, which here makes vast amounts of power from the free water of Niagara. Those of you who have visited Manhattan recently no doubt have noticed the proliferation of Edison generators and its new customers. We are reaching into private homes, public facilities and places of business. Simple generators placed every couple of miles proves that direct current is easily controlled and a viable motor for the growth of industry." He fell silent a moment. There were, actually, serious issues with sparks from the power lines through neighborhoods, but no one dared interrupt him. "There is a second version of electricity. As different from the first as belladonna is to mother's milk. I speak of alternating current."

Some more applause erupted briefly in the rear seats, the cheaper seats, where the younger men sat, the backers of alternating current. "You applaud, my friends, but for what? A scientific quirk. A creation of Nature like a shark, murderous by nature and helpless to change. It produces a dangerous level of voltage that defies control. The beauty of direct current is that it is stable. It travels only a short distance. Beyond ten miles there is no danger of electricity being unleashed. For, while we have made a great tool of electricity, it can just as easily be our undoing. Careless use of direct current could, in theory, kill, but there are natural limits on how far it can travel, and therefore natural limits on its danger." He paused for dramatic effect. "Alternating current can be manipulated to travel well beyond the generating source. And containing it is a far from perfect science. Let me give you a demonstration."

From the crowd, some rumbling, some laughs, of the lower, cruder sort.

A man in a white shirt and collar but no tie or jacket, a burly man out of place amongst the engineers, appeared on cue to take the handle of the generator. He also carried under his arm a puppy, a small black dog with floppy ears, in a wire cage that he set on the table. At Edison's cue, he began to crank the generator. The crowd fell silent.

"While my associate generates alternating current, let me point out another device necessary to the transmission of alternating current. This is a small voltage transformer. It is an essential part of the transmission of alternating current. It takes a lower voltage, which is how it must travel in the wire, and raises it. How much and how easily is it controlled? We don't know." Edison leaned forward with a look of urgency. "It could easily bring a killing voltage into your homes. A level of power that would do this to your children." And without warning, Edison turned a small knob on the transformer, picked up a rubber-covered cable with a flat metal edge and touched it briefly to the tail of the puppy.

It yipped, a high, thin shriek. And smoke rose from its fur. A minute later the stink of burning meat spread through the hall. The puppy had collapsed into a dead pile of fur.

The audience was quiet. A deep sigh, approaching a growl, could be heard from Tesla. He was shaking his head.

Edison directed the cage with the dead puppy be passed among the first row of the audience, verifying that the puppy was dead. At the end of the row the last viewer handed the cage with the dead puppy to the assistant, who took it behind the stage. "That, my friends is part of the unstable danger of alternating current. We cannot contain it. Direct current remains under our control. It is the safer form of power and the one this country will move forward with. Thank you for your kind attention." He sat behind his podium to scattered applause.

Tesla stood. He was a foot taller than Edison and half his age. His English was accented, but he spoke well. "Gentlemen of the American Institute of Electrical Engineers. My thanks for your kind invitation to speak." He paused a moment and took a drink of water from a glass at the podium. "The demonstration that Mr. Edison has just given us only proves one thing. Dogs are not a good means of transmitting electrical power."

A wave of laughter passed through the crowd; it was hesitant, for the object of the laughter was either a dead dog or America's leading scientist, neither of whom inspired laughter.

"Direct current has served us well during this early stage, our learning phase. To accomplish what Mr. Schoellkopf," he rolled the letters as would a native of Germany, "has is a great example of commercial application of science. I wish him every continued success."

Another wave of applause passed over. Schoellkopf nodded his thanks to Tesla but stayed seated.

"Mr. Edison has just shown us that voltage transformers can raise or lower the voltage in the transmission line. This is the great benefit of alternating current. It can flow at low voltage for miles. For tens of miles. To Buffalo easily. And further. And when it is needed, one connects it to a voltage regulator, a copper coil essentially, and one immediately has high voltage. It is thus suitable for incandescent light, for arc light, and for manufacturing applications. It may seem new and frightening, but it is well within our power to control. And once it is controlled, it will transform our lives even more than it already has. Do you want to see another experiment?"

The young men in the back applauded loudly. Tesla walked back to the alternating current generator. The same burly fellow reappeared and handed Tesla a small object which Tesla took in his right hand and held up. "The current regulator is, of course, key to maintaining safe amperage. And the current regulator is as safe as," he shrugged theatrically, "as direct current." He got some chuckles. He held aloft a light bulb. "A carbon light bulb," he explained to the house. He waited for the generator to get a few spins in it. "I am now turning the voltage regulator down. Down to twelve volts. Down from a hundred. And, more importantly, the amperage is turned down to six amps. And watch me."

"I do take one precaution," said the scientist, and from behind the podium he produced two simple sandals with thick soles. "These are cork-soled shoes, to be sure I am not the electricity's favorite path to the ground. Wearing these, let me show you how alternating current is our servant, not our nemesis." Tesla held the bulb in one hand and took the same cable with which Edison had killed the dog in his other hand. The bulb lit and Tesla smiled. "I need not explain to you all what is happening here," he said. The back row began applauding. "I'm not experiencing any heat. I feel a little tingle, but it could be the honor of being in your august presence." He smiled charmingly. The bulb's light ebbed, brighter one minute, dimmer the next. Tesla turned the knob. "Let's take it up to twenty amps." After a minute of continuous light, Tesla let go the cable, set the bulb down, and shook the assistant's hand.

"Let me show you another example." He set the bulb down and bent over the table a moment, working with wires. He held a cable in each hand and nodded to the assistant to crank the generator. The audience gasped as blue flickers of lightning traveled over Tesla's body. It crackled in his hair, which rose as though a stiff wind blew it straight up. Tesla walked slowly from one side of the stage to the other, the blue crackling lightning flowing over his body, giving all a good view. When he finally returned to the table and set the cables down, the hall erupted in loud applause. Edison kept a stony grin on his face as Tesla took his bows. "I hope you leave this evening remembering that alternating current is safe, if used scientifically."

She got out of Horace's second-best suit as soon as they were back in the stone house. The bedroom was bright with electric light, but now she looked at it as the killer of small puppies. The linen with which she'd bound flat her modest bosom came off and she let herself go natural for the evening, just wearing a cotton shift. The demonstration had confused and horrified her. She nearly cried out when that bastard Edison killed the puppy, and her contempt for the hardness of men grew when no one else protested. She went down to the kitchen, sat at the table and wrote it all down while it was fresh in her mind. In thirty minutes of intense writing she captured it, then got up and chopped a piece of ice from her icebox. She held it to her forehead, then her neck.

Horace had lingered at the hall and shortly after she was finished he arrived. "Is he going to a kill a dog in every city in this country?" she asked Horace, as though her lover was Edison's secretary. "I've decided to disconnect our lights," she said. "I keep thinking of that puppy."

"It's a stupid trick. I don't know why he persists in doing it. It seems to go over better in New York City, where he pretty much is the power source," said Horace. He opened the ice box and poured himself a glass of milk. Sighing with delight, he finished off half of it. "As for disconnecting the lights, let's leave them on a little longer. At least until my company starts generating. Then we can switch." He finished the milk. "Did I tell you that Mr. Adams has cancelled the contest, the hundred thousand dollar prize?" June shook her head. "They didn't get anything that fit the bill, but the gentleman we hired to evaluate them wrote up his own design, which might work. For alternating current. I think they were leaning towards it anyway, and after tonight's demonstration, from the talk I heard, I think our future is with Mr. Tesla's method."

"That's good news," she said.

"I forgot to tell you, I've been promoted, sort of."

"Promoted?" She embraced him. "That's wonderful. What do you mean, sort of?"

Horace poured more milk. "Well, I told you the canals are being dug, and they are being lined with millions of bricks." He set his empty glass down to free up his hands to tell the story. "About a month ago the head mason came up to Mr. Agutter, our bookkeeper. He said we were out of bricks. You could have knocked Agutter over with a feather. 'I just paid for five thousand bricks, not two days ago, bricks delivered by train,' he said. Then the head mason says, 'we got just two hundred bricks left and that won't last us a day.' Apparently it isn't the first shortage we've had. Mr. Agutter was asked to take up my tasks, and I take up his. He had more to do, and he earned more. I guess they think he might be stealing."

She kissed his forehead. "I'm happy for you, though Percy Agutter is a rock solid old Episcopalian and not the sort I'd think of as a thief. Now, if the bricks keep getting stolen, what will happen to you?"

"I don't intend anything to happen," said Horace. "Percy didn't like to move from his desk. I intend to move around and keep my eye on things."

The next day she published her angry column on Edison and learned from the stories published in the other papers that there was a ground-swell among the leading engineers for Tesla. Lester met her late in the day in her office. "I just wanted to console you. You confronted Mr. Edison and no one, not one person, has thrown a brick through our window. Will you make it home all right?"

She looked left, then right, then stuck out her tongue.

The next day Lester knocked on her door. "I've been invited on a tour of the Adam's construction site. They were pleased with your column. They've finished blasting one tunnel and it's being lined. It's quite a site. Can I interest you?"

June was re-reading her old story on the Loyalists. She got it out periodically, polished it a little, thinking that someday she would publish it, when she was satisfied with it. She was capable of polishing her writing for years. Good thing for deadlines, she knew, or I'd never get my copy finished. "Yes, I hear they're going through a lot of bricks."

Lester nodded. "So it's a date? We're to be at the entrance tomorrow at one for a tour. Wear good walking shoes."

"George Kilgore," their guide introduced himself. George was in his late twenties, and his spectacles and suit indicated that he worked at a drafting table, not with a trowel. "I'll be leading you today. Please watch your steps when we get into the yard."

They were permitted past a wooden gate covered with NO ADMITTANCE signs, and the journalists had their first good look at the hole in the earth. Cool air flowed up from its damp, dark emptiness. It was like standing at the edge of the falls in the dark of night with no water passing over. "How deep does this go?" asked June, fighting vertigo.

"A hundred and eighty feet, more or less," said Kilgore. "Basically as far down as the American falls. You see that gate?" They saw a steel and wood barrier near the river's edge. "When this canal goes into service we'll take that down. There's a wing dam we'll put in place, and that will help funnel the water in. It will fall as far as it would naturally. When it reaches the end of its trip it will spin the paddles of a turbine."

"And that will create the alternating current?" June ventured.

Kilgnore nodded. "Absolutely right, Miss Lockwood."

She beamed. Lester wasn't speaking, his own attack of vertigo threatening the safety of his luncheon pork chops.

Kilgore led them to the edge of daylight. There were pumps working and pipes carrying water. "That water in there?" asked Lester, hoping to sound intelligent.

"Yes sir. There's water pouring into the tunnel constantly. We've got a generator going full-time to keep it dry."

June walked to the wall of the tunnel, and looked at the brickwork. "It's lined with brick," she affirmed.

"Yes, Ma'am. We expect when we're done we'll have used nearly twenty million bricks." Kilgore lit two kerosene lanterns and they began walking along a railroad track on a descent. "When the company first tried to tunnel, some years ago, we blasted the rock free and took it out and didn't appreciate how much water we'd be dealing with." The journalists nodded. "We had a lot of cave-ins, walls collapsing."

They could hear work ahead. "Just to put your minds at ease," Kilgore now had to yell, and his voice echoed, "we're not blasting today." A laborer guided a mule, pulling a wagon laden with bricks past them. "Today we're concentrating on lining the walls of the tunnel. We've been digging for three days, and now it's time to reinforce it."

Another mule-drawn wagon came by, this one empty of bricks. Instead, a wooden bench had been installed. "It's a little far to walk, so I thought we'd ride most of the way," Kilgore announced. He helped June up the step, and let Lester make his own climb. Kilgore took the reins of the mule, a gentle tap of the reins and they began descending at mule-rate.

Shining the lamp at the wall, Kilgore pointed out, "we haven't covered all of this area with brick yet. You can see the layers of rock, limestone alternating with shale. The shale is where the water comes from. The nearer to the river, the shale is porous with water. That's why the pump is going."

"Twenty-four hours a day?" asked Lester.

"That's correct," said Kilgore. "The river never stops. And we're on a very aggressive schedule. We even worked on New Years Day. Mr. Adams and Mr. Rankine want this built as quickly as is humanly possible." He pointed out the brick. "First we blast, and then we clear a path and use these mule carts to move out the rock. Then we bring in lumber and reinforce the tunnel. Once it's safe, we use a mix of concrete and rock to patch over the shale as best we can. Then we lay brick. We've got brick five layers deep all the way down."

"That's a lot of bricks!" Lester said, trying to sound funny. "Will it hold back the water once you start up the plant?"

"Yes sir, the pressure from the river water coming in will be greater than the pressure from the shale."

June rolled her eyes; more science. "How much of the river will be diverted?" she asked.

Kilgore started to answer, then looked at June and smiled, awkwardly. He finally said, "in the neighborhood of sixty-eight hundred cubic feet per second."

She stared back. "How much of the river is that?" she asked.

"A drop in the bucket, Ma'am," said Kilgore. He then pursued a detailed history of how that particular stretch of tunnel was dug during the bitter winter and how ice had been a huge problem. "Three men died building this particular stretch."

They didn't follow the tunnel much further; they'd seen bricks, they saw laborers laying more bricks, they were impressed with the mammoth engineering project. Kilgore drove them back up to daylight and they were shown the trench being dug and lined with concrete. "Eventually, of course, we plan to transmit this power. We're committed to alternating-current at this point. In this trench, which will eventually reach to Buffalo, will be a copper cable, with a protective coating of lead. The current will travel via this cable, with transformers at each site to raise or lower the voltage as needed, depending on what they use the power for."

It was late in the afternoon when they returned to the paper. June went to her office, shut her door, and from the outside one could hear her typewriter keys whacking paper, moving as quickly and rhythmically as the piston of a locomotive. What she had seen had alternately thrilled and depressed her. *"I cannot help but worry over how much of the falls we will enslave to generate electricity. Today we may be partaking sparingly of the river, but if electricity becomes popular, we'll need to divert more and more water. When will it end?"*

She typed two pages, read it several times, and thought about her past lessons with business. She had already been demoted to columnist from managing editor. If she raised a cry over electricity, where else could they put her? Worse, what would she do if she didn't have this paper to give her a reason to get out of bed?

She put the column in the same drawer with her story on the Loyalists.

Another sticky evening in August, a year later, after editing Ethan's latest factory story—the Niagara Food Company, using state of the art generating power from the river to make bread, boring copy but apparently the public ate it up—she locked up and went home. Normally the stones helped cool the house in the summer. Tonight, though, the air was heavy and warm and she sat in her parlor reading. There was more street noise than usual, and it was simply too hot to sleep. The windows were wide open but there wasn't any breeze. Horace was atypically out.

Drifting in her windows were sounds of ringing carriage bells, distant conversations she couldn't make out, and the whistle of an evening train arriving. There were a lot of people in town tonight, so the restaurants and the theaters were in full swing. She read yesterday's *Buffalo News*, page two, local news, skimmed the *News'* version of the same New York story the *Courier* would print tomorrow, then lost interest.

There was a woman out there somewhere who laughed like a horse. And the men she was with weren't much quieter. She almost nodded off but she couldn't sleep now, because either the horse-laugh woke her or she kept herself awake waiting for it. And giggling when she heard it. *You're too old to giggle,* she gently scolded herself. She rubbed her eyes and thought of going out, of finding that raucous bunch of people, or at least walking. And wondered where Horace was at this hour.

It was only ten-thirty and she did just fine on only a few hours' sleep. Sitting in the dark, glancing out the window—her carpenter was right, she never sat on her porch—she pulled herself up, set aside the News, and put on her favorite dress, a plain cotton with short sleeves. It was cool and would capture any hint of breeze that touched her.

In the middle of Falls Street she paused in quiet amazement at the revelry taking place tonight. Fireworks were lighting up the sky, the street was filled with crowds spilling out from the taverns, reminding her of the bad old days. "Hasn't been this rowdy since the state took over the falls," she said to no one. So many fireworks, so much food, so much beer, and so many people making so much noise. What was happening? Then she remembered the parting words of Ethan as he had trotted out the door today. "Happy July Fourth, Miss Lockwood!" Of course, July 4th.

Around the rapids were lanterns and arc lights as the nighttime diversions made their money off the celebrants. A few barkers fought with their voices for the spare pennies of the tourists who came out in the daylight to see Nature's antics, at night to see Man's. The lights were on and, from the Goat Island Bridge, June saw the mist of the falls silhouetted by the intense beams. The mist rolled gently and the arc lights threw the river into hazy, moving shadow, making it alive in a form more spiritual, more sensual, than wild. Her eyes, tired from proofing copy, were starting to hurt from the yellow glare of the light. She looked down and rested them on the water, white foamy currents rolling over boulders, dimly reflected in the light but iridescent in the night.

She walked on, crossing the bridge and stepping off onto Goat Island where much the same show she'd left behind continued. On to her favorite spot. She was pretty fearless about walking alone around the falls. The island was too familiar to her for any shrub to hide someone. She could see where a leaf had fallen since her last visit. Reaching her spot, she glanced around for any strangers, then removed her shoes and stockings and let her feet soak in the chilly river water. "Ooh," she gasped, the chilling joy as she'd anticipated.

She was writing the news story of the year, and it was proving a stressful story to research. It was taking time for her to gather her facts, even using the newfangled wire to request information from New York, an expense Lester wasn't happy about, but she was certain she was investigating something important. It was about a man she had met a couple of months ago, a self-styled entrepreneur named William Love. He had come rolling into town last spring with great bravado, which June found common but very unbecoming in a businessman. Loud, boastful men belonged in front of the bazaars, hawking people in. Niagara had a bumper crop of businessmen, and June had met most of them, and Love was just a cheap sideshow barker in their midst.

He was well dressed and he had a southern accent; he didn't raise an eyebrow in Niagara Falls. He wore a green linen suit and a pristine white shirt, gold tie tack and cuff links and shiny, shiny leather boots. That was William Love. He was balding on top and had a dark bushy beard. Fairly tall, not thin, but not stout; he could not be called noticeable for his form.

But he had a skill. He knew the language of business, of financing, of lending, of risks and return on investment. He could speak to bankers and investment houses as though he was one of their own. He rode the New York Central from New York City to Niagara Falls and someone later swore he started the trip without twelve cents in his pocket and when he stepped down onto the platform in the falls he had the financing for Model City and a pre-paid return ticket. But there was a lot of that kind of talk afterwards.

Love arrived alone that day in May in 1893. "Boy. You there," he hailed a small black boy who scurried through the crowd and took the handle of Love's suitcase, struggling with it as he followed Love out of the depot. "Boy," Love asked, his voice a cultivated imperious tone, "where is the finest hotel in this town?"

Pausing to catch his breath, Levon Robinson studied Love. If the man was really interested in the best, then he wanted either the Cataract or the International, and they were close by, which meant a short trip and a small tip. A longer trip was the Kaltenbach, which was also a guaranteed nickel for bringing in the business. "How long you staying, sir?"

"I may never leave," Love said, never taking his eyes off the cloud of mist that rolled above the nearby cataracts.

"Uh-huh," Levon nodded, and hefted the suitcase. All day long he heard voices, some textured and trained to earn money through volume or guile. Love fit right in. If the suitcase held all the man's clothing he was a man of modest means, and the case itself looked battered. "I think the Kaltenbach House would be comfortable, sir. And they can offer you long term rates."

"Kaltenbach it is. Lead on."

The streets were filled with the first wave of the tourist season, and with the businesses that catered to them. It was unpaved but illuminated, boasting light poles alongside the pounded earth, light generated by the Schoellkopf plant, itself a tourist attraction. The nighttime traffic of 'light gawkers' had kept Falls Street almost as busy at night as during the day. Shops now stayed open until well into twilight.

Love was only one of many well-dressed men, but was probably the fastest talking one on the street that day. Rather than engage a cab from the line by the depot and pay Shylock rates, Love let the black boy struggle with his case along the crowded boardwalk, using the suitcase as a breakwall. All the time he was talking aloud, to himself. "Three dry-goods stores within a block, eh? Boy? How many newspapers are printed in town?" Levon briefly raised three fingers as he struggled his way through the sea of legs. "Three papers? And electrical streetlights. I'd read of them. This city has the services for a community twice its size. Excellent. Must find a banker soon. And an assessor."

The Kaltenbach came into view, just as Levon's arms were aching from the load. "Boy, what is your name?"

"Levon, sir."

"Le-von," Love pronounced each syllable like a book of the Bible as they stopped on the boardwalk before the hotel. "How much do you earn in a day?"

Levon felt wary. "Thirty dollars," he said, his best take times five.

"Well," answered Love with smiling skepticism, "I can see I'm in the wrong line of business."

Levon said nothing and wore his expectant smile. "Have you any idea what my business is?" Levon took a guess: grifter, no-account, hustler, gambler...

"I am an entrepreneur," said Love, rolling out the word with an exaggerated French roll. Hustler, Levon decided, holding out his hand now. Love ignored it. "I am here to establish Model City. It will be the first of its kind, a planned industrial community whose power will be drawn from the limitless energy of the Niagara." Love turned to point at the invisible river beyond the buildings and people. "I have in my pocket," he tapped his chest, "a prospectus that has the backing of the New York State legislature, granting me riparian rights that will permit me..." Levon's eyes were glazing over, "and will eventually repay initial investors a conservative return of one thousand per-cent."

Levon blinked, realizing his tip hovered in limbo. "Levon," Love made his pitch, "I would be a sorry example of a businessman if I failed to offer you an opportunity to improve your lot in life. Your invaluable service to me today is easily worth... say, twenty cents," cheap hustler, Levon noted, "but I am prepared to convert that into a five dollar investment certificate in Model City." Love's hand dove for his other pocket and he smiled patronizingly. "And here is the certificate."

"Sir, please," Levon cut in, "I surely appreciate your generosity but I'm no businessman. I just like's to get my pay, so can I have the money, please?"

Love's hand came out with a bundle of papers and peeled off one like a dollar bill from a roll. "But you don't appreciate, my boy, that I am immediately improving your investment astronomically. That, in addition to the increase this stock will show within the week," Love pitched hard, a bead of sweat coming down his forehead, "means a payoff this Sunday of at least thirty dollars. When you go to service on Sunday you can tithe a week's wages and still buy yourself the finest meal in town."

Was it the challenge? He must have had at least fifty dollars in cash on him, since he'd sold a dozen stock certificates on the train ride coming up. So Love had enough to pay off Levon, but it was the kind of man he was, trying to go through life printing his own money.

"I still prefer thirty cents, sir, please." He tried to up the ante even as he was scanning the street for O'Connor or Flaherty, the two cops with the morning beat. Love was frowning. Fishing the coins from his pocket with an effort, Love held the coins just out of reach in one hand, his certificate in the other. "I want you to fully appreciate the opportunity before you make a hasty decision, my boy. Here's the few coins your labor has earned and here is a piece of the future, and I am being exceedingly generous to take so much of my valuable time explaining this opportunity to you."

Levon caught O'Connor's eye, said officer having just stepped out of a tavern. Love saw him too, and pursed his lips. Handing Levon the money, he stuffed his certificates back inside his coat. "Very well, little pickaninny, ignore the future. More than most white men would do for the likes of you." Seizing his suitcase himself, Love walked smartly into the hotel.

"Grifter, Levon?" asked O'Connor, his beefy face flushed.

"Yessir, you got here just in time," said Levon. The officer patted the boy on his head and Levon started back to the station.

Love announced himself in the offices of every paper in town. He talked his way into Lester's office while he changed his typewriter ribbon. "I would advise you to keep an eye on me," he said to Lester, "as I'm going to put this town on the map."

Lester allowed himself a smile. "We think people find us without much trouble," he said. "What sort of business are you engaging in?"

"A project to develop a new community, a model city," Love almost got revved up, but Lester had sent the signal to June to call him, standard practice around the office for rescuing people from the most desperate of the attention-cravers.

"You're needed on the first floor," said June, concealing her smile. "Something about a misspelling on the front page." Lester excused himself and ran to the privy. Love reluctantly left ten minutes later.

Choosing not to assign a reporter to interview Love, two days later Lester read a gushing story about him in the *Power City Daily*, a rival that sold best in the business circles. "They can have him," he said to June. "His plan is to dig a canal across the countryside and, where it falls over the escarpment, create a man-made falls, which will provide cheap electrical power to create a model city that he calls," and Lester struck a melodramatic pose, "Model City."

"How original," she answered dryly. She wondered: should they have covered this? The charter, that is, not Love. She hated to be scooped, even with fools.

"This is my collateral, Mr. Hogan." Love pulled a fat envelope from his attaché, extracted a well-folded legal document and set it on the banker's desk.

Hogan was a nondescript middle-aged man, balding, a neatly barbered fringe of brownish gray hair circling his head, muttonchop sideburns, and the collar and tie of a businessman. He was captain of a bank he'd built with borrowed money, grown with small loans to local businesses and holding savings accounts for the workers crowding into town. His desk should have been that of a poet in a garret somewhere, sheets of paper in piles, one pile spilling onto another, a pot of ink standing open. Love's document unfolded slowly on top. Barricading the paper flow at the desk's edge was a heavy silver pen stand. The stand held two fountain pens. Both were missing. "Don't mind the mess," Hogan said, "I know where everything is."

He picked Love's document off the top of the mound. Opening it cautiously and letting his eyes trickle down its length, Hogan's eyebrows furrowed, his mouth frowned. He studied the paper for several moments longer than was comfortable for Love, trying to comprehend it. Legislative boilerplate repelled his vision, made his eyes slide down to the elaborate signatures at the bottom. Love stood and took a slow, measured tour of Hogan's office, and of Hogan's desk. On top of the pile on the bank president's desk was an article of eviction from...? Love couldn't make out the address. Hogan got up, mumbling, "excuse me, won't you?" and left the office with Love's document. Love, one eye on the door, carefully scanned the papers.

Eviction notice, seizing a rooming house on River Road. Under that, a balance sheet from Niagara Alkali. Negotiating a loan?

Ah! Monthly profit statement for Power City Bank. Love scanned the first page, one eye on the door, turned to the second, then the third. The banking crises begun in March over whether federal paper money was backed by gold was hurting this bank, hurting all banks. There wasn't enough gold just now in the world to prop up the currency of a country that was printing more and more money. The result was inflation. The year had started badly and to tighten their balance sheet they were probably calling in all marginal loans. And the sheet on Niagara Alkali? He couldn't make sense of the numbers. A footstep outside: Love dropped the report, backpedaled to the window with its view of Falls Street, and smiled at Hogan on his return.

"My apologies," said Hogan. "My attention was needed by the head clerk."

Liar, Love thought. *Nobody came for you. You had my document viewed by the lawyer next door to be sure it was no forgery.* "No problem, Mr. Hogan. You must be a busy man and I'll try to conduct my business as quickly as possible and be out of your way."

"What form of business are you considering?"

Love took up a Napoleonic pose by the window. "As you have my charter from the state, you appreciate that I have a plan endorsed by the legislature.

Not strictly speaking, thought Hogan.

"My plan is to channel river water across the county as far as the Lewiston slope. At that place another cataract will be created, a smaller and more easily controlled one. That falls will work as a power source. I intend to create a Model City in the open fields. There will be factories and surrounding the factories there will be homes, churches, shops, and schools. A true community. But a planned community, carefully developed, with managed growth. Not a spontaneous shantytown that dies out in a few years. A city that will last." Love paused to let Hogan catch up. "I am suggesting that Niagara could provide the power and land to re-define how our society develops."

"Your notion is certainly interesting," Hogan began with a variation on his rejection statement, "but my bank is more concerned with profits than with initiating social changes. I—"

"Profits are at the core of my city," Love interrupted, sensing rejection and repackaging his speech. "I am a social planner second, businessman first. I expect to build the city of the future, and it is a businessman's future." Hogan closed his mouth, listening. "In five years this city will make rich men of us all. Across the country, perhaps the world, wherever free land and water still exist, others will seek to copy this plan and become millionaires. Let me explain." Hogan provided a sheet of paper and a pencil as Love first described, then sketched, a city plan. Nestled around the base of the man-made falls would be tunnels, cut into the slope, and through them the river water would be funneled into turbines. These turbines, enormous machines, would power Model City and its industries.

"We are already using this method to generate power from Niagara," Hogan pointed out at one point, "we've done so since 1881, a plan our bank has invested in. Heavily. You must have heard of the Schoellkopf plant? It's been profitable but there are limits on what can be done with electricity. And until more applications are discovered I'd be reluctant to duplicate our investment with this version."

Love forged on. Factories were concentrated near the east side of the canal for ease of wiring. Homes would be built for the workers—

"We tried that in Echota," Hogan again interjected, "without profit. Sir, social planning does not thrive when one needs a profit."

Love bore on, desperately spinning visions. Vision, however, was not in short supply in Niagara.

Hogan wondered if this man knew anything about Niagara. The region was, in 1893, more firmly planted in the 20th Century than in the 19th. Planned communities had already been tried. Technology? Love claimed to be a visionary but every idea he'd suggested so far could have been pulled from the local papers. Visionaries, especially those whose dreams subsisted on electricity, streamed into Niagara. Most returned to whatever hole they'd crawled from. A few were able to bridge their dreams to reality. Very few were able to convince Hogan or his competitors to finance their dreams.

"Key to this project is this," Love finally concluded, and Hogan, glancing at his watch with relief, smiled obligingly. Love, sweating through his shirt, having peeled off his suit coat earlier, picked up his grant and flipped to the third page. "I have rights to as much of the Niagara as I wish to draw," he said, pointing out the key text.

Hogan waited—it was true and of little importance; charters were rather easily come by. Most recipients didn't have the money to exploit their charters and so the rights were rarely exercised.

"Everything happening to Niagara Falls can happen to my community. We can learn from what has not worked here. The same investments, the same growth, the same fortunes. There is one distinction. The State of New York grants these charters without charging for the power in any way." Hogan nodded—this was all very pedestrian to him. "I am going to dig a canal from my site across the country side to this site. When the water reaches the Escarpment I will have created another Niagara River and another Niagara Falls. But, unlike the state, I intend to charge for the right to use this water."

"Just think of the revenues uncollected every time the state gives away a piece of Niagara," Love pressed, almost hissing with greed, for here was the heart of his plan, and almost the last piece he could play.

Hogan wondered what was powering the man. "What prevents investors from simply going to the state for further free water?"

Love felt the tug on his fishing line. He sat down, for now he could land his catch. "Contrary to the state leaders' opinions, the Niagara is not an infinite source of water power. What I have here," he tapped his charter, "many entrepreneurs have won. But it is about to become very rare. Within a month the state will announce the end of open charters."

Hogan's eyes grew and his posture straightened. "End of open charters? Impossible. Why?"

"The efforts of the commission to regulate development along the river," answered Love, "they have recently mustered support in the house, and if you have kept up with the news from Albany, three requests for charters in the past month were rejected."

"Rejected?" This made Hogan blink. He had not kept up with the news.

"I would venture to say that the era of free water is closed. And that makes this charter rather valuable. Excellent collateral, don't you agree?"

Hogan sat quietly for a couple of minutes, working through Love's story.

As the banker began to search for a paper in the mound, Love looked over the office furnishings. Leather overstuffed chairs, brass fixtures, electric lights. His office in Model City would look like this—but bigger, much bigger.

"Sir, speaking strictly hypothetically," Hogan said, after fetching a pen from a teller, now scribbling notes, "pending verification of your news, if I then persuade the bank's directors of the merit of your request, how much of a loan were you requesting? And in what installments?"

"I would need start-up capital to survey the land and purchase it outright. In two weeks, say, ten thousand dollars." He ignored Hogan's glance. "Within three months I would require another twenty thousand to begin digging the canal." Love reeled in his catch, pausing to sink the hook fatally deep. "Of course, I also need sound advice from someone knowledgeable about local property values. And I can't think of anyone better suited than yourself." Hogan glanced up from his writing again as Love produced another stock certificate, the one Levon had spurned. "If you would consent to serve on my board of directors, Mr. Hogan, I would be honored to award you preferred stock in my chartered company." Love gently set the stock certificate on the top of Hogan's pile.

The banker cautiously picked it up, looked at the seal, and Love's flamboyant signature, and said, "I would like to arrange a meeting for Friday, sir, at eleven in the morning. That will give me the opportunity to present this at the Wednesday board meeting. At that time we may be able to set final terms on this. . . most interesting investment."

Love strolled out, his charter in his pocket, smiling.

Hogan confirmed the charter, and the legislature's new mentality about river rights, thanks to a telegram to a contact in Albany. So, the banker decided, he's got the goods. His charter will be worth thousands in a month, and probably close to a hundred thousand within a year or two. A hundred thousand in deposits was Hogan's dream. Though Love's dream project was as ill-conceived and poorly thought out as were most of the projects that had come to him in the past seven years, some of the dreamers had succeeded. Niagara Falls was on the cutting edge of technology, mostly because it produced vast pools of electrical power for very little money. Industrial magic that would have been impossible ten years ago was working now. The companies lining up along the river were creating new products and new uses for electrical power everyday.

So he'd advance Love fifty thousand. If he actually started his project, which was amazingly unoriginal, it would last him less than six months and either he'd be successful in blasting the canal, or he wouldn't. If the canal were actually being dug, then he could borrow more against the work finished. If Love was as poor at executing his dreams as were most of the other dreamers, then in six months the charter would be the bank's. Either way, Hogan felt comfortable with the arrangement.

Over the years, June found she picked up the best news leads just by chatting with the businessmen who stopped by the paper, sometimes to place ads, sometimes angling for a story if they felt publicity would help them. Six months after Love visited the paper, she first heard the rumor. It was from Tom Yansen, manager of the new Niagara Brewing Company, sharing a rumor, "Love is running out of money." He struck a match and lit himself a cigar, and one for June. "You look at that project up the river, see the kind of payroll he's got to meet," said Yansen, "and at the rate they're digging that canal you know he's a good year away from actually generating profits. I'm amazed he talked Charlie Hogan into a loan. From what I hear, Love also has loans from some New York banks."

That Love was a poor businessman was clear when he widely announced his plans after getting the money. He publicized that he needed to buy "hundreds of acres of land to dig a canal from the Niagara across the peninsula, to create a man-made falls and generate electrical power in the process." He also announced that he'd raised "hundreds of thousands of dollars."

"Well, hell, might as well say 'pick my pocket,'" said Horace, reading the story at the kitchen table. "Y'know, land prices up there doubled overnight." June nodded, finishing cutting up potatoes and carrots and putting them in the pot. Stew was one of the few dishes she felt competent making. It seemed the pot did most of the work.

"If he had a brain, or his own money, he could have waited for the prices to come down," Horace said.

"It's my understanding that he has almost no capital of his own, just money raised from investors expecting dividends soon, and loans with interest due. So he bought the land and now he's run short of money." She added a chunk of coal to the stove and stirred it up. "He travels back and forth to New York, to calm the old investors and sing up more."

"Well, I hear work on the canal isn't progressing much. Oh, did you put onions in?" Horace sniffed. "You know I don't like onions."

"Just one for flavor," June said. Horace sulked.

June did her work well. She explained the outline to Lester Davidson one late afternoon. "To fulfill this project, Love needs a hundred or more strong backs for digging. Healthy labor is in short supply here, between Carborundum, and Castner's and Union Carbide, and Rankine's power company, hiring men as fast as they can make the trip here from Europe, so Love has been forced to ship up more immigrants from New York, housing them in a tent city at the site, and all of that was more money spent than was planned."

Lester lit his pipe and nodded; so far this was common knowledge.

"I'm going up there tomorrow to look around," she announced at the end.

Lester frowned. "Are you sure that's," he paused to pick the right word. "Are you sure that's safe?"

"You wanted to say 'are you sure that's wise,'" June accused him. "And the answer is, perhaps not, but I'm going anyway."

It was a warm day and, while the walk was good for her, she did have to pause a couple of times in shade to cool off. As she neared the work site, traffic increased; wagons passed her coming from the site, some filled with shovels and other tools, some with laborers. At least four wagons fully loaded with laborers passed her, making her wonder if Love's labor problems were easing. Though each driver stopped to offer her a ride, she declined.

When she reached the canal it didn't look very big. It was about twenty feet deep, and twenty feet wide, and it went about a hundred feet. "I've seen bigger ponds," she said in amusement. "Deeper, too." It was a news-gathering trip, so she found the foreman's office. It was a wooden shack with a dirt floor and was filled with big tables covered with charts, plans and surveys. There were two men inside when she knocked on the wall by the open door.

"Can we help you?" asked the bigger one, dumbfounded to see through the door a middle aged woman dressed for the city. "Mr. Love ain't in today," he thought to mention. "This is his foreman, Mr. Krajewski."

"Thank you, I'm not here to see Mr. Love. I'm June Lockwood, from the *Niagara Courier*, and I'm just taking a look around." The introduction had the desired effect. The two men suddenly glowed with excitement, wondering what they needed to do or say to get into the newspaper. "I understand that the canal is a little behind schedule?"

"Well, yes," said the gruffer one, Krajewski. "We was supposed to be a half mile complete," he conceded, "but we've had a terrible hard time. Finding good men who want to work for a living with their backs, digging, that's been real hard," he labored with his diction, getting the words out past a heavy accent, "and finding men who are experienced with nitro is very hard. But, to be truthful, even if I could find a hundred men who would do fair day's work for day's pay, Mr. Love don't own the land a half mile up yet. In fact, we're within ten feet of the property line. We're moving rocks and smoothing out the part that's done."

"And how many men do you have?" June asked, "I saw three wagons on the road."

The other man, with glasses, perhaps the bookkeeper, cleared his throat as though public speaking. "We got about seventy, seventy-five men. Only ten from around here. Got thirty from Black Rock and Buffalo, and about thirty-some that came up from New York and Mr. Love's supposed to be bringing up another fifty from there any time now. But Mr. Krajewski is right, we can't use more men until the land is clear to dig."

She had learned what she could, so she spent a minute getting their names right. She started back towards the Echota Station, recalled the train was most of an hour off, and despite the inappropriateness of a woman wandering a work site, she thought to walk around and see if the men were as lazy as rumor had it.

There were just four men in the ditch this afternoon and they seemed most concerned with finding relief from the summer sun. They were sturdy looking, but they weren't doing hard labor. One lay flat in the shady corner of the ditch, two others were leaning on their shovels, chewing tobacco and spitting juice as dark as the muddy water in the puddles. A big wheelbarrow sat untended with a little dirt in it. One man stopped trying to reach the itch in the middle of his back, grumbled and picked up his shovel and slowly added dirt to the barrow. "Suit yourself," said another. "I don't lift my tail for nothing," added the one lying in the shade.

A minute later Krajewski came by on horseback. "Get up and fill that barrow!" he yelled.

The workmen looked up at him; compared to them he was a short, round man. One especially brawny laborer hefted a shovel like it was a flower to show his muscles. "If you'd like to get off yer own lazy ass, maybe you'd come down here and show us what you had in mind," he jeered.

"If you aren't. . . to work, you. . . be fired!" retorted Krajewski in his labored English, intimidated by them but refusing to run.

"Listen to that Polack trying to sound like he can speak our language," sneered another one. "I might as well be fired," said another man, "you figure out when pay day is going to be yet? I don't dig another shovelful until I get what's owed me." At that the foreman tapped his heels to the horse and left.

June heard the train whistle blow in the distance, her signal to go, but she couldn't help herself. When Krajewski was gone, she stepped out of the line of trees she'd been observing from, and got their attention. They looked startled, and tried to nod and tip non-existing hats. "I'm sorry to be eavesdropping on you, gentlemen," she began, then introduced herself and asked, "is what I've heard true, that you haven't been paid yet?"

"Payday's four days late," answered the slightest built of them, sounding like he'd had more education than the others. "Normally we get paid on Saturday, and that's been the rule since we started here three months ago. But Saturday past we was told that Mr. Love was late with the payroll on account of some important meeting in New York." He sounded skeptical.

"But they said we'd get double wages next Saturday," added another, who was clearly counting on it. "Which better happen."

June thanked them and made her way back through the woods and the pathway to the train station. The train had just left the station, she could see the last car disappearing towards the falls. *No matter*, she thought, digging out a pencil and a pad of paper she carried, *I've got some news to write*. She wrote it out before the next train came, read it on the ride back, rewrote it in her office, but was still unsatisfied.

"Would you read this?" She stood in Lester's doorway. "It's a little controversial." Love was a businessman, an entrepreneur, and these people were afforded kind treatment in Niagara Falls. Others had invested and failed, but failed honorably, and were treated like crippled soldiers, while June was writing about a man she thought was a charlatan from the outset. That, she thought, or a fool. She had an unshakable sense that the story must be true, even if it was negative, and knew that writing the story as she knew it was a mortal sin. In William Love she sensed her own swan song, but she felt a need to pursue this story to the truth, and the fallout be damned.

That night Horace came home late again. "Dear, you look exhausted," June said. He nodded, his jacket dirty, his shoes muddy. "Where have you been walking? In the tunnel?"

"Precisely," he said, first pulling off his dirty shoes, then dropping in his favorite overstuffed chair like a sack of bricks. "I've been tracking each shipment of brick, and going into the tunnels when I can do so unobserved, and counting them. Estimating, actually." He drank the glass of milk she poured for him. "In the past three months we have ordered a million, five hundred and thirty thousand bricks. I have the payment vouchers." He pulled a slip of paper from his pocket. It was smudged with mud and sweat, and on it Horace had scribbled numbers. "We have been losing a full third of our orders each month for the past three months. Probably more than that, but that's as far back as I can count. Someone, or some collective, has been stealing enough bricks to build a neighborhood of houses."

June's mind, God help her, started writing the story. "Do you have any suspects?"

Horace finished his milk with a gasp for air. "I have two suspects. Andy Wilberforce, who runs the supply shop, is the most logical one. When bricks are needed, the foreman sends two men to our supply depot. Andy gives them what they ask, but they sign a voucher for what they've taken. I get the vouchers, and I don't have enough vouchers for all the bricks that have disappeared. So Andy is my first suspect. A gruesome character named George Tandy is my other suspect."

"His name is familiar," said June.

"He's known to the police." Horace's watery eyes were half-shut with weariness. "He's mostly a brawler, but in his younger days as a thief as well. I made some inquiries with the police."

"How do you propose to stop this?" she asked, slipping fully into 'interview' mode.

Horace looked at her from the corner of his eye. "You can't write about this. At least not until I've figured it out."

She frowned a little. "All right. But how do you plant to catch them?"

He looked distant, thinking a moment. Then, "the only way I can think of is to hide in the brickyard and see who takes away a load of bricks without signing a voucher."

The next night Horace came in at four in the morning, dead-tired and dismayed. "I fell asleep," he admitted to her in bed. "I slept from about one until just half an hour ago. I need to take some coffee with me or something to keep me up."

The second night she lay awake as long as she could. She fell asleep after the clock chimed three. And at dawn there was a knock on her door. Pulling on her housecoat, she briefly checked her hair, pulling it back in a bun as she did more and more for convenience. Opening the door she saw Officer Pomer.

"Does Horace Pepper live here, Ma'am?"

"Yes."

"Are you his wife?"

She hesitated slightly. "Yes."

"Then I have some bad news."

The officer's English was rough, but she got the story. Near dawn a laborer fetching a stack of bricks found Horace's body. His skull was crushed, probably with bricks.

"Take me to see him," she said. She started out the door, but Pomer gently barred the way.

Pomer shook his head. "It's not a good idea."

"Take me to see him!" she screamed in the officer's face, and pushed past him.

He followed her down the street, sunlight just filling the street. Tears streamed down her face and people who knew her stopped to ask her if she was alright. She didn't hear herself but she was screaming Horace's name all the way down Falls Street.

Horace's body was covered with a tarp. She burst on the scene and before anyone could stop her she pulled it away. She could barely recognize his crushed face, and someone had taken the extra pains to stab him twice in the chest. She dropped to her knees and took his already stiffened corpse in her arms.

She was cried out when she let his body rest on the dirt, and her dress was smeared with his blood when she walked into the Police station with Officer Pomer's help. The station was as quiet as the streets. "Please, sit here," asked Pomer, and for the first time she did as he asked. The officer knew her. "Miss Lockwood? You've got blood on you."

The sound of her name sprang tears to her eyes. Pomer spoke softly to the watch officer and his jaw dropped. "Miss Lockwood, I'm so sorry." She fell to her knees. She caught her breath and screamed. The officer came out to help her up, her cry summoning two others from the back. "He's been murdered!" she screamed.

"It's Mister Pepper," Pomer explained again. "With the Adams company. A fellow, named Agutter, came by a little while ago. They found his body in the brickyard."

They got June to sit, gave her a sip of brandy, and sent a man to the paper. Alma and Lester showed up, Alma having begun crying on the way. June looked up at them, having calmed somewhat, and in their embrace began crying again. Somehow she got home and into bed but it was all a blur.

A day later the police arrested Tandy. Under the shack he slept in they found buried a bloody shirt, and after a day of vigorous police questioning they extracted a confession. June went to his arraignment in the city court, a building she knew well. "I want to see him," she told Lester. "I want to look in his eyes and see if he's a murderer."

Tandy was led in in shackles when the judge called out the case. He was not tall, but broad and well muscled. His scalp had been shaved and he had half the teeth God gave him and a black eye, courtesy of police interrogators. He stood before the judge and heard the charges. "George Tandy, you are charged with murder in the first degree. You are accused of beating to death Horace Pepper, an employee of the Power Company. How do you plead?"

"Innocent." His voice was a deep, feral growl. June walked over to the defense table and stood behind it. When the judge denied him bail, he was turned around and was face to face with June.

"Did you kill him?" she whispered. She looked into his dark brown eyes but saw nothing that shrank from her stare, nothing like fear or remorse. She saw a dog caught biting a man.

He looked at her as though she were a woman of the street. "You ain't much to look at, are you?" he said. The cop yanked on his shackles and he was dragged back to jail.

On the way back to the paper she was dry-eyed. "What did I expect to hear him say?" she asked Alma. "Yes, I killed him and I'm sorry? He'd just pleaded innocent. But they've got evidence on him. I expect he'll be hung." She wished that made her feel better. It didn't touch the emptiness Horace had briefly filled.

Having been beaten to death, Horace's casket was nailed shut by the coroner. "Now, Mrs. Pepper—"

"I go by June Lockwood," she said softly.

"Oh." The undertaker, with a hint of accent, perhaps Italian, wrote that on a slip of paper. "He was a wounded soldier?" He had seen Horace's damaged leg.

"Yes. Wounded in the Wilderness Campaign." She felt a wave of tears coming.

"I can get a uniform for him."

"No," she said, probably too firmly. "Bury him as a gentleman. In a suit." She left the room abruptly to keep her tears private. The undertaker understood. He had what he needed.

June found a photograph of Horace and set that on his enameled black mahogany casket, set on sawhorses in the front room. She received condolence calls from William Rankine and Dean Adams, dressed in their best black suits. Others came over two days of viewing, but June had no memory of it. For the first time she used one of the empty rooms to sleep in, the one farthest away from the public room.

When they lowered his coffin into the earth, she let fall a clod of earth, stepped back, and walked alone back to her house. She shut the door firmly and went to bed.

She let her mind roam as she rested on the Hermit's Rock that evening. The night air was alive with insects but they didn't seem to care for June's taste. She wondered what time it was; the colored arc lights on the Horseshoe Falls had turned off a little while ago so she knew it was late. As she rose and hopped back to dry land and put on her stockings, she heard someone coming. She wasn't without fear, but common sense required that she see them before they saw her. A moment later a man stumbled from the woods, sprawling on the path. 'Drunk', was June's immediate assessment, and she tensed.

"Maybe I should kill him. Would they pay me to kill him?" the man asked himself, crying through the alcohol. He pulled himself to his feet, oblivious to his danger, and started an unsteady walk down the pathway to the three islands. June followed at a safe distance. "Emmeline, I've failed you," he cried, "I lost it all. Every dollar. I don't know what to do now." He kept going out on the path until he was at the water's edge. "I'm sorry. Emmeline, please remember me kindly," he said the last almost in a whisper. Dropping his billfold on the last rock, he walked into the water.

"Sir!" June called out, "stop. You'll drown. Sir!"

He continued, knee-deep in the river. There was no stopping him, she knew, and she tried to look away, but she watched as he stumbled, fell forward, saw his arms swing wildly as the current caught him and pulled him. "SIR!" she screamed as the moonlight's reflection showed him being pulled by the rapids. He was out of sight in a minute. June stood at the water's edge, one foot out, then the other, then stepping back, trying to gauge her chances of wading out and rescuing him, but he was already gone. She strained her eyes trying to see if maybe he'd caught a hold on the odd rock or stunted bushes that somehow grew out there on exposed rocks. After some time had passed her horror faded and weariness set in. She saw his wallet, hesitated a moment, then picked it up. Tucking it under her arm, June ran most of the way off Goat Island. Back in the village she walked briskly and finally, limping after raising a blister, got to her home and fell asleep on her bed, fully clothed. For the first time in her life she had feared the falls.

Morning sunlight woke her at eight, a little later than her norm. She remembered last night and felt a wave of crying come upon her. She wasn't a crier, so she looked around to find something else to think about. The wallet. Still holding it, she looked at it as though it had come from beyond the grave. Opening it cautiously, she pulled out two letters, one from a Miss Emmeline Sanderson, one unsent, presumably by the suicide, five one dollar bills, and a paper that unfolded into a stock certificate in William Love's Model City Project, representing a $200 investment. She opened the letters, blushing at her violation of privacy. His name was Jeffrey Edgemere, Emmeline was his fiancée and he had recently quit his job as a bank clerk in Syracuse to turn his savings—apparently an inheritance—into a fortune sufficient to earn Emmeline's hand. And he had met William Love and had given the Model City man his money.

"Oh, no." She might have cried for the poor man, but her goal this morning was to not cry anymore. But with everything she knew now about William Love and his Model City, with her distrust for him now solidly backed by the facts, she could only cry when she remembered the drunken man throwing himself into the river. "Stupid, stupid man," she moaned softly. Then a question formed in her restless mind. *What forced this poor fool to kill himself? How did he know his money was gone?*

June readied herself for the outside world and pressed on. Instead of the *Courier*, she went to the International Hotel where, everyone knew, Love was ensconced in a costly suite. At the front desk she caught the attention of a clerk. "Could you tell me if William Love is in?"

After thumbing through a wad of index cards, the clerk shook his head. "No, Mr. Love checked out late last night."

June's eyebrows rose. "Checked out? Left? Not returning?"

The clerk nodded. "He did leave a forwarding address. Would you like it?"

She read the address; a lawyer's office in Manhattan. Not likely she'd actually find the entrepreneur there. This was just for creditors.

"This is the only address he left? Did he leave any luggage? Did he leave any messages? What time did he leave last night?" she interrogated the clerk. A small crowd grew behind her, so the clerk answered with 'yes' and 'no' and 'no' and "I don't know," with a hint of impatience. "Thank you," June said listlessly as she stepped away. She was rebuilding the scenario. Perhaps Jeffrey Edgemere came to visit Love last night. Love had been in New York for two weeks, so June knew, apparently trying to scrape up the cash for the next payroll. June also knew there was a bank panic in New York, risky loans coming due, Love's no doubt one good example of them. So perhaps he came back empty-handed yesterday. He presumably told Edgemere that the investment was either gone or maybe he just lied and said the project was behind schedule and no dividends could be paid yet. Something, but apparently not enough to hide the truth.

June hit her office in the *Courier* like the Lord's whirlwind, dashing past a chorus of "good morning Miss Lockwood." She wrote the only draft with a clear head, checking her notes once or twice. Typing it out, it filled five pages, and she looked it over again for a while before walking into Lester's office. "Good morning, Miss Lockwood," he customarily greeted her.

"I've finished my story on the Model City Project, Love's project. It's falling apart as we speak." She handed him the story.

He girded himself for a painful read. He leaned against his desk and rested his forehead in his hands as he scanned the first page, looked up at her, then began to read it carefully. He hadn't been looking forward to this. After two pages of careful reading, he glanced up at her. "I don't know if I can print this, Miss Lockwood. It's potentially libelous to Mr. Love."

"Please just finish, then we can discuss legal issues," June said, a little brusque.

"Can I have a little while to read it in private and then we can discuss it?" he asked. June reluctantly nodded and left.

He leaned back in his leather chair and read the story through without stopping. William Love was depicted as a charlatan, the Model City Project a fool's errand, and his financial backers as either naïve victims or out-and-out morons. Davidson started circling in pencil the parts he was most concerned about. Most of the way through he realized there were only four unmarked sentences. He sighed; June was an institution at the *Courier*. How to broach an institution with a cardinal law? He walked next door to her office, where she was reading the *Power City* rag.

"I've read it," he said, as though it were an obituary of an old friend. She was silent. "It's a strong piece of writing," he said, but knew his usual blandishments were useless. She had her poker face on. "If I publish this, the paper could be sued by half a dozen local businesses, and if we're unlucky enough to be read in New York, by a couple of very powerful businessmen there."

"Am I wrong?" she asked, knowing the question was an oversimplification. "I know I got the story right."

Davidson scratched his balding scalp and sat in the other chair in June's office. "I have no doubt you've gotten your facts right." He was quiet a moment, then said, "you were the managing editor for twelve years, June." He looked at her and asked, "imagine someone else bringing this story to you then. What would your concerns be?"

June was thoughtful. "Years ago I wrote a story about a man who was going to dig a canal through the old village, let the water fall back into the Lower Gorge, and harness the river's water power for industry. He was going to make a hundred thousand dollars within five years. There'd be a dozen new businesses in town and lots of jobs. That's what he said, and I put it in the paper. We printed it." June considered lighting a cigar, but decided not to test Lester's nerves further. "Within a year that man was bankrupt and had lost fifty thousand of other peoples' dollars without creating anything. I think about that, and wonder how many people lost money because they believed what they read to be true."

Davidson nodded. "Good point. We have been careful to support business. More importantly, we're a respectable paper and we have a good reputation." He paused, picking his words carefully. "I can tell you that if I had the chance to change stories we've printed in the past, I would. Not because we've given approval to bad ideas by printing them, but because we could have been more forthright occasionally and given more... qualified support to business." He set her story on her desk. "Is there any way you can rewrite this and not make the reader believe the Model City Project has collapsed?"

"But it has. And he sold a lot of stock locally, and those people deserve to know the truth while there's any hope of them getting their money back," June argued. "If, in fact, there is." If Lester had a few twinges of conscience over what he'd printed in the past, June had a dozen. And maybe she was guilty of trying to clear her conscience with one big blast, but it was far better than hiding from those memories for the rest of her life.

"You don't know for a fact that the stock is worthless," Davidson argued.

June considered that for a moment. "I have a suggestion," she replied. "Hogan lent this man at least fifty thousand. Right now he either knows where Love has run to and how he's going to get his money back, or he's scared for his bank. Let's go call on him. If he can redeem this stock certificate," she had Edgemere's, "I'll pull the story completely."

"Okay."

"And if he won't, you'll print it as is?"

Davidson wasn't a happy man. He didn't like to think a woman was bullying him. "We'll print the story, perhaps with a few modifications."

They rose together and headed for the Bank of Niagara. The street had the usual congestion, tourists, travelers and tradesmen and horses and a very few cars. The Bank of Niagara had its offices in a wood frame building two blocks from the *Courier*. With June by his side, Lester opened the door for her and they entered the quieter atmosphere of the bank. Hogan could usually be seen at his desk in the far corner; today his desk was empty, even of papers. "Could we have a moment of Mr. Hogan's time?" Lester asked the clerk.

The clerk, a woman barely twenty, had a distracted look. "Mr. Hogan is ill, I'm afraid. He is at home and we don't expect him in today. Could you come by tomorrow?"

Davidson frowned and June brightened. They stepped outside and hailed a cab that took them a fifteen minute ride to Hogan's house. It was a new home, wood frame with marble steps, and a beautiful garden, along Gill Creek. The servant that answered their knock, older than Hogan and at least as well dressed, said, "he's just received some very bad news. He's not up to having guests. I'm very sorry."

"Our cards," Lester produced a calling card. "We're from the *Niagara Courier*," he said, "and we're about to print a story that suggests the Model City Project has lost its financial backing. Does Mr. Hogan have any comment?"

The servant left with the message, and returned quickly. Tersely, as if to mirror the sentiment as well as the message, he said, "Mr. Hogan says you may print what you wish, it is your paper." They got back in the cab and rode back to the offices in silence, June brimming with excitement, Lester with anxiety.

Davidson struggled with the text for two hours and finally sent it all to typesetting; there was no particular sentence he could lance that would pull the teeth from this story. "I'm not afraid to tell you," he said to June after the paper had been put to bed, "I'm not looking forward to tomorrow."

June was being more considerate of her successor. "You've done the right thing, Lester. I'm proud of you, and I'm proud of this paper."

It was on her way home that evening that June remembered Jeffrey Edgemere, and his death, and that she was the only witness to it. *What does that say about me*, she wondered. With his wallet, she went to make the report. Suicide at Niagara Falls was not rare.

"So you saw Mister Edgemere go into the water?" asked the police officer, silver-haired and a little hard of hearing.

"Yes," June admitted, embarrassed, "I tried to. . . well, I asked him to stop. He was drunk and I. . ."

"You did what any decent God-fearing person would do," said the officer. He wrote the report on a piece of yellow paper, dipping the fountain pen every line for fresh ink. June couldn't read his handwriting and wondered if history would ever know of Jeffrey Edgemere's fate. After taking the report and the victim's wallet, the officer wished June a good evening and she headed back to her home. She stayed in that evening, tried to read a book she'd bought on the Holy Land, then looked at a framed picture of Horace and her in front of the falls. They had indulged at some point shortly after he'd returned, and she'd mislaid the picture until recently. She kissed her fingertips, touched Horace's face, then went to bed early.

When she reached the paper the next morning she'd forgotten about yesterday's tension; it was like that. A story would foment stress among the editors, then it would go into print and their fear would be for naught.

It didn't last. Thirty minutes after their morning edition hit the street, Ethan Sinclair came bursting into the offices. "The police have a riot at Model City! The workers have demanded their wages and there's no money. They're waving copies of our paper and screaming for Love's blood."

June paled. Davidson quickly sent Ethan back to the riot with a photographer. "I was afraid of this!" he scolded June. "The bank's just opening. We better warn Hogan."

Hogan was at his desk, reading the *Power City* paper. He stood when they entered. "Good morning, Miss Lockwood, Mr. Davidson," he said in a weary voice. "To what do I owe the honor?"

June held out a copy of the *Courier*. "You may want to read our first page, Mr. Hogan." He took the paper and began reading.

"Good God," he said after the first paragraph. He sat down and read a little further. "You printed this?" he accused Davidson. "You wrote this?" he glared at June.

"It's truthful," June said, feeling defenseless as Davidson also glared at her. "Everything in that story is true."

"Truth takes different forms," her publisher waffled.

Hogan had stopped reading. He was shaking his head, pulling out folders that said LOVE and MODEL CITY on them. His hands were shaking.

"I'm sorry if our paper has caused you embarrassment, Mr. Hogan," Lester was apologizing, "we do feel the obligation to print important news, and we try to save innocent people's reputations."

"Well you've done a damn poor job of it today!" Hogan erupted. "To say that a huge project that our bank has given major backing to is bankrupt? You don't think that damages our reputation?"

Outside, the sounds of people, running and yelling, came nearer. Hogan broke off from tongue-lashing these fools to go to the door, open it, and lean out cautiously. He shut it fast. "It's a mob!" he yelled to the tellers. "I'm locking the door. Put all your cash and negotiables in the safe. We're closing early today." Hogan dug out a large skeleton key and locked the front door, and as June and her editor watched, the four tellers rushed to a doorway in the back with canvas sacks.

"It's going to be a run," June said, in a diminished voice, not proud of her work.

"No, it isn't," Hogan interjected. "If I was stupid enough to remain open it would be a run. We're just closing for a day or two to let people forget about this nonsense you've printed." He crumpled the paper in his hands and threw it hard into a waste paper basket. "Please excuse yourselves. We have a back door that's inconspicuous. That way," he pointed, and they hurried out, into the alley. The tellers had already disappeared.

Cautiously reaching the street, they saw the crowd. Love's ditch diggers had come to town, a crowd of about fifty men. A cop, Officer Pomer, was blowing furiously on his whistle, reaching for his pistol, yelling, "disperse! Go to your jobs! Go about your business!"

"We got no jobs! You got our payroll?" "You get paid this week, copper?" Pomer, the first Italian cop on the city force, hesitated to shoot at the ditch diggers, some of whom he knew.

"Go back to work," he pleaded with them. "It'll all get straightened out. If you don't disperse we'll have to use force."

A second policeman appeared, Officer Sinclair, with a shotgun. Sinclair hesitated not a second. BOOM! His first shot was aimed overhead. A shell ejected. A rock was thrown, wide. Sinclair aimed a second shot in the direction of the thrown rock. BOOM! "Aowwwww!" a rioter howled, falling to his knees, his hands covering his face. A hail of rocks rained on the police. One struck Pomer in his right temple and spun him sideways. As he fell to his knees his pistol was taken from him and fired at Sinclair. Sinclair backed up quickly, emptying his gun into the mob as Pomer fell under their rocks.

"Lester!" June hissed, and she dashed out into the mob, bending over Officer Pomer. Turning to stare at her editor, she drew him out on sheer force of will and he helped her drag Pomer into the alley. The mob was chasing Sinclair, who was running in the direction of the Police Station while trying to reload, the ditch diggers screaming and throwing stones at him, when around the corner came a horse-drawn wagon complete with bars.

"It's the wagon!" The crowd stopped and scattered, as the wagon was also carrying five more armed policemen who immediately opened fire on the men. A volley of gunfire left June's ears ringing, a fog of gunpowder briefly shrouded the street. When it dispersed six more men were down as though sleeping, two of them sprawled obscenely, flagrantly dead. Others were crawling for cover with blood streaking down their shirts and pants. From the alleyway, June held Pomer's bleeding head in her lap, smeared with his blood and her own tears. Davidson had disappeared. The crowd had run, the police had given chase. The street was relatively quiet, but for the groans and cries of men lying in pools of their own blood.

The bystanders had run into shops while the riot ensued; they were now returning to the scene with morbid curiosity. Finally June saw her editor come running. An ambulance was following him. "Here!" Davidson was yelling, "he needs medical help!" Two other cops picked up the bloody, unconscious officer, gently laid him in the back of the ambulance. Then they slapped the reins and the ambulance pulled away, leaving the bleeding and still workers for someone else to tend to. June began trying to stop the bleeding of the nearest wounded man. She was joined soon by women, summoned by the grapevine, and they began carrying off their wounded. By noon, June was smeared with blood and dirt, and was grateful no one had shot her.

June caused a stir when she entered the *Courier*'s office, then recalled her plain blue dress was smeared with blood. "Miss Lockwood!" "Are you all right? Is that your blood?" Shaking her head, she went into her office, shut the door, and cried. She had written a solid story. It was one of the best pieces of research she had ever done. She had delivered important news to the community, had acted as a responsible journalist.

So why was she crying? Over the havoc her story had wrought? Because she knew the wounded Officer Pomer and some of the workers? Ignoring the concerns of the staff, the inquiring knocks on the door, she went home a little later, unable to concentrate, saying almost nothing but, "good day. See you tomorrow," to Ethan and Lester and the two women typists.

Letting herself in to her house, she shut her front door behind her and leaned against it. These wonderful stone walls—could they keep the world out?

Sometime later she changed her dress. She kept hearing the angry workers, the sick crunch of a rock denting Pomer's skull, kept smelling his blood. Shaking with the morning's memory, she tried to sleep but couldn't. Two glasses of claret didn't help either. She left the dress in a tub full of water to soak. Late in the day she examined it. Though the bloodstain would fade, she asked herself, "where on Earth would you wear this again?" She cut it into rags. Then she collected the rags and burned them. It was dark when she grew hungry, and she decided tonight was a good night to eat at the Temperance Hotel's restaurant. It was an occasional treat.

"Did you hear about the riot today?" her waiter asked. "Cop got killed, that's what I heard. Also five or six of the mob. They were Love's men. They hadn't been paid in six months. They broke into the bank, but didn't get any money. The cops arrested a couple, charged 'em with murder." June's face was frozen. "So, what can I get for you tonight?" She had lost her appetite, apologized for the inconvenience, and went home to snack on bread and milk.

The glass of milk reminded her of Horace, as it always did, and she sniffled a little at his memory. Solace evaded her at every turn. She finally sought it in the one source that never failed her. She went to the Hermit's Bath and spent most of the night there, not sleeping, thinking about the riot, and thinking more and more critically of what she had written. She smoked a cigar in the twilight, and it helped a little. *Irresponsible* was what she kept thinking, then she would defend herself with the thought *I'm too old to be irresponsible. But my article was a public service*, she thought. Then she remembered the dead men in the street. She returned to her home when the horizon began to grow light, less haunted but still dazed. She dozed for a few hours, rose late, and when she arrived at the paper late in the morning she was not surprised to find a note on her desk. 'Please see me immediately,' signed Davidson.

"George Hogan opened for business late yesterday afternoon," Lester told her when she reported in, "because about fifty of his customers, including Tom Yansen, were threatening to call the police and arrest him for theft." He cleared his throat. "So he reopened. Within an hour his assets were completely depleted. He had twenty-thousand in gold and silver and it's all gone." Davidson rose and shut the door. "He does have backers in New York City, investors who provided his initial financing. But, as it happens, there's been a bank crisis in New York and Boston this past month. Some banks are closing and most are calling in any loan that isn't rock solid. George sent wires to his backers, but however they answered they didn't wire him funds. He still owes about seven thousand to depositors that probably won't be repaid." Lester looked a good ten years older, not having slept. "He came to my house last night and told me that I could expect a visit today from the Chamber of Commerce." Davidson sighed, rubbed his own tired eyes. "I don't know exactly what to expect, but I know that we derive seventy percent of our income from paid advertisers. So I'm going to listen very carefully to what they say."

June bowed her head as if in prayer. "What would you like me to do? Do you want me to attend that meeting?"

He wanted her to quit. "I'm sure you don't want to, and I don't think you being there will help. They'll be here just after lunch, so why don't you leave in a little while. It will probably be a quieter meeting without you."

She was smelling her flowers and watching some bees at work when she saw Lester come walking down the street. "Are those called lilacs?" he asked.

"I don't know," she answered. "They were here when I moved here."

"You don't read much Walt Whitman, do you?" he teased.

"No, I don't care for poetry," she said, smiling for him. "These are lilacs? They bloom every year. I didn't know they smelled so sweet. I should have smelled them before." She stepped indoors and invited him into the parlor. She sat, he remained standing. "They want my head, don't they?"

He looked at the toes of his well-shined boots. "That's about the size of it. There were over thirty there. All of our regular accounts, and George Hogan."

She nodded. "Did it matter that my story was completely accurate? Didn't that matter?" She knew it didn't, knew why it didn't, and felt abashed that it was her last refuge.

"I think you understand that the accuracy of the story didn't really enter the discussion at all. It centered on the role of a newspaper in the community to uphold the community, to work to its advantage. I won't embarrass you with a full report. They called it irresponsible. Hogan suggested that a former society reporter had no business trying to do an expose on a bank, or any business, as you lacked the, I'm quoting here, proper education and training, end quote. There were more than a few references to your gender, but that's small potatoes."

She ground her teeth, wishing she had a cigar. "And my fate?"

He sat on her overstuffed sofa. "I didn't promise them anything. I'm the managing editor of this paper and I won't have my business decisions dictated."

She looked out the window at nothing to avoid looking him in the eye. Lester's decisions were rarely his own.

He looked around the room, and for the first time appreciated how old it was. "I never appreciated how, uh, quaint this place is." He looked at her again. "My point is this. You are a firebrand, but you are also invaluable to this paper. What I wish to propose is that you stay on as a tutor, a mentor. I'd have to edit anything you wrote, and you know I will have to reign you in where you've previously been free to write what you want. Can you stay under those terms?"

"Can I," she said, but choked up. Clearing her throat, she tried again. "Let me think about it today. Thank you for coming by." He left, and she sat alone in her parlor. Every line she wrote would be carefully scrutinized and lanced. She would never be permitted a word at all controversial, and as June thought over her editorial history she knew almost every word she had ever written was a little controversial.

I've lost Horace. If I lose the paper all I have is this house, and I don't think that's enough to see me through old age. Her decision made, she mourned the part of her she'd just buried, and remembered then that she had set aside a project once, a special project for her to begin the day she quit working. The diary she'd found, her 'guest register', still resided on her bookshelf. It was her responsibility to add to it; she had kept every edition of the *Courier*, and in most of them she had written some lines. She had planned this for her retirement, presuming she wasn't found dead at her desk at the paper. Her plan was to clip the work she was proudest of, add that to the diary as her entry, and then she would feel her debt to history paid.

A chapter with the diary of June Lockwood extended the diary of Nehemiah Cleary, and of Sawyer Jackson. She dug out the decades of newsprint over the course of three days and realized that she had to be selective. Very selective.

Miss Danielle Dowling Carteret Simpson... survived because it was her last deb article. Blondin's shoes? Sure, it started her career. The two years' worth of editorials calling for the state to buy out the tourist traps were best summarized in a long piece she did on the dedication. Then she selected one of the dozens of pieces she had done on the various stunters. *With these years Niagara Falls grew from a village into a city, and into an industrial power*, she annotated. *Because people are foolish, they attempt foolish activities...* she introduced the stunters. As to the importance of generating electrical power; *If I had thought in advance of the impact of electrical power on this region I might have been less zealous in these pieces... but what's done is done...* she apologized for her many vigorous challenges to the community to begin development of electrical power.

It was a rainy week, and June spent it reading her career and clipping the best bits into the diary. The diary couldn't contain it all, so she added a book of clippings. *The continued diary of the Stone House, as annotated by June Lockwood.*

And when it was complete, when she felt she'd had the privilege of editing herself to her own standards, she tucked the clippings into the back of the diary, which wouldn't close completely now.

From a stout rubber-encased cable the power flowed. It ran up through a hole in the wood plank floor and up the side of a thick oak post. The floor was two hundred yards long and another two hundred wide, and on it rested ten stout square brick ovens. The cable ran up the wall and across the ceiling, braced against the bare ceiling beams, and at a junction of black glass insulating bulbs, ten smaller cables branched out across the ceiling to hang down like pythons and deliver five thousand kilowatts to each brick oven.

"It's very warm in here," said Ethan Sinclair, his young, clean-shaven face red and damp. He scribbled notes for his story.

"That's because we got ten five-thousand-kilowatt lines in here firing up ten ovens to about a thousand degrees each," answered the foreman matter-of-factly. He was striding from oven to oven, brushing aside the tender of each and examining for himself the heat gauges mounted on each brick oven. He didn't seem to feel the heat, though he was sweating through his dirty cotton shirt. The reporter, suited up as though interviewing the President, was sweating profusely, from both the heat and from his obvious fear of the power and the equipment surrounding him.

"What if one of those things blew up?" He followed close in the foreman's wake as though he might otherwise be drawn by a fiery vacuum into the nearest oven.

"What happens if one of these ovens gets too hot?" The foreman glared at him. "It blows up!" he thundered with a mischievous curl to his lip.

"How hot would the oven have to be?" asked the reporter a moment later, his writing hand frozen by the last answer.

Examining another gauge, the foreman answered without turning back, "the oven would have to be way over fifteen hundred. And I don't know exactly," he added with emphasis, "because I've never had one blow up."

The timer on an oven finished then, its loud whistle blowing a jet of steam. Ethan leapt back as the foreman and the tender donned smoked-glass face protectors and thick cotton gloves. Using the iron hook on the tip of a long wooden pole, the tender expertly unfastened the latch of the kiln door and, swiveling the hook to catch the lip of the door itself, pulled it open.

Intensely hot air, 'dry as the winds of the Sahara', gushed out. The foreman, undeterred by the heat of the hourly ritual, used another tool, a square plate on a long pole, to pull out of the oven a red hot tray of what would be caustic soda, mainstay of 'many important' industries. What important industries the reporter didn't know and wasn't about to ask the surly foreman, but the stuff must have a purpose. As for the 'winds of the Sahara'?

"Poetic license?" Ethan pleaded.

He sat now in a hard wooden seat facing Miss Lockwood. The cooler, cluttered, editorial room of the *Niagara Courier* was in stark contrast to the 'cooking room' at Castner Electrolytic Alkali. In the hot, dry, noisy factory room, with spilled grains of yellowish soda packed in the corners and gusts of hot air rushing from the ovens, the Sahara metaphor must have seemed perfect.

Miss Lockwood's pencil lanced his best line from the first paragraph. "There's nothing wrong with being poetic," she was telling the reporter as her eyes struggled with his prose, "if you are writing poetry." She drew a heavy line through a major part of his second paragraph. "Here," she paused, smiling, "this is the kind of detail I want." She read from his typed copy, "the ovens are of red brick with stout iron doors that glow dull red while the soda cooks. The ovens can contain up to a thousand degrees, sufficient to turn the shallow trays of briny water into caustic soda." Lockwood looked at her young reporter with a school teacher's loving gaze. "That's good detail."

With almost half his reportage intact, Ethan dutifully retyped his story—a promotion piece on the latest company to build near the new power plant. He had written a story like this once a month or so for a couple of years, as long as he'd been on staff. It was a duty, not a pleasure. He was waiting for his chance to do 'literature'. Miss Lockwood had read his poetry, and she kindly said it wasn't bad, but it clearly hadn't moved her. She had promised to print a poem of his about the falls, whenever he finished it. The poem was in its third year of gestation. Today Ethan wanted to get outside and 'feel my inspiration'. Happily he was a fast typist and he dropped the Castner Electrolytic Alkali Company's write-up in the print box on his way down the steps and out the door to a warm July day.

A hot and stifling night two days later woke June before sunrise. Sweating in her bedclothes, she decided she'd gotten the sleep she could expect. "Let's go sit with the hermit." Putting on a light, shapeless cotton dress, compromising modesty with the stifling heat, she walked the quiet streets to Goat Island, smiled as she always did every time she stepped onto the bridge without paying the dollar, and walked without haste to the far side of the island. This dawn she saw no one at all as she walked through the woods and emerged on the pathway along the Horseshoe Falls. Down the pathway she knew by heart, she reached the rocky bank and looked for the boulder on which she'd spent years toying with death. Her hand flew to her mouth and she stared.

The boulder was almost high and dry. The water marks on it were down a foot. The Hermit's Bath was down by almost half. She had seen water levels change through the seasons, spring and fall being the most dramatic, but never so much and so suddenly. "What's happened?" she asked aloud. The day water no longer flowed over the falls had more than once been used as a joke or dare that the world was coming to an end. June's mind was logical enough to know the world wasn't coming to an end, but she sure as hell wanted to see why the river had lost almost half its force.

Lester was attending a funeral in Indiana so she was filling in as managing editor. Returning home, preparing for her work, she was preoccupied by the mystery. As she stepped into the offices of the *Courier*, Ethan greeted her. "Miss Lockwood. I was able to photograph the opening this morning. There must have been thirty photographers there but Mr. Rankine's people made sure I had a good clear shot."

Shaking her head, she asked, "what was it you photographed this morning?"

"Mr. Davidson assigned me to the story before he left," Ethan explained, his excitement slightly diminished. "The new electrical generating plant. This morning two more generators were activated. They've doubled their capacity in one stroke. It's amazing. Megavolts of alternating current. In another year we'll produce enough power to light up New York City! Or Boston!"

"That's very impressive," she said, in a voice even and cool. She retired to her own office and, uncharacteristically, shut the door. Sinking into her seat, she struggled with her despair.

Today the cataract was only half as powerful, half as loud, half as forceful as it had been yesterday. Her favorite little spot, sparkling with danger, was as dangerous today as a glass of lemonade. After reading through Ethan's stories, explaining as simply as possible how the power would be generated, she nodded. It was all there. The engineers gave details on how much water would shoot into the underground tunnel once the additional generators were installed. She just hadn't paid it any attention. It was a great day for business.

She left work late, after sunset, and went back to the Hermit's Bath. Others either weren't saying anything or, being tourists, didn't notice how the falls had been choked by half. *And I cheered them on*, June admitted. God, she wanted to die.

That evening she watched the lights from Canada light up the mist of the Horseshoe Falls, waited for them to blink out, then in the solace of the moonlight thought carefully for most of the night about her final years. "Teaching Ethan to be clear, not poetic. Is that my last challenge?" She thought of something she'd told Horace. "Someday," she once confessed to him, "I'll leave the *Courier* and I think what I'll be proudest of won't be the writing but that I wrote in a room where one could hear the roaring of the falls."

When dawn came she hadn't convinced herself that she had the energy or the interest or the conviction to teach cub reporters, or to move to Buffalo or another larger city and write, or to try to enjoy what would be a quiet retirement. "I've had it up to here with 'business'" she announced to the rapids. So she stepped into the water of the Hermit's Bath, felt her heartbeat pick up, and wondered how quickly the waters would carry her, how much it would hurt, how long she would remain conscious.

June Lockwood died, in her sleep in 1923.

> *For forty years, she worked for the Niagara Courier, moving from society reporter to managing editor. She was a strong voice in support of community improvement and progress. After her retirement in 1894 she did some traveling, but returned to Niagara Falls and became a regular contributor to the Courier through letters to the editor. Her crusades against entry into World War I and in favor of a municipal water treatment facility to combat cholera were typical of her self-less dedication to her community. She will be missed.*

The ditch that William Love did not complete remained an empty ditch until chemical industries came to Niagara Falls in the twentieth century. They began using the ditch as a dump. Very little was known about what went into the dump. The legacy of Model City would not be known for another eighty years.

The City Comes Down

F reshly washed, the Cadillac glistened from its black top to its chrome hubcaps. The driver carefully navigated Erie Avenue, rolling in and out of potholes, the Caddy out of place on a street of humbler, older, mostly dirtier cars. And the neighborhood got worse with each block west of Portage Road. When the driver turned down Third Street, he pulled to the curb before a rambling two story property. It was very old and unkempt, lots of windows broken, the roof sagging, walls bowing out, nothing quite symmetrical anymore. The driver, tall with short wavy black hair, dressed smartly in a blue suit, turned off his car, made sure it was locked as he got out, and tried to look at the old house from different angles without stepping into the yard. For the driver's shoes shone like his car.

Around the corner a minute later came a Plymouth Fury, navy blue and a little scratched, five years older than the Cadillac. Pulling to the curb behind the Cadillac, another man got out, in a cheaper suit, hair almost to his shoulders, carrying a briefcase. "Mister Spallino?" he called to the well-dressed Caddy owner. "I'm Wayne Davidson, with Falls Realty. Am I late?"

Their appointment was for 12:30, and both watches read 12:25. "Thanks for meeting me here, Mr. Davidson," said Joe Spallino. "I'm curious what you can tell me about this property."

Davidson set his briefcase on his trunk and retrieved the listing sheet. "Well, it's been on the market for," he did the math, "three and a half years, since 1960. And it's got a lien on it from the city for back taxes."

"How much is the lien?"

Davidson hunted another sheet of paper in his chaotic briefcase. It took a minute, and the realtor stole a glance at his customer to gauge his interest. Spallino was looking at him. "Here we go," he said, trying to show self-confidence. He was just starting in real estate, having barely fed himself as a car salesman. "Taxes in arrears are now $3,208.57."

Spallino nodded. "And what's the property's price tag?"

Davidson smiled, the way they'd trained him in car sales. "Well, the last owner died without a will three years ago. She had no family. If you're interested, you can probably get this for the taxes and a few fees for title transfers."

Spallino nodded. Reading from the listing sheet, "assessed value is $3000." He looked at the house. "Can I get this reassessed? After paying off the taxes? I can't see it over half that."

"Would you be using a loan?"

"No, cash."

"Ah, of course. Well, with a loan, of course, the bank would require an assessment." Wayne was new at this and this was his first cash buyer. He thought through the usual procedure. "But we can get it re-assessed anyway. I can't promise you what the assessment will be, of course, but you're right, it'll probably be lower than when the property was occupied, given its current condition."

"What's the square footage?"

Davidson glanced at the listing sheet. "It's got over three thousand square feet. Everything in three's," he tried to joke.

"What would you say the property is, about an acre?" Spallino asked.

Davidson shaded his eyes as though he was seeing a great distance. "About that." Then, to be sure, he looked at the listing sheet. "An acre and a couple hundred square feet more." Spallino wasn't showing much emotion one way or another, no great curiosity, but he kept asking for numbers. "This is a great property for rental income. You can turn a place like this into four or five small units, for a fairly nominal amount."

"This is a tear-down," Spallino said, a bit curtly. "You'd have to be out of your mind putting a dime into renovating this. It's only good for the land. Nevertheless, I always take a look inside something I plan to buy. Did you bring the key?"

Davidson, befuddled now as to whether he had an interested party or not, dug out the key to the front door. Shoe shines be damned, they walked through the front lot, sinking into some mud in the process. "Colonial era sidewalks leave a lot to be desired, huh?" Davidson joked, as much for himself this time. He was pretty sure his client had no sense of humor.

Spallino, taller by almost a head, reached the front door first, turned and waited impatiently for Davidson. The realtor got the key into the lock, and it turned stiffly and slow. He pushed the door open.

Dust rose and swirled with the hint of breeze raised by the outside. Spallino stepped in carefully, testing the weak floorboards and picking a pathway. Empty of furniture though, oddly, someone had dragged in a tire. The plaster was stained and swollen from leaks, crumbling where they touched it.

The boards creaked under him, and Davidson was barely a hundred forty pounds. "Real fixer-upper," he joked to himself, as Spallino was in the other room. "Want to see the basement?"

"No, thank you," he heard from another room. "Kids have been having beer parties in here."

"Let's hope that's all," said Davidson, checking his watch. He had an open house on Porter Road in the Town of Niagara in half an hour and he was hoping to grab a sandwich on the way. *C'mon, guy, shit or get off the pot. You're right, it is a tear-down. So either you want the land or you don't. Why we're inside at all is a mystery to me.*

Spallino came back to the front room from a different way. He already owned a dozen properties in this neighborhood; he'd bought them all within the past six months. It was cheap land, and with the new mayor and his promises to rehabilitate downtown, buying land down here looked like a smart investment. "Yea, it's a tear-down. Mr. David-son, find out exactly what the fees are to transfer ownership. I'll do the back taxes and I'll pay for the assessment, but I won't pay more than ten percent over that for fees. Think we can do business?"

Davidson beamed. "I believe so. Barring unforeseen hurdles, I can probably bring the title by, say, in four days?" Spallino nodded agree-ment. "I need to get to the city hall records department, pull the title, and get the tax office to update its records. Just paperwork," he said.

"Very good." Spallino shook Davidson's hand and walked back to his car, pausing before getting back in to get a paper napkin from his front seat and wipe off a gob of mud from his heel. Tossing the napkin on the ground, he got back in his Cadillac and drove off in a powerful roar.

"Last place on earth I thought I'd sell," said Davidson, his spirits suddenly buoyant. The best part was he'd done nothing besides put a sign on the property and list it for a week in the classifieds. Spallino had called him. "And a three hundred dollar commission." He might be late for the open house. He didn't care anymore. He'd unloaded the old stone house on 3rd street. "When they hear this one in the office, I'll be a god."

Del Nichols woke to see the backlit display on his Big Ben alarm clock: 6:10 a.m. Through the high, rectangular casement window he saw it was light outside. He closed his eyes, hoping to sleep until at least eight, since he had no job to go to. But it was a steamy August morning and his basement apartment was already suffocating, and he was awake at six-ten a.m. because Mark, the upstairs tenant, got up at six-ten. Based on what Del could hear through his ceiling, Mark couldn't find his shirt or his new baseball shirt, "the one my mother gave me for my birthday," and finally he couldn't find a clean bowl for cereal.

"Your stupid New York Yankees shirt is in the dirty clothes bin, you slob, you wore it yesterday," Del said to the ceiling; Del liked the Pirates.

Mark didn't hear him. Mark was a big guy, a couple of inches taller than Del and at least twenty pounds heavier, and he hefted hot water tanks for a living, so Del avoided trouble with him. But, in addition to his other infractions, Mark never parked his pickup truck squarely in its space, usually crowding into Del's space. "If you can't find your car keys you may find them hanging from your mail bin, where I saw them last night. I could have tossed them under your door, but that meant going up two flights of steps, and that was too much effort." He rolled over but the squeaking footsteps and thumps were just as loud. "I wanted to throw them in the storm sewer, but that meant going outside, which was also too much effort."

He looked at his dark walls. In the army he only had a few square feet of his own and he'd put up no pictures, no posters, nothing. Now a civilian, he had an apartment of blank walls. They looked better at night, in the dark, with the hope of a life splashed across them. Like walls in other people's homes, with pictures of friends and family, photos of places, art, something reflecting back a life lived. He'd moved in a month ago, and he knew every time the sun rose he'd just see bare walls, plaster painted many times. Worse, in day light there were small holes where pictures once hung.

Mark left at six-thirty, his truck roaring like a beast awakened, and his wife, Angela, was quiet until seven-thirty. Del could conceivably doze until then. Angela rose, showered, dressed and ate to the sound of her collection of Motown, but once awake Del found it hard to get back to sleep. Especially in the heat. So he got up and brushed his teeth. His jeans were on the floor beside his mattress, which perched on his box spring flush on the floor. "Sheeee-it," he cursed as he pulled on the stiff, sticky denim. His bare feet stuck to the linoleum floor tiles. *Next time get the top floor*, he lectured himself, *open up the windows and catch some breeze.*

It was his first civilian apartment after a twelve year hitch in the army brought to a sudden, ungraceful, ending when MPs found a bag of pot in his footlocker at Ramstein, West Germany. It was a couple pounds of mediocre weed, certainly enough to distribute. And Del had been selling it, just to his friends. During his three weeks in custody he wondered which of them turned him in; he was certain the army couldn't have found it without help. They sent him home in July with no pension and pitiful savings, but that was his fault.

So he took this dingy, eighty-dollar apartment, including heat which was no great deal in August, because it was cheap. And because it was just a few blocks from the apartment where he'd grown up, though the neighborhood was less familiar now, and he was used to living close enough to the falls to walk there, and he was just ten minutes from the Upper Rapids. He had a ten by twelve bedroom, a nine by twelve living room with the illusion of more space from adding a dining 'nook', and a kitchenette so small one had to stand in the dining 'nook' to cook. *But how much space does boiling water require?* he asked. It was just possible that army cooking was better than his. His tiny bathroom was walled in flat gray ceramic tile with mildew growing uniformly along each tile. Brushing his teeth, he spit into the sink, somehow missed and saw a gob of toothpaste hit a tile. The toothpaste was white and highlighted the gray mildew. *I guess I should try to kill the mold*, he thought, as he usually did when he saw it in the morning.

A neon tube flickered slightly over his sink. He caught his reflection. Having let his hair grow a little, now that Uncle Sam wasn't dictating such things, it was longer than he remembered it ever being. It curled around the nape of his neck, which he didn't mind, and hung well into his eyes, which he also didn't mind, but he could hear his mother and father, parenting him from the great beyond, "if you want to get ahead, you have to look businesslike." He vaguely wanted to 'get ahead' of where he was, but he didn't look very businesslike.

Nor did he feel businesslike. He hadn't slept well and he wasn't going to shave this morning because it was too much effort on little sleep, and now he thought he looked old even for thirty. *I look like shit*, he decided, *and shaving won't help*. A few more hours' sleep would be nice. And I'm going to the Employment Office, where one is supposed to look ready for work.

His apartment was in an elderly three story brick building on 3rd Street. His six year old '63 Rambler was snug in its parking space on its designated bit of pavement. It was considered a 'blighted' neighborhood, in part thanks to the dirt-cheap beer in the tavern across the street and its patrons' habits of mistaking parked cars and buildings for urinals, and because a tornado could level the entire block and run up a tab of maybe ten thousand dollars for ten properties. All the buildings, including his, needed paint or repointed bricks, or new windows, and the ground was layered in litter which was widely stained yellow. But it didn't matter, if one read the papers or listened to the news, because the city was going to demolish it all.

Turning on his radio, he selected FM. "This is Tom Virgo on WJJL, the Voice of Niagara, and coming up, from Percy Faith, 'Go Away Little Girl.'"

"The only place where radio is duller than AFN," he complained, and pushed a button. The station changed. He got a snippet of Henry Mancini, then Frank Sinatra, punched the radio buttons without looking at them, hit a country-western station and got Johnny Cash, and thought of getting an eight-track tape player. "Buy something cool, maybe the Beach Boys," he planned. "But with what for money?" He had only three hundred dollars in the bank, which, with his current lifestyle would cover about three, three and a half months of rent, cheap food, cheap beer and lots of TV. No movies, no eating out. Pretty boring.

The state employment office in Niagara Falls was on Pine Avenue. Being one of the main commercial streets, traffic here was a fair barometer of the city's health, and on this August day in 1969, the city seemed to have a virus that was turning into something worse, some virus that closed businesses and left empty houses. Block after block, he saw empty windows, hand-lettered GOING OUT OF BUSINESS signs, and small parking lots restricting parkers to customers, and weeds were taking back the lots. The only crowded lot was for the state employment office. "God, this place is depressing," Del said to his rear view mirror.

Last week his 'job counselor' of the day regaled him with what was intended as a pep-talk on taking what was available. What was available, that is, to a guy who drove a truck for the Army and was now on the street with 'bad paper'. What was available was temporary work, pushing brooms in the factories along Buffalo Avenue. It paid poorly and folks were starting to hear about the hidden dangers of chemicals. He'd taken three days' work of this sort, pushing brooms. It padded his wallet a little. But it was boring.

God knows he'd learned to deal with boredom in the army, but he was back in the world, where people owned Corvettes and Cadillacs, ate in good restaurants, and had nice homes. He was learning again to be envious. So he did a few of these day jobs, then decided to get off his ass and look for real work. And it had been a tough hunt.

Parking his car between a badly rusted pickup and an Oldsmobile as dinged as the Rambler, he turned off the radio. Into the land of false hope, he braced himself. He was wearing his civilian uniform, a sweat-shirt and jeans and sneakers, and his fatigue jacket. The last piece got him a little more respect than he could get without.

He pushed through the glass doors. The small waiting area had plastic chairs. Posters covered the walls, warnings of the dangers of drug abuse alternating with state and federal notices thick with legal boilerplate on the rights of the unemployed, on labor law, and other concepts out of place in a room designated for the desperate in a town with rising unemployment. Your right to sue your employer for religious discrimination. . . went one poster. It made Del smile. In this town? You'd be hooted out of the place as a fool, giving up a good job because the boss didn't give you Good Friday off. Del registered, then sat and fished a section of the *Niagara Gazette* from the heap of paper on the table. He was looking for the comics when he heard his name called. *Oh no*, he saw, *I got Grimsby*.

Grimsby was an old man with a bad toupee and a voice sculpted by years of smoking. He was hardened by life, his body fossilized, curled stiff and reluctant to bend at any joint. When he sat, his head faced forward, and to move his head he moved his entire body. To turn his head, and face the next out-of-work soul meant his withered left hand had to use his desk as an anchor to push his rolling chair to the right. He was a believer in the employment model whereby the next person through the door was the right one for the job on his desk. Del interviewed, after Grimsby's urging, for jobs as a vacuum salesman, scrub jockey at a car wash, and finally took that temporary job for three days pushing a broom in Carborundum's weaving room, to shut Grimsby up.

"Mister Nichols, you were in here last week, is that correct?" Grimsby was looking through his thick glasses at Del. As though there were precious jobs to be rationed, and one dared not visit the well more often than one's allotted turn.

"Yes, I was," Del said. He'd thought showing such initiative would improve Grimsby's opinion of him, perhaps translating into a referral to a decent job. "I was hoping," he shrugged as though confessing to a petty crime, "you might find me a job."

Grimsby fired up his desktop microfiche reader. The blue and white display was hard for Del to read. Watching Grimsby lean forward and peer into it, like watching a hockey game on a tiny screen with terrible reception, Del found he didn't trust Grimsby's reading skills. He'd noticed job descriptions asking for a high school diploma and giving credit to servicemen that Grimsby roamed past. "You want a day of work at Union Carbide?" Grimsby asked, blinking as he got nose to screen.

"One day?" Del shook his head. "I've done it. Not worth it for the cancer I'll get in ten years from working there." He knew he was pushing one of Grimsby's buttons, but he didn't want any more temp jobs, and the old man pushed off from his desk to look Del over for a good old pep talk.

"Mr. Grimsby?" The receptionist was calling. Grimsby gripped his desk and turned to look at her. "Mr. Grimsby?" she called again, fetching him with a wave of her hand.

"Be right back," he promised Del, and got up and walked slowly, with a pronounced limp, to the receptionist's desk.

Del leaned forward and got a better view of the microfiche. Scanning quickly, he skipped through job titles. 'Engineer. . . Business Manager. . . Engineer. . . shit,' he swore, and he worked the fiche carrier like the reader on a Ouija board, hoping to find magic. Glancing over his shoulder, he saw Grimsby occupied with someone off the street, a black woman with a wildly colored headband and huge hoop earrings. He was going to be a minute. Del studied the fiche more methodically. 'Construction. . . Demolition crew.' He stopped. 'Truck driver. . . contracted for Urban Renewal in Niagara Falls. Possible long term employment. HS, Spec. consideration veterans.'

Yes! Del found a pencil and scribbled the phone number on the back of one of Grimsby's business cards, and since Grimsby wasn't coming, he scribbled the address as well. Demolition of Buffalo, Inc., had the contract for the long promised urban renewal project in Niagara Falls. "Long term employment for sure," Del said to himself. And special consideration for veterans. He saw Grimsby was now trying to speak with the woman, who was using the F-word liberally, clearly upsetting Grimsby. "Thanks, ma'am," Del said softly, waving as he walked out.

He stopped at his apartment to shave, after all, and put on clean jeans. Then he walked to the address, just a few blocks away. The company was in a trailer parked in the New York Central railyard, which he knew well. The trailer had three windows, and air conditioning units stuck out of two of them. He hadn't called ahead, and wondered, a little late, if Grimsby wasn't supposed to be calling on his behalf. Too late to worry about that. He knocked, and a young woman opened the door.

"Yeah?" She was a young Italian girl, dressed in spotless denim and a white V-neck shirt, showing off her plump hourglass figure. She must have liked what she saw, as she beamed at him. "C'mon in, you're letting the heat in."

"Sorry. I'm here about a job with the demolition crew."

"Have a seat. Mr. Janese?" She called through a flimsy doorway and he heard a man's voice. "Guy here to join the crew?"

"Have him fill out an application, then send him in."

"You have experience in demolition?"

Del nodded. "Yea, the summer before I enlisted I worked for a guy who was demolishing a warehouse." He was lying. He'd never worked demolition, but it was his best paying option right now, so as far as he was concerned he'd never worked anything but demolition.

Frank Janese read Del's application. Janese was fifty-something, and he was a magnificent fifty-something in his perfectly barbered silver hair, carefully trimmed moustache, and spotless, creased denim. "You got a referral card from the Employment Office? I'm supposed to get a referral card."

Del gave him the business card he'd taken from Grimsby's desk. "This is what he gave me. You can call him. He'll remember Delbert Nichols."

Janese took the card, glanced at it, and set it on the desk, his mind moving on. "What branch of the service you in?"

"Army. Twelve years in Europe, mostly driving trucks around Ramstein." Special consideration for veterans.

"You ever smoke dope?"

Del panicked. He really wanted this job. It was close to his lousy apartment, it was outside work, which suited him, and it potentially paid better than the Buffalo Avenue hellholes. His palms were getting sweaty and he realized he was licking his dry lips. "Did I ever smoke dope?" he repeated the question, looking at Janese as though there were subtleties Del didn't completely grasp.

Janese set the application on his desk. "Yea. I asked if you ever smoked dope?" His brown eyes were framed in jet black eyebrows and when his face set in a frown it was scary. "It's a yes or no question."

Del looked down at his dirty sneakers. "Sure. When I was a kid." He looked up at Janese. "But not anymore." That was pretty close to true. He felt he'd been in a prolonged adolescence during his hitch.

Janese's frown eased up some. "You ever in one of these peace marches?"

Peace marches. The protesters against the war in Vietnam were making the daily news on a regular basis. They marched in the falls and in Buffalo, mostly around the university campus and the ROTC offices and the recruitment centers. There were also daily denunciations of the protestors by mayors, governors, those in power. There were daily reminders that some folks hated the war, some folks hated those other folks, and some, like Del, were confused and undecided.

However imperfectly his army years had ended, he felt some loyalty to the corps, but from everything he'd read and heard about the Southeast Asian conflict, it was a bad place for American boys. So he was still making up his mind how he felt about the war and suddenly his loyalty to the war hawks was a condition of employment?

"No, I've never been in a peace march." He felt like he'd just had his dick squeezed by Mr. Janese, like he'd been fondled. *You got no business asking that kind of question,* he thought. *I wish I had taken part in a peace march, I wish I'd given a damn. Being safe in Europe I just smoked dope and ignored it. I don't need this fucking job. I don't want to work for a shithead like you anyway, Mister Creased Jeans.*

But Janese seemed satisfied. He picked up a walkie-talkie. "Nickie? You got a minute? I got a guy here for your crew."

The radio hissed static. "I'll be there in a minute."

A minute to kill. "So how you like Germany?" Janese asked, smiling. He made Germany sound like the town two hours east. The interview was over, now it was just two guys shooting the breeze.

"Beer was good." Del was still steaming with anger, and was struggling to suppress it now that he was on the verge of a job he wanted. Fortunately, Nickie was not far away. The door opened, and Nickie stepped in, in soiled jeans, dirty t-shirt, hard hat, and well-used gloves. He had silver hair under his hat, and he hadn't shaved that morning. Nickie could be Janese's father.

"How you doing," Nickie asked, pulling off a glove to extend a strong hand. Del began to stand. "Nick Gallo. Nah, sit, take it easy. You'll never hear me say that again." He meant it as a joke. Janese handed Nickie the application. He looked at it for a moment, then gave it back. "Ever drive a truck?" Del nodded vigorously. "Ever use a jack-hammer?" Del froze, then said he hadn't. "You'll learn. We're starting by excavating the old hydraulic canal. It's going to be the footings for the new convention center. We'll eventually be pulling up this railyard," he indicated their present home. "That's why I asked about the jack-hammer. We're going to be pulling down everything for a dozen blocks going that way and that way," he indicated the river and the gorge. "I'm looking for guys who can do the job and show up on time every day. How long you in the service?"

"Twelve years."

"Honorable discharge?"

He hesitated. "General discharge."

"Fuck a general's wife or something?" he seemed more amused than concerned.

"Something."

There might have been a brief bit of dead air as Del remembered it later. "Okay, someday we'll have a few beers and you'll tell me." Nickie scribbled something on the form. "Take this out to Gina. Tell her you start tomorrow, she'll get you started on the forms. It's insurance mostly. Job pays four-fifty an hour, we work a ten hour day. Okay?"

Del nodded; if Janese was a shit, Nickie was his redemption. "Okay." He shook Nickie's hand again, then Janese's. He had the job. He was smiling.

"We start at six-thirty. Don't be late your first day, okay?" Nickie grinned again, then left.

Janese handed him a folder of forms and sent him back out to Gina's desk. Alone with her, he couldn't help noticing her. She looked barely out of high school, and deeply into cosmetics and jewelry that interfered with her hands. Her dark hair and olive skin were a pleasant view. Her perfume was like hair spray in his throat. "'Kay, you fill this out, and this part, leave this blank," she riffled through the forms, her long, painted fingernails somehow separating sheets, her bracelets clanking, "and you don't need to fill this out, I can do it." She smiled broadly at him. *I think she likes me*, Del thought, *but I'm at least ten years older than her*. He usually thought of good, long-lasting couples as being of similar age and race. That was starting to change too, except in Niagara Falls. Thanking her, he started out the door. "Bye," she called, and stood to show off her figure, in case he missed it the first time. "Welcome aboard."

He celebrated by buying steel-toed boots at Goodwill. Awakened next morning by the same steamy heat, he had coffee, then decided he should eat something. He looked in vain in his bare cupboards. Out of cereal? Right, that was dinner last night. Crap. He had a loaf of bread, but no toaster, and he wasn't up to using the electric burner to carefully toast the bread, so he just folded a couple slices and chewed it down, then walked the three blocks to the trailer. It was another humid morning and at the end of the block he was sweating just from walking. He was in his newest jeans and an old shirt and his new-ish boots.

Nickie was standing by a dump truck, finishing off a cruller, a steaming cup of coffee in his hand. He waved Del over. Inside the cab were two others, both younger than Del. The engine was idling loudly, the cab littered with paper coffee cups, cigarette ash and butts and the remains of a box of donuts. Nickie pointed to a huge guy behind the wheel. "That's Al."

"Call him Pig Mac," said the other guy, and got punched in the shoulder by the driver. "I meant Big Mac," he grinned.

"He's Leon," said Nickie. "Call him Leon. This is Del Nichols, the new guy I told you about. Good to see you can read a clock." He smiled slightly. "You'll start up by the river." He pointed across the rail yard. "You can almost see it." He handed Leon a clipboard with a city map clamped on it. "They dumped trash in the canal to fill it in '56. We're digging it back out and taking it down Buffalo Avenue, down Hyde Park Boulevard, dumping it here," his index finger rested on a lot on the north side among some factories. "Leon will be using the front-end loader. You and Al will be hauling today. Any questions?" he asked them all.

Leon took the clipboard. "You afraid I'll excavate the wrong site?" he teased Nickie.

"I'm just hoping between the three of you there's one guy that can read a map," Nickie said, that hint of a smile touching his face. "If you have any problems, give me a call on the radio. Okay?"

Leon opened the cab door and Del climbed in and Al rammed the truck into gear without benefit of clutch, giving Nickie a pained expression as the truck pulled away. "Why do you do that?" Leon asked him.

"Because it gets under Nickie's skin," said Al. He had a crew cut, the build of a serious weight lifter, and a vacant, potentially mean smile on his face. "So, Del, you a faggot like Leon?"

Del, shoulder to shoulder with Leon, glanced at him for his reaction. Leon smiled. "You're just jealous 'cause Gina let me get into her pants."

"What would she want with a faggot like you?"

Leon stuck his middle finger upright in Al's face. "Poor horny Al. Gina wouldn't let you lick the shit off her ass. Keep it up and I'll scratch your ear with the bucket."

Del tensed, but both guys laughed, as though this was their usual morning banter.

"So, Del, want to know why fatso here gets called Big Mac?" Leon asked. Leon himself was not a body builder, but his clothing had certainly seen some action. "We go for lunch, see how many Big Macs he orders. His record is ten."

"Eleven," Al corrected, making a left turn. "I threw it up, but I got it down first. And don't call me Big Mac, call me Al."

He was forced to slow down as a young black man in dirty pants and a torn blue t-shirt crossed Erie Avenue in a leisurely fashion. Rolling down the window, Al lit into him. "C'mon, c'mon, you fucking nigger, move your lazy ass."

The black man was no match for Al, much less Al in a truck, but he stood defiantly in the street until Al was forced to stop, then pressed his meaty palm on his horn. Del winced. The black man was alone, and Del wondered if Al would bully him if he had friends.

Leon reached behind the seat, got out a scuffed hard hat with 'Big Mac' written on it in black marker, put it on the owner's head, then smacked it. "Stop that!" Al let the horn fall silent. "Damn, you're giving me a headache in record time today. You want to try to make a good first impression on Del, or do you want to confirm that you're a complete asshole and start a race riot?"

Al spun the wheel slightly to cut around the walker who had stopped and flipped Al off, with some body language for good measure. He gunned the engine. "Neighborhood is a shit hole."

Del nodded slightly. The Falls Street—Erie Street stretch of downtown had crumbled. His parents once talked about the thriving South End when they were young, but somehow the prosperity had escaped, leaving empty buildings, businesses limping towards failure, and more and more CONDEMNED signs.

It was only a five minute ride, though it seemed to last an hour with Al's stream of rude insults. "Fucking ghetto, now it's just nigger-town, they torch the buildings in their own frigging neighborhoods, y'know. The firemen should come down one night the next time they torch one and make sure one fire takes out the whole fucking neighborhood. Burn it to the fucking ground."

"Shut up, please?" Leon asked. He turned to Del and spoke as though Al were in the back, "I just ignore the asshole. See, of the two of us, I can read, and I earn twice what he does."

"Bull-shit," said Al, but with more humor than anger. He hit the brakes hard and made his passengers bob forward slightly. "Everybody out."

The old hydraulic canal once diverted water from the upper river, behind the falls, across the peninsula of downtown, and then let the water plunge down onto the turbines of the Schoellkopf Power Plant, a brick institution at the bottom of the gorge. In 1956 a rock slide swept the power plant away, with minimal loss of life but completely destroying the power plant. The canal that fed it was filled in a couple years later with whatever was at hand. And now it needed to be emptied.

There were two front-end loaders and two dump trucks parked behind a factory, with a scuffed up Johnny-on-the-spot. "Okay," said Del, feeling he should prove he had a voice. Al whistled at him, and when Del turned he got a hard hat in the face. It left his nose tingling. "Thanks." He wasn't smiling when he said it, because Al was.

"Keys are usually tucked in the visor," Leon said, as he headed off to start up the loader. He stopped, remembering something, and turned to Del. "Just a warning. If you need to use the toilet, make sure Al isn't around. He likes to tip it over with someone in it." Del nodded.

He started the truck and felt the familiar rumble of the diesel shake the truck gently, like a big dog beneath him. He shifted, worked the stick, and got a feel for the clutch. It wasn't a new truck but it was running smooth. He thought of testing the hydraulics, raising the bed, but he could see that Leon was already in motion, positioning the backhoe to dig, and he heard Al's air horn; he was indicating that Del should pull up next to the scoop.

It all came back to him; the truck was not much different from the army's equipment, just painted black instead of gray. He pulled up and waited.

The bucket blocked out the sun when Leon raised his scoop, and then the truck shook as dirt and rock fell in. Del waited for three more loads. Then Leon waved to indicate he was full. Grinding first gear, Del got rolling.

It was great, driving down Buffalo Avenue in a heavy truck, the factories lining the street. He fit right in. "Better out here than in there," he said, and kind of hugged the big wheel in his hands. The vibration he got from the wheel when he drove over train tracks was vaguely sexual. It was so cool to look down at the civilians in their little sedans. From Buffalo Avenue he went down Hyde Park Boulevard, which meant taking it slow as more cars roared past him. Stop-lights every couple blocks made for slow going. He'd just start gearing up to third when the next light would go yellow and he'd have to brake again. It turned a fifteen-twenty minute ride into a good half-hour. It would be worse at rush-hour. "But what the hell, I'm working again, making decent money. And I'm not in the army anymore." Still, what was that empty feeling?

He found the dumping area, marked by company signs. Driving over the muddy ground, lugging it in second gear, he reached the back of the lot and began to wrestle the wheel to turn the rig around. "Back it up to the end, dump it and pull out," Leon had instructed him. Using his side-view mirrors, he got into position and pulled down on the lever to raise the bed. He heard the engine's pitch change as it powered the hydraulic pump, felt the bed break free as it rose. He counted to three, that being the rule he'd been taught by Uncle Sam, and slowly rolled forward in first. Through the mirrors he saw rocks bounce out, and dirt falling. Pulling forward about twenty feet, he left a fairly neat pile. Stopping, pulling on the lever to let the truck bed back down, he heard the motor lugging and, just as the bed was almost settled, he saw Al's truck come rolling in. And then the truck stalled.

He worked the starter for a few minutes without success. Getting out, climbing up on the front bumper, he lifted the hood. The usual parts, the usual wiring. He didn't really know much about engine repair, and he saw nothing wrong. "Problem?" Al called from his truck cab.

"It stalled."

Al let his mean smile blossom again. "I don't think it stalled. Check your fuel gauge."

"I just started it. It said 'full'. I haven't gone ten miles." Al's evil smile was graduating into chuckles, so Del got into the cab with a sick feeling. Sure enough, the fuel gauge had gone from F to E in one short trip.

"The tank leaks. Why do you think I made you take it?" Al laughed deeply; he'd waited forty-five minutes for this. "We got a five gallon can in the shed over there, for emergencies. Just make sure you fill it up again," he added sternly, as though Del had brought this on himself.

Son of a bitch, Del thought. Being hazed wasn't so bad, but he could tell Al was the sort of prick who lived for it. Stuck me with the truck with the leaky tank? Fine.

When he returned with, however fleetingly, full tanks he asked Leon, "does Al know the tank on this is leaking?"

"Oh yeah, dipshit tore through the yard at forty, hit a rock or something and punched a hole in it yesterday." Leon said. "The way he drives it you'd think it was demolition derby time. It's going in for repairs tomorrow. Nickie said just run it today, and keep refilling it, 'cause we're behind the eight-ball in clearing out this ditch. Nice of Al to fuck up the tank and stick you with it."

"Yeah, good ol' Al. I wonder if he'd notice if I pissed on his seat at lunch?"

"Well, I'll take a dump after you. He'll have to notice that."

When Al rolled up twenty minutes later, he got out with coffee and McDonalds hot apple pies for them. "Hey, sorry to hear your fuel tank leaks," he joked with Del, "here's a little something to make up for it." He gave him coffee and a pie.

Del took a cautious sip.

"Taste okay?" Leon asked, suspiciously, sniffing his own cup. "'Cause he's been known to take a whiz in people's coffee."

Al rolled on the ground with laughter.

They stopped for lunch and drove, in Al's truck, to McDonalds. True to his word, Al ordered four Big Macs and tried to swallow each in two bites. Doing so produced a small pile of shredded lettuce and a puddle of 'special sauce'.

"Nickie said you were ex-Army," said Al, coming up for air. "You in Vietnam?"

"No," Del said. He sucked on the straw in his Coke until it rattled empty. "I just drove trucks around West Germany." He made a point of looking around at the lunch crowd. Some black, some white, a few people in suits, more people dressed the same as he, in dirty work clothes.

Al nodded, a little dismayed. "I almost got drafted, I got called up to get my physical. But I got flat feet, and all they want is guys for the infantry, so they didn't take me."

"Shithead here wanted to go," Leon said, in an exchange they apparently ran before. "Guys all over the country are breaking their arms and legs to stay out, and you wanted to go." He shook his head.

Al looked a little dark. "Well, at least I wasn't some college faggot."

Leon tried on a weary smile. "Anybody who can get into college is, by Al's measure, a faggot." He ate a French fry. "Until last year I had a college deferment. I was taking Psychology at Brockport. But it's all bullshit. It's just a party school. I guess I lost interest. I want to earn some money to take a trip around Europe. I'm going to go to France, Germany, and last of all, Italy. I think I'd like to live there. I want to see something besides the falls, and Vietnam isn't my first choice."

As though Leon had never spoken, Al pointed out a guy in long hair, wearing a t-shirt bearing the peace symbol. "When I was here earlier, getting coffee, I got stuck in line behind one of those freaks. He had an American flag sewed into the ass of his jeans, and he's wearing a peace symbol around his neck. I wanted to grab that symbol and just choke him with it. Those faggots are destroying the country."

"If you watch the sky over there," Leon pointed towards the river, speaking to Del, "and you see the mist from the falls, sometimes it looks like one of the clouds from a Road Runner cartoon. When Wile E. Coyote falls off a cliff." He smiled stupidly at Del and shrugged. Del laughed. Al swallowed the last of his last Big Macs and threw the wrapper at Leon.

"So you drove trucks around West Germany? You'd rule the road, wouldn't you," Al said, fascinated with some macho image of driving a big truck in Germany like the lord of the manor.

"I drove trucks. I hauled gasoline and diesel fuel mostly."

"Did you ever drive snowplows?" Leon asked. He was dipping his French fries into a puddle of ketchup. "I always thought Germany got a lot of snow."

Del shook his head. "A couple of winters were snowy, but they only get a couple of feet of snow the whole winter. We get a lot more here."

"No shit," Leon said, nodding. "See, if I'd already gotten to Germany I'd know that. So why'd you come back here?" It was a challenge to Del's powers of reason, but Leon meant it innocently. "I mean, the only real work around here is the auto industry, which is laying off, or the factories on Buffalo Avenue. And I don't know what the city thinks it's doing with this urban renewal thing, but they aren't going to revitalize," he waved his hands to mimic the grand gesture of a politician, "downtown by smashing it down and building a convention center. The Canadians still have the view, and it still gets frigging cold here in the winter." Back to the question: "so why'd you come back here?"

"My family is from here." They are, both of them dead now, he thought, buried in the cemetery next to Hyde Park. "I was eighteen when I signed up. All I knew was that I needed to go somewhere every morning and I was done with school. My guidance counselor said I should try the service, so I go in the service. I didn't see much there except for Ramstein." Jesus, what a loser, he thought. "So, anyway," he added, then finished off his French fries.

They sat back for a moment's rest in the uncomfortable molded plastic bench. They weren't the highest paid guys they knew. They weren't the smartest guys they knew. And they were pretty dirty. But they had jobs, and they'd just eaten lunch. Leon, the only one wearing a watch, a simple Timex held snug by a leather band with elaborate snaps, held his wrist up. "It's time to finish digging out that ditch," he said to Al, "if you can avoid destroying a second truck in two days, we might just finish the job today."

Al, showing no inclination to getting up, released a deep belch that drew a few offended glances. "Ah. See, the problem with you, Leon, is you're always trying to finish a job early. My old man taught me better. If you want the work to last, don't go busting your ass to finish early. Nickie said they were trying to clear the ditch as far as the railroad tracks by a week or so. So we got a week or so. And we get paid by the hour. So take it easy." That said, he got up, picked up his tray, a lake of 'special sauce' topped with the paper wrappings of his lunch, and shoved it forcefully into a visibly overflowing garbage bin. Leon and Del carried their trays across the floor to an almost empty garbage bin, meanwhile watching Al use his plastic tray as a tool to compact the trash.

"Man loves his work," Leon said with a smile. Del laughed, a little harder than he intended to. And he could feel some muscles aching already.

He was laughing at a Leon joke when he got out of the truck at six that evening. Dear God, I'm tired, he said to himself, and he walked the three blocks to his apartment in a fog. Showering felt so soothing he almost fell asleep in the tub. At seven he put on a pot of water to boil. As soon as the first bubbles rose from the pot he emptied a box of spaghetti in it. It took some effort to stand there and stir it, then to heat some store sauce in a pot he took dirty from the sink. When it was finished he inhaled it.

The news was the anti-war marches, that and the latest footage of the Vietnam War. Soldiers humping along some country road, helicopters flying in formation over rice paddies, some window gunner spewing bullet casings like popcorn. Presumably there were targets somewhere out of the camera's range. Or maybe he was just firing the gun to give the cameraman some exciting footage.

"I managed to miss that show," he said to the TV. Thank God. I discovered marijuana in the United States Army, driving trucks. If I was facing life and death everyday I probably would have discovered my way up to heroin. Whatever took me the deepest, held me the longest. In West Germany there were never important dangers, just petty bullshit. He smoked marijuana purely out of boredom. And, if he were honest with himself, as a possible way out. A passive-aggressive approach to a discharge, fortunately his service record was good, even a commendation or two from war games. To simplify the process, his captain offered him the general discharge. So the boredom ended. He still liked pot, but he hadn't smoked it since coming back. Truth was he couldn't afford it.

Five minutes later he was stretched out on his bed, TV still on. With the overhead light in his bedroom on, with the upstairs folks loudly enjoying a movie, he fell deeply asleep in his jeans.

"Okay, change of assignment," Nickie announced to them the next day. "I got a couple of bigger trucks coming up from Buffalo today. They can carry twice what you guys were moving, so you're done hauling dirt. It's time to start with the houses. I'm going to be starting two more crews this week, trying to catch up."

Del saw a look of dismay on Al's puss. His tactic of prolonging the work had failed.

Nickie produced a clipboard with two pages, documents typed with carbon paper, stamped in red letters CONDEMNED. "Here's the address," he used a pencil to circle it: 626 Fifth St. "Take this truck to haul the debris to the same dump as you used yesterday, but keep it in a separate pile. Leon, you used a bulldozer, right?"

"Sure," Leon said.

"It's just a ranch, so a bulldozer should bring it down. For tomorrow I'll have the wrecker up here with the ball on it, because tomorrow we have to knock down a triple decker, but Leon can break the house. Del, you use the bucket to pick up the mess, Al, you use the truck and take it to the dump. Got it?"

"Fuck, I know how to drive a bulldozer," Al complained. "Why don't I get to drive the bulldozer?"

"Cause you put one of my trucks in the shop, asshole. Think I'm going to let you drive even more expensive equipment?" Nickie said, giving Al a rare frown. Al looked away.

Del didn't know how to use the bucket, but he figured it would explain itself. Al drove them to the site, swearing even more vividly on the way, and his passengers ignored him.

The house was abandoned, plywood nailed over the doorway and windows. Leon pulled a crowbar from a tool box in the truck and while Al sat and listened to country music, Del helped Leon pry the door open.

"We have to double check that it's empty. Bums start moving into these houses when they're abandoned, and Nickie doesn't like getting in trouble by burying them," he explained facetiously. "We also want to make sure there aren't any gas or electric or water lines still live." The plywood came loose, and Leon put the teeth of the crowbar between the door and frame and gave it a body shove. The door squeaked open.

Stepping inside, Leon called out "hello?" He went around the front to the living room, Del went in the back, to the kitchen.

The windows were nailed over, the kitchen lit by light seeping between the boards and now pouring in from the hallway. Del pulled open a silverware drawer, then the drawer below that. He found an old book. The binding was faded but he deciphered *Roads of Destiny*, a collection of O. Henry short stories, bound in blue cloth, the pages yellowed and the cover water-stained. On the binding, a spine label from the Niagara Falls Public Library. It was small enough to fit in his pocket, snugly.

The kitchen cupboards were empty, for the most part, a few of the doors missing. A gaping spot and patterns of dirt showed where the refrigerator sat for years. A doorway on the side led down a flight of narrow wooden steps to the basement.

"Hello, down there," Del called, hearing Leon's voice from the front. He looked for a light switch, flipped it up. No light. He thought then that a flashlight would be a good idea, but decided he could navigate by what little light was leaking in through the mostly broken basement windows.

Damp and dank, it smelled moldy. Two wooden beams ran the length and width of the house and a third beam stood at the juncture. Old wiring wrapped in cloth insulation traveled the rafters, wrapped periodically around porcelain knobs. In the far corner he could see fuses and a fuse box. Check the power, he remembered. Overhead he could hear Leon's boots on the linoleum. "Del?"

"In the basement. Do you have a voltage tester?"

"I'll get it from the truck. You find the fuse box?"

"Yea, that's where I am."

"Okay, there's no gas line going in, so see if you can find the water and make sure it's turned off."

He found the pipe behind a broken chair. The iron faucet head wouldn't budge either way. He went up to the doorway and called out, "do you have a wrench? I found the water but it's stuck."

They met at the water valve with a tool box. Selecting a monkey wrench, Leon got the faucet to turn and then they heard water running. Turning it back, "I guess it was off." He found the voltage tester and tested one of the fuses. "Power's off. I guess it's all over but the wrecking."

They left the door open on the way out. Al was still listening to the radio.

Leon started up the bulldozer and raised the blade until it met the edge of the roof. Diesel smoke pouring from the exhaust, he revved the engine and the treads chewed up the dirt as he pushed tentatively. Cracking, like a small gunshot in the air, the wooden gutter crumbled against the blade. The roof buckled and the wall gave way. Leon pushed deeper and the roof began sagging, breaking around the blade in pieces.

Del was fascinated by it. Then he remembered he still had to figure out the machine he was sitting in. With a little experimentation he got the bucket to scoop, raise, and turn. By that time half the house had crumbled into the basement, a hole covered with roofing shingles over which hovered a cloud of old plaster dust. Leon was chewing up the rest of the lawn driving around the front.

Del got the scoop moving forward, but on his first pass he missed the pile completely. He thought he heard Al yell something, but fortunately the diesel engine drowned him out. On his second try he scooped up a chunk of roof, chunk of wall, and some dirt. Al had moved the truck around his side, so Del got it almost all into the truck. By the third scoop he was moving almost all building debris, and almost all of it ended up in the truck.

"Not bad for a virgin," Al called to him. "See you in half an hour."

There was more wreckage than could be moved. Leon stopped, leaving one corner of the house still standing. He turned off the bulldozer and walked over to chat with Del.

"Al comes back later each trip," Del said, after turning off the loader. "He took an hour on the last trip. We could do it in a half-hour, easy."

"That's my boy, make the work last," Leon said. "Nickie's not kidding about being backed up. If Al doesn't shake a leg, he might end up picking up trash by hand for the city."

Del fished out the book. "I found this in the house."

Leon took a look. "O. Henry," he smiled in appreciation. "He's a very entertaining writer. Ever read his stuff?"

"I don't remember."

"He loved to have stories with a twist, a surprise ending. He was a master of the short story."

"Thought you studied psychology?"

"I was thinking of minoring in literature," he explained. "Well, you found some free reading material. Enjoy. One of our few perks."

At five Al managed to return with the empty truck, and they still had a couple loads of debris. "Nickie's going to be pissed we didn't finish," Leon said.

"It'll be here tomorrow," Al said, contentedly.

But it wasn't. Del woke near midnight to the sound of fire trucks. The air horns and the high whine of the sirens drew him out of his apartment. He followed a thin stream of curious people walking towards the excitement. 350 Seventh Street was burning. The firemen were setting up a couple of lines to keep the flames under control. Del glanced at his watch—1:47 a.m.—and scolded himself to get to bed. The debris was like a huge ashtray by then, dark and smoldering, and drenched.

He walked home and tried to get to sleep, but he kept seeing the roof buckle that morning against the force of the bulldozer. *Does this mean I'm in love? With demolition?*

He spent more time the next day loading the sodden, burned debris into the truck. They finished early, and Nickie came by and told them to go home. "We're behind, but it's Friday. Next week we've got a couple big buildings to start. Come back ready to work," he said with a look at Al.

With the ease of an experienced chef filleting a salmon with a trusted knife, Beth Reuther snapped open the *Niagara Falls Gazette* and inserted the bamboo rods that, once trussed, hung the paper from its appointed place on the rack like a spitted lamb. It was eight fifty-three, seven minutes before Elliott, the custodian so unresponsive the library staff thought him mute, unlocked the heavy front doors of the Carnegie building.

At eight fifty-eight, Walter Morrow slipped in through the Staff entrance with his brown lunch bag. It was humid and Walter walked to work; he was heading for portly and his short sleeve shirt, straining at the buttons, was stained dark at the pits. He came through the Reading Room with sweat beaded on his forehead and made a beeline for the *Gazette*.

"Do you keep a deodorant in your office, Walter?" Beth asked as his wake washed over her.

"Why?" Walter thought of himself as the absent-minded professor. It worked for him sometimes, such as in being late to work and to staff meetings. It worked less well in personal hygiene.

"Do reason," Beth said, speaking through her mouth.

Walter was her first date when she came back to Niagara Falls from Boston. He was then the newly hired local historian, about twenty pounds lighter, and elated at escaping what he'd expected was a life-term teaching public school. He referred to his three years at crumbling Trott Vocational as 'my years as a lecturer' and a casual listener would think Trott Vocational was, perhaps, the University of Trott.

"Is this today's?" he opened the *Gazette*. She nodded. "I attended a meeting of the Urban Renewal Agency," he said with a cold dryness, as though that excused any tardiness, "and listened to them signing death warrants on sixteen properties. At least one was an art deco classic on Jefferson Avenue. Why am I here?" he asked melodramatically. "I'm a historian in a city demolishing its history."

"I'm been asking myself the same question," she said, though she didn't think he was listening.

The only answer she came up with was her father. I promised myself when Mom died and I came back I would only stay a year. She'd earned her library degree at Simmons College in Boston, then got a job at the Boston Public Library and she was happy. Returning to Niagara, the only work she could find initially was cashier at Slipkos, at ten cents above minimum, and she laid the groundwork for a move either back to Boston or to Philadelphia, or Washington, or her real dream, the Southwest. She left books about them lying around the house where her father would see them, and subscribed to the *L.A. Times* to assess the rents and the employment picture. Her father said nothing, still in shock over the death of his wife. And while he shuffled through the house, pausing often to gaze at her graduation photo with the three of them, she couldn't bear to leave him behind.

Then the library job opened up at the public library. The staff of four was down one due to retirement. She interviewed with Mr. Laker, predecessor to her current boss, Mrs. Koenig, and was sure she'd blown the interview. The opening would rotate her through the magazine collection, book buying, regular reference and typing up index cards. "What sort of journals would you add to our collection?" Mr. Laker asked during the interview. Beth, after her years in Boston, tossed out her favorites. "*Mother Jones, Open Cell, Ramparts.*" She saw her prospective employer's eyebrows arch. "And, of course, *Popular Science*," she tried a save.

She got the job, she learned, because Mr. Laker was impressed with her Boston Public Library experience. Six months later, Mr. Laker took a job in Buffalo, and Mrs. Koenig was hired. Beth's job included work on committees to add books and journals and records, and Mrs. Koenig declined almost all of Beth's selections. Her co-workers, Abigail Roosevelt, Danielle Vernon and Linda Gallagher, were born and raised locally, and she was by ten years the youngest of them, and by almost a hundred and eighty degrees the most radical. Abigail was the senior librarian, working in her early sixties in hopes of replacing Mrs. Koenig. "You're our resident lefty," Abigail liked to joke to Beth. "Token lefty," Beth usually said, when out of hearing. She stopped making suggestions for the collection. She worked on not smirking when Abby or Linda offered suggestions from the *Reader's Digest Library*, or to beef up the romantic fiction section. In all fairness, the stuff did circulate well. Danielle just typed index cards contentedly in the back.

Three years of this. Her father was so cheered when she got the job it almost negated his wife's death. Almost. And only for a couple months. Beth wasn't and had no intention of becoming her mother, or of retiring from the Niagara Falls Public Library. But the latter didn't seem likely anyway. Mrs. Koenig was already mentioning openings she'd heard of at Niagara University, or the University of Buffalo, "and of course, the new community college is growing." Go where a leftist would be more welcome, she seemed to be saying. "It wouldn't hurt," suggested Danielle one day, resplendent in an almost floor-length blue dress she'd made herself, "if you wore a skirt."

That was why she accepted Walter's stuffy, clumsy offer of a date three years ago. She thought he was another lost soul who must move on or die. But after three dates it was painfully clear that Walter was quite the opposite, grateful and clutching tightly to his lifeboat of a job in the library, which only death would pry from his fingers. His mother was in a nursing home and when he managed to manipulate a 4-F status he almost danced to work. She said 'let's be friends'.

She experimented with women as sex partners, and while it had clear benefits over heterosexuality, there weren't many women lovers to pick from in Niagara Falls and the dearth of choice left her wanting. A lingering effect was that she was tarred as a lesbian, her years in Boston sealing the diagnosis, and her dating life went the way of her dreams of living in New York, or Boston, or London, or the moon. And Danielle, Eleanor and Linda, none of whom she'd ever grown close to, spoke to her as little as possible, treating her as an exotic, to be feared, a tropical spider interesting to watch, from a distance.

A young man came in, wearing a Niagara Falls High School jacket, and she was soon helping him find books on Vietnam.

Saturday morning Del woke with that good feeling of a day off. It was raining, so he drove up to Goodwill and bought an umbrella. He drove back, parked in his spot, and walked to the river, or more precisely its bed. The Army Corps of Engineers had dammed the American falls, diverting the water to the Horseshoe, to study the rock face. Del was trying to study it too.

From Prospect Point, he splashed across the bridge to Goat Island. It was almost the same, but never quite, the rock face changing ever so slightly and resetting Del's sense of time from human to geologic. This pilgrimage had eased him back into civilian life, and through the stresses of job hunting. Employed now, he watched the water pour over the Horseshoe and wondered how people got the guts to go over in a barrel. "I guess you can't be afraid of getting wet." While heating a can of soup back in his kitchen, he saw the book lying on his scarred counter. "Well, according to the check-out record," he said to the book as he opened the back cover, "you were last checked out April 2, 1954." He glanced at a couple pages, but short stories held no interest for him. "Might as well return you," he decided.

He saw her first. She had a pleasant face, blonde hair she grew to her shoulder blades and dark brown eyebrows. He thought she died her hair, but he never spied dark roots. She was date-stamping magazines at the circulation desk when he came in. She looked up and he turned away, pretending he was studying the building. The Carnegie library had a cozy, circular flow. The book shelves were neatly tucked into a crescent, the second floor a balcony over the first, with a glass floor to let light flow. Had he ever visited the library as a teenager? He thought so, he had a memory of borrowing a record once, but it all looked new to him this morning.

"Can I help you?" asked Beth. She saw a stranger, a man her own age with hair covering his ears, curling around his neck. She loved long hair on guys. He was cute, she decided, and when he spoke he had a nondescript accent, perhaps once local but not anymore. That made him more interesting.

"Yeah," Del said, realizing that he was smiling and looking into her eyes. *I haven't spoken socially to a woman in a while*, he realized. He'd satisfied his urges in the army by visiting a brothel. There was a girl, she said her name was Gretchen and maybe it was, and after sleeping with her many times there was a bond of sorts. And Beth bore a resemblance to Gretchen. And as he remembered that he was standing in a library, not unlike a church, he banished thoughts of German hookers. He handed over the book. "I found this in a, in an old building I was demolishing," he corrected himself.

She glanced at the book. "Yep, definitely one of ours. Checked out in," she looked at the back, "1954." Looking at him with a smile, "are you sure you're finished with it?" It was this streak of sarcasm that surfaced periodically that she tried and failed to suppress.

"It's not checked out to me," he said, "I don't even have a library card."

"Oh," she said, nodded understandingly, and put the book aside. "And you're proud of that?" What was making her talk like this? Perhaps because the guy, someone she hadn't seen before, was smiling more and more at her no matter what she said.

"Now, now, Beth, the man returns one of the lost sheep you aren't supposed to put him in the stocks." The speaker was a man, a little older than Del. "I'm sorry to butt in, but did you say you found this in an old house you were demolishing?"

"Yeah," said Del. "Del Nichols," he introduced himself.

"Walter Morrow, local historian," Walter introduced himself with that collegial air. "Mr. Nichols—"

"Call me Del," he said. "Yeah, I'm on a demolition crew. We were knocking down a building over on Fifth Street and I found this in a kitchen drawer."

"Oh," Walter said, as though this had great meaning. "How many houses have you demolished?" He seemed stressed.

"It was my first, but I guess we've got a lot of work ahead of us," said Del. He noticed Walter's distress then. "Is there a problem?"

"Well," Walter said, "I've been very," he hunted for a word, "concerned that in the demolition phase we may lose some local history. I mean, we've already lost local history. They built a parkway over Porter Park, where Fort Schlosser was, and where the Old Stone Chimney stood." He shook his head. "So now that the buildings are coming down, I'm just wondering what else we're losing."

"What might we be losing?" Beth asked, a conversation she'd had with Walter, but one to which she wanted to hear Del's side. Enjoying the role of devil's advocate, she said, "not to be snotty, but the area they're destroying is pretty run down. I'm glad to see the city finally doing something."

"The South End is the oldest neighborhood in the city. God knows what we're losing," Walter rebutted as briefly as he could. He was surprised at Beth.

Del sensed he'd upset Walter, sensed he'd provoked a grudge between the two of them. Looking for an escape, he saw an army recruiting poster on the wall—'Start your future now!'—and a chuckle escaped.

Beth stood there a minute, stuck. Walter was sulking, and Del had just looked away with what sounded to her like a contemptuous snicker. She felt mean, and a little stupid for provoking Walter, and she glanced around for an escape.

Walter excused himself and went upstairs, to his office.

Del, relieved the pompous sounding guy was leaving, smiled at Beth. "So I don't have to pay any fine or anything?" he joked.

"No, no fine." She beamed, relieved that Walter was gone. "So you're on a demolition crew?" she asked.

"Yep," he said. Never thought it was a way to meet women, but what the hell. "Want to hear some demolition stories?" He couldn't believe he said that.

She surprised him a little. "Sure. But I am at work," she said, laughing lightly. "I'm Beth Reuther," she blushed, "I hadn't introduced myself." He gently shook her hand. Her eyes looked up at the wall clock. "And if you can stop by at two o'clock, I'm only doing a half day."

"Perfect." And it was.

Del showered again, put on a clean shirt, and alternated looking at his tiny black and white TV and the clock until twelve-thirty. "Should I have lunch?" he wondered. "Will she be hungry? Probably. I'll wait."

She met him at the library entrance. "Right on time," she said, "I'm always impressed by punctuality." She wore a plain white blouse with some lace around the neck, and a long skirt, a concession to her co-workers. He remembered to open the car door for her, then got in. "Where should we go?" she asked.

"Well, you wanted to hear some demolition stories," he reminded her, "but I've only been doing it for three days. The first day I helped dig dirt out of the old hydraulic canal, which isn't real interesting. Then we started demolishing the house on Seventh Street, but before we could finish, kids torched it. So I'm a little short on material." He pulled onto Main Street. "Hungry?"

"Starving," she said. "Hey, there's a McDonalds. I don't eat in them much, but what the heck."

Having already eaten as much McDonalds as he wanted that week, he kept his smile on as they parked.

The house was a plain two story Victorian on Elk, near 1st. A large handmade sign reading ESTATE SALE was taped and stapled to the front of the partly-enclosed front porch. Del tested a push mower, its wooden handle weathered and cracked, coated with corrosion every-where except the edge of the cutting blades. The mower started stiffly but then spun with a menacing flash of sharp metal. It shared the tiny lawn with two old bikes, curved fenders snugly molded around the flat tires, and a collection of heavy looking wrenches, iron blackened with old grease, and wood planes shiny with use and age. Prices were written in black ballpoint on scraps of masking tape on each item. "A dollar for the plane," Del said, picking one up. "My father had a couple of these. I know he paid more than a dollar for them."

"Where's your father?" she asked gently.

"Both of my parents died when I was in the service," he reported, "carbon monoxide. It was accidental." He stopped walking, remem-bering the time, details returning. He'd driven by the old apartment a couple of times since coming back. It was just three blocks from where he lived now. But the old apartment, the last of four his parents had rented while Del grew up, was now the very model of urban blight.

It was an old-fashioned four unit building, with cedar shingles and a peaked roof. He remembered it as being clean and kept up. Now it was vacant, boarded-up, and a fire on the first floor had been extinguished but not before scarring the building. "I have an Uncle Leonard in Florida. I came home for the funeral, but Uncle Leonard was the executor of the estate. I guess the planes either went to Goodwill or to Florida."

She nodded sympathetically. "My father has one, but I bet he'd like these," Beth said, reaching for her purse. "I'm going to buy all three of them." Del picked them up and they went inside to pay.

"Can I help you?" The sales woman was young, with short, curly black hair, and a kind looking face. "I guess you're interested in the planes?" Beth nodded. "Have you had a chance to look around?" she asked. "I can hold these for you," she indicated a space behind a folding metal table set up in the living room, holding the cash box and a notebook to record sales. "I mean, you just hit the lawn. There are two floors, an attic, a basement, and a gardening shed." She smiled in amusement. "If you need any help, my name is Sue Davies."

They drifted through the dining room, where a gate-leg table was covered with dishes and figurines. A few shoppers drifted by, and two other women with name tags offered Beth help. "Just looking," Beth said, smiling.

"Let me know if you need any help," said the second saleswoman, very businesslike. "My name is Mary Moore."

"What are they, working on commission?" Del asked softly when they were alone.

A box of silverware was open for inspection. Beth counted pieces. "They've got a setting for twelve, if you don't want enough forks."

"Is this silver or steel?" Del asked, taking a closer look at the stamp on a knife. "Oneida. It's steel. Too bad. I hear you can get a good price for silver."

"When will you be demolishing this house?" Beth asked, looking around the room.

"I don't know until the day comes what house we're working on," Del said. He looked at the house as though he could sense its date with the wrecker. "Janese is the boss. He says we're working first on properties the city already owns. The ones that are abandoned, I guess. And there's a lot of them. This one is probably down on the waiting list."

"Janese," she recognized the name. "I went to school with a guy named Janese. I didn't like him." That was stupid, she thought. To change the topic a little she asked, "how many guys work with you?"

"There's three of us on our crew, actually two adults and one jerk, but I know the boss has other crews. Know anyone who likes to work outside and smash things?"

She thought of it for a minute, pretending she had muscles that, hefting a sledge hammer, would make light work of a brick wall. "It would probably be fun for a day," she said. "But I'm on Civil Service and giving it up for a job that won't last me until retirement isn't wise." After saying it she felt a sick sensation, as though she'd just hit a dip in the road. *Am I really thinking of retiring from the Niagara Falls Public Library?*

The kitchen held a rich collection of ancient appliances with cords of wire wrapped in cloth insulation. "This waffle iron cord has been repaired once or twice too often," Beth said, lifting the cord. It was rigid, encased from the plug to the iron in black plastic tape. "Doesn't even bend anymore."

"Let's plug it in," suggested Del, "and watch the lights dim while the air fills with the smell of burning electrical tape."

"How romantic," she fawned. "Go ahead, plug it in. Chicken," she gently taunted him as they left the kitchen and its dangers behind.

The second floor bedrooms, rich in dark molding and dark with old wallpaper that seemed to swallow the light, were also thick with dust. They began sneezing repeatedly. "I think I'll pay for my tools and get some fresh air," Beth said, gasping for air.

"We didn't do the attic," Del said, looking up.

"I'll wait outside," Beth said. "I got my money's worth. You go ahead, tell me what you see." She started down the staircase.

Dating etiquette dictated he follow her. But he was curious about the attic, and decided that he could take her at her word. The attic steps, metal folding stairs with long, dangerous looking springs, groaned and swayed under his weight. Fortunately the attic light bulb was on. Unfortunately, the dust problem was much worse, and the heat was trapped just under the rafters. Standing almost upright, he pulled in his air through his mouth. Sweat broke out on his forehead.

The attic was pretty bare, but among some other junk there was a box labeled '10 cents a book'. Reading from the bindings, he discarded

Modern Animal Husbandry and *Almanac and Gazetteer—1914.* "*Peyton Place.* That's a keeper," he decided. And the last book was *Reunion of the Grand Army of the Republic—1893.* He thumbed through it; Civil War stuff. "Sure, why not." He took his books and left the attic.

She was sticking the toe of her shoe in the dirt of the neglected flower bed along the side of the house when he came out. "This soil is dead," she said, shaking her head at the lack of upkeep.

"Got your tools?" he asked.

"They're in the car," she said. The thought that the car was, however briefly, common property for them, made him smile with the thrill of a relationship. "What do you have?"

He was deciding whether to let her see him with a copy of *Peyton Place,* when she took them out of his hands. "Oh, like your reading a little steamy, do you?" she teased him. "But," she read the title of the Civil War book, "not too steamy."

They started up the Rambler. Del made two turns out of habit and they were on Goat Island. "What a good idea," she said. "I haven't driven around the falls in," she paused to think, "maybe not since I came back from Boston. That was two years ago. I don't even remember what's down here anymore."

"Well, there's the falls," he risked a bit of sarcasm, then retreated into better behavior. "I probably come down here once or twice a week. You know they've shut down the American falls, right?"

They were driving by the dry channel. "Oh, right, the whole Army Corps of Engineering thing. What have they come up with?" she asked with mock concern, "how will they save the falls?"

He was following it on the news while he was unemployed. "Well, they're still studying it, but they suspect if you pull out all the boulders at the base of the falls to clean it up, the falls might collapse. The boulders are keeping it up. That's just a theory," he added. He pointed out the wall of dirt that pushed the river towards the Horseshoe Falls.

"You should've been a tour guide," she said.

He shook his head. "I used to think so too. I looked into it before I joined the army. It's like being a waitress or a salesman. They give you a lousy salary and you have to pull commissions out of the tourists. And kickbacks from whatever souvenirs they buy. Which gives you incentive to drop them at souvenir shacks. Plus you can only make a living from it during the summer. You have to do something else to survive for two thirds of the year."

"I didn't know that," she said, with a reverence for pure fact few other than a librarian could summon. "Those are the Three Sister Islands, right?" she asked as they drove along the Upper Rapids approaching the Horseshoe.

"That's right. And do you know what that rock is, by the First sister?"

"The Hermit's Bath."

"See, you know your falls," he congratulated her. "You just needed a refresher."

"So how long were you in the military?" she asked.

"Twelve years. I signed up on my eighteenth birthday."

"Was your father in the military?"

"No, he drove trucks for a living."

"So why the military?"

Trying to remember himself at eighteen, he recalled talking with his guidance counselor shortly before graduation. "You've taken the vocational training courses, not the college prep," the guy said, a flabby man with a black flattop and an American flag tie pin, his name forgotten. "Well, you can probably get in at the Tonawanda Chevy plant, or at Harrison Radiator in Lockport. And there's Carborundum, Hooker Chemical. I know someone in Hooker's personnel office. Want me to give him a call?"

He dared for the first time to say, "I was hoping to do some traveling. I was hoping to see, like, California." Surf boards, the Beach Boys, girls in bikinis.

The counselor nodded understandingly. "Well, I tell young men like you every day that the army made a man out of me. Have you considered enlisting?"

Back with his date: "I didn't have a lot of choices," he said to Beth. "So I signed up. And when I was looking at my thirtieth birthday I'd made Sergeant but I was still driving trucks, and I still hadn't seen California."

Beth looked at him oddly. "Uh-huh? So you left when your hitch was up?"

"I left a little early. With a general discharge," he said.

Her eyebrows rose. "How come?"

He looked at his new book on the Grand Army of the Republic. "I smoked a little pot. And I had about five joints in my footlocker when it was searched. They offered me a trial and punishment, or a general discharge. I took the general discharge."

Her eyebrows came down; he was, after that brief scare, harmless. "Where did you serve? I hear in Vietnam everybody smokes pot."

"Yea, well, I was in West Germany. And a fair number of guys smoke pot, but the army does crack down now and again." He looked at her and blushed. "Want me to take you home?" She surprised him with a kiss on his cheek.

It was odd being finished with a date at five in the afternoon, but Beth explained that she needed to get home and "help my father." Help him how she didn't say. He'd picked up hints that her father was ex-military, and that he might have a disability of some sort, but she'd changed topics when he started asking. She laughed at almost every attempt of his to be funny, and he thought she could tell he was enjoying being with her.

Since he'd picked her up at the library, that's where he let her out. "Uh," he started thinking of the next date as he stopped at the curb. She opened the door, got out and then opened his back door to get the wood planes.

"What do you do with yourself on Sundays?" she asked, looking serious.

"Nothing," he answered.

"Would you come out to my house for dinner?"

"Sure. Thanks."

"What's your phone number?" she asked, hunting a pen in her big purse. He gave her his number—at least one of them was giving up a phone number—and she wrote it carefully on the register of her checkbook. "I'll call you tonight and give you directions. Do you know LaSalle at all?" He shrugged. "My father's place is right behind the Red Barn on Pine Avenue."

"I know where that is."

"Okay. I'll call you later."

He barely remembered the ride back to his apartment. He descended the steps into his basement room remembering how the sun shone on her face, one of the funny things she'd said. He didn't remember the joke well, just the laughter. And what stayed with him was her eyes. He pondered the image a moment and realized that she didn't seem to pluck her eyebrows, and that made her eyes fuller, livelier, prettier. And she had offered Sunday dinner. He looked in his bathroom mirror and thought: *her dad is ex-military and I've got shaggy hair. Do I have time to get a haircut? She'll certainly notice. What'll she think of me? Being respectful? Being a chicken?* Like he'd always done in the face of tough decisions, he walked away from it. He felt the need for a relaxing turn on his sagging couch and found *Peyton Place*.

She called him at seven and gave him directions, and said, "if you could wear a dress shirt, that would be nice."

"A dress shirt it will be." He found his old white shirt, or what remained of it. The collar was frayed and when he put it on it was too tight. He caught Beirs still open and bought a new one. He picked up a cardigan sweater to complete the costume.

The Reuther home was a modest Cape two lots behind the Red Barn restaurant on Pine Avenue. Beth met him at the door on his first knock. "Hi," she beamed, and kissed him on the cheek again. He smiled, wondering how close they were to the real thing. "C'mon in."

The back door opened onto a mud room, where he began untying his shoes. "Just wipe 'em off," she hinted. She led him past the washing machine and dryer and into the kitchen. The room was steamy, with aluminum pots on the stove top electric coils. He smelled roast beef and potatoes and saw gravy.

"Dad, this is Del Nichols." Del looked from the food to Beth's father.

Frank Reuther was sixty, looked eighty, a little paunchy, almost exactly Del's height, leaning heavily on a cane in his left hand. He was wearing a white shirt with a tie knotted tightly. He wore thick aviator rimmed glasses and his breath stank of cigarettes. "Mister Nichols?" He offered his right hand, and his grip was strong. "My daughter tells me you're former army?"

"Yessir," Del said, falling back into the habit.

"Served where?"

"West Germany, sir. Ramstein Air Force Base. I was in logistics. Drove a truck a lot, hauling fuel for tanks."

"Nothing wrong with that. Them tanks need fuel. I was in West Germany shortly after the war, but I got sent to Korea when the Communists acted up, then Vietnam. Field artillery. Good to see my daughter found a grown man who's served his country." He started turning away to take a seat at the table. "Damn hippies she brings by almost turn my stomach."

He looked at Beth; it was her turn to blush.

She picked up a plate of mashed potatoes and followed him to the table. "Dad, I brought Walter Morrow for dinner, once. He's the local historian at the library, and I'm not dating him. Remember? You wanted to talk to him."

"Whatever you say, boss," her father said, seating himself with a little difficulty. "Del, look at these shoes. Know where I got them?"

Mr. Reuther was wearing Keds high-tops with fresh white laces.

"Daddy, you promised you wouldn't wear those," Beth said. Looking at Del, she said, "I think he robbed some kid playing basketball."

"Hey, Del can probably use a good set of sneakers. Know where I got these?"

Beth retreated into the kitchen. Del shook his head, smiling.

"Goodwill. A dollar a pair. I don't think they were ever worn. They got a lot of bargains at Goodwill," Mr. Reuther advised, his eyes alive with the joy of his cheap sneakers.

"I shop at Goodwill, too," said Del. One couldn't boast of that just everywhere. "My work boots, they're steel-toed. They were three dollars at Goodwill. I'm pretty sure somebody wore 'em before me, but they're a good deal."

"I like this man," Mr. Reuther called to his daughter. "Knows the value of a dollar."

Beth was a fairly good cook; Del preferred his meat without a crust, but the way her father tore through the beef it was clearly to his liking. She maintained the conversation, asking her father questions about his service for Del's enlightenment, then asking Del questions about growing up on Ferry Avenue, gentle ones about the military in West Germany, almost never allowing her father to ask Del a question. She seemed to have him under control.

"I spent a year near Tan Son Nhut," Mr. Reuther said to Del. "We can win that war, you know. Ship all the protestors over there, give them a gun, wait for Charlie to fire at them and see what pacifists they are."

Del smiled noncommittally and Beth interrupted with a non sequitir library story. He noticed a portrait on the dining room wall, Beth receiving her high school diploma, her beaming father in his uniform, and a woman that might be her mother. Beth saw him looking and nodded. Mouthing, 'mother', she got up to serve her father more roast beef. "You haven't eaten your peas, Dad," she nagged him gently.

Mr. Reuther left the table without comment when he finished his third portion of roast beef and went slowly but steadily down the basement steps. "He's got a little office down there, with his Army books and a reading chair and a TV. It's his space." She held his hands in hers. "You made his day, telling him you shop at Goodwill. Dad always said the army was a great career but a lousy way to make a living." She smiled. "You didn't really get those at Goodwill, did you?"

"Yes."

She smiled even broader. "I thought you were just sucking up to him." He helped her clear the table and she scraped the leftovers into the garbage. "Every pair of ice skates I had as a kid came from Goodwill. I always wanted figure skates, but some year all they had were tubular skates, hockey skates. So I learned to skate both ways."

"What kind of skates do you have now?" he asked.

"I don't skate anymore," she said. "I was always lousy at it."

He washed a plate and handed it to her. "Still dirty," she handed it back. He scrubbed it again and handed it to her. "Still dirty," she said, suppressing a grin. He gave it a fresh squirt of soap and lathered it and rinsed it; it sparkled. "Still dirty," she giggled.

They finished the dishes and wandered back into the dining room. "About the picture. My mother died while I was in Boston. It was really hard for my dad. He doesn't like to talk about it."

"How?" he asked softly.

"Cancer. She had a job in the mail room at Hooker Chemical. A crummy job, in my opinion, but she liked it. Then she got cancer." She frowned and blinked her eyes a couple times. "I wish she was still here, she could really keep Dad going. Now all he does is go down in the basement, park in the recliner and watch TV."

"You're doing a good job," he said softly. She looked up at him, blinked away the residue of the tear that had formed there, and surprised him with a closed mouth kiss.

They walked out to his car.

"Thanks for coming. He likes a little company for Sunday dinner."

"He's okay. Not too fond of the protestors. So what," he started, then said, "when do we—"

"I'm working tomorrow, from noon until seven. Stop by after work, okay?" she gave him another peck, on the tip of his nose. "I have ironing to do. Bye." She went inside.

He barely remembered the ride home.

He tried TV but his mind was a whirl of dinner, of Beth, of the day. *Maybe I'll do better reading*, he thought. He found *The Grand Army of the Republic*, he got a Genesee from the fridge and sat on his badly padded couch and picked up the heavy book.

Lifting the cover, a section of pages came up with it. A folded piece of old brown paper, dry and frail, slid on the surface of the page. He carefully unfolded it.

It was in longhand, written with a fountain pen.

> *November 1812—This warrant is for the arrest of Private Nehemiah Cleary, former Company Clerk for the Lewiston Encampment, who resides near Fort Schlosser in a stout Stone House, near Judge Porter's homestead. Cleary is to appear before the Senate in Albany to answer questions concerning the nature and quality of supplies provided the militia in the Lewiston Encampment.*

At the bottom was an illegible signature.

He studied it for several minutes, absorbing new details with every look. The edges were crumbling, in fact the fold almost broke the paper in half. The ink was certainly from a pen, and not a ballpoint. It smelled like the attic. "Fort Schlosser." He once knew local history, and he hadn't forgotten it all. "That puts it in the War of 1812 or earlier. And a 'stout Stone House'?" He knew of one old stone house in the neighborhood; maybe that was it. It was standing empty, just a block and a half away, where houses were being knocked down. "Holy shit," he said, his voice a whisper, as though shit was truly holy.

He dreamt of Beth that night. They were driving around town in his Rambler and she was taking pictures. "They're demolishing everything," she kept saying, making him stop in front of a newspaper stand, and then at Slipkos so she could take a picture of it, with women pushing shopping carts through the doors and around the parking lot. Then they stopped by Prospect Point. "They aren't demolishing the falls," he argued, but she was insistent. When his alarm woke him, he still remembered the dream, a rarity for him. *I don't know whether I should tell her about this or not,* he pondered as he pulled on a dirty sweatshirt. He was smiling at the memory when he got to the dispatch yard. Though Al lived out in the Town of Niagara, and Leon lived up by Hyde Park, Del was always the last to arrive.

"Delbert is smiling," said Al, grinning in his usual rude way. "Did he get laid?"

After a week of working with him, Del felt entitled to shoot back. "Yeah, and I never thought your sister was my type."

Leon laughed and punched the dash. "Whoa, good one, Grandpa!"

"Get in the fucking truck," Al said.

He has no sense of humor, Del decided, and he thought of trying to pull the punch after the fact but he suspected that might just make things worse. "Where we headed today?" he asked Leon.

"Number three-sixty-one Second Street," Leon read.

"That's just around the corner from me," Del said. "I'd go home for lunch, if there was anything there to eat. It's kind of weird to be pulling down buildings in the neighborhood."

"If they're tearing your neighborhood down, it can't be much of a neighborhood," Al said, in a tone both rude yet somehow concerned.

Sounded like he was willing to make peace. "It's slipping, that's for sure," Del said. "So what are we waiting for?"

"Nickie's got another crew starting today," Leon said. "He wants us all working on the same building, it has to come down today."

"From what I hear, the city's bought a lot of property and they have to clear downtown out. If they don't get their asses in gear and flatten, like, a hundred acres, we lose a bunch of federal money," said Al.

"You read that in the paper?" Leon asked, and Del knew he was setting up Al for a crack about being able to read.

"No, my old man sits around all day, listening to the radio and he told me," Al said.

Nickie drove up in his pickup, and behind him was a dump truck. "Okay, everybody follow me," he called out. "It's just a couple of blocks, try not to get lost."

They pulled up to the old apartment building. It had burned a few days ago, the familiar scorch marks and destruction marking it as a weak member of the herd. A dumpster sat in the parking lot like an albatross. A crane with a wrecking ball was already in the parking lot, as were a bulldozer and two trucks. Nickie was directing the new guys, who were climbing out of the truck.

"Uh oh," Leon said softly as Del walked with him, Al a few feet behind.

Del glanced back at the new guys and saw Leon's concern. The new wreckers included three black workers. Del caught, then released breath. Maybe it would be okay, maybe Al knew enough to mind his manners at work.

"Leon, Del, Al, this is Sonny, Tom, and Ed."

Sonny and Tom were standing together with poker faces and hands shoved into pockets, saying very little, and saying it mostly with facial gestures. They were both muscular. Ed was older than all of them, his face greased from days unwashed, and Del wondered if Nickie hadn't hired him from some soup kitchen.

"Leon, Del, Sonny knows how to handle the wrecking ball. You all got trucks today to haul debris. Except Ed, you and Al, I want you to go through the debris at the dump and pull out the copper. The place is supposed to be full of copper pipes."

Del and Leon looked at each other. Al was taken off driving and put on scavenging copper pipe? Not good. They didn't even look at Al, they could sense his growing temper.

Nickie drove off and they got to work. It started smoothly enough. Sonny clearly knew what he was doing; he moved the iron ball smoothly, the engine roaring as the ball hit the building. There was efficiency of movement in how he worked the handles, precisely. The crane moved like it was an extension of his arm, and he punched through the roof and then banged on the walls, knocking it down neatly. Nickie drove by twice, stopping the second time to cheer them on, unheard of.

Al rode to the dump with Del and put on country music at high volume. Del preferred rock, but he ignored it. When they reached the dump, Al sat in the truck while Del maneuvered and upended the truck bed. When the truck was empty, Del came to a stop and let the engine idle, waiting for Al to climb out.

"I'm thinking of quitting this fucking job," Al said finally. "I got a cousin in Florida, and he says I can stay with him while I find a job. You ever live in Florida?"

"No. I'm still trying for California." The radio blared 'Stand by your man' for a minute. Finally Del asked, "you getting out?"

Al ignored him and sat until Tammy Wynette was done. "You see that nigger running that wrecking ball?" he asked, looking out the windshield. "I could do that job with one hand tied behind my back." He was simmering and Del didn't know which way he'd blow. Finally Al popped the latch on the door, kicked it open, and climbed down.

Del sighed with relief and drove off a little faster than usual. Turning the radio knob until he got a Canadian station that played full-length album tunes, he was finally enjoying himself. An hour later he was back with another load and Ed was sitting on a rock. He had a small pile of pipe stacked nearby. Al was nowhere to be seen. "Lose your buddy?" Del called to Ed. Ed waved back, like he was deaf.

At lunchtime, Nickie drove up to the demolition site with bags of food from Burger King. "Anybody see Al?" Nobody had. "If he walked off this job I got five people waiting in line," said Nickie, as though Al was hiding nearby. "I need you guys to jam this food down and get back to work, double-time."

"Is there money buried under this place?" asked Del, comfortable enough now to risk joking with Nickie. "What's the hurry?"

Nickie grinned back. "Well, Army Boy, it's taken the city about five years to get their shit together. And now we got a ton of money from the Feds, all tied into cleaning out the South End, which is officially a slum." A dozen eyes glanced at Sonny and Tommy, hoping the comment slid by. "So we're on a timetable, and they keep changing the dates. First everything had to come down by December, then by November, next they'll tell me it has to come down by October. Which means I hire a hundred more guys. Del, if you can get the cooler out of the truck bed it's full of pop. Don't get dehydrated."

As Del retrieved the cooler, Nickie's walkie-talkie called him, and he started up his truck and squealed his tires. "He's only going two blocks," Leon said, "what's the frigging hurry?"

Al showed up at the demolition site just as they were finishing up. "Where the fuck've you been?" asked Leon. "Nickie's looking for you."

"Nickie can go fuck himself," Al said, and he said it loud, though Nickie was long gone. He saw the cooler and flipped the top open.

A minute later the air was splintered with Al's loud use of the 'N' word. In just a few seconds the work crew was gathered around the truck bed, where Sonny was standing. "What the fuck did you say?" asked Sonny.

"I said, you're drinking my Coke," Al said, in the highest dudgeon he could muster, but in a softer voice.

"That ain't what you said," said Albert. "You said, 'Nigger, what you doing with my Coke'? Ain't that right?"

Leon stepped forward. "Al, you stupid shithead, here's your Coke." He opened a fresh one and handed it to Al.

Al took it, then threw it at a stretch of standing brick wall, the soft drink burst in a spray of carbonation.

"I heard his mouth. I better hear an apology," Sonny said.

Del looked at Al. "How about it?"

Al looked at a sea gull that was exploring the debris. "Sorry." It came out flat, without feeling, but Sonny decided to nod and walk away.

Al sat at the site and gradually drank most of the pop in the cooler. Shortly before quitting time Nickie rolled by. Al saw Nickie's truck and decided it was time to run off.

The site was cleared and the crew was walking slow, wiping sweat with dirty hands and sweat-soaked shirts. "Good job, boys," said Nick. "Go get a good night's sleep. We got two houses to bring down tomorrow. And if anyone sees Al, tell him to stop by the trailer when he feels like it, for his last paycheck. He's fired." Nobody said anything.

Beth wasn't working that morning, he knew, when he entered the library. He knocked on the Local History door and was turning the knob anyway when Walter invited whomever in. "It's Delbert Nichols. I brought in the O. Henry book."

Walter nodded and waved him in. "I remember. How are you?"

"Okay. I found something else," Del said, and handed him the letter.

Walter took it, sensed its age and frailty, and set it on his desk with care. "Where did you find this?" Del explained. "Nehemiah Cleary?"

"Ever hear of him?" Del asked.

"No. Never."

"Fort Schlosser was in the War of 1812, right?"

"It predated the war, but that was when it saw action, yes." Walter went into a trance. With the letter flat on his desk he was pulling one book from a shelf, thumbing through it for something, sometimes nodding and writing something, sometimes putting the book back, disappointed. Then he read the letter again, reacted to something else, went looking for a map, or just studied the letter. This went on for ten minutes, Del watching him at work, hoping to learn something.

"I was thinking of the stone house, the one on 3rd. You think that's the stone house they're referring to?"

Walter paused, eyes locked on the letter. Had he heard the question? Was he struggling to balance the odds, the likelihood that the stone house of the crumbling South End was the same structure referred to in this ancient arrest warrant? Del was tempted to wave his hand to see if Walter was still awake.

"Oh," Walter said suddenly, as if time had just restarted, "that's got to be the place. That's my assumption, anyway."

"No shit," Del said, grinning. "That's so cool."

Walter's distracted mind found that amusing. "Yes, I guess it is cool. But there's a," he paused, hunting for the word, "a problem."

"What problem?"

Walter found a folder and pulled out a piece of newsprint. It showed a map labeled 'Master Plan—Urban Renewal Agency—Niagara Falls'. "This was published by the *Gazette* three years ago." He set it on his desk, next to the letter. "This part, called 'Rainbow Center', is eighty-two acres to be cleared in the South End, close to the Prospect Point Park. Here," he pointed out an aerial photograph of the South End, "is what they call Project Number One, and this is Two, and so on. See the white lines outlining the projects?"

"Those are the areas being cleared," Del said, recognizing the neighborhood he was working in, living in.

"And here is the stone house."

"Fuck." Del blushed; the word got tossed around at work. "Shoot. It's in Project Twelve."

"Square in the middle," Walter said. "You were right the first time."

They looked at the letter, at the faded ink on the brown paper and the date, 1812. The grainy black and white aerial photo showed the inn as one of many tiny buildings at five hundred feet. Surrounded by other old buildings, the neighborhood was outlined in white.

"Where are you working now?" Walter asked, his eyes still studying the photo.

"We were working here," Del touched the place in the photo, a block from the stone house. "But we're not moving in any logical pattern. We did a building here," he touched the first house, north of the railroad yard, "and we just did one here, yesterday," he touched the apartment building south of the rails. "But aren't they supposed to be saving the historic sites?"

Walter nodded. "Oh, yes, they are. The United Office Building is on the National Register of Historic Places. And St. Mary's is safe, even though it's squarely in the middle of Project Twelve. And the Shredded Wheat factory is being preserved, even though it's well outside the project areas."

"So we just show the urban renewal guys this letter and they put the Stone House on the protected list?" Del asked, just knowing it couldn't be that simple.

"It's not that simple," Walter said, looking wistful and sad.

"But they can't wreck the house if it's full of history, can they?"

Walter said nothing for a moment. He glanced at his watch. "Do you have a car?"

"Yeah."

"I walk to work. If you don't mind driving, I can show you an example of a place full of history."

They drove up Main Street, then over to Falls Street, passing within a block of Del's apartment. "Up to Quay Street," Walter directed. Del stopped, third in a row of cars waiting for the stoplight. The off-ramp for the Robert Moses Parkway was to their right as they passed through the intersection. "Take this right, right here," Walter said urgently. Del made the turn, into a small parking lot.

Walter got out and started walking. Del followed him onto the grassy shoulder of the parkway off-ramp. Cool wind off the river made the eighty-degree day more comfortable. Cars roared by on the parkway, and the factories of Buffalo Avenue, with their smokestacks puncturing the sky, stretched out behind them to the horizon. It was a noisy, uncomfortable place to be a pedestrian.

Walter was walking towards the parkway, headed for a small copse of trees and what appeared to be a barbecue pit. Del followed, hunched a little against the wind. "What're we doing here?" he asked Walter when he reached him.

Like the Ghost of Christmas Future, Walter pointed to the barbecue pit. It had a brass plate embedded in it, which Del knew to be an unusual ornament for the average barbecue pit. "Built by French, 1750, 100 FT. Westward is Fort Little Niagara's Barracks, which they burned in 1759."

There was more to it but Walter said, "it's the oldest masonry in the region, aside from Fort Niagara. But more to the point, it's the site of Fort Schlosser. It more or less indicates where the Portage Road began. It's arguably the most important historical spot, besides Fort Niagara, in the region. And it's under the off-ramp of the parkway." He paused as a truck roared by. "They built a parkway over the city's most historic point. And it's only standing where it is because losing it completely would be even more embarrassing." Walter was releasing a deep anger. "This is an example of being in the wrong place at the wrong time." He turned to face the factories, the crumbling downtown. "So to answer your question, yes, they can wreck the Stone House, even if it's full of history."

It was on its last legs, the ridgeline sagging and shingles missing. If there was once a lawn it was now purely weeds and wild flowers, growing tall and unrestrained. Elm, oak and maple trees, untrimmed for years, grew together in a canopy that shielded most of the house from view.

"Are you sure about this?" he asked.

"Of course." Beth let the car door fall shut.

It was a week after he'd found the letter and taken it to Walter. He'd demolished three more houses that week. Beth's father was admitted to the hospital for some tests on his lungs, Beth dividing her time between work and the hospital, so today was their first date in a week. Del tried for a movie, some darkness and a chance to explore kissing. But Walter was now a man possessed, and it seemed Beth had caught the sickness. So here they were.

Since finding the letter, he'd driven by the house half a dozen times. He'd pulled to the curb and looked it over, but found he was too timid to approach it himself, on foot. Beth was more courageous.

She found a path amongst the weeds. "C'mon," she cheered him on with a smile, "I want to see if we can get inside."

"Inside?" Inside a clearly locked up house? "Isn't that breaking and entering?" he asked, making a joke of it.

"Nobody lives here," she said, turning to encourage him. "C'mon, it's an adventure. You go into abandoned houses everyday, right?" And she laughed, at the adventure, at the excitement of it. She'd had damn few adventures since coming back.

The walls were made from fieldstone and mortar. A wooden door, constructed of six planks bound with large iron nails, the heads rusting. Tugging on the wrought iron handle, she felt not a hint of give. She made her way to a side window that was just three feet off the ground. Pressing her face against a pane of glass, shading her vision with her hands, she peered inside. "It's empty," she said. "Big surprise. Do you see a way to get in?"

Del was looking out for the police who would stop them, demand identification, then take them away in the back of a patrol car. But traffic was light on a Saturday afternoon in a neighborhood without entertainment, a cloudy day threatening rain. "Get inside?" he asked. Stop looking like such a chicken in front of her, he scolded himself.

He stomped through the tall weeds, exploring around the side. "This place is big," he said. The front of the house, two stories tall, clearly had four rooms on the second floor. Obscured by the trees, the house kept going down the block. "This must have been an inn. It's huge."

The back door had a modern lock. It was quite private, they having pushed through a fir tree that offered full camouflage. The blouse she was wearing was worn and he could see the shape of her breasts, and that something had made her nipples erect. As she smiled mischievously, a beam of sunlight fell on her face, and she was beautiful. Here they were, alone, outside, in a private place. Del felt himself getting aroused, knowing nothing between them would happen, not today anyway, but aroused nevertheless. "This place is huge," he said, in case she'd missed hearing him the first time.

Beth nodded, looking up at the wall and the windows above. "I want to get inside." They tried to open the windows they could reach, but they weren't budging. Del discovered a bulkhead door. "It's a walk-out cellar."

"Yes, you see those in New England a lot," Beth said.

"That's right, you lived in Boston."

"Yep."

"What was that like? Boston?"

"It was cool. I liked it there."

He almost asked 'why did you come back?', until he remembered the experience.

She knelt to grab a cellar door handle, braced herself, pulled and the door rose. She had some muscle on her. "There."

Del felt like a complete wiener. At the bottom of four steps was a wooden door. It had an old latch with a simple key-lock.

"Crap," she said.

"Wait a minute," Del said. He went back to the Rambler, dug in his small box of tools. Taking a standard and a Phillips, they unscrewed the latch, and the door opened, scraping hard on the floor. "We're in."

The basement was pitch black. The small windows, layered in dust and webs, let in no light; that and the uneven dirt floor forced them to walk slowly and carefully. The open bulkhead doors provided a short pathway of light and they navigated beyond it by hand, like finding their way in a cave. Blinking in the dark, the room slowly lightened and they saw a staircase. The steps were narrow and the risers uncomfortably high. Beth went up first, giving Del his first, close-up view of her butt. He saw her panty lines right in front of his face and savored the moment. Then he banged his shins on the risers and forgot about her butt. She worked the knob, and daylight shone down on them.

The house smelled of mold, of damp wood, and perhaps a tad of old urine. She really didn't want to touch anything, to pick up the smell or the decay. The floor was broad pine boards held by square nails. The walls and ceiling were plaster, interspersed by pine planks, now dark with dirt and spider webs filling the corners. They heard cars driving by, radios playing, people's voices, the guttural roar of trucks. Most of the small window panes, with the ripples and bubbles of a simpler time, were broken. Some were smashed, some still held but had holes in them the shape of the stone that smashed through. Crunching underfoot, the floor was littered in glass shards and the stones that had done the damage.

On the second floor the windows were in better shape, thanks to the protective tree branches that grew too close to the house.

Kids had been breaking in for years. Small fires had been set in the fireplaces that almost every room had. Empty beer bottles, mostly smashed, added to the danger the floors posed to bare feet.

The front door led to a huge room, the public room of the inn. In there the floorboards were pitted and worn. Beyond the public room was a slightly smaller room, perhaps for dining. This room's ceiling had four glass globes for electric light. Two were broken, two intact, dust covered, with dead bugs trapped in dense webbing.

She began sneezing. "Choo! Choo!" She found a tissue in her purse and blew her nose, but that triggered another burst. "Choo! Choo! Choo!"

"You need some fresh air," Del said.

She waved her hand no. She turned her back on him, and blew her nose like a French horn. "Thad's bedder," she said. "Press on."

The kitchen was next. Aside from the public room, the kitchen had the next largest fireplace. The cabinets were quite empty, their doors gone for firewood, the remnants in the fireplace. Off the kitchen was a doorway that descended into a root cellar, part of the basement. It stank powerfully of urine. "Someone goes in here regularly," she guessed.

The rest of the house was single rooms, with one on each floor converted into a bathroom sometime in the twenties, to guess by the claw foot tubs. The old fixtures were mostly smashed, and the floorboards were stained from old flooding.

It smelled of dust, of mold, of decay. Like a book left in a summer cabin by a screen window. Dampened and dried, frozen and thawed, yellowed by the sun. Hinges were dried, boards warped, and most doorways opened only with a struggle. The ceilings on the second floor were stained from episodes of leaks over the years. On the walls were maps of old pipes from the age of central heating. Scavengers had pulled most of it out to recycle copper, unconcerned with residual water still in the system, causing more stains.

The explorers were smeared with dirt and a wispy clot of webbing in Beth's hair, when they opened the front door from the inside and stepped out. Del sneezed, and sneezed, stopping only when Beth found another tissue. He blew his nose and saw the color of the house in it. He smelled the mildew on his hands, he smelled it on her. "Kind of dusty," he said. "You've got some in your hair."

"Get it out, get it out," she whined, her first sign of girlish weakness.

"I'm not sure my hands are any cleaner than what I took out."

"I'd rather have your hands in my hair than that," she said, and he took that as a good sign. "I'm starving. Want some food?"

He nodded. Time for this date to go mainstream.

She promised to make dinner in his apartment, without first visiting his kitchen. "Today I've seen empty cupboards for the first time in my life," she said in amazement, opening his kitchen cupboards. "The Stone House and here. I don't know anyone else with empty kitchen cupboards."

"I only cook for myself," he pointed out.

"You have, let me count," she pointed at the small stack of cooking pots she found. "One, two sauce pans, one real cooking pot, and," she lifted a stout, black skillet, "the most disgusting iron skillet I've ever seen." She looked at him. "Besides macaroni and cheese, and frying up a steak, what do you eat?"

"Spaghetti," he added, and had to look in his freezer. "I got some TV dinners."

"Can you take me to Slipkos?"

She led him through the aisles and they assembled a meal of chicken, potatoes, and a salad. She also grabbed a few spices. They filled his apartment with the smell of cooking for the first time.

"This is really good," he said, savoring the smell of the baking chicken, "it's almost as good as my spaghetti."

"Almost?" she responded to his challenge, "almost?" Fortunately Del had soft couch cushions because she grabbed one and swung a haymaker at him, which bounced off the back of his head.

"This means war," he announced, and grabbed a cushion, but she had broken into a run and he swung and missed. Chasing her through the apartment didn't take long, and then she was cornered, holding up the pillow like a shield. He held up his hand, as if for a truce, so she lowered her guard and he bopped her gently on the head. "Now we're even," he said.

"One is never 'even' in pillow fights," she warned, but disarmed to check the meal.

First they ate, and they had no leftovers. They turned on the TV and lay on the couch. Legs entwined and faces rubbed with cushions, he kissed her with the hope of making love, and she kissed him back with the possibility.

"Can you stay tonight?" he asked.

"Well, I'm over eighteen," she said. "But he takes my absence better if I give him three days' warning. It sinks in. He doesn't wonder where I am. And I don't have a good 'last minute' excuse. Can you think of one?"

"The library doesn't run a midnight shift, does it?" She shook her head. "What if I had a car breakdown up in, say, Toronto, and called you to come get me?"

"Well, he'd expect me whenever I got home."

"Tell him you'll be staying overnight. Tell him," Del searched the walls of his apartment for a creative spark and remembered again that they were blank.

She sat up on the couch. "This is ridiculous. I'm twenty-nine years old. I really should have my own place, but I live with my father so I can take care of him. That makes me his nurse, but not his slave." She got up, got his phone and dialed. "Dad? Yeah, I'm going to be, uh, staying over a friend's tonight, I didn't want you to worry. Her name is Kelly. Kelly Hutchins. She's new at the library. Well, she lives in Buffalo and we're going out to a late movie and I just didn't want to drive home late. I don't know why she lives in Buffalo. Yes, I guess she does have a long commute. Anyway, don't wait up for me. Bye."

She hung up, blushing deeply. "I don't know if I'm more embarrassed at lying to my father or at you watching me."

"Kelly Hutchins? Do I have long hair or short hair? And am I cute or homely?" he asked. She stuck out her tongue. He made a calculated risk and picked her up in his arms.

"You have short hair," she said, kissing his ear, "and all in all, I guess you're not too homely."

The next morning, a Sunday, they had toast and coffee and ate around the dirty dishes of the night before, and Beth turned on the television to catch the news. "Today, the Department of Defense reported that the Republic of Vietnam. . . " and footage of soldiers marching and helicopters buzzing a jungle made Del yawn.

"So what do you think about the war?" Beth asked.

"I don't know," he said. She frowned. "What?"

"It's a country in a civil war, and we have no business there," she said.

"How do you know that?" he asked.

"Do you read much?" she asked. "Besides *Peyton Place*. Coming to the library to hand in priceless historical artifacts is noble, but I never see you check anything out." She was toying with him but there was grit beneath the game.

"I don't read very much," he admitted. "I was never much of a reader."

"Would you read something if I asked you to?" she asked.

He didn't mean to but he rolled his eyes. "I guess. What?"

"I'll give you a choice," she said. "Tomorrow, after work, you come by and pick me up and I'll have some books for you to pick from. Okay?"

"Okay." They did the dishes, they turned off the TV. They went for a walk around the falls, and they came back to the apartment for more sex.

"Now you have to take me to the library and I can get my car and go home. My father likes his Sunday dinner. As you know."

"I do."

The railroad station was once the heartbeat of Niagara. It was such a fixture of the city it rivaled the falls themselves in peoples' memories. For a century it carried people to and fro, into Niagara Falls and out to the surrounding towns of Echota, LaSalle, and the Tonawandas. For a lifetime the old men sitting downtown heard the ear-splitting whistle, felt the rumble through the pavement. As ten-year-olds they smelled the engine's smoke; now their ancient faces scowled as they heard the metal rails scream as they were torn from the ground. Some gathered by the police sawhorses that marked the border of safety.

Three days of the promised jackhammer work left Del feeling like a cross between Superman and Jell-o. Two popped blisters and a strange dream involving vibration and he was ready for a change. He got it; he and Leon and Sonny spent a day with cutting torches severing the iron beams inside the building. Today Sonny worked the wrecking ball, but it was slow going. The railroad station didn't want to go down. He swung their heaviest ball five times without much to show besides bruised bricks, each strike aimed to knock the building into next Tuesday. How could a brick building take such a pounding as the wrecking ball was giving it? The crowd cheered for the building with each hit, as though encouraging an aging prizefighter. Sonny took broader and broader swings, moved the crane to hit other angles, and finally knocked holes through the brick walls, but still couldn't collapse the old place. Then he hitched up the seven-fifty weight, raised the iron ball high, over the top of the one story station. And let it fall. It broke through.

"Are you okay, sir?" asked a cop who turned from the battle to see an old man struggling to stay upright and gripping the sawhorse for balance.

"My poppa," the old man's voice was a whisper, "I used to meet my poppa here, every day. The 5:19. Everyday but Sunday." He sniffed, gurgling. He was ancient; eyebrows grown wild, jowels sagging, deep furrows framed his upper lip, and he rubbed at his nose with his bowling shirt sleeve, mopping it up. Before he turned away from the cop his cheeks were streaming, and he slowly walked across Falls Street to sit on a bench with others gathered to watch.

By the time the ball finally slammed through the weakened iron supports and left the work to the bulldozers, the old man had gone home to his daughter's. But others stayed and watched.

⌒⌒⌒

"Uh oh."

Marilyn Grabowski, city council secretary, was at her seat early for the meeting. Marilyn was forty this year, and had started dying the gray hairs blonde, instead of the dull dark brown she was born with. She liked to think she looked like Dinah Shore, but no one else ever mentioned it. She was wearing her 'uniform' as she called it, a white blouse, ironed to perfection, a blue scarf tied around her neck, and a plain brown skirt that went below her knees.

She sat in the middle of the table so she could hear everyone. Tonight's meeting, on a sticky summer evening, brought the smell of sweat, of aftershave from those who went after their five-o'clock shadow, and always of tobacco. Her warning was her first reaction to the sight of a group about thirty strong. Some were carrying signs. GOING BROKE said one, BUDGET IS A KILLER was another, and LACKEY BURNS $$$. Marilyn would have warned the mayor and the city councilors, but the Property Taxpayers League was a regular fixture of late. There were just more of them tonight.

She checked her steno pad; it had a good thirty blank sheets. She knew from past experience that the Taxpayers League wouldn't be saying much that was original, and from one speaker to the other the only variance would be in volume and personal insult. However long the meeting went, thirty pages ought to cover it.

The women peeked into purse mirrors, trying to maintain their hair-dos in the humidity. Men were so fortunate, she thought, all they had to do was put on a clean shirt and comb their hair. Collecting in the hall-way, they were talking softly amongst themselves. That wouldn't last; if the meeting started late they'd get loud. Eventually they'd get loud anyway. They'd been to more meetings than she had, and they were all ages. They would make the mayor and the councilors file past them, and they would invade the room when the meeting reached the 'New business' entry on the agenda, even though their business was hardly new. Seven o'clock. Marilyn's family should have finished the dinner she left in the refrigerator for them, meat loaf and mashed potatoes. She hoped her husband, Keith, a foreman at Carborundum, was heating up vegetables for their son, Keith Jr. For her dinner, an hour ago, Marilyn ate the half of a meat-loaf sandwich she'd brought with her. If she ate anything more than half she'd have an upset stomach. That's what these meetings did to her.

She felt bad for Mayor Lackey. Given that he was Irish, with that gift of the gab and then some, and she knew from working around him that he spent more time in front of the mirror fixing his hair than any woman she'd ever known, but he was so lively. There weren't enough lively people in the world. People like Lackey entered a room and the entire room knew it. She found she liked him in spite of him. A heavy door creaked, the echo just audible over the chatter in the hallway. "They're coming."

Lackey came out first, followed by Bill O'Brien, Guy Proulx, Francis Lyon and Tony Ingrasci, all in business suits. Like they were running a gauntlet, they passed through the crowd and into the council chambers.

"Were they meeting in there?" asked a woman, her voice rising in suspicion.

One man glanced at the brass plate over the door the men had come from. "They might have, but they might have just been getting ready for a long sit-down. That's the Men's Room."

"Current item," said Proulx, tonight's chair, "two hiring requests from the Fire Department."

"What're you going to hire them with?" "They're overpaid!" "You can't keep ignoring us. We're not going away!" The crowd heckled.

"This is getting completely out of hand," said Councilman O'Brien, loosening his tie. "We've spent forty minutes trying to get to a vote on hiring two deputy commanders for the fire department. If you look at our agenda, at this rate we'll be here until tomorrow morning. If we could meet in executive session we'd get this work done faster."

"I have no objection to meeting in executive session," said Lackey.

"The public has the right to attend these meetings. You go into executive session you're breaking the law." The challenge came from the man with a sign reading BUDGET IS KILLING US.

"The public can attend the meetings, not disrupt them," Lackey retorted sharply. "You can also speak, if you do so in an orderly manner. This is not an orderly manner."

Proulx tried to interject. "We're talking about the budget, and the fire department's need for two deputy commanders. The motion was made to approve, and that's when you—" he pointed to the Taxpayer's League member, "interrupted with a question. You have to ask to be recognized first. Do you understand?"

The protestor shook his head and raised his hand in dismissal, uninterested in playing by Roberts Rules. Another protestor, perhaps his wife, raised her hand. "I'd like to be recognized."

Lackey heaved a deep sigh. "Chair recognizes Citizen X."

"My name's Shirley Ianuzzi," she said angrily. "Not Citizen X. I live on Whitney Avenue. And I don't see why the fire department suddenly needs to have two new deputy commanders. We're demolishing buildings, right? There are fewer buildings to protect. And at the rate you're going," she glared at Lackey, "you'll have the whole downtown knocked down. So what's to protect? Why we hiring more firemen?"

Lyon, putting on his reading glasses, said, "the request was raised last year, and we postponed it because of budget pressures. There have been three retirements at that rank this year, so in a way, they've lost three already. This way they still lose one."

"But hiring them still raises costs," argued another protestor. "My property tax bill came in the mail last week and I can't afford to pay my taxes, feed my family and live in this city." That was how it was going; the protestors didn't want to deal with the depth or subtleties of the budget process, just that the bottom line was too high. And like stubborn anchors dragging along the bottom of a stream, they wanted the boat to stop.

Joe Novak, a thin slip of a guy and a twenty-year veteran columnist and reporter for the *Gazette*, was taking a steady stream of notes. This was becoming a regular event, the angry taxpayers disrupting the council meetings. He checked the time. He'd need to leave the meeting soon to put a story together for tomorrow's edition. He'd taken two photos of protestors, and they needed to get developed.

Lackey got up. "I need a drink of water," he mumbled in disgust. He walked out a side door and went, alone, back to the men's room. It was refreshingly empty. He turned on the cold water tap, and when the water gushed into the porcelain bowl he cupped some in his hands and patted his face. "What a fucking waste of time this is." He enjoyed the quiet, drank a little water, and let his blood pressure ease down.

The door swung open behind him and he heard two men enter. Their footsteps stopped when they turned the corner and saw him. He drank some more water, to have a reason not to speak to them.

"I just don't know why they can't figure out for themselves that you can't get blood from a stone," said one to the other, loudly for Lackey's benefit. "It's like they think the money's just gonna float down from the state or the feds, like they're getting all these grants for demolishing downtown. Don't they realize when they destroy a business, they lose taxes?"

"Of course we realize the demolition process destroys the tax base," Lackey said, still leaning over the sink, turning his head sideways and speaking in a voice that was half growl. "How Goddamn stupid do you think we are?" Then, raising one dripping hand, in his disarming way, he joked, "don't answer that." It left his two listeners struck dumb; was he saying they were stupid or he was stupid?

Lackey appreciated the moment of silence. He was back in control. "Do you know why your taxes are going up?" He stood up straight and held up his hands, gestures he had perfected in his years as a minister. "Not that malarkey about blood from a stone, please. Do you understand what's happened to the city in the past ten years?"

They were each in their late forties, early fifties, both had shaved and missed a few spots; both clearly worked with their hands, not their heads. The mayor had asked them a question and it was like they were back in third grade, with the teacher asking them a question about reading they hadn't done.

He advanced on them as he spoke, closing the distance like the hunter advancing on prey trapped in the headlights. The chance to pound some real facts into these numbskulls was always a tempting opportunity. "Remember the Power Station in the Gorge? The Schoellkopf?" They nodded. "Remember in '56 it was destroyed by a rock fall?" They nodded quickly. "Well, that cost us a lot of cheap power. And it was a private company, one that paid taxes. Losing it hurt the tax base, badly. The state and the federal government are building a new hydro facility, but it's going to be publicly funded, and to do it they took a lot of land, land that is now and forever off the tax rolls. And the Parkway also took land off the tax rolls."

They were good students, they were quiet and listening. Lackey was close enough for them to smell the peppermint gum he chewed to cover his coffee breath.

He indulged in a hint of a smile. "Well, we lost twenty percent of our taxable land, but we don't lose that much responsibility for fire protection, for police, for garbage, for all the services. Inflation being what it is, you need to take in more money just to keep things even. So, I figured we might try to revive downtown, which I think we can all agree has become pretty run-down?"

They nodded, one leaning against a wall now, the other with a hand on the nearest porcelain sink. They might have been watching the fifth inning at Hyde Park.

"So for the next several years we need to pick up the balance by raising residential taxes. Once we get the downtown rebuilt, we get that convention center up, we add those hotels, get that office space built and leased, we'll be pulling twice as much out of downtown as we used to. Then we can roll residential taxes way back. That's my plan," Lackey said. "And I thought it through carefully before presenting it. I don't think there's another way out." He paused; they weren't nodding in agreement as they might in church if he'd just praised God for something, but they were quiet and seemed cowed. *Had he gotten through?* "Do you see what I'm trying to say?"

They glanced at each other. This was a rare moment; Mayor Lackey was actually quiet in their presence, having asked them a question, and seemed willing to wait quietly for their response. There were thousands of people who'd never believe this moment occurred. The older one, with less hair and thicker glasses, finally said, "I don't know about what you just said, Mayor," and Lackey felt fully in control again, "but I just can't afford these tax hikes. It's that simple. If you raise them again, I'll sell my house and move out to the Town of Niagara."

They had come in to relieve their bladders, but this encounter had pushed that out of their minds. They turned and left. And Lackey listened to them leave. *If you raise taxes*, he thought, *some of them will leave. And there's not much to draw people into the city these days, so when these people sell, housing prices will drop. As the prices drop, assessments drop, and tax rolls drop. It was a downward spiral. It was a race, in fact, between getting downtown rebuilt before the city collapsed in on itself.*

Meanwhile he really had to return to that damn meeting.

Marilyn Grabowski's pen hovered over her steno pad. In one ear she was hearing an angry woman calling Lackey and the councilors, "a bunch of empty-heads. You got empty heads. You're hearing one of us after another telling you we can't pay more taxes, and here's the budget for next year and the taxes are going up. You guys," Marilyn stopped taking shorthand, "got shit for brains."

She blushed for the rude woman. Lackey smacked his wooden hammer on the gavel. "Meeting is adjourned. We don't need to sit here and take this abuse." More protestors were waiting to speak, and Lackey's announcement got them howling. "I said it's adjourned. Are you deaf as well as stupid?" She blushed for the mayor. It was ten o'clock, and these people were capable of going late if the council let them. The council had a fifty-two point agenda and they'd never gotten past item nine, the fire department request. She heard the mayor call for a motion to adjourn.

"You can't just adjourn because you're tired of hearing the public," said Guy Proulx, the Mayor's primary adversary and almost certainly candidate for his job. "They're telling us the truth and we're not responding."

"Fine," Lackey snapped. "You stay and listen to them. I'm tired and I want to go to bed. Will someone please make a motion to adjourn?"

Lyon rolled his tired eyes, blinked twice to clear them, and raised his hand slightly.

"Motion to adjourn is made," Lackey said crisply, "second?"

O'Brien raised his hand. "Seconded. All in favor?" Everyone but Proulx raised his hand. "Let the record show that by a vote of four to one, the meeting was adjourned." Marilyn was making the familiar scribbles in her notebook. "Have a good night, everyone," said the mayor, and he strode out the side door.

He heard voices following him, but nobody was so undignified as to run, and he walked fast. He thought he heard "dumb Mick" echoing down the hallway, but if he did he just smiled. He was the Mayor.

The next day was his real pleasure in life, a meeting of the Urban Renewal Agency, of which he was chairman. He saw the same faces, as the councilors all sat on the board, but they could close these meetings, and did. He arrived early, and saw Lyon and Proulx talking. "Good afternoon, gentlemen," he beamed, sitting at the same table as yesterday, the others seated pretty much the same, but this time with no angry homeowners. "I'm pleased to say I went home, had a nice Scotch, watched a little television and slept like a baby."

They chuckled agreeably. "What's first on the agenda, today?" he asked.

"Joe Spallino asked to speak to us before the meeting about his proposal for downtown," said Proulx. "He's sure with our backing, the project will fly."

Lackey scowled. "I thought this was settled. I thought we settled this last year. Is my memory failing me?" He looked at Marilyn, keeper of the notes. "It was Joe Spallino, wasn't it?"

Marilyn nodded. "Mr. Spallino approached the board last June, actually. I can get my notes on it, if you like."

Lyon was in a golf shirt, and the sky was cloud-free. "Joe came in here last year, we all remember. He had a plan to build a big hotel, put a nice restaurant in. You sent him packing, Dent."

Lackey looked at the councilman. "Francis, you know the plan. We do everything full-sized. We're salvaging the most useful real estate in the city, eighty acres a stone's throw from the falls." He pulled a little on his tie, loosened the knot. "I've spent God knows how many days on trips to Albany and New York and even Washington, talking to anyone that would listen, building the case for rebuilding this city." He paused, perhaps for breath, perhaps for dramatic effect. "They didn't have to give it to us, you know. It seems like every American city has a crumbling downtown. There are lots of mayors shopping around for state and federal money to give their local economy a booster shot. We did it. I did it. And I'm not giving up all this land in little chunks here and there to your friend or his friend or his cousin, to build some Goddamn little hotel and restaurant. We need to think big."

Proulx held up his hand. "May I interrupt?" Lackey glared at him but nodded. "We know the plan, we've heard the lecture. The convention center is being designed, and the demolition is picking up speed. Everything is going according to your grand plan. But Joe Spallino has a lot of good friends, with a lot of clout. Are you telling me that we can't even let him speak to us?"

"What the hell for? Look at our agenda. The owners of the Candlelight Lounge think their shitty little bar should stand in the middle of where the convention center is planned. They won't bargain, they won't be bought out, we have to start taking it by eminent domain. There are two more properties in the same boat. There's four properties here we have to review buyout prices on and check against the budget." Although he wore a watch, the mayor looked at the clock on the wall.

"Francis wants to play golf today. You want to kiss Joe Spallino and make him feel good, or get on with our work?"

Proulx looked at Lyon, who shrugged. "Let's give Joe a few minutes."

"Fine," Lackey hissed.

Joe Spallino came into the meeting in a blue suit coat and off-white shirt but no tie. "Gentlemen, it's a pleasure to see you again," he began, setting his briefcase on the table and shaking hands all around.

Lackey got up to meet him. "Joe, how are you? Always a pleasure to see you," he said warmly, beaming, close enough to exchange hugs. "What can we do for you today?"

"Well," he said, making eye contact with each councilman, "I took my plans for the hotel and restaurant back to the drawing board, so to speak. I remember what you said about dreaming big," he said. He sounded like a chastened schoolboy anxious to show he'd learned his lesson. "And I reviewed my plans, got in touch with the bank, dug out some money I'd stashed under my mattress." He added a little chuckle and they chuckled with him. He displayed a drawing some draftsman had done for him, a white print in blue. "Here's the hotel. Instead of a hundred rooms with five stories, I went another floor for a hundred twenty. Instead of just a restaurant, I added a lounge over here on the side. Course, I'll need a little more land for parking. And on this side, I added a mini-golf. The total amount of land I need goes from four to four and a half acres, but I got Power City Bank ready to write a check. I showed you the numbers last year, and they'll just get better with this addition. I just need you fine gentleman to give me the letter for the land. What do you say?" Spallino finished with a broad smile.

They looked at their copies of his plan, circulated as he was talking. Lifting the first stapled sheet, Proulx nodded. "So you'd go to a hundred and twenty rooms? And a mini-golf?"

"For the kids mainly. Sometimes teenagers out on a date will go mini-golfing. I took my wife once. She must have hit the ball twenty times getting it in," Spallino joked.

The councilors pretended to read the papers, waiting for Lackey to speak.

"Joe, the problem we had the last time isn't really addressed with this change," Lackey began. "We're building a convention center that will take eighty-two acres. Just to support that we need another eighty acres for parking garages and at least four hundred rooms. What the convention center doesn't take up is committed to the LaSalle Arterial. And, say, did I show you the plan?"

The plan was an artist's conception of the New Niagara Falls, with the to-be-built arterial sweeping along the bottom of the model, carrying traffic in four lanes around the back of the convention center, then along a boulevard lined with two parking garages that fed into retail and office buildings. At least two skyscraper hotels flanked it. Three odd cylinders stood nearest the falls, at least one of which was to be a 'rotel', an oddity, a rotating hotel.

Lackey leaned over the model, which took up a fifteen foot long table. "Where in here am I supposed to find the space for a little hotel, a little restaurant, and a mini-golf? We're looking for year-round facilities. Something that can pull in tourists year-round. Mini-golf?" he shrugged. "In January?"

Spallino's face reflected his emotions; he'd gone from hopeful to supplicant, to dismay. Now he was sinking deeply into anger and was suppressing a deep desire to smash the model of the future. "Who do you know is going to fund a project like that?" he pointed at it with disdain.

"Well," Lackey answered matter-of-factly, "the federal and state funds will build the convention center. We've gotten some calls, some letters, from hotel chains like the Hilton. Once ground breaks on the convention center, they'll be lining up to build. And the smallest offer we've received is to build a hotel twice the size of yours."

"Those are outsiders. Chains. What ever happened to local business?" Spallino asked. Lackey looked sad for him. There was nothing to say. "Why did you tell me to think bigger when I came in here last time?" Spallino asked, glaring at Lackey. "Why did you encourage me to go talking to banks and see how much I could borrow?"

Lackey couldn't recall, in detail, what he'd said last June. He might have given Joe encouragement. Much had happened since then. More state and federal money came their way, and that made the convention center more of a plan than a pipe dream, and that got the ball rolling with the hotels. Perhaps he'd given Joe the wrong signal, sent him back to the drawing board, hoping he'd come up with something. But it was too late now. "I don't recall encouraging you, to tell you the truth. I didn't think a local businessman could get together the capital needed to take part in this."

Spallino was pursing his lips to keep back the torrent of anger he wanted to pour on the mayor. "You don't remember?" he got out. "Does anyone here remember?" he asked the others, who were all content to let Lackey handle it. "Does anyone here remember him telling me to 'think big'?"

"He's been telling everyone to think big," said Proulx. "Joe, you aren't the only local businessman to get sent out the door. You're just the first today." Proulx stopped there, because he was behind Lackey in this area, and as much as he liked seeing someone try to rip into the mayor, he didn't dare let himself be seen as a supporter of these relatively small projects. "Joe, there will be other opportunities when this project is done. If you're smart, you hold onto your money. If this all works, you'll have a chance to spend it."

"Oh, it'll work," said Lackey, looking sideways at Proulx. "It'll work. But Guy's correct, Joe. When it takes off, you'll have your chance to get in on it. But not just now."

The angry developer packed up his papers silently, accepted a handshake from Proulx and Lyon, and left the room, perhaps shutting the door harder than necessary.

"Well, that's done with. Now, did anyone here today hear me encourage him to come back again?" Lackey asked, trying to get a laugh. He got no response; these guys have no sense of humor.

The remaining members of the urban renewal board drifted in from the inviting outside. "It's gorgeous out there," said Morton Siegler, city manager. "Fran, you just come from golfing or are we holding you up?"

"Let's just get today's business wrapped up pronto, okay?" Lyon joked.

Angelo Medina and Harvey Shane, directors respectively of urban renewal and planning and development came in together. Bill O'Brien came in, looking like he'd been painting something, off-white paint smears on his hands. Mike O'Hara, in his usual three-piece suit, saw the nearest seat was by Bill, and pushed his chair against the wall. Beatrice Lazio came in, hair upswept, fresh from the parlor.

"Anyone know where Tom Biggins is?" asked Lackey.

"Uh, family funeral, I think," said Medina. "He called me and said he might make it, but he wasn't optimistic. It's okay, we have a quorum." Medina pulled out a thick manila folder filled with papers stapled in bunches. "Pass these around, please." A burst of sunlight filled the room. "Anybody mind if I close these blinds?"

"I like the sunshine," said Mrs. Lazio.

"You like it so much, why don't you move to Florida?" joked O'Brien.

"Well, depending on how this project works out, I might," she said dryly.

"Let's get started," said Medina. "The first page includes properties we currently own. We're making great progress since we got the process of condemning streamlined. We have sixteen buyouts to vote on today. The offers have been extended to the owners and accepted. If we approve, they get added to the list for clearance."

The room was quiet as they read. "How many acres will we have purchased with this batch?" asked O'Hara.

"Just eight," said Medina. "But now we can move much faster. If we can meet weekly for the next few months we'll be able to break ground on the convention center by the end of the summer."

"I'd like to start earlier," growled Lackey. "We've made the people of this city wait long enough."

"Let's just make sure the checks are being written for the correct amount," said Proulx.

They finished reading. "I read the total costs, over a hundred thousand today, are within the budget," said Lackey, and the vote was unanimous. "Next item, if you turn to page three, are properties we need to begin negotiations with owners on. They are not condemned, they are active on the tax rolls, so we have to first try to negotiate fair market value."

"Am I mistaken," said Shane, "or is 626 Third Street near the old Stone House?"

Medina looked into a bulging accordion file he'd left on the floor. Thumbing through several sheets, he said, "it's more than near it, it's the house."

"Owned by Joe Spallino?" said Lyon. "Joe Spallino." He glanced at Lackey, who was reading the page now, his mouth hanging open. "Good old Joe Spallino."

"Did we ever discuss the Stone House when we were reviewing the exempt list?" asked Lazio.

"It wasn't discussed because it wasn't on the list of candidates for the National Register," said Lackey. "It's just an old house. Very old house, but in bad shape, in a bad neighborhood," he said. "It's a tear-down."

"I can't believe this one's on the list to tear down," said Proulx. Any chance to put a bug up Lackey's butt. "Let's table this one until the next meeting. Who's our local historian?"

"Walter Morrow," said Medina. He looked uncomfortable. "The problem with Walter Morrow is that he thinks every property is historically important."

"Did the Stone House ever come up?"

"It did," said Siegler. "If I remember correctly. But it's in a bad place." They looked at the map. "Dead center where the convention center is going," he said. "A shame, really."

"So Joe Spallino owns the Stone House, and it's dead center," summarized Lackey. "Well, Joe was just in here and didn't leave a happy man. So, let's give him a week to calm down, add a thousand to our offer, send out the attorneys and buy it and demolish it. I don't see where there's any alternative."

They moved on to the next page.

Rainbow Center

With its engine rumbling, shaking the cab, the truck backed the flat bed trailer bearing the crane onto the vacant lot that used to be the corner of 3rd and Erie. Del and Leon scrambled onto the trailer and took off the restraining chains. With a bellow and cloud of diesel smoke, the crane's engine started; its gearbox rattled and ground its teeth and the crane slowly lumbered off the trailer.

Six days ago the vacant lot they stood in had been smashed into existence. Today the wrecking crew stood in the lot and aimed their iron ball at the three-story house next door. Tonight that house, too, would be a vacant lot.

"Okay," yelled Sonny.

"House is clear," yelled Leon, jogging from the open doorway.

SLAM! CRUNCH! BOOM! Creaking sounds, a crashing thud that shook the house to its stone basement. Plaster fell and a piece of ceiling upstairs fell. A little piece it must have been or the floor would have given way beneath it and dropped, dropped straight down to the basement—

SLAM! A supporting wall blew into dust and splintered wood. The roof sagged visibly.

SLAM! The ball crushed into the northwest corner. More outside wall collapsed, the third story bedroom was gone. The chimney fell and punched through the roof, letting light pour unnaturally in.

"Just one more, over by that supporting beam," said Sonny. The iron ball dangled on its cable, hung motionless for a moment in mid-air. The cable swung towards the house, dragging the ball in its wake, until the ball lazily crunched into the exposed ribs of the house.

The roof's ridgeline sagged, then fell. Inside, a long creaking sound slowly filled the house. The roof settled and the upper structure came down, taking down the lower structure with it, straight down to the ground.

When he met her at the doors of the library for their Saturday estate sale date, she asked him, "did you read about the Stone House?"

"What? Where?" he asked.

"In the paper."

"I don't read the paper."

She smiled. "How does a librarian end up dating a guy who doesn't even read the newspaper? Come in," she pulled him over to the Serials room, where the week's editions of the *Niagara Falls Gazette* were hung on bamboo rods. She pulled up Tuesday's, and flipped it to page three. "September 7th, 1969. Read this," she touched the story.

He sat at the table and read. "They're buying the Stone House to demolish it." He looked at her, "does Walter know about this?"

"He called in sick yesterday. He says he didn't even sleep the night he saw this."

"Taking it kind of personally, isn't he?"

"He loves history. He loves this town. He hates to see it demolish its history."

Still seems a little flaky, Del thought. "What about that letter I found?"

"He sent a copy of it to the state historical department. We called them after reading the news. They can't find it. They should have had it a week ago. But it wouldn't stop this anyway."

"But why don't we just take it to the urban renewal people? Won't they fix it?"

She looked at him. Either he was brilliant in his simplicity, or he was painfully naïve. "Take it to the urban renewal people," she repeated. "Well, it hasn't been done, so I guess we should cover all the bases."

"Is Walter here today?"

"No, he's a department manager," she said, with a hint of jealousy, "he doesn't have to work weekends. But I think he'd enjoy a visit. Let me give him a call. Do you mind not going to another estate sale today?"

"Sure. I'm not even done with *Peyton Place* yet."

Walter's apartment was a second story in an immense old Victorian off Pine Avenue, close to Haeberle Plaza. There was an intercom by the door. "Walter? It's Beth, and Del is with me."

"Oh, hi," Walter's voice limped from the speaker, "I'll buzz you in. Leary will greet you. I'm upstairs."

They opened the door and a Labrador-based mutt greeted them with licks. "This is Leary, Walter's dog. Named for—"

"Timothy Leary?"

Walter was in the attic, a low-ceilinged space which he'd made into a reading room with almost no headroom, a challenge for someone as tall as he. He walked hunched over from the pile of cushions he'd been sitting on by an eyebrow window that looked out on the street. He was drinking a Strohs. "Hi folks," he greeted them sadly, "thanks for coming over. Want a beer?"

"Sure," they said.

"Still upset about the house?" she asked. He nodded.

"I have to admit I didn't read the news about the Stone House until just recently," Del said.

"I pointed it out to him about twenty minutes ago," said Beth. "Del has a unique strategy. He wants us to simply present the urban renewal agency with the letter. See what they do."

Walter shook his head. "I wish that would work but I know what they'll do. Nothing is what they'll do." He took another swallow of beer. "When they got the first grant, when they knew the downtown project was going to get funded, I was invited to be on a committee that looked at all the property in the South End and determined what shouldn't be demolished. We spared the United Office Building, which was nice. We spared the Nabisco Factory, which I thought was kind of cool, saving a factory, but when I mentioned the Stone House, which we know goes back to at least the Civil War, they hemmed and hawed, then they voted to send some real estate assessor to look at it. He wrote up this report that said, probably accurately, that the place was falling down." He sighed again, running his hand through his hair. "And unfortunately, most importantly, it's right in the middle of their planned convention center. And it doesn't have the clout of St. Mary's. So the vote to save the Stone House had one vote for, the rest against."

"Do we know, or did we know, that it was the oldest house in the city?" Beth asked.

"We didn't then." He curled into a partial fetal position. "And the letter isn't exactly the gold standard of proof. I doubt it will matter, but," he looked at Del, "maybe you have the right idea. We should at least give them a chance to see it and react to it."

"I told you," Del said to Beth, poking her gently in the ribs, and they drank beer. "Do you know someone to call?"

"Morton Siegler is the city manager, but Mayor Lackey's the real guiding light on this renovation," Beth said, "and I don't think he wants anything to stop construction of the convention center. They've been talking about how it's going to double the tax base in the city." Walter snorted in disbelief and she smiled at him. "But from what I read, Guy Proulx is his biggest opposition. Why don't we show it to him?"

"Couldn't hurt. Eventually the entire agency needs to see it. But I guess we could start with him, and get his reaction to it." Walter was perking up; he even got out some pot he saved for special occasions. Del impressed Beth with his rolling abilities, and a little while later they cracked open the window a little.

"We need a name," Beth said, "our happy little group needs a name."

"The urban renewal avengers," Walter suggested.

They shook their heads. "No, no, something funny."

"The librarians!" Walter offered.

"I'm not a librarian," Del pointed out.

"I'm not either. We could become honorary librarians," Walter suggested.

"The Scavengers?" She suggested.

"Forget it," said Walter, falling into a giggling fit, "forget it."

Guy Proulx was also a teacher at Niagara Falls High School, and agreed to meet them Monday afternoon after classes. Del took his first day off, and found he liked putting on a dress shirt on a weekday. What he wasn't expecting was the anxiety attack from following Walter into the school. He hadn't been in it for twelve years, but it shrank him back to eighteen the moment he stepped through the doors. "Hello!" he called out. "Man, it echoes."

"Yes, it does," Walter agreed dryly. Del said no more. Walter led them to the teacher's lounge, where a man not much older than Del was drinking a Coke while reading papers. "Mr. Proulx? I'm Walter Morrow, with the local history department."

Proulx was dressed in white shirt and blue tie, and when Walter announced them he tucked the student papers into a battered leather case. "Hi, Walter, have we met?"

"I was on the committee that reviewed historical properties in the South End." Proulx nodded, whether he remembered or not.

"And your friend?"

"This," Walter said, "is Delbert Nichols. He actually found this document I wanted to show you."

Del shook the teacher's hand, and Walter gently presented the letter from the manila folder it now called home. Proulx looked at it briefly, then stopped packing up his materials and sat at the table and read it over again.

Lining the walls were lockers, much like the outside hallways, but inside the lounge the smell of tobacco was legal. A framed photograph of President Johnson hung in the corner, with an American flag on a pole topped with a golden eagle beside it. The flag reminded Del of the news footage last night of students marching against the war. There was talk of a huge demonstration being planned, to try and provoke a nationwide strike against the war.

"This is fascinating," said Proulx, studying the paper. He looked at Walter. "If I understand this correctly, a private in the militia was under arrest, and he grew up in the Stone House?" Walter nodded.

"If I remember correctly, no records prior to the War of 1812 exist?" Walter nodded, less enthusiastically, "so this, by implication, means the Stone House existed in 1812, and likely some years before then." Walter nodded vigorously again. "Wow. So the Stone House is really the oldest building in the area, outside of Fort Niagara."

"Exactly. Exactly," Walter said. "And if we'd had this evidence back when we were marking sites to be spared demolition, I think this would have made a difference."

Proulx looked at Walter skeptically. "You think so? Keep in mind where it is."

Walter wasn't stoppable. "Can we stop the demolition of the Stone House? With this new evidence?"

Proulx looked at the paper again, this time like it was a bad report card. "I don't think so. See, we accepted money from the state that requires clearance of condemned properties by certain deadlines that are coming up fast. On the other hand," Proulx thought out loud, "this isn't yet city property. Joe Spallino owns it. God knows why. But you might want to talk to him, since it's still his property."

"Mr. Proulx, I actually work on one of the demolition crews," said Del. "What happens when you try to buy a property for demolition, and the owner refuses to sell?"

"We try to negotiate a price," said Proulx. "We'd rather have a happy ending. But if the owner won't accept a reasonable offer, which is usually decided by the assessors, say if the owner thinks he can make a killing by holding out, we start condemnation proceedings."

"How long does that take?"

"It used to take forever. We've got it down to about six months."

Walter was back in his frowning mode. "So what kind of time does that buy us?"

Proulx clarified it. "It's August 31st. They want to break ground on the convention center next month. If you can get Spallino to drag out negotiations for a couple of months, Lackey has to begin condemning the property. That would push the ground breaking back until almost Christmas. With the winters we get, that effectively pushes it back until early spring. Which would certainly bust his balls."

"But it doesn't save the house," said Del.

"Nothing is going to save the house," said the councilman.

On the ride back to the library, Walter was like a man on his third pot of espresso. "Not good enough! Not good enough! We must find another plan of attack!"

"He said straight out." Del said. "Nothing will save the house."

"He's just a councilman, not God."

Back in the library, Beth was in the Technical Services area, typing catalog cards. Through the door, Del could hear the typewriter keys going thwack! thwack! thwack!, followed by a muffled 'damn'. He watched Walter tear through the Reference Room, pulling down a thick volume labeled *Serials Listing*. Paging through it, Walter touched a line of text and found a pencil to scribble with.

"I thought so. The Buffalo Historical Society has the complete records of the papers of the Buffalo Historical Society," Walter announced with a smile. "And they have it indexed."

"Indexed," Del repeated the foreign word. "And we care because?"

"We need to quickly research Nehemiah Cleary's history. Find out anything we can about him."

"Why?" Del asked; Walter is getting flakier by the second.

"You heard Guy Proulx, right?" Walter asked, his gentler nature returning, his brows furrowing in concern. "Nothing can save the house. That means that that letter, by itself, won't save it. But we know a name now. We know the name of someone who lived in that house, and he was noticed by history. He hit the radar. So now we hunt with other radar and see if he hit it anywhere else."

Del's mouth was hanging open. "I'm missing something. Radar?"

"If Nehemiah Cleary turns out to be locally famous, or to have done something for which he should be famous, that might drum up popular interest in him. And that would save the Stone House."

"You sure?" Del asked, still skeptical.

They both heard the manual typewriter striking the card through the door. "It's a good thing Beth is a superb reference librarian," Walter said with a wry smile, "because we can never read her catalog cards."

"Why does she have to type catalog cards?" Del asked, happy to have something new to tease her with.

"Everybody on the library staff rotates through all the jobs. Except, thank God, me," said Walter. "The Historical Society is closed tonight, but open tomorrow. What are you two doing tomorrow night?"

"Well, they're showing *The Green Berets* at the Strand, and it's bargain night," said Del, and Walter winced. "Or we could do the historical society."

They got to the Historical Society at 5:30. The building, a Romanesque structure, bordered Forest Lawn Cemetery, where thousands of militia and regulars once encamped, vainly awaiting General Smythe's order to attack as Van Rensselaer's army collapsed fifteen miles north.

Del and Beth let Walter lead the charge. He knew the building and made a bee-line to the reference desk. "Can I help you?" asked the archivist, a middle-aged, shiny bald man.

"Walter Morrow, Niagara Falls Local History."

"Hey, I keep meaning to come up there. Good to meet you. Josh Weinberg." Walter started with a very general explanation, but now they were working with another trained bookworm.

"Do you think Cleary was at Queenston?" Josh asked.

"Definitely." Walter showed Josh the letter.

"A-ha. Okay, a lot of local men were at Queenston. A militia roster from Lewiston might confirm that." Josh was making notes on a scrap of paper as he spoke.

"What we're looking for, in particular, is something that would save the house," Beth said. "We now know it's the oldest in the city, but all we know is what's in this letter, that Nehemiah Cleary lived in a stone house, and that he was in trouble during the War of 1812. Something about supplies."

"'Cleary is to appear before the Senate in Albany to answer questions concerning the nature and quality of supplies provided the militia in the Lewiston encampments,'" Josh read. "Problems with camp supplies? That rings a bell," he said. "Ever read about General Smythe's Black Rock encampment? There are lots of complaints about the supplies. Lots of them. Everything from the guns to the butter. And the commissary agent was Augustus Porter. You've probably heard of Porter?" They all nodded. "So Cleary was somehow involved in the supplies." He led them into a room whose door read 'Microfilm'. "We've tried to put everything that old on micro," explained Joshua, "there isn't a lot, but somewhere in here may be the information you need. How much time do you have?"

"Not much longer," Walter answered glumly.

"Let's start with the war," suggested Joshua, "hey, Leo?" The security guard in the hallway walked around. "I'm in micro if anyone needs me." They followed him into a room filled with metal filing cabinets and watched him quickly, efficiently, sort through three drawers and collect four reels. "I'm afraid we only have three machines working tonight." Seating Del and Beth at one reader, Walter at the other reader, Joshua placed a reel on each reader. "This," he said to Beth, "is muster lists. This would at least tell us how long he was in the army, within a month or four."

"Month or four?"

"Payrolls were irregular, and names didn't always show up, what with desertions and deaths. The original muster book will at least tell us if he joined."

"This," he set up Walter's reader, "will be correspondence between the officers. Some of it is actually log sheets from the local forts." He picked up a third reel and sat at another machine. "This one should tell me anything Albany was up to at the time."

"What if we strike out?" Beth asked.

"If we do, well, things couldn't get much worse," said Walter, "in terms of historic preservation."

Del cranked the plastic wheel and the microfilm squeaked as it was pulled through rollers and under the glass plate. Images scrolled across the opaque screen. "'Government Payroll Record'", Del read, "June, 1812, through May, 1815. Continued on next consecutively numbered film.'" *This won't be much help*, he griped to himself, but cranked up to the listing 'Lewiston, Commanding Officer, Colonel Stephen Van Rensselaer'. As he began to turn the crank he groaned loudly.

"Problem?" Beth asked, not taking her eyes off the screen.

"It's all handwritten."

"Yes," she said, "there was a chronic shortage of typewriters in 1812."

"And there were a lot of volunteers."

"Suffer in silence," she suggested, smiling.

A few minutes later, without warning, Nehemiah's name rolled up and surprised them, mostly because they could read it. It was a confident signature, one of trained literacy. "Okay, we got him," he said, touching the name on the screen. "We found him in Lewiston." Del's heart pounded. Josh and Walter came over to look at the screen and see Nehemiah's name, nod, then return to their own reels.

After forty more pages of hard-to-read film of nineteenth century handwriting, Del found his mind wandering. Stifling a yawn, he noted it was already ten to nine. Rubbing his eyes, he tried to read the screen. *Fortunately, Beth seems to eat this stuff up.*

"Here's something," said Josh, hitting the print button. It was near closing. Walter tried to read Josh's screen from his seat; the chairs were a snug fit. "The Senate did call for an investigation into the supplies. There's nothing here about how it turned out, but they were not happy with the situation in Lewiston."

Walter, having found nothing, cranked his film faster than the loving couple, looking for the next Lewiston payroll. There wasn't one. *Everybody's finding stuff but me*, he griped.

They finished their rolls. Del got up, rubbing his eyes. "Can I take a breather? This is giving me a headache."

"Sit here and cheer me on," Beth said, and he closed his eyes and held her hand in both of his. "The forts' logs are grouped. That helps."

"Wonderful," he whispered.

Joshua got called away to help a patron. Beth's eyes flitted over routine entries in the log of Fort Schlosser in July, 1812: eighteen months from any fighting. 'July 12th. Most of the villagers are moving to Black Rock in wagons. Fear of invasion. Guards doubled, leaves restricted.'

"Look at the time," Beth said, looking the clock on the wall to relieve her eyes. "We have to go."

"Fine with me," said Del. He looked at Walter, who was studying his screen like the cure for cancer was buried somewhere in it. "Walter, we're calling it a night."

Walter sighed, but rubbed his own tired eyes. "Did you finish your roll?"

"Not quite."

"Well, make a note of how far you got. There's another roll here we didn't get to. I'll leave a note and ask Josh to hold the reels. I'll come by and finish them."

They dropped Walter off, and Del was vaguely planning an intimate moment with Beth, but she cut him off with a quick kiss in the driveway. Her father's bedroom light was on. "Dad's up. See you tomorrow."

She found her key to the back door, but to her surprise her father hadn't locked it. "Dad?" she called out, finding the light switch in the mud room, then into the kitchen. "Dad? You up?" She listened. His TV wasn't blaring from the basement, he must be asleep. He didn't usually leave his light on. She went upsatirs and peeked into his bedroom. "Dad?" She felt rising anxiety, and tried the bathroom door. She knocked clearly; nothing would bother her father more than the embarrassment of his daughter seeing him on the toilet. "Coming in," she announced, waited a heartbeat or two, then opened it.

Colonel Reuther lay on the bathroom floor, unconscious, and Beth cried out, "Dad!" She knelt to check his pulse. He was alive. Apparently he'd been sitting on the toilet and, perhaps, fainted. She got a towel to drape over his waist and something caught her eye in the toilet bowl. The water was vividly red. There was a faint smear of it on his leg.

She called for the ambulance, opened the door, and went back upstairs to wait with her father. "Beth?" he whispered, as though asleep. "You home?" he asked, not opening his eyes. Outside, Beth heard the ambulance arrive.

"Up here!" she called out the window. "It's my father."

The colonel drifted off in the time it took for the medics to get up the steps. They checked his vitals, then got him onto the stretcher. "He's going to be all right, Miss," the medic tried to comfort her. She drove behind the ambulance to Memorial Hospital and followed her father's gurney into a bay of the emergency room. The bright fluorescent lights hurt her eyes. She glanced at her watch. Eleven-thirty. It was past her bed time. The medics had checked his blood pressure immediately, and started a transfusion.

Now a doctor swept in with a nurse following. "Are you his daughter?"

"Yes. Beth Reuther."

"Are you the one that found him?" the doctor asked as he and the nurse again took blood pressure and pulse and temperature. "We've got a contusion here," he pointed out a bruise on the colonel's temple to the nurse, "I want an x-ray of that." To Beth he asked, "where was he?"

"In the bathroom. On the toilet," she added, in a softer voice.

"Possible heart attack," the doctor advised the nurse. To Beth he said, "a side effect of a heart attack is that it feels like peristalsis, the call of nature."

"But the toilet seemed to have a lot of blood in it," Beth said.

The doctor's brow furrowed and he examined the colonel's rectum. "Yes, there is blood here. Patsy," he addressed the nurse, "let's get the cardiac workup, but let's get some blood work stat. Miss Reuther," he said, "you may want to go home and we'll call you."

"Oh, I'll wait. I'll wait out there," she said anxiously. Her father remained unconscious.

"Well, it's been a busy night, and your father is stabilized, but," the doctor glanced at the clock, "the x-ray is backed up and I'll need some tests on his blood before I have any idea what's going on, and that's not going to be done before breakfast."

The nurse turned to her and led her out of the bay. "I promise, we'll call you as soon as he's conscious. There's nothing you can do. Go home, and try to get some sleep."

She found herself back in the parking lot, looking up at the night sky. Leaving felt wrong, leaving her father in the hands of strangers. Then she remembered that horrible sensation of utter helplessness she felt, kneeling by her half-naked unconscious father. And sitting out the night in the waiting room depressed her so she surrendered to a wave of tears. The crying passed, but left her with a headache. She got in her car and drove home. Once there, she thought to call Del, but now the clock read 1:15 a.m., and she knew Del had to be up very early. *I'll call him from work*, she decided. Then she remembered the messy bathroom upstairs. She got out her sponges and Clorox and by the time the bathroom was clean again she fell asleep in her clothes on her bed.

Walter took an hour of vacation and left work early for the Historical Society the next evening. He picked up where they'd left off the night before. Beth had stopped on October 13th, 1812, but Schlosser saw no action in the Queenston attack and recorded the least accurate rumors— 'we are in Canada and are marching a thousand strong towards Fort Erie. Great agitation in barracks, a clamoring to march to the Lewiston camp and take part. Orders are to remain. The British are in full retreat and may attempt something desperate.' Walter smiled in hindsight, cranking more slowly.

The village was almost empty by late November when an entry read; 'Pvt. N. Cleary, reported missing from army in October. Killed by sentry on Portage Road.' His throat choked a moment. "Oh no," he whispered. He hit the print button. "Killed?" he read again. "A deserter?" He sighed in despair. "That's not going to save anything."

The colonel was sitting up in his hospital bed, reading the *Gazette*, when Beth walked in. "Hey, Dad," she smiled, and though the colonel was decidedly against public displays of affection, he hugged his daughter. "How you feeling?"

"I feel fine. I want to go home."

"Did the doctor come by yet? He said he was going to do some tests."

"I think he came by real early. I was kind of dozing." He looked very sleepy still. I wonder what they're giving him? she wondered.

She stayed with him until he nodded off again, then went looking for the doctor. She settled for his number, left a message to call her at work. She went back to her father's room and, still asleep, she kissed him on the cheek and left for work.

Desperate to find something he could use, Walter sacrificed a sick day and drove to the University of Toronto. The delights of the city tempted him, coffee houses and young people with long hair and posters calling for the U.S. to get out of Vietnam, but he was on a mission and, like a swan finding Capistrano, found the library and its microfilm. The massive bound index made his arms ache carrying it back to a table to read. Softly he said, "calling Nehemiah Cleary."

An hour later, having worked through the entire index with every relevant term he could conjure, he had another list of references to check, mostly general correspondence on the War, nothing specific. "This is turning into a serious long shot. I'm going to need stronger glasses if this keeps up," he said, which was a problem. Glasses were expensive and his health insurance didn't cover it. Maybe I can get my mother to pay for it. Call it a birthday present.

"First reference." He cranked the film up to the appointed page, which was just 'correspondence'. "'October 19th, 1812. From Governor-General Drummond to Major General Roger Sheaffe, in command of Fort Erie. Regret to report that the stolen payroll was briefly in our possession. Two New York deserters were arrested in possession of the payroll. They were properly tried and found guilty of the crime. One, identified as Pvt. Lucas Joseph, was executed.' Walter winced. 'A second, N. Chery, escaped custody during an artillery assault following the trial. He is still at large. If found, his original sentence was twenty years hard labor. As presiding officer at his trial I recommend the sentence be changed to death, and that it be carried out immediately upon re-capture. Our search continues.'

Walter stared at it. "Could N. Chery be N. Cleary?" It could, he knew; it must have been almost as hard to read this handwriting in the original as it was in film. And it mentions the other soldier, Lucas. The mysterious N. Chery stole a British payroll, and a month later was dead. *It only costs a dime*, he encouraged himself, pushing the print button.

The other citations led him to a series of letters for paymasters, all testifying that the payroll due on October 21st was delayed and one of the thieves remained at large. Search parties scoured River Road in vain. Fortunately, payrolls were sufficiently irregular that the troops were only mildly outraged.

Light angling in near sunset reminded Walter he was finishing off his sick day. He looked out a nearby window, at an oak tree growing in a courtyard, to rest his eyes. He looked down his list of citations, what a detective would call 'leads', most of them crossed off. *Call it quits soon*, he decided, yawning.

The sun was setting as he neared the last of the citations and wondered whether he should be feeding the meter. "The *Niagara Advertiser*, the *Newark Gazette*, the *Pelham Gazette*, the *York Messenger*. Probably all old war stories. I might get lucky," he coached himself to push on. He thought to glance around, self-consciously, and see if anyone heard him speaking to himself. He noticed other patrons, whose own lips were moving.

Two hours of reading the reminiscences of old soldiers, learning more about the war and the Loyalists, not a bad thing for a local historian, and he found another piece to the puzzle. 'I served under Captain Richard Lightfoot, His Majesty's Royal Army, during the War with the United States. The strangest event of the war, to my recall, was an evening I went with two of my men, Captain Lightfoot and a Yankee named Mr. Cleary to sell rusted muskets to the Rebels.'

'I had taken the muskets from a barn in Lewiston. . . '

Bottles of Genesee sat untouched on Del's kitchen table as they began to compare stories. "Here's what we know. The man who purchased the bad supplies was Judge Porter," Beth said. "Nehemiah Cleary was the company clerk, but before he could be questioned in the matter he died in November, 1812, killed by a sentry on the Portage Road. That's from the microfilm we found in Buffalo."

"Right. But he didn't die in November," Walter said, barely suppressing a smug smile, handing out the copies he'd made in Toronto, "he was involved in the supply scandal, perhaps unfairly, and he staged a strange act of revenge on Judge Porter the following spring. Read this."

They read the story, frowning and looking up at each other. "How common was the name Cleary in 1812?" Del asked.

"It may have been misspelled as 'Chery'," Walter noted, passing around the copy.

Del looked at the sheets with Beth, utterly bewildered at the contradictory evidence. "How could we have two versions of this guy's life?" asked Del.

"Welcome to the world of local history," Walter said.

Beth went to the bathroom. Walter sat in silence, shaking his head slowly. When they all returned to the living room, he finally broke the silence.

"I have a question," asked Walter. He looked at them as though he'd already asked it.

"Speak, Walter," said Beth. *No woman I know could marry him without killing him within a week,* she thought. *God knows I couldn't, to my father's relief.*

"It's possible there were two Nehemiah Cleary's back then, but let's assume there was only one in that time and place. One of these stories is wrong."

"That's not a question," Beth noted. She was tired and she'd expected this adventure to be concluded in measures of black and white, not gray. Since it seemed to be a fruitless adventure anyway, it was starting to bore her.

Walter ignored her. "If Cleary stole the payroll, that would explain his arrest—"

"In Canada," said Beth, "the payroll was British. He was also arrested by New York."

Walter nodded. "Right. He was at Queenston." He looked at Del and Beth and they nodded. "He came back, and had a run-in with a sentry near Fort Schlosser, so he wasn't among those held captive at Fort George." They all nodded, but just slightly. "Reported killed, but not killed, he went back to Canada. Since there's a still a war on, why did he go to Canada?"

"Actually, looking around at our world right now, that's the only part that makes sense. There's a war on, and the men are going to Canada," Del said, going for levity. She smiled at him. Walter rolled his eyes.

"He went to Canada because he knew he was under arrest, however unfairly, in New York," Beth said. "And must have found safe haven there, somewhere."

Nodding, Walter added, "and somehow arranged for this strange act of vengeance the following spring." Walter looked at his friends. "Right?"

Del asked, "but is there anything here that would bring people into City Hall screaming to save the Stone House?"

After a moment's thought, they all said, "No."

"I have an idea," said Beth. "Walter, you've been fretting all along that in the course of demolition we may be losing historical artifacts. Of all the homes in the South End, the Stone House is the one most likely to confirm your worst nightmares. So let's go to Joe Spallino, tell him some or all of this, and ask if he minds if we search the house."

"Search the house?" Walter asked.

"Search it, Delbert-style," Del said. "Pull up loose floorboards, pull down cabinets, punch holes in walls, look for anything. Kind of demolish it, from the inside. Just so we can be sure when they, when we, demolish it that it's just old boards and stone and plaster."

Walter nodded sadly. "Sure."

Joe Spallino was a businessman and it took Walter a couple days to get in touch with him. "Mr. Spallino? I've been told that you're the owner of 626 3rd Street? The old Stone House?"

"That's correct. What can I do for you?"

"Well," Walter identified himself, "the city wants to buy the property, if I'm not mistaken, to demolish the building and build the convention center there." Spallino m-hmmed. "Well, I was on the committee to identify and preserve historical sites, and I strongly suspect we missed one. And you own it."

"Really?" Spallino asked. He was taking the call in the office of the Funeral Home he owned on Portage Road. He had other businesses, but none of them afforded the privacy and quiet of the mortuary. "It's supposed to be the oldest house in the city, but nobody can prove it."

"Actually, I think I can," said Walter. "But that's not why I'm calling." And an hour ensued, with Spallino reluctantly absorbing more local history than he had a taste for. Walter tried to take shortcuts but Spallino, a tenacious listener, would interrupt with 'what's that?' or 'who's that?' and Walter would backtrack to explain a war, or the Portage, or who Augustus Porter was. He tried to tell Spallino about where and how he and the others had assembled the pieces of the story, but that's when Spallino said, "okay, I think I know enough. So why are you telling me all this? I can't donate the house to your, what are you, the local history society?"

"Not," Walter said, "not quite."

"Whatever. The city needs the land. It's right in the middle of where they're building the convention center. And they've called me already, and made an offer, which I'm going to refuse."

"You are?" Walter asked, hopeful. "Are you going to refuse to sell them the property?"

"Hell no," said Spallino, "that's why I bought it. I don't want it. But they offered me six thousand for it, and I know they can do better than that. So we're going to. . . negotiate."

"Oh," said Walter. "Well, then, since you don't want the house, since it's going to be demolished anyway, would you mind if I searched the house first? I have a feeling there might be some historical artifacts in there."

Spallino thought it over. "Search it how?"

Walter swallowed; his mouth and throat were dry. "Well, to be honest, we'd like to pull up floorboards, maybe drill a few holes in walls if we think we're on to something."

"Who's 'we'?" Spallino asked, sounding suspicious. Walter explained. "Oh." Spallino sounded bored again. The phone line was quiet in Walter's hand, and he thought Spallino had hung up but he could hear a radio playing somewhere in the funeral home. He heard Spallino breath, a piece of paper turn over, and then heard, "I got an appointment with the urban renewal board next week, Thursday. I'm optimistic I'll walk out with a deal. So you got a week. I'll write you a note that says you aren't trespassing. Stop by tomorrow and pick it up. That make you happy?"

"Pretty happy," said Walter. "Thank you, Mr. Spallino."

"Yeah," Spallino's mind was already elsewhere, "my pleasure."

Six guys from the day shift at Hooker were having a beer after work at the Jetport Lounge; they voted 5-1 to demolish Falls Street. They also voted 6-0 to then send the wreckers over to Russian to do the same to the Kremlin.

"What I like is that maybe in another year I can drive downtown without getting mugged," said a husky, bearded forklift driver whose haircut was modeled around his CHEVY cap.

"Ever get mugged?" asked someone.

Looking at the questioner with passing annoyance, the driver continued speaking. "I don't go downtown there at night without a baseball bat under my front seat. And I use it," he swore solemnly to his beer.

"Hope you do better down there than you did on the league or you be one dead honky." That got enough laughs to save the ass of the skinny guy with the scraggly beard sitting by the TV set; he was all mouth, no brains.

"Chickenshit," muttered the batter.

"One thing you know is going to come out of this is jobs," said an older guy, quiet until now. His gray hair and beard made him look rather statesmanlike against the hunting vest he wore, "I drive up and down Military Road all day, take loads all over the place, and I see the public works guys out at the Dunkin Donuts all sitting and drinking coffee while I'm working. City Hall gives you a job to go over and paint the benches in front of the park, y'know? They send ten guys to do five benches."

More laughter.

"So what are they going to build down there?"

"I heard they got plans for a big casino, like in Las Vegas."

"Where'd you hear that?"

"Was in the paper. Some councilman talking about it."

"No, no," said the disbelievers, shaking heads, draining glasses.

"Sure," insisted the guy with thinning hair, "they're building casinos, and they got a revolving hotel planned, and they're going to enlarge the airport. This place'll be under a runway in three years."

"Who's the jackass said all this?" asked the oldest one again.

"I don't know. Read it somewheres, I forget. Think it was one of the Buffalo papers."

"It's against the law to gamble in New York," reminded the big mouth by the TV.

"They change laws when they feel like it," said someone else.

"Hey, I don't mind casinos. They'll bring some money into town. And clean up downtown. I got no argument with getting something cooking downtown, bring in lots of money."

"No money you'll ever see."

More drafts were set up, another conversation began. Then the Bills game came on and everybody started groaning.

The next morning, Del and Leon and Sonny arrived at 630 Third Street. Sonny was playing a cassette tape of Gospel music Del could have done without, but he'd come to like and respect Sonny, a divorced father of six whose children were all down south in Alabama. "I mail them money every week, so's they know they got a daddy," Sonny admitted one day, after a hard day's work. They were sharing a six-pack. "I did some drinking and carousing when I was young and their mama left me and took them back down to live with her folks. Which was probably the right thing to do." Sonny was a deacon in a church over on Highland Avenue, and invited Del, and Del always politely declined. He let Sonny play his Gospel, figuring it was the closest he would get to church anytime soon.

So anyway, Leon was towing the crane on a flatbed with his truck, Del following in his truck, Sonny riding with him, off to demolish a triple-decker. They parked in front of the house, plenty of parking space. "Hello, anybody home" Leon did his usual announcement after stepping through the entry that had no door.

"Who's there?" came the response, followed by the sound of a pump-action shot gun, which stopped Leon in his tracks. "Turn it off," Leon called out to Sonny, who'd just fired up the crane. "Turn it off!"

A family of three was still living in the third floor apartment. By the time Social Services got someone over, the *Niagara Gazette* had a reporter inside checking the spelling of the unemployed man's name and a photographer shooting the house at a distance, next to the crane, 'under siege'. After half an hour became two hours, Del and Leon and Sonny went to lunch early.

"I'm Linda Sinclair, I'm with Social Services," the caseworker introduced herself to the to-be-homeless. "Did you get any mail from the city?"

"Here," said the young woman, in her late twenties. The letters were carefully stacked on top of the bookcase in the main room by the battered black and white Zenith with the coat hanger antenna. Her husband, a little older, sat in a paint-scarred kitchen chair, smoking and looking angry.

Sinclair looked at the mail and tore the oldest one open. "Yep, this is the warning." She tore the others open. "These are all warnings. Did the landlord come by and say anything?"

"We don't ever see the landlord," said the man. "We just mail a money order to a post office box."

"Why didn't you open these letters?" she asked, in the best non-threatening tone she could muster.

The reporter joined in the questioning. "Is this a protest? Do you have any comment?" It was a time of protests, and how cool if this was one right in town.

"No comment," the man said. "Ain't no protest."

Did the caseworker have a comment? "No, Social Services reserves comment," said Sinclair. She addressed the woman. "Why are you still living here, knowing the building is to be demolished."

"Demolished?" the woman asked. "Knocked down?" She was shocked, so was her husband. The caseworker showed the letters to the wife and pointed to the crane out on the street.

"Can't read," she finally admitted. "Neither can he." The man lit another cigarette, mustering some indignation.

So 630 Third Street was evacuated by three-thirty, with the help of Del and Walter and Sonny, and the family was put up in a motel with cable for two months while they found another apartment.

And the next day they started up the crane.

"We almost bought that house." The couple in their forties sat in their Plymouth behind the two other cars waiting for the policeman directing traffic to let them pass. One lane of traffic was closed, occupied by the crane and dump trucks. Behind the cop was the trailer that had delivered the crane. The crane was in a gravel driveway that led to a collapsing garage in back.

515 Third Street was already abandoned. The windows had been nailed over with scrap pieces of plywood and one sheet had been torn half off. "I wonder if they took that light fixture in the front hallway. I bet it was worth a lot of money."

Built to house the workers that stoked the fires of power along the river, the house was over eighty years old. It was one of seven houses on the block built from the same set of plans. It had its interior paint changed thirty-nine times, from whites to off-whites to yellows to brown to kelly green, to shades of blues, back to off-whites, then a brown that was left on so long it peeled. Then white again, two coats, to cover up the brown. During the Second World War a young bride was trying to fry fish with margarine when she felt false labor pains, got distracted, and the soot on the walls required new paint.

515 didn't have much good soil. That was the only acceptable explanation for the Carborundum foreman who owned the house in the early fifties and couldn't get so much as a pear tomato to grow in the backyard. "The soil is dead." "Do you mulch?" "Sure I mulch!" "Do you weed it?" "I weed it every night after my ice cream!" "Does it get sunlight?" "I cut down a tree just to make sure." "I don't know what to tell you." "I tell you, the soil is dead!"

During the early sixties a young couple managed to eke more than a few stalks of cannabis from the dead soil. They painted—several colors at the same time, as a matter of fact. One room became the Jackson Pollock room; you can guess why. These folks were eventually evicted.

The neighborhood got poorer. The house was cut into apartments and painted again. Now the cupboards didn't close anymore and the screws holding the face-plates to the electric plugs had to be excavated from under a rainbow of old layers. The couple in the Plymouth, seemingly the only people who had not painted 515, was long gone when the wrecker's ball swung. It took them a little while to bring it down; yeah, it was probably all that paint.

When Walter turned the key in the door they all heard the bolt pull back with a 'click'. Pushing on the heavy doorway, he got it open about forty-five degrees before it stuck on the warped floorboards. Beth stepped in, holding a sturdy plastic flashlight in her gardening gloves. Del was the last in, carrying a metal case flashlight he'd borrowed from work.

They turned back to see Walter standing in the doorway, his eyes downcast and his lips moving. "You alright, Walter?" Beth asked.

He finished his silent meditation. "I felt," he spoke slowly, uncomfortably, "I should apologize to the spirits of those who lived in this house. I feel like I've just entered a cemetery."

"O-kay," Beth said, in her most understanding tone.

"Do you do that every time you go into a historic home?" Del asked, and no matter how he phrased it it came out mean. "I don't mean it to sound like it does."

"It's okay," Walter said, and he fought a little with the lock getting the key out, then had to shove the door to shut it. The house seemed to go on forever, in relative darkness. "There's a lot of space in here. How do we do this?"

"Let's not split up," Beth said, joking nervously, "it feels a little weird being in here."

Sunlight lit up the windows, but seemed to be swallowed whole. Del turned on his flashlight, and Beth added hers. They lit up the floor, which was littered with chunks of old plaster, bits of broken glass, and dark chunks they could only guess at. They looked up at the ceiling. Dark stains overlapped, cracks traveled across it, and in the corner the plaster had fallen, looking like something had crashed through from upstairs. "Lot of water damage," Del said. "Probably the roof leaks, badly."

Walter, with no flashlight, tried the surface mounted switches. "Is there power running to the house, do you think?" he asked.

"I doubt it," Beth said.

They moved methodically through the rooms, testing switches where they found them. A few fixtures still had bulbs, most were smashed, the bulb base embedded in the sockets. They looked down a hallway at four doors for four rooms. Opening each door gave them a fresh burst of moldy air. Each room was small, with windows cracked and streaked in dirt. Empty and bare, in the last one the ceiling had completely collapsed and they could look up and see the second floor. "They weren't kidding," Walter said. "This place is in terrible shape." Almost an hour of careful exploration later, they were sure no power flowed in the old wires.

"Got a confession for you, Walter," Del said. "This isn't our first visit," he indicated Beth.

"Oh, you big mouth," Beth said, blushing and suppressing a smile.

"You guys borrowed the key before?" Walter asked.

"The basement has an outside door. We just let ourselves in. But we didn't even go this far."

They returned to the front room. "I smell urine," Beth said, her nose wrinkling.

"Well, you know you can't buy beer, you can only rent it," Del joked. She gave him a sickly smile. "Between kids breaking in for beer parties and bums using it for shelter, a little urine isn't too shocking. Look out for the ca-ca."

Beth was the first up the stairs. They creaked a little, but the banister was sturdy in her hand. "This is probably the strongest part of the house," she said, testing it. From the landing she saw the bowl shape of the floor, the result of two centuries of settling. "Watch your steps," she warned. "This floor would fail the marble test."

Walter explored a front room. "This room is larger than the ones downstairs. Maybe this was for the family." Again they saw exposed wood in the ceiling where the plaster had fallen. There was an old switchplate on the wall by the door, and a surface-mounted outlet on the floor molding.

Del pinched a piece of exposed wire. "If you did turn on the power here, you'd blow a hundred fuses in a minute." There was a closet in the corner and the door still hung, knob still mounted.

Walter pulled on it and asked for light.

Beth gave him her flashlight and he shone it in. "Steps," she said.

"It's an attic," Walter said. "Last one up is a rotten egg."

"Don't try walking up there, Walter. These ceilings are all collapsing," Del warned. He heard Walter's hesitant footsteps slowly creep across the ceiling over his head. "Well, don't count on me to break your fall."

"Do you have a crowbar?" Walter called down.

Del went out to his Rambler and returned with the tool. Climbing up the steps, Del joined Beth at the top landing, looking at the ancient flooring. Overhead was the roof, hewn from pine, still round and knotted, now sagging badly. Some of the rafters had cracked years ago.

"Clearly you have the best medical coverage," Del said and handed Walter the crowbar. "Here."

Walter knelt by a floorboard and Del saw why it caught Walter's eye; it had a little shine to it, as though it had been pulled up many times over the years. It also had a round headed nail. Walter got it up with a shriek from the nail. Something was folded inside, tucked in the space between two rafters. Retrieving it, Walter's hands shook a little as he opened it. "Silver certificates," he announced, disappointed, thumbing the bills. "Someone's collection of silver certificates."

"Which, technically, belong to Joe Spallino," Beth reminded him.

"Right," Walter said. He shoved the bills into his coat pocket. "Remind me they're there," he asked her. Standing, he explored further, boards creaking and other boards shifting as his weight challenged the old wood.

"Be careful, man," Del said again. Walter was heavier than he, which would make him hard to haul out.

"There's something over there," Walter said. He shone Beth's flashlight into the far corner where, in fact, there was an old wooden box.

"Maybe the boards are stronger nearer the edge," Del suggested as each of Walter's steps made the rafters echo with squeaks.

Walter reached the wooden box. "It says 'Wendts Dairy' on it," he read, with dry amusement. "And there's a. . . " he paused, looking closer, "a couple of books?"

"Anything by O. Henry?" Del joked.

Walter picked up one. "This is more of a journal." He stood, hefting the box and its contents. "Well, we found some reading material." His next step broke through. He dropped the box in front of him and it landed on its side, spilling its contents.

"Aoouuuww!!" Walter's leg went through, stopping at his knee. "Ouw. Oh, God. Oh, something's stabbing me in the leg. Oh shit."

Both of them were at his side then. Del tore away boards on either side of the hole and they saw that a splinter had wounded Walter in the leg. "Oh, Jeez, you're bleeding," said Del. "Does it hurt?"

Gasping, Walter nodded. "Damn right it hurts." They tried a couple of combinations, turning this way and that, and asking Walter to turn his leg a little. He shrieked at every move.

Del had seen a couple guys injured in the service, though none in a situation as unique as this. "Okay, Walter, I'm going to pull your leg up. I don't see any alternative. So try to take as much weight off it as you can. Ready?" Walter nodded. "One-two-three!"

Del pulled and heard Walter gasp, but he kept the pressure on and the leg came up, with a small splinter forced through Walter's calf. Blood stained his sock and Walter was pale. Del did his best to pick up Walter, but he bumped him or jostled him with every step. Midway down the steps, Walter broke free. He limped down, falling the last step. "Meet me at the car," he said through clenched teeth. Trying to run on one leg, he dripped blood on the steps as he took the flight in two leaps. "Oh shit!" he cried out as he hobbled across the front room and out the door.

Sitting in the back of Del's Rambler, Walter lay back and took deep breaths. "Okay, man, we'll have you in the emergency room in five minutes," Del promised, getting his keys out.

"Did anyone get the box?" Walter asked. "I'm not leaving without the box."

"All right, all right, I'll be right back," Beth said, dashing back inside the house.

She stepped inside again, alone this time, and realized she forgot her flashlight. *Just where I didn't want to be,* she thought, gulping. She climbed the stairs, ascending into deeper darkness. *I should go get the flashlight,* she thought, but thought of Walter bleeding in the back seat. Just get your fanny up there and get back. She tried to pretend she was walking down Main Street at high noon as she retraced their passage back to the front room. The doorway to the attic remained open, with a dark stain of Walter's blood now on the wood. She jumped up the steps and at the top she hesitated just a minute before poking her head into the attic.

It was cold up here. She didn't notice it the first time, with the adrenaline pumping, but an early autumn chill was in the air. Over there, about fifteen feet away, was the Wendts Dairy carton, on its side, with a book flung onto the floorboards, open, some of the pages bent double. It wounded her to see the book in that condition. She got to it, aware of the protests of the flooring. There were two bound volumes, and the box itself was a little heavy. *Leave the box,* she decided.

Creak.

I didn't do that, she knew. "Del?" she called. "Del?"

Creak. Then again, coming from below. *Oh shit,* she whimpered. Looking around, she saw just one tiny window, around the front, facing west, and the car was parked on the north side. *I could kick the window open and scream,* she thought, still standing, waiting, listening. *But what am I screaming about? We searched the house and. . . there was that stink of urine. Pretty fresh smell,* she thought. Tucking the books under her right arm, she slowly returned to the attic steps and stopped.

Creak. Not coming from the room this time, and then again—cre-e-e-e-ak, cre-e-e-e-a-k, and more sounds, but retreating, heading away. Away. She descended the steps, one at a time, thinking to talk loudly, but afraid to make a peep. Peeking out the doorway, the room appeared empty. She got to the next doorway. There might be another creaking sound, but it was from way down the hallway. She was just two steps from the staircase. She leapt at the steps, awkwardly catching the banister in her left hand and scampered down.

She burst out the front door, panting and sweating, stopping when she was most of the way to the sidewalk and looked back. The first floor looked dark through the windows and the second floor was screened by the branches of trees that had grown up around the house. *I know what I heard*, she thought.

"Here you go," she presented the volumes to Walter. "Let's get out of here," she said to Del.

"Did you lock the door?" Walter asked.

"No," Beth said, and Del glanced at the deliberate tone of her voice.

"We'll take care of it," Del said to Walter. "First things first. Nobody's going to break in there."

"My God," said Walter in the back seat a block later. "Oh my God."

"We'll be there in a minute," Del promised. "If I had a siren I could do better."

"No," Walter laughed, a little shrill, "it's not my leg. These books. They're not books. They're diaries. The inside cover. Look at this." He held up one volume, propping the cover open with his thumb.

Beth saw a familiar signature. "Nehemiah Cleary. Mister Good penmanship."

Del tried to look at the signature while watching traffic. "I can't see it. I can't see it."

"You can see it when we get to the hospital," Beth promised, reminding herself, not for the first time, of her mother.

By the time they pulled up to the ER entrance, Walter was going into shock and Del's back seat had a blood stain on its artificial upholstery. "Man, you know how hard it is to sell a car with blood on it?" Del pretended to complain. "And you're not even famous." The splinter completely pierced Walter's leg, sticking out the other side. It looked gruesome. Walter looked pale and close to fainting.

"Walter, Walter, you hear me?" said Beth. Walter looked her way. "Stay awake, okay?" In the hope that teasing would rouse him, she asked, "you sure you don't want to just get some peroxide on it?"

"Why don't I just park out front and we can walk in?" Del suggested as they parked by the ER doors. Walter's eyes were half-closed and his lips moved but he wasn't speaking.

They helped him out. A nurse saw them and fetched a gurney. They helped her get Walter on and watched Walter disappear into an examining room.

"I guess we can go back and lock the door now," Del said. "And read the diary."

"You drive us back, I'll start reading," said Beth.

Del locked the front door and Beth said nothing, preferring to read Nehemiah's tale. "He was a Loyalist. His parents were Loyalists too," she reported.

"Loyalist?" Del said. "So was he on the British side at Queenston?"

"No," said Beth. "He was on the American side, because he came from what would be Niagara Falls, New York. His parents moved here when the area was British. Then the border moved but they stayed."

"Why would he join the American side, though?" Del wondered. "If he—"

"I'm only about ten pages in, but he was twenty and he sounds like he was just desperate to get away from home," she said. "It was easier to join the New York militia, since he was in New York."

"Just seems bizarre," Del said. "So desperate to get away that he joins the nearest army to fight in a war, even though it's not the side he wants to be on. I'm just thinking of guys trying to stay out of the army to stay out of Nam. Timing is everything."

"Yea, being in the right place at the right time. Or the wrong time." Beth buried her face conspicuously in the diary, and let a couple of Del's emptier comments go by without response. It was a Tuesday, just one in the afternoon of their day off, and they went back to Del's apartment. Beth marched in and parked on his uncomfortable sofa and opened the diary and continued reading.

He remembered the other volume in the car. He retrieved it, and began reading June Lockwood's story.

"There are pages missing," Beth said a few minutes later. "Augustus Porter was not a saint. He's delivering these decrepit muskets to the militia. Nehemiah has gone to find his captain, and there's a page torn out. Who would tear a page out?"

Del, thinking of the house and the fireplaces, said, "maybe someone was using it to start a fire? There are other uses for paper I'd rather not go into."

Beth frowned. "Yea, but these were in a box in the attic. Whoever's living in that house isn't keeping these books in the attic for firestarter. Or toilet paper."

"What do you mean 'whoever's living in that house'? Did you see someone?" Del asked.

Beth explained the sounds. "I didn't' see anything or anyone, but I know I heard something or someone moving away."

He nodded. "Well, probably some tramp is using it for shelter. And we probably surprised him. But I'm glad you mentioned it." He thumbed through June's diary. "This one's by someone named June Lockwood. She moved in during the Civil War and stayed until she died."

Beth looked up at him, confused. "June Lockwood? Who is June Lockwood?" She thumbed through her book and saw a gap in the narrative, then a change in handwriting. And there were sheets of paper stuck at the end, almost falling out. "Okay, Nehemiah's part stops about here," she held an inch of pages together, "and who is this now?" The room was silent as she skimmed a page. "Someone named Sawyer Jackson." She looked at him with the light of discovery in her eyes. "My God, Del, these are all written by people who lived in the house. It's a history of the house."

Del raised his eyebrows. "Cool."

It was lunchtime at the Red Coach Inn, from whose front windows one could see the rapids and hear the falls. "Good afternoon, Mr. Mayor, Mr. Medina, Mr. Siegler," the maitre'd greeted the city's political triumvirate. "Your table is waiting." He led them to a generous table in the front, set for four.

Lackey's eyes lit up as they walked by the dessert cart. "Save some room for the chocolate cake, Mort," he reminded the city manager.

Siegler smiled. "I'm trying to drop fifteen pounds, Dent. I'm trying to get into a thirty-four waist again."

Angelo Medina took the seat furthest from the door, facing it. "I spoke with Joe Spallino yesterday, and he should be here. Did you bring the papers, Mort?"

Siegler pulled out a thick, tri-folded document from his inside suit coat pocket. "Of course, never travel without paperwork. And you talked with him about the dollar figures?"

Medina nodded. "Yes. He wouldn't commit to any particular offer, but agreed to meeting. We generally agreed that we wanted to buy the property and he wanted to sell it to us. It's just going to be a matter of money."

Lackey, in a brown suit that fit him a big snugly, couldn't resist a jab. "When isn't it a matter of money?"

"Can I get anyone a drink?" Their waiter, a young man with hair parted in the middle and tied tightly behind, appeared.

Lackey gave him a flash of disgust for his long hair. "I'm feeling like a martini."

"Seltzer for me," said Siegler.

"Martini," said Medina, then held up his hand. "No, make mine a Seagrams, straight-up." He did like martinis, but not after Lackey ordered one.

They were trying to count how many properties had been cleared so far when Joe Spallino arrived. He was jovial, knowing that his investment was about to pay off. "Martini for me, Joey," he said to the waiter. "Dent, Mort, Angelo, good to see you." Handshakes all around. "Did we order lunch yet?"

"Not yet, Joe," said Lackey, smiling, "but you sound like you're hungry, so you start us off."

"Steak, please, rare, with baked potato and sour cream," said Spallino.

"That sounds good," said Lackey, "make mine the same."

"I'll take the fish," said Siegler. "Broiled, not fried."

"Fish is healthy food," said Medina, kidding the city manager, "broiled or fried, what's the difference. I'll do the steak, but no baked potato."

"Steak fries?" offered the waiter.

"Yeah," said Medina. He'd just had his suit tailored and it felt good.

"So, Joe, do we want to talk before we tear into the red meat or after?" asked Lackey.

Spallino laughed politely. "Well, gentlemen," he addressed them all, "I spoke with Angelo yesterday, as I'm sure he told you. This is about the property on Third Street that the urban renewal program needs to clear. It's an old house, falling apart. I am happy to sell it to you. But I'm a businessman and I can't let go of equity or I am denied entry into heaven."

More laughter. "We understand," said Medina. "I guess the delicate issue here is just how much equity you feel you have in the property, Joe." He took a swallow of scotch. "We know what you paid for the lot, as it's a public record. We're prepared to double that, which gives you a handsome profit."

"Seven thousand?" Joe said the number. The mayor and city manager nodded and Mort began reaching for the papers. "Normally, that would be a generous offer, Angelo, and I respect that you're doing the city's business, and you need to come in under budget if you can. But I bought the property on spec, and I have to tell you I can't let it go for under twenty-five thousand."

Mouths hung open. "Twenty-five thousand?" Lackey repeated. "You strike oil there, Joe? There's not a property in that neighborhood worth that." His anger flaring in spite of his smile, he asked in a softer tone, "you pull that number out of your ass?"

Mort leaned forward with his benign, accountant's smile. "Gentlemen, we're all businessmen here, and at the end of this meeting we all want the same ending. Joe, we all know you don't intend to do anything with that land." He took a sip of seltzer to relief the bubble of indigestion forming. He burped lightly. "You bought it to sell to us. We're buying, but we're not made of money."

Angelo stepped in. "Joe, just to be sure we're all working from the same deck, you know that if we can't come to an understanding here, today, that we," he indicated the city leaders, "have to go back after this lunch and call the lawyers, and begin condemnation proceedings. We take it by eminent domain and you'll get maybe four hundred over what you paid for it." He let that sink in for a moment. "Nobody wants to see you in that situation," he added. "We've had some differences in the past, but we all live here and we all want the same thing. So what's your real price?"

Spallino's martini arrived and he took a third of it in one mouthful as the deputy urban renewal director spoke. Eminent domain. "I don't think there's a real or unreal price, Mr. Deputy Director," he added the title to make clear the talks were growing less friendly. "And if you pursue condemnation proceedings I'll make it a point to spend twenty thousand at least on lawyers to slow you down to a crawl." He took another drink. "I know you'll win," he said, conceding the point, "but if you don't win soon, you lose more time than you can afford. So then, I kind of win. So let's get back to numbers, not threats. Twenty-five is what I want. I'll consider going to twenty-two-five, with the understanding that, once you get the big project going, I am on the short list for projects after that."

Lackey smiled, not his 'election smile' but the one he used buying cars. "Well, we're making progress, Joe. And I know I can speak for the others in saying that you are definitely going to be tops on the list for local projects."

Medina cut off the mayor. "Joe, we have a limited budget and a lot of property to acquire. See, the state will build us a new boulevard from the end of the Robert Moses. A new boulevard to go through our new city, bringing all those tourists in with their money. The state will pay for the road, but we have to clear the land for them. And they have a deadline and we have limited funds. I don't think we can go a penny over seventeen."

The food arrived, but nobody touched a fork. "So what are we talking about," asked Mort. "Twenty two for Joe, seventeen for the city. Five thousand dollars isn't enough to create trouble." He reached for the paperwork. "Dent, I can probably do some creative numbers with the accounts, free up some cash. Joe, can we meet in the middle? Twenty thousand?"

Joe was an experienced poker player; inside he was exulting at getting over fifteen thousand. He took another sip of his depleted martini. "I consider everyone at this table a friend, and that kind of money should not get between friends. Twenty thousand will work for me."

They grinned, shook hands, Mort got out the paperwork and scribbled the number on the form and Joe quickly scribbled his name on the right line, as did the others. "Another round over here," Mort ordered. When the drinks came, he raised his seltzer. "A toast, gentlemen, to the city and its visionary leaders and businessmen. We can't lose."

And finally they got to the steaks. And the fish.

Joe Spallino was enjoying a cigar after dinner in his den when his phone rang. "Hello," he answered, gruffly as was his style, but a little happier than usual.

"Mr. Spallino, this is Walter Morrow."

It took Spallino a moment but he remembered. "What can I do for you, Mr. Morrow? Did you get to look in the house?"

"Yesss," Walter said, his voice thick with urgency, hissing like a snake. He was at home, his wounded leg, purple and swollen, closed with several stitches. Parked on his couch, with a half-finished bottle of Strohs on the coffee table before him and cold coffee in two other cups on his end table, he had both volumes in front of him now, and he had read it all twice. After Del and Beth brought over the volumes he'd done nothing but read them. He could barely manage to tear his eyes off the volumes now. He was also a little disoriented from painkillers. "We actually found some papers in the house, with some amazing information. The house is incredibly important to the city. Its history is as rich as any building still standing. I need to talk to you about preserving the house."

Spallino closed his eyes, anticipating an upset geek. "Mr. Morrow, I have some bad news for you. This afternoon I reached a price with the urban renewal agency. They own the house now."

Walter closed his eyes in anticipation of agony. "You sold the house. Do they plan to," he hesitated to say it, then felt embarrassed at the empty air, "demolish it?"

"I believe so. If I hadn't sold it to them, they were going to condemn it. If you have an interest in saving the property, you need to talk to the urban renewal agency."

Walter threw a coffee cup at his wall in anger. "Thanks for letting us look at it," Walter said, his voice hollow, remembering his parents training to be polite. Spallino said he was welcome, goodnight, and the phone went dead in his hands. "Shit."

Del found the letter in his mailbox after work Wednesday night. He took it inside but didn't get around to reading it until he had started dinner. Tearing it open, seeing the seal on top, he knew it wouldn't be good. 'This building has been purchased by the Niagara Falls Urban

Renewal Agency. . . and all leases are forthwith cancelled.' He sighed. *I knew this was going to happen*, he said to his pot of spaghetti, *I've even been expecting it. But now it means I need to find another place to live. What a pain in the ass.*

The bar across the street was empty now, and that morning as Del left for work he saw another demolition crew pull up in front of it. Tonight, on his return, he saw just a pile of broken building. *Fortunately I didn't plant any perennials.* How much money did he have in the bank? He'd saved as much as he could, almost two hundred dollars, knowing he'd have to pay more rent. *I should pick up the* Gazette *tomorrow and see what's available*, he planned. *Nothing down here, unfortunately, nothing where I can walk to the falls.* The old neighborhood was fading fast.

When the spaghetti was done, he wolfed it down as was his custom, and decided that, it being a warm September night, he'd walk around the falls. Beth and Walter and he had read both of the diaries. He knew about June Lockwood, and how she loved to walk around the falls, and it gave him a bond with her to know what they shared. That evening he walked in the fading light to the Hermit's Bath.

"So the water used to pour through here twice as fast," he said. "Twice as high. None of these rocks would be exposed. That would be interesting to see."

"It certainly would," he heard. Turning, he saw Beth.

"I thought you went to see your father," he said.

She joined him on the pathway. "I did. The doctor isn't saying much, but I did a little reading and I'm waiting to hear the word 'cancer.'" She sniffed, took his arm and let him hold her. "Everything is just shit and then you die."

He tried and failed to figure out what to say. Joke? No. Something equally depressing? No. 'I love you'? Maybe. Was he prepared to say it? "I love you," he said, as though it was an offering of crumpled flowers.

She sniffed again. She drew in breath, as if to speak, but walked along in silence.

Oops, he thought, *I've overdone it. Now she's trying to deal with her father's illness and me slobbering my affection on her. Stupid.*

"I think I fell in love with you the night you came to the house in that cardigan. It was so unlike you, but I'd asked you not to wear your fatigue jacket," she said, holding his hand tightly in both of hers.

They kissed, then walked. "Did you see the news? The demonstrations in Washington?" he asked, just making conversation.

"No, I didn't see any news. I was with my father."

"I was talking to Leon today. He got his letter from the army," he said. "He has to report for his pre-induction physical."

"Oh. Does he want to go?" she asked.

"He's like me, doesn't really know what's happening, but it doesn't sound good."

She let her breath out, plans for a speech that she just cancelled. "Let's just walk."

He told her then about his eviction notice. "I knew it was coming. They demolished the place across the street."

She seemed grateful to have something to think about. "How long do you have?" she asked.

"Uh, ninety days, I think." He could have been talking about when his next oil change was due.

"You can get more. You can delay that at least six months, probably more," she insisted.

"Why bother?" he asked. "I can find something else in ninety days. I think. The rental agency only let me sign a month-to-month lease. They said the area was scheduled for demolition, they just didn't know when. Maybe you can help me find a new place?" he suggested, hoping for a safe, new direction for them after tonight's awkwardness.

"We'll find you something," she promised, and then they kissed, and kissed some more, and it developed into an embrace, and then he was feeling aroused and began holding her tightly. The squawk of a police car cruising by, the amplified voice, "take her home, lover-boy," broke their mood.

"You heard the cop," she said, blushing, "take me home, lover-boy."

Lackey was reading a list of property assessments for houses being set up for demolition. It was a Thursday morning, a day without meetings, a rarity. He was sipping coffee and enjoying a rare donut when Marilyn buzzed him. "I have a Walter Morrow here, and he would very much like to speak with you."

"Morrow? He's our local historian, right?" Lackey tucked the assessments in a desk drawer and closed it. "Okay, he's caught me on a quiet day, send him in."

Walter was wearing a tie and an ironed shirt. Lackey met him at the doorway and shook his hand. "Thank you very much for seeing me, Mayor Lackey. I know I didn't have an appointment."

Lackey nodded condescendingly. "Come on in. What can I do for you?"

Walter was carrying his rarely-used briefcase, which he set on a coffee table. He took out the diaries and set them on Lackey's desk. "Would you be so kind as to glance at these for a moment?"

Eyebrows raised, Lackey opened the first one. "Nehemiah Cleary? Should his name mean something to me?"

"He was the son of the builder of the Stone House."

"I see," Lackey said, and his eyebrows dropped and furrowed as they did when he argued over line items in the budget. He patiently flipped through the pages. The handwriting was impossible to read. Here and there a word popped out, 'Porter' and "Lewiston' and 'Van Rensselaer'. He saw the diary changed authors. 'Sawyer Jackson' and more hard to read handwriting. Blinking to ease his eyesight, he looked up at Morrow, who was gazing into a mural of the falls that hung on the wall.

"Can I ask what this is all about?"

Walter explained, getting up periodically and finding sections in the diaries to point out. Going through the years, Walter built a history of the Stone House. "It's without question the oldest house in the city. It has seen the War of 1812, the rise of the Honeymoon era, and the coming of electrical power. June Lockwood edited a newspaper here for years. I did some looking at the *Niagara Gazette* yesterday and they've got a file on her. She was quite the civic figure. And they all lived there. It's like a time machine of the city."

The mayor let the diaries fall shut and leaned back in his leather chair. It was a comfortable seat, one he'd sat through many a political scrap with. Today's was small potatoes given some of what he'd dealt with, but he'd been hoping for a rare, quiet day. "Walter, this is very interesting," he tapped the diary with his manicured fingertip. "Where did you find these?"

"Well, with Joe Spallino's permission, we went through the house a week ago and dug around. I found these in the attic." He almost added his war wound story, but it would be a distraction.

"Really," Lackey said, feigning interest. He looked at Walter. There was a hint of the puppy-dog in him. He was a big guy, but he had puppy-dog eyes. He was soft. Soft and useless. "Walter, this doesn't change anything."

Walter walked a fine line, a tightrope between respect for the mayor, for his own civil service position, and on the other hand the power, the burning flame of his convictions. Under it all was the fact that Lackey on more than one occasion piped up that the anti-war protestors were communists, unpatriotic punks; Walter's politics were decidedly to the left. "The Stone House is the most important building in the South End. If we demolish it, we demolish our history."

Lackey shook his head. "I'm not happy about it, but this city needs to find a tax base, one that mixes tourism and industry. Monuments are wonderful, for tourists, but this one's really in a bad place. And," he opened the first diary, "did you say Cleary's family were Loyalists?" Walter nodded. "Loyalism doesn't swing a lot of interest these days, y'know. They were the losers. People aren't coming a hundred or five hundred miles to see a monument to Loyalists."

"But—"

"Sir?" It was Marilyn on the intercom. "Call for you, from Mr. Medina. He wants to hold a special meeting to approve more properties? Says the deadline is getting close."

"Okay," Lackey said. Picking up the diaries, he handed them to Walter. "Thanks for bringing these by, Walter, but it's too late. We need the land more than we need the stories." He stood to shake hands. "I need to take this call. Can you see yourself out?"

Stunned by his sudden and complete failure, having indulged in a hope of success, Walter nodded, and put the diaries in his briefcase and walked to the door, hearing Lackey pick up the phone, "Angelo, how are you," with his deepest chuckle.

She woke up while he was showering and she seemed a little quiet, maybe embarrassed, mumbling 'good morning' and collecting her clothes. "I have to run home for a change," she said, pulling on her shoes, "I'll call you later, okay?"

"Sure," he said. They kissed quickly before she bolted out the door. Maybe she's not a morning talker, he thought. Maybe she doesn't do this very often herself.

"Good morning, Sergeant," Sonny greeted him as he arrived in the yard. Anymore there were a dozen crews working, and they got called up and assigned buildings. The yard had a half dozen bulldozers, a dozen trucks, a fully mobilized army of destruction. "You smiling a little brighter today. Yo' girlfriend take pity on you?"

"Good morning, Sergeant," Del answered. He had been a sergeant when he was discharged, and though he hadn't told his bosses the story of his discharge, he told Sonny one day while they were waiting for a welfare couple to get evicted from an apartment. Sonny told him he had a good story. And, incidentally, he'd been a sergeant in Korea before the war ended.

Leon came back with a clipboard with the order for today's destruction. "Anybody know the significance of 626 3rd Street?"

Six-two-six? "I know that address," Del said.

Leon looked dour, something new for him. Most days he took delight in smashing down the old and decrepit, the eyesores. "It's the old Stone House, Del. My old man told me it was the oldest house in the city. And today we're supposed to smash it down."

Del took the clipboard to see the address for himself. "No," Del said. "We can't. My friend, sort of, Walter Morrow. He, and we," he told them, as quickly as he could, what they'd found.

"Call him," said Leon. "Let him know. Just in case." And rather than climb into the truck and fire up the engine with the glee of the big game hunter out to track T-Rex, Leon got in and turned on the radio. "There's a pay phone over at—"

But Del was already jogging to the little convenience store where they bought drinks.

"Hello," said Walter's answering machine, "I'm at home, recuperating. You can leave a message and –" Del pressed the receiver down to end the call. What was Walter's home number? He dialed the Reference Desk.

Beth answered. "Niagara Falls Public Library. Can I help you?"

"You've only been at work ten minutes and you already sound tired," he teased in a gentle tone.

"Hi," she answered, her voice switching from officious to happy. "Aren't you supposed to be bulldozing a house somewhere?"

"That's the problem," Del said, and explained.

"Good God, no!" she said in alarm, then thought to look around for patrons. "Walter's home today. I guess he's a lousy patient. He's supposed to stay off his leg, but he keeps hobbling around and the wound got infected. Did he tell you he talked to Mayor Lackey?"

"Lackey?" Del was impressed. "Wow. How did that go?"

"Well, based on what you're telling me now, not well."

"Do you have his home number? Can you call him and at least tell him it's," Del found his voice fading a little, as though he were announcing the death of a family member, "it's D-Day."

"Sure. Uh, drive slow," she said. "Take the scenic route."

"I'll go by way of Miami," he said, and they chuckled without energy. "I'll talk to you later," he finished in a hushed tone. He hung up the receiver, turned and looked across the expanse of pavement, broken up by the rails. Looking left, then right, he saw vacant lots and the remaining buildings, and he could hear the diesel motors of the demolition crews rumbling like thunder coming. He liked this job. He liked working with the equipment, he liked being outdoors. He'd come to enjoy pulling down decrepit, abandoned buildings and replacing them with open space and blue sky. He didn't even mind having to apartment hunt. But this morning he felt a persistent sadness that ate at his breakfast. Like getting the telegram, in his barracks in West Germany, that his parents had both passed away from monoxide, his father starting up the car on a cold day, neglecting to open the garage door, and going back to the kitchen and forgetting the car was running.

He wasn't the crying type, he hadn't cried in West Germany and he felt the thought of crying now would be foolish, and embarrassing in front of Leon and Sonny. But he walked back slowly, a gusting wind suddenly at his back, pushing through his fatigue jacket.

"Ready to roll?" Leon asked from the truck cab.

Del got in the passenger side and pulled the door shut. "Go slow, will you?"

Leon looked at him. "You all right? This building's got you bummed out, doesn't it?" Del nodded. Sonny, driving the other truck that pulled the bulldozer, honked his horn at their delay. Leon waved him to go on, and Sonny's truck rolled past them, slowly, the weight of the dozer thumping hard as the trailer rolled over rails and potholes.

"Let's roll," Del said. "Sooner we get this over with," he started, but didn't finish.

At Walter's insistence, Beth left the circulation desk in the care of a student assistant and picked him up, then drove him the five blocks to the stone house. They got there ahead of the wreckers. Down the street they saw the enemy coming. Walter finally used the crutch the hospital lent him and Beth helped him climb out of the car and onto the sidewalk, where he sat in front of the Stone House. "Non-violent protest," he called to Beth and waved her over. "Two is better than one," he said, tugging her down.

She hesitated, then knelt and sat. "I hope this doesn't get on the news," she said, thinking of her father in the hospital, watching TV and seeing her. "Should we link arms or something? I'm new to this."

"No need," said Walter, "but I should warn you I called the *Gazette* and WJJL before you got to my house. We should get some press coverage."

Del saw them first and he smiled. Then Sonny saw them and frowned, his universal reaction to white people behaving oddly. Then Leon saw them. "What the fuck is that?" he asked.

"That's Walter Morrow, he's the local history expert at the library," Del pointed, "and that's my girlfriend."

The truck pulled up and stopped. "What's this all about?" Leon asked with a smile, climbing down from the truck.

"This house is the oldest one in Niagara Falls. It's a cornerstone of local history, and we can't let you demolish it," Walter said. "We're prepared to stay here until you drag that bulldozer away."

"O-kay," said Leon, and he got back in the truck. Sonny was finding some Motown on the radio, settling in for another siege. "Nickie?" Leon called on the radio. "This is Leon. Nickie, we got a problem."

"Nickie here. What's your problem, Leon?"

"We've got protestors."

Del turned off his truck and joined them. "Whose idea was this?" he asked. He wasn't sure he was amused. He wasn't angry, but he was a little embarrassed. Beth held out her hand, and when he took it she gently pulled him down next to her.

"It's both of our ideas," she said, which wasn't at all true, but she liked Walter and somehow this was becoming the most important moment she'd had, and might ever have. It wasn't a march of thousands, with police and violence hovering nearby, it wasn't the messy business of war and protesting war. It was an old house, one with far more history than anyone could have guessed, and maybe they could prevent the bulldozer from destroying it. It wasn't her idea, but she liked it the more she thought about it. "Sit down next to me?" she asked.

Remembering his job interview, remembering the low tolerance his employer had for demonstrations, for nonviolent protest, he thought, this could cost me my job. She looked up at him in a needy way that cut right through him. He grunted a little as he knelt to rest his butt on the curb. "I might lose my job over this," he said, like it was last week's news

"Same here," Beth said. "I was thinking about you losing your apartment. My father's in the hospital, probably for a while. You could move in."

"I don't want your father's room," he said as nicely as he could.

"I wasn't talking about my father's room," she said, blushing even as she tried a come-hither look. "Do you find this sexy or stupid?" she asked softly.

"Little of both, but keep working on it."

"Guys?" It was Walter. "This is a sit-in, not a love-in. Oh wow!" They looked up. "It's the news guy."

The news guy trotted up from a car with WJJL painted on the side. "Tom Virgo, WJJL *News*," said Tom. "Which one of you is Walter Morrow?"

Walter raised his hand. "What happened to your leg?" asked Tom.

He explained. "And who are these folks?"

"I'm a librarian, with the public library," said Beth, her voice a whisper in the presence of the microphone.

"I'm Delbert Nichols, I'm supposed to be demolishing this building."

said Del with a wry smile.

"Walter, you left a message that said you'd found a priceless historical document," Virgo said. "Could you explain?"

Walter was sitting on his briefcase, it being softer than the concrete. He got it out from under him and retrieved the diaries. "These were written by the people who lived in this house," he pointed behind him with his thumb. "Starting with a Loyalist named Nehemiah Cleary," and he opened the front cover of the first volume to display Nehemiah's name. "It also proves that this is the oldest house in the city. And it would be a sin against history to demolish it."

Virgo was holding the microphone to Walter's mouth during his speech. Now he turned to Del. Sticking the mike in his face, Tom asked Del, "as the guy supposed to demolish it, what do you think?"

Del's voice choked when the mike hovered in front of it. "I think he's right," he got out.

"So local historian Walter Morrow has initiated a sit-in on the front steps of the old Stone House," Virgo narrated for his audience, "in which he is joined by local librarian," he paused, turned to her, cupping the mike and whispered 'your name?', then spoke for his audience again, "local librarian Beth Reuther, and demolition man Delbert Nichols. Nobody wants this house demolished. Nobody," Virgo paused for emphasis, "except the city."

Drawing a finger across his neck, Virgo smiled. "Perfect," he said. "Guys, that was great. Now I'm going to hunt down Mayor Lackey and get his reaction."

"We'd be interested in hearing it ourselves," Beth said. "Did anyone think to bring any food?"

The *Gazette* sent over a stringer to interview them. "But if the city needs to rebuild itself, aren't you standing in the path of progress?" she asked in a kindly voice.

"The city can rebuild itself, but if it doesn't preserve its history it runs the risk of forgetting its past," Walter said, a line he was cribbing from a forgotten source read in his college days. "Do you remember what happened to the old stone chimney?"

The reporter smiled. "Do I? Be grateful Joe Novak isn't here. So, Mr. Morrow, do you believe your sit-in will prevent the city demolishing the house?"

"That's our hope," Walter answered.

About that time a police car rolled up. It approached quietly, but turned on its lights and siren when it stopped. The sound seized control of everyone for a moment. Del and Beth both stood up and stared as one cruiser came to a stop five feet from them.

A cop with ample gut and a gray flattop haircut got out, put on his hat, and strolled over. "Good afternoon, folks," he began, "my name is Sergeant Fiske. I was told there was a disturbance going on here. I'm guessing you folks are the disturbance. What's going on?" He was businesslike, neither angry nor amused.

"We're trying to prevent demolition of this house," said Walter, his voice now subdued in the presence of police.

"Is it your house?" asked Sergeant Fiske. Walter shook his head. "Do you know who owns it?"

"Niagara Falls Urban Renewal Agency owns it," Del volunteered, holding out the clipboard with the demolition orders on it.

"And you are?" asked Fiske. Del explained. "And you're part of this, uh, demonstration?" Del nodded. "Okay," Fiske said, one hand pushing up on his cap. "And you are?" he asked Beth. She answered. "I see. And who are you again?" he asked Walter. Once he'd gathered all their names, Fiske didn't look happy, nor angry, just confused. "Are you the only member of the demolition crew here today?"

"No," Del said. "Leon? Sonny? Could you come over?"

His coworkers had debated joining Del, but chose to sit in the truck cab and listen to the radio. They climbed out. "Gentlemen, your names?" Fiske gathered more information. "Are you prepared to demolish the house?" he asked Leon.

"Not while Del is sitting in front of it, no," said Leon, smiling.

"Okay," said Fiske, sounding pleased. He looked at the historian, the librarian, the demolition guy, and the house, and walked back to his car. Sitting down behind the wheel, Fiske took his radio in hand and began a conversation with his shift supervisor.

A few minutes later Nickie arrived in another truck. He was, by far, the unhappiest visitor of the day. "Nichols! What the fuck—" He saw Beth and said, "Sorry. What the heck is going on?"

Up until now Del had been enjoying the early October sunshine, the media and the befuddled cop, and Beth sitting next to him in a cotton dress. Now he looked punished. "Hey, Nick. I, uh," he stood, looked at the house behind him. "This is the house you sent us to demolish today. And the other day we," he indicated his companions, "went inside and did some looking around. We found some diaries. They prove the house is the oldest in the city. I," he hesitated, "I can't wreck this house. It should be a museum or something. Wrecking this place is wrong."

Nick saw Leon and Sonny, now skulking in the truck. Whistling and waving his hand, he summoned them. "Okay, boys, you weren't going to demolish the house because Del parked his ass in front of it, but now Del is going to move his ass," Nick looked at Del with the full force of his dark eyes, "because if he doesn't he's fucking fired." He let it out, including the 'fuck' in front of Beth, so Del would know he meant business.

Nobody spoke. Nobody breathed. Then Leon said, in a gentle, conversational tone, "Nick, even if Del moves, what about these other two?"

"Not a problem," Nick said. "Officer?"

Fiske, who had finished his talk with his supervisor and was meditating on his options, got out of his car, a bit reluctantly. "Sergeant Fiske," he introduced himself. "And you are?"

"I run the demolition crew and I'm ordering my man to get his ass out of the way. And when he does that, if these two don't follow him, arrest them!" Nick ordered.

Beth held Del's hand tightly. Walter, the only one still sitting, looked up. "I'm injured," he explained.

"Arrest them," Nick said.

Hostages for History

WJJL led with the story on the noon news, and Virgo's deep, resonant voice gave the incident even more drama. "A sit-in demonstration has erupted at the site of the old stone house on Third Street, reputed to be the oldest house in the city. Marked for demolition, the protest began with a sit-in by local historian Walter Morrow, librarian Beth Reuther, and oddly enough, some of the crew ordered to demolish it." "This is the city's history," Walter was heard pleading, "come down and see the diary for yourselves!"

Joe Novak was covering for the copy editor when the *Gazette* reporter handed in her copy. He checked column length, then read the all-important opening sentence. 'Protestors hostile to downtown urban renewal did their best to interfere by occupying an abandoned and collapsing building." Joe's forehead wrinkled in surprise. He glanced at the reporter, then read on. 'Local historian Walter Morrow and public librarian Betty Rooter were among the protestors. Costs from the delay to the Urban Renewal Agency's interrupted schedule were estimated at ten thousand dollars'. He frowned. Four paragraphs later, after quotes from Mayor Lackey and the police, the final sentence read: 'A diary, allegedly written by early settlers, was found in the house.'

"Is this really all there is to this?" asked Novak, who had heard WJJL's story. "Did you get a photo?"

The reporter, a part-timer who would never make full-time, glanced at her watch. "I forgot my camera. If you're interested, go talk to them yourself. They're still there." She was late for an interview for a real job, she didn't have time to do any follow-up.

He got his jacket and picked up a spare camera and told the receptionist, "going for a walk, over to the big sit-in."

"The what?"

Leon had picked up the first diary, read and turned pages reverently, and now he was as lost in its story as was Walter. "No way do I drive a bulldozer into this building," he said, sitting now in the weeds next to Walter.

"See?" Walter smiled, pointing at Leon. "Now we just need to do this with every member of the urban renewal board."

"Good luck," said Del. "Leon, by joining the demonstration you probably just kissed your job good-bye."

Leon, without looking up, said, "I just got my pre-induction paperwork, so either way I probably have to kiss this job good-bye," and kept reading.

A light rain began falling. It would make more sense later on, when they looked back on how it happened, to say it started because it rained. Del had the key, and he opened the front door.

Seeing the protestors go in the house, to Fiske's mind the wrong outcome, he began walking towards them as fast as he could without breaking into a trot, which he considered beneath his dignity. If he caught them, he'd have to arrest them, which was another reason he let them outrun him.

Del relocked the door from the inside and they retreated from it. Walter bumped into the banister and bruised his wound. "Ouwww," he gasped, dropping on the first step, leaning against the wall and gasping as stabs of pain shot up his leg.

"You all right?" Leon asked Walter. He nodded through clenched teeth.

"Open the door," Fiske said.

"Del?" Beth called, her anxiety rising by the moment, her eyes on the door.

He stood next to her, but she didn't want to be hugged, so he tried to hold her hand, but she pulled away. He settled for standing next to her.

"Think he'll break the door down?" Walter asked, looking at all of them.

Del touched his lips with his upright index finger—shhhh—and Beth burst into hysterical laughter. "He saw us run in here." Then Fiske appeared in the window, shading his eyes, looking in. She waved in a slight way. She could easily lose her job over this. She'd left the circulation desk to a clerk—which wasn't so bad—to join a protest against the city's urban renewal program, which was professional suicide. *Walter was a little safer*, she thought, but not that much. It helped that he was male. *They can type up a list of replacement librarians in two minutes,* she fretted. That she was finally having an adventure dawned on her, but she couldn't get past her job security.

Leon was looking out the other window. "Nickie's kicking the bulldozer," he reported with a touch of mirth in his voice.

Beth was well into a panic attack. This was an impulsive decision and she had little history of impulsive action and this wasn't a good start. To make a bad situation worse, she was accustomed to her ten o'clock snack and it was noon and she was starving. "Anyone got anything to eat?" she asked, feeling her blood sugar plummet.

Walter's thigh throbbed. Shots of pain were traveling up his side, draining his energy. Outside, the siren of an arriving ambulance rose in volume. The diaries were tucked into Walter's briefcase, which he kept one hand on. "We should barricade the door," he said.

"With what?" Leon asked, looking around. "There's no furniture. We've got no tools. What do we build a barricade with?"

"We don't need to barricade it yet," said Del. He tugged on the handle. Beth backed into the entry to the dining room, looking as though certain death was outside the front door. He smiled at her and said, "I just remembered I have a bag of cookies in my truck."

"What are you waiting for?"

The rain built into a good downpour, one they'd be feeling inside the house soon. Del went out the basement door, crept around to the front, climbed into the cab of his truck and reached behind the seat. Feeling the cookies, and a crowbar and hammer he kept there, he grabbed all three and was on his way back in when Fiske spotted him and called him over. "Yes sir?" Del answered, holding the tools and cookies and feeling foolish as he got drenched.

"That fellow with the bad leg," Fiske said, "he's inside?" Del nodded. "The ambulance is here for him. And I spoke with my superiors, and I'm sure you know you have to leave. You ready to come out?"

"I don't know. Let me go in and ask them," Del suggested.

Fiske gave him a look. "I'm not stupid, son. If you guys are refusing to leave, I will figure it out eventually. And if you refuse to leave, I'll have to go in after you, handcuff you and haul you away in the paddy wagon. You have any prior arrests?"

Del shook his head. "No, sir."

"You sound like former army to me," said Fiske, proposing the bond of veterans. "I was in Korea."

"I left the army a few months ago."

"Viet Nam?"

"West Germany."

"You ever in trouble like this before?" Del shook his head. Fiske looked sad and fatherly. "What I don't understand is that you're grown people acting like angry teenagers. This stunt is something I'd expect from kids. You got jobs, you got families and you're otherwise responsible adults. You don't belong in a situation like this."

"I don't really have any family," Del said softly. "And when I locked us inside I pretty much lost my job."

"You know what I mean," argued Fiske. "Guy like you, former army, you could be on the force if you wanted. Instead, here I am, this close to arresting you. That's crazy."

Del nodded. *Would they take me with my bad paper? Maybe.*

"Well, go ahead and get out of the rain. I don't have enough room in my car for all of you anyway, so I'm going to call for backup." He looked to the north, towards the police station. "They'll be here in about ten minutes. That's when you have to decide if you're coming quiet or," he tried to think of a snappy finish, but couldn't, "or not."

"I understand, sir."

Del went back inside, stumbling a little on his second trip through the dark basement. *What the hell am I doing here? Beth's inside. That'll have to do for now.*

"You got wet?" Beth asked. Del's hair was dripping, and the gray sweatshirt was a darker shade. He handed her the bag of cookies. "Bless you."

"It's raining," said Walter, holding out his hand and catching a drip from the ceiling. "Man, the roof on this place is like, well, a roof that hasn't seen much repair in two centuries."

Del handed Leon the hammer and took the crowbar in both hands. "Officer Fiske told me that the paddy wagon is on its way." He gave the front door another tug. "We now officially need to barricade it. We need to do both doors. I brought these," he indicated the tools. "Let's try to find some loose lumber, with nails still in it."

"Maybe there's some in the basement?" Walter asked. "Otherwise I guess we could start tearing down a wall," he said, looking unhappy. "In order to save the building we had to destroy the building."

Del and Leon went into the basement and, after pulling down many spider webs, found an old coal bin. Pulling it apart carefully to avoid the need for a tetanus shot, Del pried out the broadest boards he could find, and discovered painted letters on the underside. 'Ft Shlosser'. "Did he mean Fort Schlosser?" Looking now for writing, he found another one. 'Cleary House—1795'.

"What's with the names?" Leon asked.

And Del remembered Sawyer Jackson's plan to put up signs to mark the village's historic sites. The paint was faded and Sawyer's penmanship with a brush a little tough to decipher, but that's what it was. "These are actually kind of historical themselves," he said, setting them down. "Let's use the ones without writing."

As they came up the steps to daylight, they heard another siren. "That's probably the backup Officer Fiske called for," guessed Del.

"Backup?" Beth repeated, pacing in the public room, back and forth and pausing to look out the windows. "We require 'backup'? We don't have any guns. I didn't refuse to leave. I wasn't even asked."

"I refused for you," said Del, and he ignored her look. He and Leon fitted a board across the door, and started driving in the ancient nails. "Damn." He tried to drive a square-headed nail into the doorframe, but the nail was bouncing out, so frail was its grip in the old wood. "This isn't going to stop anyone."

Beth sat down a step just below the upper landing, six steps above Walter, as far from them as she could be and still see them, holding her head in her hands, and flinching with each swing of the hammer. She finished off the cookies. "Aren't we supposed to be protecting this house? You're driving nails into it."

Walter twisted around on his perch to face her. "Beth, I'm sorry I bugged you to bring me over. If you want to go you should go. I don't want you to get in trouble—"

"I'm already in trouble, Walter," she snapped. Looking out the window she said anxiously, hopefully, "but if I leave now I might be okay."

Del looked at her. His primary reason for being here was her. If she was leaving, what business did he have here? He thought briefly of his job, wondered if it was beyond saving. "Going out front means certain arrest," he deduced. "Why don't we try sneaking out the kitchen door," he suggested.

She was angry with herself now. *You always made your years in Boston sound like your years on the Paris Barricades. Here's your first real chance to defend a barricade and look at you.* She couldn't help it. The thought of repercussions that could affect her job was suffocating. She was learning some limits today. "Okay," she said, breathing easier, anxiety easing. "If I get back before Mary Lou goes to lunch, nobody has to know I was here."

Del looked at Walter. Despite the man's obvious pain, Del couldn't get past Beth's fear and Walter as the cause. Looking at his co-worker, "Leon, I'm going to take Beth back. You want to come out with me? The cop's a veteran, and he knows I am too. If we walk away I bet there won't be any trouble."

"What about Walter?" Leon indicated Walter.

"There's an ambulance out there for you," Del said to Walter brusquely.

"I'm not leaving," Walter grumped.

"Suit yourself." Del climbed the steps to Beth, and she got up and hugged him.

Leon stayed at the door, trying to get another old nail into the wood. "Well, I'm probably fired too," he looked at Walter, "and there's nothing out there for me but my pending army physical, so if it's all right with you, Walter, I'd like to look some more at these diaries."

"It's your call," Del said. "Nail in the back door and the basement door, too. As well as you can."

The house's moldy smell was much stronger with fresh rain leaking down through the walls and dripping from the ceilings. The kitchen door knob turned stiffly. He tugged hard on it and the door opened slowly, scraping on the floor. Putting some muscle into it, they got it open enough for Beth to squeeze out.

A burst of light from a flash blinded her. "Hi, I'm Joe Novak, from the *Gazette*," said the waiting reporter. "I thought I might see you here." He held up his camera and fired off another photo of them together. "Which one of the protestors are you?"

She blinked her eyes. Now there was a photo of her in the house, as a protestor. "Would you be willing to burn that picture to save my job?" she asked Joe.

"Are you the librarian?" the reporter asked.

It's because I'm a woman, right? She nodded. "How do you spell your last name?"

"Reuther. R-e-u-t-he-r," she said, leaning against the door in defeat.

"Not Rooter?" He wrote it down. "Well, I could burn this picture, Ms. Reuther, but WJJL already broke the story, and you were mentioned by name."

She closed her eyes in defeat. She'd forgotten about that radio reporter. "Shit," she said softly.

"I think you'll find that you might be safer with the picture. It would look bad for the city to fire you because you took part in a protest."

"Obviously you don't work for this city. I'm supposed to be at work right now," she added.

"Like I said, 'JJL already identified you by name," he said.

She shrugged, acquiescing.

"And you are?" the reporter asked Del.

"I'm with the demolition crew," Del said, and spelled his name.

They stood in the doorway, still sheltered from the rain, as the reporter, unsheltered, tried to protect the scribbles on his pad. "Why don't you come inside?" she suggested.

Del stood his ground a minute, but she looked at him and smiled, and he knew she'd regained her composure. She was staying, so he was staying. They stepped back from the doorway and let him into the kitchen.

Looking around, Joe thumbed the latch on his camera to advance the film. "So this is the old Stone House. Kind of a wreck, isn't it?"

"It sure is," she said. At least her blood sugar was better. "Let me introduce you to the rest of our outlaw band." She smiled at her joke as they led Joe into the front room.

A bullhorn not five feet from the front door erupted and made them jump. "This is Sergeant Fiske. I'm ordering you to leave the premises. This is your last chance to leave without being arrested for trespassing." His distorted voice echoed off the front of the house. "I'm counting down from ten." Fiske felt cold rainwater running down his neck, and felt dampness invading his shoes. Two officers waited behind him with extra handcuffs.

"Anybody wants to leave, now is definitely the time," Walter said. "I'm staying, but don't stay on my account."

"Trust us, Walter, we're not," said Beth.

"Hey, Walter, I heard I might find you in here," Joe greeted the historian with a smile and handshake.

"Hey, Joe." Walter's spirits skyrocketed when he saw Joe. He knew him from being the *Gazette*'s consultant when questions of history arose in the press room."

"Is this the famous diary? Could I see?"

"Absolutely," Leon handed him the first volume. "You should start with this one."

Joe began reading. He turned the pages slowly, taking his time with the faded handwriting. Rain dripped on his jacket, but he didn't seem to notice.

"It's really cool, isn't it?" Walter asked him.

Joe nodded, to be polite, but kept reading.

"Later on, a tour guide named Sawyer Jackson takes over," Walter said, "and this diary is by a woman reporter named Lockwood."

Joe nodded but never took his eyes off the diary.

"One." Fiske finished, like he was counting inventory in a storeroom. "One," he said without the bullhorn, sounding disappointed. He blinked away rain as he raised the horn again, "as of now, you are all to consider yourselves under arrest for trespassing."

"You want us to break the door down?" asked Officer Minucci. He was a powerfully built fellow, new to the force. Officer Bundy, by comparison, was slender and wore black rimmed glasses, looking more the scholar than the authority figure.

"Don't do anything," ordered Fiske. "This is a historic house. I don't want to break the door down." He set the bullhorn in the front seat of his car. The rain was soaking through his hat but he hated the way plastic looked on it. He hated protestors as a rule too, when they were youngsters with long hair, boiling over with contempt and disrespect for his uniform. He felt he was sweeping vermin off the street locking them up. But he couldn't hate the people in the house.

"So what am I waiting for?" asked the ambulance driver.

"Hold your horses," said Fiske, angry. Now what? His supervisor had told him to 'disperse them without incident, if possible', to break up the protest without letting something larger erupt. But he had heard WJJL's news story, and by the time he finished his countdown a crowd was growing. "Get the sawhorses out of your trunks, set up a perimeter to keep the crowd back," he ordered.

The officers set up the white and black sawhorses, POLICE DEPART-MENT—STAY BACK painted on in red. Behind it, the crowd gathered. Some were teenagers wandering by. Some middle-agers and retirees on their way elsewhere stopped and waited to see if anyone got arrested. And in ones and twos, people who'd heard the news arrived.

"What're they doing?" asked a teenager. His hair fell to his shoulders and needed washing. His denim jacket sported an American flag, sewn on upside down, and a peace symbol etched over it.

"See the bulldozer?" said an elderly woman, bundled up in a light canvas windbreaker with a white beauty parlor beehive under a clear plastic rain bonnet. She was smiling. "The demolition crew refused to demolish the house."

"Why? It's a dump."

"It's the oldest house in the city," said the woman. "It's been around longer than me, that's for sure. I hope they leave it alone. They're tearing down everything."

The teenager shrugged. He wanted to see the cops drag people out in handcuffs, wanted to see them resist arrest, wanted to see a fight break out, maybe someone wave the Viet Cong banner. Something interesting. Nothing interesting ever happened in the falls.

"Folks, we're having a little demonstration here," Bundy said, trying in vain to disperse them, "nothing very interesting. It's raining out, I suggest you go somewhere dry."

A few people did, but more took their place behind the sawhorses.

"Son of a BITCH!" Lackey erupted. WJJL's story, followed by Walter's call for pilgrims, was the lead story for the lunch hour news. "Protest? Sit-in? This isn't goddamn Berkeley!" He called the chief of police and got the latest. "So there's Walter Morrow, two guys from the demolition crew, a librarian, and Joe Novak from the *Gazette*? And they're refusing to come out? They've nailed the doors shut? Don't you guys have any tools of your own?" he asked. "It's city property. It's been condemned. I want them out in twenty minutes."

I'm going down there and count down the minutes myself, he vowed, and left in just his suit coat.

Marilyn watched him dash out in a huff in just his jacket. *He'll be cold*, she knew. *It's October now*. But she'd heard the news too. *Today*, she thought, *let's let the house win for a change*. She went back to her filing.

The mayor often wore a white cowboy hat and rode a white horse when he led parades. For some citizens, that was what they pictured when they thought of their mayor. When he got out of a plain blue Cadillac, wearing a business suit, not everyone in the growing crowd on Third Street recognized him. The police did; that mane of white hair shone like a beacon. Six other officers in three cruisers had joined Fiske and set up more sawhorses to keep the crowd back. They immediately cleared a path for the mayor.

"Who's in charge?" asked Lackey.

Fiske was still the ranking officer, and he stepped forward. No introductions were necessary, Lackey knew every cop on the force. "I am, sir."

"Okay, Sergeant Fiske, why haven't you forced open the door and arrested them?" Lackey asked.

Good question, thought Fiske. *But you won't like my answer.*

The crowd was growing, three and four deep, craning their necks to see. When they heard 'arrest them', they booed. They booed, the teenagers mooed like cows, and the more solid citizens among them looked angry. "Leave the house up," someone called out. And then the crowd had their chant. "Leave the house up. Leave the house up. Leave the house up. Leave the house up."

"I was told to disperse the crowd if I could, not arrest the protestors," Fiske finally said, taking advantage of the crowd's mood.

Lackey looked around. "Doesn't look like you've accomplished either task, Sergeant." This was one of those public relations crises he loved, like a fighter craved the ring. Though his job description was only part-time, he'd vowed to be a full-timer, and made himself larger than life at every opportunity. "Folks, this is a complicated situation," he called out. Nobody really heard him. "We can't just leave the house up," he tried incorporating their chant.

They misheard him, thought he was on their side now, and chanted louder.

Suppressing a bad word, Lackey gestured for a couple of officers to follow him as he walked to the front door. He was getting rained on. He could put on a hat, but that would cover his hair, which in some ways was his helmet, which he dared not cover going into battle. So, with his hair getting wet, he charged. He yanked on the locked knob. "Don't we have a key for this?" he demanded.

"The guy with the demolition crew has it."

"The one inside? Perfect."

Knocking on the door, he heard someone answer, "hello?"

"This is Mayor Lackey," he said, "and to whom do I have the pleasure of speaking?"

"My name is Leon. I'd rather not give you my last name."

"Well, Leon with-no-last-name, you and your friends are trespassing on city property. If you don't vacate the premises, I've given the police permission to break down this door and arrest you. And then I will know your last name. Do you understand?"

"Yep."

He took an umbrella from a cop. "Leon?" he called. "I'm counting to ten."

Guy Proulx arrived under an umbrella and, sizing up the situation, slid past the sawhorses and headed for the front door and the mayor. "Dent," he greeted the mayor, who smiled but not immediately. "I heard the news," he said. "What's happening?"

"Shouldn't you be teaching the leaders of tomorrow?" Lackey asked mischievously.

"Teacher's conference day," said Proulx, smiling smugly.

"Why does everyone think 'ten' is some magical freaking number?" asked Walter. "I say we stay."

"So you think he's bluffing?" Del asked.

Walter didn't but he nodded.

"You think they'll back off?" Del pressed him. Walter nodded again.

"Walter," Beth found her purse, "you a betting man? You're talking about Mayor Lackey. He's sold his soul to the devil to get urban renewal going. You think us sitting in here will stop him?"

Walter was getting more strong twinges of pain from his leg. He was on a mild painkiller and, checking his watch, it was now after one p.m. and he was due for a pill at noon. He got to his feet and hopped to the nearest window. "Look out there," he said. "We've got supporters."

"Yeah, we've drawn a crowd," Leon said. "Including about a dozen cops."

"And a reporter," said Joe. He looked up from the diary and rubbed his eyes. "I knew this house was old but I had no idea. This diary is dynamite. Can I take this with me?" he asked Walter. Walter looked worried. "I'll take it straight to the *Gazette*. What time is it?" he glanced at his wrist watch. "I think the printers can do a photo-offset print of this today. If they can't, I'll type in as much as I can before crippling arthritis sets in. I'll bring it back tomorrow morning. And we'll publish it."

"You'll publish it? Really?" asked Walter, perking up.

"Really," promised Joe. It was also high time for an objective observer, like himself, the fifth estate, to leave the barricade before getting arrested, which wouldn't do anyone any good. He collected his notepad and his camera, glancing at his notes to be sure he had everything he needed. "I'll go out there and talk to the cops. I know all of them, and Fiske is a pretty good guy. Maybe they'll give us more time. And when I publish some of this," he held the diary, "we might get more people out here. That just might save this place."

"You think so?" asked Beth, skeptical. "What about us? Can we get out?"

Joe looked outside at the waiting demolition equipment. "It would help if you stayed here."

They followed him to the kitchen door. Officer Minucci was now stationed by it. "Coming out," said Joe, and he squeezed his way out the narrow opening.

In the public room, using the hammer gently on the old window frame, Del and Leon pried it up. It moved unevenly, stopping a foot up at an angle. They gathered at the window as Joe came around front.

It was chilly. Joe saw Councilman Proulx in the crowd and felt a little better. It wasn't just Lackey's show now. "Mayor Lackey, Mr. Proulx, Sergeant Fiske," Joe approached them. "What's new?" he tried his usual opening line.

Whatever Joe said, they couldn't hear him in the house. They saw Lackey shaking his head adamantly, then saw Fiske holding up his hand, perhaps appealing for calm. Joe displayed the first diary. Lackey reached for it but Joe casually tucked it inside his jacket. There was more talk. Proulx talked just with Lackey for several minutes.

Then Fiske got on his radio. Nickie got led through the crowd to talk with Fiske and Lackey. Nickie listened calmly, he didn't seem too upset anymore. Lackey held his hands up as if in disgust and walked away. Joe and Fiske and Proulx shook hands and Nickie shrugged. The ambulance driver was sent away.

Joe came to the window. "Proulx talked the mayor into waiting you out. He's assured the mayor that, this being an old house without power or running water or other conveniences, and it being October, you'll be ready to come out soon. You might not even need to keep the front door nailed shut. I'm off to the paper to get as much of this diary in print as I can. I'm also going to write the most heard-rending appeal for the salvation of this house I'm capable of. We publish it and see what happens."

"But we stay inside?" Beth asked, dismayed, "that's part of the deal?"

"Well, the police will have a detail here tonight, technically for your protection. But if they report the house is empty, I fear the worst. Think of yourselves as hostages for history."

"Joe," Beth asked, "can we at least arrange to get some food in here? And some blankets? Some heat?"

"Fiske already thought of it," Joe said. "He's making arrangements. He kind of likes you guys, but he doesn't want you know it."

Then, as the afternoon waned, a long time passed when nothing changed. The rain made the chilly air feel colder. Since the house was built prior to the concept of central heating it had fireplaces in most rooms. Fiske came into the kitchen to talk with them. Looking around for himself, he took in the water damage, the vandalism. "I wondered what it looked like inside here," he told Del. "Somehow I pictured it in perfect shape, even though it's clearly not from the outside. The news said the house is from 1812?"

"At least," said Del. "Want the grand tour?" He walked the officer through the downstairs, and took him upstairs, showing him the attic where they'd found the diaries. They saw their breath in the attic.

"How about we turn on the power and get some space heaters?" Del suggested.

"You sure about that?" Fiske studied an outlet, mounted on the molding, trailing thick, cottony cord. "A hundred and twenty watt heater would probably start a fire. You'd make the mayor very happy," he said, allowing himself a smile. "We've got some chow on the way. And the Red Cross is getting some blankets."

They squeaked their way back to the public room. Fiske knelt in front of the fireplace and looked in, trying to see if the damper was open. "Probably a couple of birds nests up there." He lit a match and they watched the smoke draw up. "Seems to draw. I'll get you some firewood for tonight."

"What if it gets below freezing?" Beth asked.

"Well, according to the weather report it shouldn't. But if it does, you might want to consider giving up," said Fiske. "I'll be back," he promised, going back out the kitchen door. A few minutes passed, and officers Bundy and Minucci delivered armloads of firewood.

The temperature fell into the forties and the sun set. Beth being the only scout in the group, she got a fire started on the second match. The chimney drew well, and the smell of wood smoke was a pleasant change from mildew. They huddled close, crowding each other for heat in the small space, so she built a second fire in the kitchen fireplace. That let her and Del have a fire to themselves while Leon read the second diary by flashlight, annotated by Walter's interruptions.

Hot pizza arrived, with bottles of pop and some hot coffee in a thermos. "The mayor said not to make you comfortable," said Fiske. "So tell him the pizza was cold and the pop was warm." He cracked a half-smile. "I got Seven-up and Coke, I wasn't sure what you preferred. Normally I like a Vernors with pizza." A new cop, his nametag read Quarcini, arrived with piles of blankets. Fiske handed Del a Coleman lantern and three heavy department-issue flashlights. "Ever use one of these?" he held up the lantern. Del shook his head.

"I have, Sergeant," Beth said.

"Okay," Fiske said. "I'll be going home. If you have any problems, you might want to ask your girlfriend," he teased Del. "Corporal Quarcini will be on detail until midnight. I'm not sure who pulls the second shift. All set?"

Beth smiled. *Except for a hot bath, a change of clothes, a television, my warm bed?* Then she thought to ask Fiske to call her father, in the hospital, to explain where she was. *Was that the best course? The police calling?* "Sergeant, could you call my father, tell him where I am? He's at Memorial Hospital. He wouldn't be listening to the radio and I'm not sure he'll read the paper."

"Certainly."

"Thanks, Sergeant."

"Sleep tight."

Lackey drove by late that night. Firelight flickered in the windows of the Stone House, an image more than a century old. A police cruiser was parked in the street, sawhorses lined the sidewalk, but the crowd had dispersed for the evening. The bulldozer and trucks still blockaded the front of the house. He wished he had his trench coat as he stumbled through the weeds to the back door. Stubbing his toe twice, scraping his arm getting through a bush and hearing material tear behind him, his mood dropped from bad to foul. "Corporal Quarcini?"

Quarcini was under a tarp, watching a battery-powered TV. "Mayor Lackey?" He turned off the TV and stood up. "How you doing, sir?"

"Shitty," Lackey said. "They still inside?"

"Yes sir. Most of them."

"Most?"

"We worked out an arrangement for them to come out, one at a time, and use the toilet in the Esso station over there. It's supposed to be demolished but the water's still running. This place doesn't have running water anymore."

Lackey wasn't interested. "Listen to me, and pass this on to the other shift. If they leave the house empty, you call this man," and he gave Quarcini a card with Nickie's number. "Call him whatever the hour, tell him the house is empty. Understand?"

"Yessir."

She woke in the darkness, under a blanket, spooning with Del. A noise—creeeak, creeak. Someone leaving the room. Adrenaline pumping, she reached for the flashlight by her head, found the switch, and aimed the powerful beam at the table.

Three pizza boxes were stacked. There were supposed to be four. "Del," she tapped him gently on his head, "wake up." It took a couple of hard shoves. "Del?"

Flinching from the power of the flashlight, Del covered his eyes. "What?" he asked, very grumpy.

"Someone else is in the house. I heard them a minute ago. And one of the pizza boxes is gone."

Sitting up, mumbling 'what' not as a question but as a statement, he looked around. "Nobody's here."

"Somebody was," she said. "C'mon, we have to look around."

"They took pizza?" Sure enough, there was a box missing. "That was the pepperoni," he whined. "I wanted that for breakfast."

"C'mon," she called him from the hallway.

He tied his shoes on and followed her. They could see their breath in the glare of the flashlight. A few embers were all that was left of the fire. Looking into the rooms, one at a time, they found nothing.

"What's up?" asked Leon, and they both jumped.

"Missing pizza," said Del. Leon looked at him, then Beth. She explained. They explored the first floor, finding nothing. Their footsteps creaked loudly as they climbed the stairs, and Walter called out. "Hunting pizza," Del answered.

In the front room, the one they used to reach the attic, they found the pizza box, empty. "See?" said Beth. "Someone is in here, besides us."

"Like I said before, it's probably just some tramp," said Del. "He saw the pizza and took some."

"He left us alone," Leon pointed out. "Seems pretty harmless."

"Let's go back to bed," Del said, and they trooped back to their fireplaces. Beth got back under the blanket with Del, but she didn't sleep anymore that night.

At dawn, the roar of diesel motors just outside the front window woke them all. First Del's truck was backed away, and then Leon's truck and the bulldozer were driven off. "They're taking away the bulldozer," Walter said. "We've won!"

Nickie was out there, and a couple of guys they didn't know were driving the rigs. The hostages watched from the front windows as Nickie directed the equipment to the abandoned house next door. "Uh-oh," Walter's joy faded. A crane arrived, got into position, and began using its wrecking ball, demolishing the roof and upper story. The hits shook the air and made the panes in the stone house rattle. Nobody slept anymore.

About an hour into that, more equipment arrived, this time a truck and backhoe. The Esso station across the street was its target. First the backhoe went to work, digging up the old storage tanks in the lot. Then a bulldozer was delivered and it started with a tentative shove at the service station.

"That's our bathroom," Beth said. "They're destroying our bathroom."

"Did anyone need to go?" Leon asked.

"There goes the sign," Del said, watching the bulldozer take down the tall aluminum Esso sign pole. The crash made them all flinch.

Joe came by at nine with several cups of coffee and a box of donuts, and lots of newspapers. "Hot food everyone, hot food."

"This is wonderful," Walter said, biting into a glazed donut and savoring the heat from the coffee, "any word from the warden when we can go home?"

"Well, the good news is today's story." Joe distributed copies of the *Gazette.* "Look at the picture. It's above the fold." There was a black and white shot, by Joe, of the bulldozer and trucks barricading the stone house. Under it was an introduction by Joe, followed by two columns of excerpts from Nehemiah's diary.

> *Saving the Past—Joe Novak*
>
> *'Loyalists populated this country before it became part of New York State. Loyalists who loved this country, but didn't feel safe with the rebels. The oldest house in the city, the Stone House on Third Street, was built by one of these Loyalists. As part of the city's urban renewal program, almost every building in the South End has been targeted for destruction. This includes the Stone House. In all fairness, there was no direct proof of the house's age until recently. A diary kept by the builder's son, Nehemiah Cleary, who grew up in the Stone House, was discovered recently by Walter Morrow. Here are some passages. . .'*

"This is good stuff," Walter said.

"Thanks," Joe said, "but I couldn't help noticing that they're demolishing everything around you." Another crash filled the air.

"Including the gas station," said Del.

"Which robs us of our nearest toilet," said Beth. "Did I mention the loss of our toilet? You guys can piddle in the sump in the basement but I need other arrangements, and soon." She was sleepy as well, and though she'd stirred up the embers and fed them fresh wood, the fire wasn't keeping her warm anymore.

"The demolition is keeping the protestors to a minimum," said Joe. "Lackey isn't stupid."

And then they heard more sounds of equipment, and of demolition, from behind the house. From the back they could see the house behind them also being demolished.

"We're surrounded," said Walter. He bumped his leg again, and turned pale from the gut-wrenching pain it delivered.

"Walter?" Leon called him, "you just went white as a sheet. How's your leg?" Walter lay passively on the floor, and as Leon tried to pull up Walter's pant leg, he choked off a scream. "I think he's ready for that ambulance ride."

Watching the ambulance leave, Beth made a decision. "Del?" she said, "I was thinking, I really need to get to work and talk to my supervisor. In hopes of saving my job? But I'd feel awful if they demolish this just because of that. Since you don't have a job anymore. . . "

Leon looked at Del. "They're leaving it to the men-folk again. It's our turn to hold the fort."

"You realize you might not be able to get back in," Del said. "We're trespassing, and there's a cop out there."

Beth nodded ruefully. "I know. And I bet Walter wasn't thinking of that or I'm sure he wouldn't have left." She looked around at the house. "I need to go, but I'd feel better about going if you promise to stay. Okay?"

"Okay," Del said, "could you arrange for a ten gallon jug of water, a couple toothbrushes and some toothpaste? And maybe a camp stove, so we can heat some water. If we're settling in for a siege, we need supplies. And I'd like to wash my face, at least."

He couldn't quite believe the situation he was in, though he understood every step he'd taken. But now his primary reason for it all was asking to leave him behind.

She hugged him tightly. "I'll be back with everything my car can hold." She squeaked with delight when she went out the back door.

"Miss Reuther?" It was a disheveled young man whose jacket said WHLD, standing behind Corporal Quarcini. "Are you abandoning the siege of the Stone House?" She pretended she didn't hear him as she eased past the sawhorses and, grateful she usually wore flats, started a rather unfeminine run to her car. The reporter called after her, but let her go.

She started up her Dodge Dart and headed home. She was sleepy, felt dirty, her hair especially. Her mouth tasted slimy. And her father was in the hospital, and she'd abandoned her boyfriend to a cause she'd dragged him into. *This is not your finest hour.*

She let herself in the back door. The house was quiet, deathly quiet. No distant television noise floating up from the basement. *I'll stop by and see him in the hospital before I go to work*, she planned, *try to explain it to him.* She let the hot water run much longer than usual. For years her father's frugality conditioned her to the shortest possible showers. That morning she sat in the tub, let the hot water pour down on her, and for no clear reason, she let the shower mask her tears as she cried.

Dressed, hair vigorously towel-dried but under a scarf nevertheless, she called the library and left the message with Mary Ann that she was running late but would certainly be in no later than ten. Then, bracing herself, she headed off to Memorial Hospital.

He was reading the *Niagara Gazette* when she entered his room. The other bed was empty. "Dad?"

He set down the paper. "Is what I'm reading true?" He held out the paper and jabbed with his right index finger at the Stone House story. "You left work to join a protest?" He'd never looked at her that way before. Perhaps, she thought, this was how he tried to frost a subordinate he truly despised, who'd done something despicable, something to shame the army.

She tried to smile. "First tell me about your test results. Next time you should go for the private phone, it's really irritating having to call the nurses' station and leave messages."

"I'm going to die someday," he said dismissively, "damn doctors just can't say when. What about this? Is this where you were? All night?"

She wished to God she could act her age, but she couldn't. She apologized. "Yes, that's where I was. Didn't the police come by? I asked them to. Yes, I ended up sleeping there. In the kitchen," she added, but stopped when the story headed squarely towards being the tale of the only woman sleeping in an abandoned house with three men. It didn't sound very good. She backtracked then, and tried to make it all sound like an innocent adventure, an unexpected trip to Crystal Beach. Nothing to be concerned about, though it was so sweet of him to be concerned. She stopped, awaiting his response.

"That's the biggest line of bullshit I've ever heard out of you," he said. She stared, as though he'd slapped her, for Dad kept a pretty Christian mouth and she couldn't remember him ever directing a profane word at her. "You're usually very responsible. Why didn't you call?"

"There's no phone in that house, or electrical power. Didn't the police call?"

"So what if they did. There are pay phones, right?"

"We couldn't leave." Why not, he asked. "Well, technically we were trespassing and if we left we wouldn't," she dropped it. He wasn't interested in the house, or any issues stemming from it. What was worse, she'd been out all night at a protest? "I wasn't in any danger, Dad. I was with Del. You met him. He's an old army guy, like you."

His eyes narrowed. "Lots of old army guys want nothing but to get a girl like you in the sack the first chance they get."

Her eyes narrowed. "What's 'a girl like me', Dad?"

"Oh, someone not so young anymore, not married."

"You're calling me an old maid?" She began laughing, but it made him swell with anger. "Someone desperate for a man?"

He looked ugly then. "You said it, I didn't."

Her father had never spoken to her as a man before. "I'm not that kind of girl," she said quietly. "I thought you knew me that well. I'm not desperate for a man, and I'm only thirty. That's not old."

"Your mother and I were married eight years by the time she was thirty." It was rare for him to even mention Beth's mother. He was going well out of his way to be harsh.

She was tired, she was running late. Her patience was done. "Well, maybe you should have waited. Maybe you should have dated more."

He raised his hand as if to slap her, forgetting perhaps that he was propped up in a hospital bed, but stopped as she stared him down. "I didn't have sex with anyone last night, okay? Not that I have to tell you anything."

"I am your father," he said.

"Big deal," she said, and turned to leave the room.

"Don't you leave the room while I'm speaking to you," he ordered. "Get back here."

"I'm not a kid, Dad. I'm an old maid, remember?" She wanted them to both laugh, to put this, somehow, behind them.

"You're acting like a common whore," he said, the meanest, unkindest thing he could think of.

She couldn't believe what she was hearing, or what followed. "Screw you," she said. It felt terrible. It made her chest ache. But it was done and it worked; he shut up. She left his room and kept her eyes locked on the distant 'EXIT' sign by the stairway.

Leon and Joe went off to explore the house. Del could hear their voices echoing and the house creaking around them. Trying to take his mind off his dirty clothes and scummy tasting mouth, he read the paper. "She's right, I should read this more often," he said. "I especially miss the comics."

A creaking noise from a difference source tickled his ear. He lowered the paper slightly and saw someone looking over the second floor banister at him. "You can come down if you want," he said as gently as he could. "I won't hurt you."

A woman of indeterminate age crept down the steps. Her hair was cut short and uneven, but whether it was gray or just very dirty he couldn't tell. Her clothes were in layers, a corduroy skirt on top with long underwear and denim under that for petticoats. She had more long underwear, with a flannel shirt and what looked like a lengthy t-shirt showing below her waist. Under all that clothing she was stick-thin. "Hi." Her voice was lifeless, the minimum communication from one remote satellite to another.

"You like pizza?" Del asked.

"I prefer it hot, but I was real hungry. I'd pay you for it but I got no money just now." She sat on the top step, where Beth perched. She was wearing gloves with the fingertips worn away. She had just a few teeth, her lips retreating into her mouth. "They're tearing this place down?"

"Trying to. You been living here long?"

"A year or so." She stretched and yawned, pulling up her filthy sleeve. Del saw the start of a scabby needle track.

"I tried using a needle," he said. "Twice. It freaked me out. But I smoked a lot."

"I don't do it much," she lied. "You carrying?" she asked, her voice hesitant but hopeful.

"No, not any more," he said. Just now I wouldn't mind a joint, though. "So where would a guy with no job and no apartment stay in this town?"

She looked outside as a bulldozer roared close by. "Used to be a lot of places, when it's warm, but they're knocking a lot of them down." She tucked her fingernail in a corner of her mouth and chewed on it, and looked out at the sound of a bulldozer tearing a wall down barely twenty feet from the house. "God, that's awful sounding."

"It is. What's your name?"

"Why you care?" She looked at him carefully. "I don't tell guys my name. Sometimes guys fuck me when I don't want to. They always start by asking me what my name is." She flinched when a truck bounced in a pothole, the bang rattling the windows. "I need to get straight. I got to go. I can't stand this." She got up and said, "what's your name?"

"Del."

"Bye, Del. I wouldn't stay here long. I hear they're tearing it down." She came down the steps, keeping as far from Del as she could, and crept out the back door, sliding along the walls like a camouflaged lizard, her ears plugged, the sounds of the trucks too painful to bear.

"Bye," Del said.

Walter's wound was infected, so they admitted him. "We're going to give you some penicillin for the infection, and put in a drain to get the pus out of the wound," explained the doctor, a man with thinning hair and deep pouches under his eyes. "You must be in some pain."

"Well, yeah," Walter said. "Since yesterday."

"Well, you know," the doctor began to lecture him, "we can only give you the pills, you have to take them." Walter nodded as the doctor explained again the dosage of the antibiotic, one every three hours, preferably after eating. He swallowed one immediately, though his stomach was empty. "That might make you a little queasy," the doctor warned.

"I'll take queasy over what I'm feeling," said Walter.

They wheeled him into a second floor room overlooking Ferry Avenue. Outside his window he saw a stretch of row houses, a cozy little house set unusually far back from the street, and on the corner a massive Victorian. Traffic was light. He couldn't see the three blocks away where his friends were in the stone house.

A knock on his door; in came a guy he didn't recognize but a voice he did. "Hi, there, Sam Philco from WHLD. You're Walter Morrow, the guy who discovered the diaries of the old Stone House, right? You work at the public library, right? Mind if I ask you some questions?"

God, he talks fast. "No," said Walter, "I don't mind. But the pain killers might make me a little sleepy, so ask fast."

"Is the Stone House the oldest house in the city?"

"Absolutely. The diaries prove it."

"Those are the diaries that Joe Novak began publishing in the *Gazette*?"

Walter nodded. "It's radio," Sam said in a lower voice.

"Yes, those are the diaries."

"Did the Urban Renewal Agency know about this?"

"I personally met with Mayor Lackey four days ago and tried to explain this to him," Walter said, a yawn escaping. He stopped himself then. He wondered if he still had a job. If he shut up now, would that matter? "I told Lackey the Stone House was, without doubt, the most important building in the South End. He said it didn't matter. He needs the convention center more."

Sam was watching the needle of a sound gauge as Walter spoke. When he finished, Sam said, "wow, that's really heavy." He waited through another of Walter's yawns. "So what's saving the stone house today?"

"I have friends who also read the diaries. They're staying in the house, refusing to leave."

"And the police haven't arrested them? Why is that?"

Walter shrugged. "I think they expect us to get tired and cold and hungry and leave on our own." A deep wave of sleepiness pulled him

down. "My friends aren't going to leave until we know the house is safe."
A minute later his eyes rolled up and he fell deeply asleep.

"I think that's all we have time for today," Sam dictated. "Thanks to
Walter Morrow, local historian at the Niagara Falls Public Library."

Beth got to work by nine-thirty, half an hour late. Her mail slot had
messages. One from Mrs. Koenig, her supervisor. One from the Property
Taxpayers League. *What do they want?* One from her father, dated yesterday evening. *He called here trying to find me?* Her eyes filled with tears.
She wadded the message up and threw it out.

Not being one to wear mascara, or, today, any makeup, she blinked
her eyes clear and went to Mrs. Koenig's office.

Mrs. Koenig was a matronly woman who always wore dresses and
combed her graying hair parted from the side, cut just barely shoulder-
length. She was a hard worker, but had a maternal instinct for her staff.
Beth was a challenge for her, with her big city attitude, and the only
other degreed librarian on staff. She looked up from reading Library
Journal when Beth knocked at her open door. "Come in, dear."

Beth stepped in, facing Mrs. Koenig's desk, a steel gray destroyer. "I
have this message from you?" she said, holding it up.

"I remember," she smiled kindly. "Could you close the door?" Beth
obliged. "Thanks, dear." She put the journal aside. "I heard the news story
yesterday on WJJL. And then I saw the front page of the *Gazette*. On one
hand, it explained where you ran to," she gave Beth a look copied from
first grade teachers, "and it reminded me that you never know someone
as well as you think." She was smiling. "Tell me what happened."

Beth felt a weight lifting. She respected Mrs. Koenig and liked her, but
also feared her. She was by-the-book and Beth's behavior had strayed.
"Walter found them in the house. Walter, and Del and I explored the
house last weekend. Because it was due to be demolished." She got the
whole story out, introducing Del in the process.

"I'm so jealous," Mrs. Koenig said, smiling. "It's a bona fide adventure,
and I've never had a bona fide adventure."

Is she kidding me? wondered Beth. *The same woman who keeps mentioning jobs in colleges? Who lined out almost every book I recommended by
Kesey and Kerouac and their band? Did I have a friend here all along?*

Then Mrs. Koenig looked down at her desk, breaking eye contact to help her complete her assignment. "I envy you the adventure. But Mayor Lackey was not amused." She made eye contact. "And he called me yesterday and he strongly requested that I discipline you." Beth nodded. "He was very specific about how I was to do that."

Mrs. Koenig glanced around her office. It used to be a closet. It was choked with shelves, with posters, and file cabinets. She barely had room for her desk and the chair Beth was using. The new library, which Mayor Lackey discussed with her yesterday, would triple their current space.

"It will be a modern showcase," Lackey promised. "But getting there won't be easy. To do so we all have to pull together. We can't show a divided front. We need to stay united."

Do you think you're leading some kind of crusade? That's what she was thinking. "I understand," is what she said. And Lackey let her go after that, for which she was relieved. She'd heard stories about him.

"I am sorry that this had to happen," she said, "but effective October 15th, you will be dismissed from the library staff."

"Dismissed?"

Mrs. Koenig nodded.

Beth remembered to breathe. "That doesn't seem fair," she got out.

"Between you, me and the walls, it isn't. You may wish to challenge this," her soon-to-be former supervisor said, "and I will testify that this was a direct order from the Mayor. But in my experience it will take a year before you get a hearing, and I can't guarantee it will go your way. If you can appeal it at the state level, you will probably win, but that will take a couple of years."

Beth felt tears filling her eyes and blinked hard to clear them.

"I can tell you that I," Mrs. Koenig was also struggling with her emotions, "admire what you did. And I'm sorry I'm such a, a coward that I didn't stand up to him. I promise you the most sterling recommendation I can write."

Beth left Mrs. Koenig's office and got to her seat at the reference desk. It still felt good to sit here, today. The conversation hovered overhead like an impending power outage, but just now she was warm, on home turf. She saw the message slip from the Taxpayers group.

"Iannuzzi residence." Beth identified herself. "Oh," said a woman's voice, "you're the librarian." The librarian, Beth thought with a smile.

"I been listening to the radio, and I saw that picture in the *Gazette*," she said, "now, is this something you're doing to irritate Lackey?"

"No. We just couldn't stand to see the house demolished."

"So who's there now? I mean, there's no phone there, so you aren't there, are you?"

"No, I'm at the library. The only two there right now are the two gentlemen from the demolition crew. Walter Morrow was injured and had to go to the hospital."

"Geez, did the cops beat him up?"

"No, no, the police were very nice, very helpful," Beth said clearly, perhaps too loudly. She looked around again but the room was empty. "Walter hurt himself finding the diaries, a splinter of wood actually went through his leg. It got infected."

"Ooh. Poor guy. That must hurt. So let me tell you why I called. Do you know about our organization?" Yes, Beth did. "Well, we've been trying to get Lackey to pay attention to our demands, without much luck. It looks like you've found a way. You think we could join the," she paused, "what do you call it? Sitting-in?"

"Sit-in. And yes, you're as welcome as we are. It's city property, we're trespassing. But I guess the more the merrier."

"Very good. That's real good. Thanks, Miss Reuther. Look for me down there later."

Beth's heart was pounding when she hung up the phone. *How many of those angry taxpayers were there?* She picked up the phone to call Del, then, smiling at her error, set it down. She looked up at the clock. Ten a.m. She was entitled to two weeks of vacation, and she wasn't sure whether or not to start at lunch time. She was starting to get angry with Mrs. Koenig, but she realized that even as her bridges were burning, she was going to have to move forward. And that was exciting.

Walter woke in his hospital bed after a wonderful snooze. On the tray by his bed was lunch, delivered while he slept. He was ravenous. He used the spoon to slurp the chicken broth, upending the bowl to get the last drops. Then he downed the grilled cheese sandwich and the milk, the first milk he'd drunk in years. His leg felt much better, and its color was healthier. There was no more throbbing around the wound but there was a tube coming out of his bandage. *I hope this doesn't hurt*, he prayed. "Ecch." He pulled it out slowly, carefully. It didn't hurt, much. Then he found his clothes in the nearby closet, dressed and, peeking around, walked with a slight limp to the elevator. On the ride down he glanced at his watch. It was two o'clock, later than he thought.

On the street, the damp chilly air made him zip up his jacket and after a little walking his leg hurt again. *It's only a few blocks*, he coached himself, and the first one was downhill. He favored his leg, hoping he wasn't being too stupid leaving the hospital. He noticed, for the first time, that the leaves were turning, and he paused to enjoy the burst of yellow put forth by a huge old birch tree. Down the alley by the row houses, he walked carefully, the pavement riddled with potholes and deep cracks. The houses on either side were old, cheaply built and falling down.

He saw the Stone House sooner than expected, as the buildings and trees and light poles surrounding it were gone. The demolition crews had crushed the overgrown bushes, the trees that had shielded the second floor, and there it was. Rambling, grayish, its ridgeline sagging badly, it filled half a city block. And it was standing alone, like a photo he once saw of a structure standing in gray rubble near Ground Zero in Hiroshima.

There were two police cars, and police sawhorses completely surrounded the building. And as he walked around the front, to see what was happening, he saw a crowd of about thirty gathered there. A few were holding signs, homemade and hard to read. SAVE THE STONE HOSE read one, the writer forgetting the U in house, sticking it in after finishing. Another sign read U.S. OUT OF VIETNAM.

He struggled past a sawhorse, his leg starting to throb again, and a cop started to cut him off, but Sergeant Fiske saw him and, to Walter's amazement and relief, waved off the cop. He tapped on the windows. "Del? Leon? Anybody home?" He hiked his bad leg up to the window sill, gritting his teeth in pain and sliding in slowly, twisting his chubby frame in a most undignified way to pass through. Inside, panting from the pain and exertion, he leaned against the wall and watched a row of cars driving by. A stream of them, fifteen in a row where there had been no traffic, drove slowly by and parked up and down the street.

People got out, with more signs, and they gathered into a group, and all in the course of a couple minutes marched up to the line of saw-horses, pushed one aside and walked towards him. Again the cops let it go.

"Everybody stand in front of the house and hold hands," said a middle-aged woman in a Jackie Kennedy pillbox hat. They started at the front door and spread out. Mrs. Iannuzzi had her own bullhorn. She mounted the front step and aimed it up to the sky. "The Progressive Taxpayers League wants Mayor Lackey to know we don't want this old house demolished." The bullhorn distortion made most of the sentence gibberish. "This is a historic house and it must not be demolished to build a pipe-dream convention center that will just bankrupt the city." She paused for emphasis before 'bankrupt the city'.

"Leave the house up. Leave the house up!"

Four vans from different TV stations arrived. Mrs. Iannuzzi knew the media.

And as the police talked to each other on radios, and the citizens arrayed themselves around the house, Del woke from a nap, curled up in a blanket in front of the kitchen fireplace, and saw Walter. "Hey. How you feeling?"

"I'm okay."

"What's going on?"

"Reinforcements," Walter said, smiling. "I don't know where they came from, but we got reinforcements."

Leon was in the upstairs room, hoping to find leftover pizza. It was all gone, but he saw the back of the door in reflected light and saw a message cut in the wood. He dug out a screwdriver to scratch away the paint. Half an hour later he read 'Claire.' *Nehemiah's work,* he realized. He was looking for more messages when he heard the bullhorn. He joined them downstairs. "What would really be helpful," Leon said, "is a battery-powered radio."

"Today we have television," Walter said, with undisguised excitement. "Why don't they come and talk to us? We're the protestors." More police arrived, adding to the numbers behind the sawhorses. The cops looked uncomfortable, talking to themselves.

"Can anyone hear what they're saying?" asked Walter, getting agitated.

A police captain showed up and spoke with the media, then left.

Finally a man in a windbreaker with CHANNEL 7 on the back headed for the house with a camera man in tow. Walter stuck his head out of the window and waved.

"He's enjoying this," Leon said, disapproving.

"Someone might as well," Del suggested.

"Hi," the reporter called to them, "I'm Irv Weinstein, Channel Seven News. And you are?" he held the microphone to Walter's face.

"Walter Morrow, local history specialist from the Niagara Falls Public Library."

"And your friends?"

Walter shared the window reluctantly. Del peered out. "I'm Del Nichols, I'm with," he corrected himself, "I was with Demolition of Buffalo, but when we refused to knock this house down I lost my job. And this is my co-worker Leon." Leon stuck his face out the window and waved. Then he retreated.

"We've read about the diary," said Irv to Walter, sounding profound. "What else can you tell us?"

The cameraman moved in and Walter and Irv talked about the age of the house, and about Nehemiah the Loyalist, about June Lockwood and Sawyer Jackson. Irv finished taping, shook Walter's hand, and left with his camera man.

More pizza was delivered around four o'clock. "Could you guys just leave us some peanut butter and bread next time?" Leon asked. "This pizza isn't good for you, y'know, not for every meal."

"And where is that portable toidy we talked about this morning?" Del asked Corporal Quarcini. "I can take a whiz into a sump hole only so long. It's getting pretty stinky down there. I have to go number two and the wreckers ruined our gas station toilet."

Twenty minutes later a portable john was delivered. No peanut butter.

The latest edition of the *Gazette* hit the street. Front page, under the fold, three columns, under the headline "Founding Father bilked Army? From the Stone House Diaries,"

Augustus Porter has long been revered as the founder of Niagara Falls. He managed the Portage Road after the revolution, owned Goat Island and the land around the falls, and built much of the early industry here. But he was a businessman first, and one of his first businesses was quartermaster to the militia in the early months of the War of 1812. And the Stone House diaries divulge a scandal Porter was involved in. . .

We expected Springfield muskets, the regular army issue, .70 caliber, which still shot a lighter load than the .75 caliber British Army musket. The muskets we got were of varying make and varying caliber, none as powerful as the British muskets and in universally poor shape. I held an ancient musket with French writing, from the days of George Washington's army, .65 caliber or lighter.

Joe distributed copies. "I'm wondering how this one will turn out," he said. "The Porter family is the royalty of Niagara County. This will probably upset a lot of people."

"You're darn right it will," said Walter, not happy with what he was reading. "We're trying to build support for this house. With all the material to work with, why did you pick this? Why not print Sawyer Jackson or June Lockwood? That wouldn't upset anyone."

"This is the real story. Sawyer Jackson and June Lockwood are good history, but this is," he tapped the headline, "actually news."

Walter said nothing else, just chewed his pizza and didn't look at Joe. The goal was to save the house. That meant keeping the crowd interested. Stories about musket and scandals involving the Porter family weren't going to win the crowd. They were almost all women out there. A love story would have worked them up nicely. *He should have asked me,* thought Walter.

The crowds wore thin as the dinner hour approached. A rusting Dodge Dart approached behind a blue Cadillac. The Caddy stopped at the sawhorses and the Dart just behind. Lackey stepped out of the Cadillac, a copy of the *Gazette* folded under his arm. Beth got out of the Dodge with a bag of potato chips and a six-pack of Strohs. Lackey saw her. "You are Miss Reuther?" he asked, his publicity smile on. It wasn't everyday he ordered a librarian fired; he wasn't sure what to expect.

"Yes, and you're Mayor Lackey," she said, not smiling.

"What's in the bag?"

"Snacks."

"For our fine men in uniform?"

"For our fine men in the house."

"Sergeant Fiske," the mayor called, and the officer made his way reluctantly from his car, where he was reading the paper. "Are we providing aid and comfort to the trespassers?"

Fiske looked sour. "I thought we'd agreed to wait them out, sir."

"Wait them out, yes," Lackey said, tugging on the bag to look inside. "Beer and potato chips? I'd join them if I didn't have other responsibilities."

She broke away, and walked unimpeded to the front window and passed the snacks through. "Del, any idea where you dropped the key?" she asked, climbing in.

Lackey opened his newspaper and held it up for the officer to see. "See today's *Gazette*? Front page?"

"I was reading it when you got here," Fiske said. "Interesting reading. Real interesting. Is it true?"

Lackey scowled. "It's a diary of a Loyalist. They lost the war. They were sore losers. Do I believe one of them when they say one of our founding fathers was a crook? No, I don't. Do you?"

Fiske's forehead wrinkled. "I don't know what to think. I think I'd like to read the whole diary when I get the chance, and make up my own mind."

The Progressive Taxpayers saw Lackey and started taunting him. Never one to run from a fight, he approached their picket line.

"Mayor Lackey!" Shirley Iannuzzi roared into her bullhorn. "The citizens of this city are going broke. We need property tax cuts."

He couldn't help himself. "What does this," he indicated the Stone House, "have to do with property taxes? Whether this building stands or falls, it won't affect your property taxes."

His logic was good, but the Progressive Taxpayers got what they were after as the TV crews came back out and rolled camera.

Nickie Gallo's desk was a mess. Half of it was covered by a broad and unstable pile of papers, chunks of it bound by staples. Each chunk represented a condemned property. The year began with a more modest, orderly flow of these forms, a flow comfortably handled by him and his niece, Gina. The pace had quickened in the past two weeks. The courier service used to bring one. Then they brought ten. Today they brought twelve.

"Ten, eleven, twelve," he counted, licking his fingertips for better traction, taking one from the big mess and adding to a series of five stacks he'd started on a table. "This is one week old, this is eight days, this is nine," he scribbled on sheets of paper. "Jesus Freaking Christ, we're falling behind." He had thirty jobs pending, with three crews. No, make that two crews—since Del and Leon joined the freaks in the old Stone House.

But the demolition orders kept coming. The state was waiting, impatiently, to build the LaSalle Arterial. And when Del and Leon bailed on demolishing the Stone House, the agency told Nickie, "take down everything around them, and keep going." Like leaving a small pile of trash behind while sweeping the floor.

He thumbed through his rolodex and found the number he wanted, his cousin Mike in Rochester. "Mike, yea it's Nickie. How you doing? Yea, well, I got more business here than I can handle. The stone house? You read about that, huh? Yea, it's slowing me down a little but that's not my biggest problem. Can you spare a couple of crews? I could use ten guys. No, I got enough trucks. Maybe a bulldozer. Y'know what I need is a couple more cranes with wrecking balls. Sure, we can do it that way. Can you get 'em on the road tomorrow? Hey, how can I thank you? You'll find a way? Hah, I bet you will."

The Urban Renewal Agency meeting that evening was in disarray. Only half the members could make it on twenty-four hours' notice, and there was no agenda. It was just Lackey, Medina, Siegler, O'Brien and Proulx. "Gentlemen," Lackey began, "thanks for getting together on such short notice. We have a crisis."

Copies of the *Gazette* were on the table. "Has everyone read the stories the paper did on the Stone House?" Medina asked.

"Certainly did. It's very interesting," Proulx said, and he sat back, resting his chin on his hand and watching them like they were rats in a cage and he was the observing scientist.

"With all the crap they print about us, it's the first time in months I've actually read the paper," confessed O'Brien. His smile faded. "My son asked me if I was going to destroy the old house."

"What did you say?" asked Proulx, amused.

"I said no," O'Brien admitted.

Lackey looked at the story through his reading glasses. "I found it disturbing," admitted the mayor. "And I wonder how accurate the story about Judge Porter is."

"Is Morrow still camped out in the Stone House? We should be talking to him," said Medina.

"Well, Walter helped Joe Novak get the story," Siegler said, "so we can probably assume it's accurate. My question is, who cares?" He glanced around. "Given everything that's at stake here, is this bit of historical trivia important?" He waited a moment. "I say no."

"What do you mean?" asked Medina. "You think if we don't say anything, it'll just, like, blow away?" He looked around the table.

"Mort has a point," Lackey said, leaning forward. "If we take the long view, when has history ever impacted this city? This isn't Boston, and it's certainly not Washington. History is important there. It's part of their industry, part of their tax base. For them, history is a dollar sign. If they started demolishing historical sites in Boston, you'd hear them raise hell. And it would be from the local businesses, the hotel owners, the restaurant owners. Because history means money there. And in Washington, picture them cashing in the White House for something more modern? Politics doesn't even come into it. Those are cities where history is part of their business."

"Niagara Falls is about the falls, and about industry. Tourists at Prospect Point, tourists riding the *Maid of the Mist,* and guys doing their shifts at Hooker and Carborundum. That's what pays the bills here. Not history."

Proulx broke in. "That's very perceptive, Dent. But I have to say, based on what we've learned in the last couple of days, that I'd like to go on record opposing demolition of the Stone House." He braced for the storm.

"Oh really?" said Lackey. Proulx was a devious bastard, he knew, and was angling for a run at his job, which was why he kept him close by. "Well, that's your constitutional right. It's a stupid decision, a completely irresponsible decision. An abdication of your position of leadership." He stopped there, and glanced at the others. "I strongly disagree with Councilman Proulx's decision. The Stone House can't be left standing. Our new city has to be built." He was red in the face now. "I'd love to hear any other opinions."

"Anyone here ever take a tour with a tour guide?" asked O'Brien, trying to be the diplomat. He knew the answer. "I wouldn't either. I figure, I'm from here, I know it all. But Lucy had cousins in from California last year and they wanted to take a tour. So we went along, we figured it would be fun." He thought a moment about that sunny day in August, of the black limousine in which the six of them rode through the traffic. "We started by coming down River Road. They kept the windows rolled up because of the smell, but they told us about how Niagara became a major industrial center because of the cheap power. When we got to the falls, the guide had a hundred stories about how high the falls was, about people like Red Hill, about Blondin walking on his high wire, and that poor kid who went over in his life jacket a few years back. Millie, my wife's cousin, asked how the falls became the honeymoon capital. Has to do with Napoleon's nephew, which I didn't know." He was losing track of his point. "We saw a lot of the falls, we went over to Canada, we did the Whirlpool, we did the Floral Clock. But we didn't stop anywhere historic. And nobody asked to."

Lackey nodded vigorously. "Exactly. This is not a city that cares about its history. It cares about tomorrow, and today. But not much about yesterday, and if it's history, Christ, according to that diary, our big moment in history was the War of 1812. Who in hell ever made dollar one from the War of 1812?"

"Apparently Judge Porter did, but nobody since," joked Proulx. He got laughs.

"Are you still in favor of letting that pile of rocks stand in the way?" Lackey asked.

Proulx nodded.

"Well, I'm clear on the value of the house to the city, which is zero," said Siegler. "However, the Citizens for Progressive Taxation have jumped on this. I heard the story on 'HLD this afternoon. They were interviewing Shirley Iannuzzi, and she was vowing they'd block demolition of the house until they were heard."

"What does that mean?" asked Lackey. "They've ruined Council meetings for the past three months. I hear almost nothing but them."

"No offense, Mayor," said Proulx, "but all you do is tell them to shut up. I don't think they're happy with that response."

"Well, we can't promise them taxes will come down anytime soon," said O'Brien, "so what else would calm them down?"

"Maybe it's time for a symbolic sacrifice," said Proulx. They all turned to look at him. "Someone from the agency. Announce that we're going to take a new look at urban renewal, and a new look at the property tax situation. Something like, 'we know there's a lot of frustration out there'. And throw them a bone. Fire someone from the board."

Lackey was looking distant, or so a stranger might think. He liked the idea. In fact, he was looking at a photo of the current board, framed on the wall. "Anybody got a dart?"

Proulx raised his hand. "I'll volunteer."

Lackey sat back in his chair and looked at Proulx, studied him with deep suspicion. "Why would you want to volunteer?"

Proulx tried to remain poker faced. He'd surprised them all. "Well, if I resign you have a unanimous vote on demolishing the Stone House."

"Right, and you have an election issue."

"Anyone else volunteering?"

Lackey was thinking months ahead, counting votes, counting wards, and planning mine fields. Proulx had just slipped past him today. He wouldn't let it happen again.

For a long minute nobody said anything. Medina said, "okay, are we supposed to be following Robert's Rules? Does someone need to make a motion?"

Proulx grinned. "Don't bother. I'll write a letter tomorrow. I'll just say I'm departing after constructive differences with the board. We're all still friends. I'm still going to kick your ass at the Porter Cup," he winked at Siegler.

"Okay," said Siegler, smiling but uncomfortable. "I think we're finished."

Walter was rolled up in two blankets, hogging the fire. He was having wild dreams. In them, he was in the public room but light was pouring in, almost too much for one sun. He was sitting in a chair, the room was furnished circa 1900, and a party was in progress. A woman sat down next to him, an old woman.

"Allow me to introduce myself. Walter Morrow."

"Jennie Davidson."

"Welcome to my party for those who've lived in the Stone House. When did you live here?"

"I lived here in 1934. I came to Niagara Falls from a small town in Ohio, me and my daughter. See, my two eldest boys came up first to work in the factories. Then, since they did well, the rest of us followed. My last day here was my eighty-third birthday. Everybody, my boys and my daughter and my grandchildren all came over and stayed a while. It was a nice time. They'd brought me a big cake and put candles on it. Not eighty-three or I couldn't have blown them out and lasted the final hours. But it was very nice, and all my grandchildren kissed me good night and all my boys kissed me and wished me happy birthday. And when they left I turned on my TV and fell asleep watching Robert Mitchum. I guess I had a heart attack in my sleep. I don't mind. It was lovely."

"What part of the house did you like the most?"

"Not a part, but the time of day. Dawn. I usually woke up at dawn and in the summer the sun filled my bedroom and the wood shone. I loved those wooden floorboards. I went down on my hands and knees and polished them, me, eighty-three. I polished them 'til they shone."

Jennie faded in a burst of light and a very voluptuous woman with almost clownish makeup dropped into Walter's lap.

"Hey, sweet baby, enough of the old lady." She began working her hands between Walter's thighs and he shifted around in his sleep, getting aroused. "I owned this place back in 1925 and ran a house of pleasure. I had so many girls working for me, different girls coming and going, we turned this town on its ear." She laughed, throwing her head back, her right hand on her chest in false modesty, her chest amplified with a low neckline and push-up bra. "And no cop ever touched us either, because there wasn't a night that the mayor or the chief of police or a city councilman wasn't visiting." She giggled, and Walter felt himself falling in love. "My best girls, the ones that stayed longest, were Cherry and Silk, they were from New York. And Lady Anne, she was from Toronto. They stayed the longest. Others came and went. I had two black girls, Cleopatra and Mahogany. I forget which was which. One was very popular with men who enjoyed French arts, I think it was Mahogany. Those girls were popular, especially with the white boys. And then there was me." Walter thought he detected a hint of a southern accent now. "I knew some tricks, I don't mind telling you. I lasted six years. God, I made money. Last night I had in this house I took care of four men, three of them half my age, and left a smile on every one of their stupid faces."

Walter, blushing and hoping she was going to take him upstairs, asked the rude question, "did you die here too?"

"Hell, no. Change of administration. The new boys ran me and my ladies out of town. I died of TB in Pittsburgh in 1930."

"What about this house did you like the best?"

"The walls, sweetie. You can't hear any kind of moaning through these walls."

To his dismay, she was gone. The light faded. A man, white haired, in a three-piece suit, sat next to him, and Walter's aroused state dissipated.

"Niagara," the white haired man was saying, "represents a unique investment opportunity. The force of the river, harnessed properly to an enormous wheel, could turn ten of the largest grinding wheels in the world. I've spent my own money developing the plan. All that I require is the land, and ten years of tax relief. That," said the gentleman with a rueful smile, "is what I told the council. They responded with the land and two years' tax relief. I agreed."

"What happened?"

"We couldn't draw the business. The Erie Canal was shipping the grain unmilled so cheaply it still paid to send it to Syracuse and have it ground there rather than do it here. I had built only two mills when my funds dried up. You see, I had counted on the proceeds of my first two to finance the rest."

"What part of this house did you like the best?"

"The main beam in the basement near the southwest corner. I hung myself from it when the town seized my mills for back taxes. For all I know there's still a piece of cord on the rafter, for the oaf of a coroner just cut it and let me fall like a sack of potatoes."

Walter woke in the dim light of downtown streetlights. He looked around at his surroundings, and was convinced, then and there for the rest of his life, that houses could be haunted. He looked at Leon, who was deeply asleep, and plotted for a while on ways to accidentally wake him up for company. Instead he nodded off.

At dawn they were awakened by the familiar sounds of diesel motors and buildings being battered to the ground. Joe Novak arrived at seven with coffee. He looked grim. "I got a few phone calls about the last entry, about Porter."

"Let me guess," said Walter sourly. "They don't like to hear bad things about the Porter family?"

Joe nodded. "History is a funny thing in this town. It's amusing, but nobody wants to stop for it. I heard a rumor last night that the Urban Renewal Agency had an emergency meeting to discuss this place, and that Councilman Proulx spoke in favor of saving it. That same rumor says that he resigned from the agency by the end of the meeting. So let me ask the tough question. How long do you guys think you can stay here?"

Del's hand went to his greasy hair, and he scratched his scalp. He and Leon were in the same sweatshirts and jeans they'd worn to work three days ago. "I'm getting a little tired of sleeping on the wood floor. And I'd love a shower. But I'm a big boy. Is there any chance the house can be saved?"

Walter pursed his lips. Joe looked at his cup of coffee. Beth yawned deeply and scratched her back, but said nothing.

"So nobody thinks our crusade will succeed?" asked Leon. He stood and stretched. "I need a shave and a bath and a change of clothes. Just like the rest of you. And tomorrow I'm expected at the Armory, for my pre-induction physical. As best I know, I'm in good health. My arches aren't flat, so I'll probably pass for Infantry. So I'm probably looking at a trip to Vietnam in about two months. As unpleasant as staying in here is, it is still better than what awaits me. And since we've found Sawyer's stupid signs, and I've found a message from someone who once lived here, in despair, I really don't want this house demolished. So I'm staying until they either drag me out, or bury me under these walls." He smiled. "Sorry for the speech."

They didn't bother voting. "Thank you, Brother Leon, for that inspirational sermon," Del said. "Uh, if you enlist before induction, you can maybe get into a different branch of the service. Get into the navy or the air force. It would at least get you out of the infantry. First call up the reserves, see if they have any openings. It's a longer hitch, but you'll be stateside."

Leon nodded. "I'd heard that but I wasn't sure." A new burst of bullhorn activity distracted them. "Now what?"

Councilman Proulx arrived at the picket line, followed by Progressive Taxpayers. He had a map, and with Shirley Iannuzzi assigning them, the marchers all drove off in different directions. When they were all dispatched, Proulx walked around the sawhorses and came up to the window. "Good morning in there." He sounded indecently cheery.

"Good morning, Mr. Proulx," said Walter. "What's cooking?"

Proulx looked like he hadn't slept much, like he was running on adrenaline. "Well, you may have heard that last night I resigned from the Urban Renewal Agency. I protested the demolition of this house." A round of clapping came from inside as the others tuned in. "This morning, working with Shirley Iannuzzi's group, we're mounting a more aggressive protest." They crowded around the window. "The city gave orders to demolish everything in the pathway of the new boulevard. Demolition of Buffalo, your old company, has about twenty more demolition crews coming into town this morning. But Shirley's people are now staking out every building in the path of the new boulevard. And they are going to stay in the buildings, just like you folks are in here. And we'll stop the demolition."

Four mouths hung open. "Is that what you wanted?" Walter asked, incredulous. "I thought you were really geared up for the new city."

Proulx flashed his version of the Lackey smile. "I have my reasons for what I'm doing. For what it's worth, I don't think we'll stop the demolition. I don't think we want to. There's far too much committed. Look at all the ground we've already cleared," he indicated with a wave of his hand. "But we're sure putting a bug up Lackey's ass." He glanced at his watch. "I'm off. Oh," he reached into his pocket, "here's a radio. Keep in tune." He handed Walter a battery powered pocket AM-FM radio and jogged back to the police line with a wave.

"What the hell is going on?" Beth asked, excited but still cranky from just rising.

"Politics," said Walter in a distant voice. "And it will be interesting to see what happens in the next couple hours. And now we have a radio."

Demolition ground to a halt. By eleven o'clock, Lackey was in emergency meeting with the remaining members of the agency. At eleven thirty, the mayor drove over to the Stone House. "Still in there?" he called.

In fact Del and Beth had found a room with a door that still shut, and took two blankets in for some quality time. Leon was in the front room, looking for any more messages from the past. Joe was at work, so Walter was alone. "I'm here," he said, sounding more subdued than he wished.

"Would you people be willing to come out if we," Lackey cleared his throat, "arranged to move this building?"

Walter stuck his head further out the window to be sure he heard right. "Move the building?"

"Put it on wheels, roll it out of the reconstruction zone. Find a safe place for it and let it stand," Lackey said impatiently.

Do I ask him to put it in writing? A witness would be nice, Walter thought, and who should come trotting up but Councilman Proulx.

"What did they say?" asked Proulx.

"You ask him," Lackey said, bristling with irritation.

"Walter? Did the mayor explain moving the house?" Proulx asked.

"Yes he did," said Walter. "I can't speak for everyone, but I think we have a deal."

Yesterday

Beth landed in Buffalo twenty minutes late, but that was mostly the fault of O'Hare Airport, which delayed the flight. The temperature in Buffalo was twenty-nine degrees, with a fifteen mile per hour wind, perfectly normal for a western New York February day but a chilling greeting for a girl who'd moved to the desert twenty years ago. Starting her day in her sunny ranch in Tucson, where she planned to retire soon as director of reference for the university, she spent the morning remembering. During the flight she tried to watch the in-flight movie but it was hard to follow without the earphones which USAir distributed for three dollars. Since it was a Steven Seagal film, she didn't care to part with the three dollars. Just as well. Old memories were returning, her paperback sat unread in her lap.

She was flying back to Niagara Falls to attend the retirement dinner of her old friend, Walter Morrow. It had been a few years since she'd last thought of her friends back east. She vaguely remembered Walter, Del, Leon and herself huddling in that old, run-down colonial inn, defying the bulldozers. *What did I do for a bathroom? And whatever happened to that old house?* She rarely shared that story. When she got the invitation to Walter's retirement party, followed by a call from Walter two months ago, it jogged her memory. She surprised herself by immediately agreeing to come back; she almost never went back east.

Two weeks ago the library lost its power and, as she and her reference staff sat in pools of daylight and waited for their lights and computers to come back, they listened to a battery-powered radio broadcasting news of war in Iraq and the protests against it. Kiefer, a young member of her staff, talked about his arrest protesting the war and asked, "you were in the Sixties. You must have seen some action, too."

"I protested the demolition of a colonial house, that was about it." She told Kiefer about the Stone House and he nodded admiringly at her and suggested she was on the same level as the solitary man, framed eternally in a TV screen with CNN logo, blocking a tank at Tiananmen Square. "Not even close," she corrected him. "It only lasted three days. We knew the bulldozers weren't coming in." Memory corrected her. "We were almost certain the bulldozers weren't coming. We had pizza and Coke delivered. The only real hardship was my dirty hair. That, and the toilet facilities."

And then she remembered making love with her ex-husband, Delbert, in that tiny room. Chilly, damp, their passion making them sweat. They had blankets but no pillows, and unfortunately for her back, Del inclined towards the missionary position. Her back periodically gave her trouble and it was always in the spot she bruised that afternoon. Even as she shifted in the airline seat it ached. Love hurts.

She remembered her fear, curling into the fetal position when the bulldozers demolished everything around the house. Plaster falling, wood creaking, crashing noises coming from all directions. It was, she thought, as scared as I can remember being. She huddled in Del's arms.

She and Del got married, had three wonderful years, and then the demolition work ended and Del got bored and went back to smoking dope. Three years of fighting and counseling later, they divorced. A year after that, she headed west.

Would Del be at Walter's dinner? Perhaps. They divorced in 1976, and when Beth's father died in his sleep in 1977, she job-hunted outside the state and ended up in Tucson in 1978. Remembering a favorite book of hers, goodbye to all that.

On the snowy, windswept ground at Buffalo, she got her suitcase and rental car without difficulty, and the airport was still in the same place with pretty much the same roads. *Not much changes here*, she thought, and it made her smile, sadly.

The retirement dinner was held at the Alps Restaurant, in the Town of Niagara, two hours hence. She had time to check-in at the Hotel Niagara—now part of a chain called Travelodge—in her youth the oldest and grandest hotel in town, her indulgence for this otherwise uncomfortable trip, and freshen up. She crossed Grand Island, and the North Grand Island Bridge, snow covering much of the landscape. She didn't see snow in Tucson. One had to go north, at least to Flagstaff, to see it. She'd never made the trip. Sometimes when you grow up with it, you get your fill. The sun was setting, backlighting the factory smoke-stacks and their clouds of airborne waste. *Kind of pretty. Too bad it isn't an artist's rendition.*

She slowed to a crawl at the John Daly exit for the John Daly Boule-vard, momentarily confused by the sign but realizing they'd renamed Quay Street. And to her right, she couldn't see it but knew it was there, was the old stone chimney.

The streets were atypically lined with parked cars. She missed the turn and ended up driving down Main Street, heading north. The roads were cracked, storefronts were empty. *I don't remember so many closed businesses*, she said to herself, making sure the doors were locked. She turned around on a side street lined with old houses; at a glance she saw cardboard in one window, a poor substitute for glass in winter. Given a moment to study a neighborhood at a long light, she shook her head. "Is it possible that it's worse than it was in 1969?"

She found her way back to the South End. The traffic here was heavier than she remembered, and she waited through a couple light cycles reaching the hotel. A huge billboard touted the Seneca Niagara Casino. *Oh, right*, she remembered, *Lackey's damn convention center.*

Built, under-used, and finally sold to the Seneca's for the casino the citizens once vowed would never open, its ice-skating rink demolished. *I liked that skating rink*, she remembered. *Only thing they built down here that I did like.* She found the former Hotel Niagara and realized that her memories were painfully out-of-date. The parking was not valet, and after she'd pulled her suitcase on its little plastic wheels from the far corner of the lot—against the wind—into the lobby, she finally found herself in a small room on the eighth floor, with paintings from Sears on the walls and advertising for the nearby casino covering the desk.

It doesn't matter, she told herself. *What you came for was the view.* She pulled open the drape, and took it in. She was, after twenty years, a little awe struck. The sunlight reflected off the water, and ice crusted the islands. "This is beautiful." Without foliage it was easy to see the geography. "There's Navy Island, there's Bath Island, there's the footbridge." She felt a deeper sense of loss than she'd expected. Fishing out the disposable camera, she took a few pictures from the window.

I hope he's there, she decided. *If he isn't I won't see him again. I fly back tomorrow night, the infamous red-eye. Perhaps I should have taken off Monday as well.* Then she remembered to check her email.

Unpacking her laptop she looked around for the presumed internet access. "Hello, front desk? I was told this room had ethernet links? E-ther-net. Yes, to hook up to the Internet. No?" She hung up. She plugged the telephone line into her laptop and, after a couple failures, managed to dial into her email, paying God-only-knew-what phone charges. The Monday reorganization meeting was moved up from four p.m. to ten a.m. "That stinks. Now it's an all-day meeting?" Her flight got her into Phoenix at eight a.m. . . . She could make the meeting, but only if she drove straight from the airport, looking like what the dog threw up. And she dared not miss the meeting. *I'm six months from retirement*, she complained to the mirror as she washed her face. *Six months.* In fact, she knew her job was safe—an age-discrimination lawsuit would keep them on their toes—but she knew her department would take a hit, and she doubted Kiefer would survive.

During her youth she had strayed into the Town of Niagara periodically, so she basically knew where Military Road was, but asking for directions and being told "right next to the Circuit City" was not helpful. Then an older man told her, "across from where LaSalle High used to be. The school's gone, but if you remember where it was, you'll be fine."

Her suit was cotton, perfectly suited for the desert but utterly inadequate for February in Niagara Falls. She grabbed her purse and did her best to run in low heels to the entrance.

It was dark but warm inside, with a smell of tomato sauce and a beery overtone. Her watch read ten p.m., Arizona time; she was right on time. Getting out the throw-away camera, she pushed open the doorway marked 'MORROW RETIREMENT', and saw three long dinner tables and, on the back wall, a banner printed on plastic—'Congratulations Walter!' She remembered the card she'd written and found the table for it. There were several wrapped items, one clearly a golf club. *I didn't know Walter golfed.* Several others were book-shaped. *Appropriate.*

And then, from behind, the doors opened again and in came Walter. It had been seven years since they'd seen each other, and Walter had added a few pounds and lost some more hair. He now had a few wispy ones waving on top, and a gray fringe. "Beth?" She smiled, she almost cried, and they hugged. "Thank you for coming," he said, "especially from Arizona."

"Thanks for inviting me." She glanced around, at the people clustered around the bar. "Is Del coming?"

Walter shrugged. "I know he got an invitation, but he didn't respond. He only lives a few miles away, he can't be skipping it because it's too far. Especially with your example."

Dinner began a little late, and Beth's jaw dropped when the dish arrived, a large, salt-encrusted roll, sliced open and smothered in thick slices of roast beef swimming in gravy. Walter said to his special guest, "I know it's messy to eat, but I love beef on kummelweck."

Beth thought of her outfit, then smiled. "Yeah, it's been a while. And it's hard on the outfit. But what the hell." Biting in, feeling warm gravy run down her chin, she set the roll on her plate, wiped her face, and looked at Walter. His white shirt was no longer white. "Walter?" she pointed.

He looked down. "Good thing I didn't wear a tie, eh?" She took another picture. They wiped gravy off each other's chins with soggy napkins, laughing and threatening each other with spit baths.

The highest ranking speaker was the current library director, Sheryl Williams, a dynamic black woman who kept her remarks simple. "Walter has a deeper knowledge of this city than any ten people you'll find. It's difficult to lose such an invaluable resource. I'm happy he's going to enjoy retirement but I won't miss waiting for him to arrive at staff meetings. Walter, I know you've got gifts over there to open, but I wanted to give you this right now."

Applause drove him up to the microphone, where Sheryl almost gave him a hug before noticed his gravy-stained shirt. Pulling back, settling for a handshake, she handed him a gleaming gold watch. "Please come by and visit, often," she said, and sat down to applause.

What a sweetheart, thought Beth. *Wonder what happened to my old boss?* She almost forgot to take a picture. Walter thanked Sheryl, thanked everyone for coming, and sat down to more applause. He was beet-red. "Walter, whatever happened to Mrs. Koenig?"

He looked up and distant. "Koenig? They gave her early retirement in the mid-seventies. I think maybe her husband and she moved to Florida. Seems we got a postcard or two." He smiled at the gleaming watch. "I wonder if I can cash this in?" he said dryly. "Probably double my pension."

"I meant to ask you, what are you going to do? Travel?"

"I've been meaning to do some writing," he confessed, looking more serious. "A book about the Stone House. I've done some digging and there were other people who lived in the house that never added to the diaries, so I'm trying to find more about them."

Oh yeah, she thought. That fiasco. "Refresh my memory," she said. "How did all that go down?"

The bar was open again and the crowd got a little louder. "Well, remember we vacated when the Councilman backed up Lackey's promise to move the Stone House." She nodded. "It was about a week later, they brought in a crew to start jacking it up. And, as always happens with low bidders, they had problems. By the time they got it jacked up there was already one crack in the back wall, starting at the foundation going up to the second floor. They got it on a flatbed intact." He took a drink of beer. "But the roads were so broken up from trucks that they had to drive really slowly to avoid shaking the house."

"Didn't they park it in the Sears parking lot for, like, a year?"

"Yes, they'd bought out Sears, and had their big parking lot, and it was the closest open space not slated for their stupid convention center. So they moved it there. Then the city got preoccupied with building the convention center and Lackey Plaza and the new mall, and the Stone House just sat there. The crack got a little wider." He took another drink of beer and someone came by, leaving early, to wish him well.

"They decided to move it over near the Stone Chimney," he picked up. "Real poetic justice. In the process of settling it on its new foundation a jack broke and the back wall collapsed." Even now the memory hurt, and he paused with a hint of despair on his face. "I've done some research since then. The house could have been moved without damaging it. They really cheaped out."

"I check in once in a while on the web. This city's been working on the cheap all along."

"Well, the winter of 1996 did it in. The weight of the snow collapsed the roof, and the walls fell in. The public room, the room we were in most of the time during the siege, is the only room intact."

She shook her head. "Well, whomever it was that said this city lives for its tomorrows, not its yesterdays, was right."

Walter glowered at her with mock anger. "I'll let that pass because I'm getting drunk."

Wearing a bulky winter coat that said TOWING SERVICE on the back, Del opened the door and hesitantly entered.

She saw him but said nothing. He was a little heavier than she remembered, and his hair was silver and thinning out on top.

"Walter?" he called out. Walter stood up and waved him over. Del was wearing glasses now and maybe didn't grasp that his ex-wife was sitting next to Walter until he was most of the way there. She was gray as well, and she wore it short, so maybe he didn't recognize her. Then he saw her, and his mouth fell open. Then he managed to put up a smile.

"Hi Beth, I wondered if you'd make it."

"Hi Del, same here. How've you been?" They were looking at each other with relief that the other had shown, and anxious after so many years without a word.

"Can't complain. And you?"

"Okay. What's with the jacket?"

"I got a business. My towing service." He half-turned and pointed to the emblem on the back of his jacket. "My girlfriend, Tammi, you don't know her," there was a brief dead spot in the air, "we got four flatbeds and a contract with the state to pull wrecks off I-190 between the North Grand Island Bridge and the Lewiston-Queenston Bridge."

She smiled. "Sounds promising. How's it working?"

"We're ahead of our bills. But I don't think I'll ever be able to retire."

She smiled amiably. "Well, you do what you can."

They met again in the hallway, both returning from visits to the bathrooms. "So how's Arizona?" he said. "Nothing like here, I bet."

She shook her head. "Nice empty spaces. And real different scenery. Of course, you have to deal with the scorpions."

"I'd love to get out there someday," he said. "I never did get to California."

"Remind me why we divorced?" she asked.

"You were ambitious," he said. "And I couldn't hold a job down. And I went back to smoking weed."

She nodded, not smiling. "I need to ask you, was it me that sent you back to using drugs?"

He shook his head. "Of course not. Good news is I've been clean for five years. Nothing stronger than beer, and only on weekends."

"Good for you," she said, and gave him a peck on the cheek.

The party droned on, people leaving in ones and twos and by ten the room was down to Walter, Del, and Beth. "Anybody remember Leon?" Beth asked. "What happened to him?"

Del smiled sadly. "Don't you remember? He'd gotten his draft notice. I remember telling him to check out the National Guard, or at least sign up for the air force or navy, but a lot of guys were doing that to avoid infantry. Maybe he was too late. I got a letter from him after he was drafted. The army sent him to Vietnam. He got killed. I don't know where, but he was dead three months after he got there. I used to have a clipping from the paper."

That dulled conversation for a moment. "The three musketeers," Walter said, drunk. "I have an idea. Who's with me?"

Beth was a little drunk herself. "I need to hear it first. If it involves taking off my clothes, no." She laughed a little loudly, then covered her mouth and blushed.

"No," Walter started again. "Let's go say goodbye to the Stone House."

Beth looked at him. "It collapsed. What's left to say goodbye to?"

"The lot was never developed," Walter said. "And the public room is still intact. Let's just go say goodbye. When will the three of us be together again?"

It took him some persistent begging, and reminding them that it was his retirement. "Del, you didn't bring me a present or a card did you?"

Del blushed. "Well, no, but it's in real poor taste to point that out."

"You can make your present to me a trip to say goodbye," Walter offered.

Del glanced at his watch. "I'm on call at midnight. You up to it?" he asked Beth.

"You got a good heater in your car?"

"I drove a truck over. And yeah, it's got a good heater."

"Let's make Walter happy," she said.

Del's heater blew hard enough to part hair. Walter rode shotgun, forcing Beth to sit between them. They drove down Niagara Falls Boulevard, noticing the big plaza for Tops Supermarket. "Tops just never goes away, does it," Beth said. "Are they really owned by the Mafia?"

"Everything is owned by the Mafia," said Del.

"Yeah, and it's all worthless," said Walter.

"Someone's sobering up," said Del. "You going to start crying on me? I don't see the guy for years and he's going to cry on me?" He wanted to give Walter a friendly shot in the shoulder, but gave it to Beth instead. "Pass it on."

"Ouch," she complained, but passed it on. "From Del."

They reached the I-190 intersection and Del geared up the heavy machine. It was noisy at sixty, so they didn't talk much. Bouncing over potholes, the flatbed behind banging, Beth felt a little like she was twenty again. *Of course, tomorrow morning I'm going to hurt in places I didn't know existed, but I've got a wonderful, eternal plane ride in which to suck down Advil.* She tried the radio but it couldn't compete with the engine.

Finally they rolled down the Daly exit. Del drove a block further, and turned right, down Falls Street. He took another right, past a decrepit house, and behind it, in a weedy lot, the truck's headlights picked up a pile of rocks. There were chunks of masonry, a low wall, and broken wood beams. "That's flooring, or the roof," said Del. "Over there is where the back was." They looked at him, surprised. "I've come by here a couple times."

They got out and the wind blew through Beth's coat. Del noticed her trembling and put his heavy jacket over her shoulders. "You'll freeze," she said.

"I never left, I'm used to it," he said, but he did curl tighter when the wind hit. With a flashlight he studied the layout.

"Over here," Walter walked down a pathway, and showed them a small shack amid the rubble. He kicked the door and it opened a couple feet, stopping dead. "It's not really safe, but we can probably step in for a moment."

It was dark, though there were holes in the ceiling through which they could see stars shining. The walls stopped most of the wind.

"Someone's been using the fireplace," Walter said, poking with his shoe at the recently burned wood.

"Guys, look at this," Beth said. Behind a propped up doorway she found a cramped space filled with a sleeping bag, a dirty mattress, and a box with some Cocoa Puffs, a box of macaroni, some plastic forks and spoons, and a dirty bowl with bits of cereal stuck to it. In a pile were sweaters and an irregularly shaped piece of canvas. "Someone lives here." Someone was trying to use this room as shelter in the winter. "Let's get out."

Silently they followed the path back, a steady wind cutting through them, and gratefully got back in the truck. "Some poor homeless guy?" Walter wondered.

"I saw a baby doll on the mattress," said Beth. "One of them might be a child."

Del backed the truck up, the rhythmic whining of the transmission filling Beth's ears as they retreated, leaving the remains of the Stone House in darkness.

"I'll stop by there tomorrow," Del promised when he delivered them back to the Alps parking lot. "I've got some camping equipment I don't use anymore. I got a sleeping bag, and a camp stove and a tent, maybe they can set it up inside."

Walter said, with an attempt at profundity, "it's still the oldest occupied house in the falls."

"Yeah," she said, not smiling. "Walter, can you let me out?" Walter opened his door and the chilly wind blew in. A kid passed them by, slogging his way somewhere. "Hey, pal?" she flagged him down. A minute later, the three of them framed, he finished off her disposable camera.

"Beth, it was great seeing you," said Del, extending his hand for a handshake.

She hugged them both, kissed their cheeks, and got in her rental.

The next day, wearing a bulky sweater under her jacket, she visited the side-by-side graves of her parents in the Catholic cemetery out by the reservoir and left a bouquet between them. She thought of that cold stone room on the flight back, a draining experience mitigated by a couple of airline drinks and two Advils. By the time the plane landed she had written out a check to the mission she found in the hotel phone book. And when the temperate air of the desert in winter greeted her at Sky Harbor, she found her Jeep, got behind the wheel, sighed in relief to be home and hoped her photos came out.

e p i l o g u e

Fact and Fiction

There was, to my knowledge, no stone house on Third Street in Niagara Falls. Nehemiah Cleary, family and friends and enemies, Sawyer Jackson, Liz Purdy, June Lockwood, and the Scavengers of 1969 are all fictional. The times they lived in I have tried to render accurately: the War of 1812, and the Loyalists populating the region, the bawdy, polluted village of Niagara in the mid-1800's, its evolution as a cutting-edge center of technology and, in 1969, the demolition of the South End, are depicted here to the best of my ability.

Some real people are depicted fictitiously. In the case of Augustus Porter I have taken significant liberties. As an ambitious business-man advancing his own plans during the War of 1812, Porter was the commissary agent for the armies of the Niagara Frontier. The shoddy supplies he provided are documented, but not widely advertised. It is indirectly noted in some sources. There are letters from officers in Black Rock about poor food, worn-out tents, lack of medicines and useable muskets and ammunition, and a footnote in *War Along the Niagara* notes that the British seized hundreds of old French muskets dating to the American Revolution from their American prisoners taken at Queenston. There was never an act of revenge by any soldier against Porter over the supplies. Nor, to my knowledge, did the state senate ever react; it was considered below standard but otherwise more or less typical for the times. I guess army food has always had a bad reputation.

The Loyalists were protected by treaty, about as well as were the American Indians. Stripped of their valuables during and after the Revolution, many left for British territory. Some, including my own ancestors, made the trip to be under the protection of Fort Niagara, then Fort George. They suffered the same as the characters I've written about. In that respect I mixed published sources with some personal family history.

I used mostly anecdotal material from published histories in "Honeymoon Capital." I didn't borrow any real people. In that respect it was the easiest section to write.

In both "Honeymoon Capital" and "Power City", I found names of companies, banks, hotels, etc. in the published histories. I took no great pain to be sure the business I mention in a particular year actually existed that year, just that it could exist in that era. The stunters mentioned were all real, though I concocted the story of Blondin's shoes to advance June's career. William Love's Model City plan is painfully well known to those who endured the 20th century crises of Love Canal.

The scientific struggle between Edison and Tesla is famous; Edison's use of dogs onstage is less well known. To the best of my knowledge they never appeared together on stage as they do in "Power City", to debate the future of electricity.

In "Urban Renewal" I changed the names of most of those in power and greatly simplified the political issues, as I wanted to focus the story on historical preservation. Having grown up then, I knew some of the history. Back issues of the *Niagara Gazette* at the Niagara Falls Public Library refreshed my memory on the chronology of events. The politics are still fresh in peoples' memories, and the dismay over the downtown's failure to thrive is an ongoing disappointment.

I do use Mayor E. Dent Lackey as well as the Taxpayer's League, by name. Lackey's vision for the city is a matter of public record. His character here is created by a blend of my memories, stories from various sources, and some emails I exchanged with Don Glynn and John Hanchette. The Taxpayer's League's disruptions of Council meetings are lovingly documented in the *Gazette*. The League never organized a showdown as depicted here.

Bibliography

In the years I've been working on this, I've read whatever histories came my way on Niagara Falls. These are sources that were especially useful.

Bowler, Arthur, ed. *War Along the Niagara*. Old Fort Niagara Association, 1991.

Dumych, Daniel. *Niagara Falls, Volumes I & II*. Arcadia Publishing, 1996, 1998.

Graves, Donald, ed. *Soldiers of 1814, American Enlisted Men's Memoirs of the Niagara Campaign*. Old Fort Niagara Association, 1995.

Greenhill, Ralph & Mahoney, Thomas. *Niagara*. University of Toronto Press, 1969.

Howard, Robert. *Thundergate, the Forts of Niagara*. Prentice-Hall, 1968.

Lossing, Benson. *The Pictorial Fieldbook of the War of 1812*. Harper & Brothers, 1868.

The *Niagara Gazette*, various issues, particularly 1969.

Records of Niagara. Niagara Historical Society, Niagara-on-the-Lake, Ontario.

The RedBook of Niagara, a Complete and up to date Guide to the Wonders of the Great Cataract (circa 1907).

Van Rennselaer, Solomon. "A Narrative of the affair of Queenstown; in the war of 1812." In *Notices of the war of 1812*. New-York, Leavitt, Lord & co.; Boston, Crocker & Brewster, 1836.

Wood, William. *The War with the United States, Volume 14, Chronicles of Canada*, 1915.

There are extensive materials on Niagara's development of electrical power on the Internet. Cornell University also has numerous historical documents scanned and viewable online.